BLACK MOUNTAIN

FIGHT FOR THE FUTURE

DAVID ARCHER

Published by Each One Teach One Publications.

First Printing: July 2023
Second Printing: November 2023

ISBN: 978-1-998871-01-8

David Archer
3420 Avenue Wilson
Suite 101
Montreal, Quebec
H4A 2T5, CANADA

david@archertherapy.com
www.blackmountainbook.com

BLACK MOUNTAIN

DEDICATION

To the children of the future.

THEME

Each generation must discover its mission, fulfill it or betray it, in relative opacity.
-FRANTZ FANON

TABLE OF CONTENTS

PROLOGUE

MESSAGE FROM THE ORACLE

It is lunar year 20XX, and the planet Ziffea is on the brink of extinction. Pollution, climate change, and the greed of one powerful corporation threaten the lives of its inhabitants and the future of the planet. The only hope for its survival—and that of its sister planets, threatened by the same enemy—lies in the hands of the Fighters. These warriors gain their power from ancient oracles and ancestral mediums who can summon the power of a supreme being named Si-Vin to imbue the chosen few with special powers to protect and maintain the natural balance of life on the planet.

It was Si-Vin, with his unlimited power, who created the four sister planets. Now, he rests in deep meditation on the surface of the star they orbit. He created the planets' life forms, some of which resemble those of ancient Earth, while others are modeled on those of other, distant galaxies. The stewards of the land, the Zlon, were created from the formless souls and spiritual energies that wander the universe after the destruction of their original worlds, including Earth. The Zlon have all the qualities of intelligent life, including the imperfections of emotional beings. Having inherited the fates tied to their previous lives, there was always a chance that the Zlon might reenact the demise of these ancient planets in their new homes. There needed to be checks and balances.

From the surface of the burning sun, Si-Vin therefore created six oracles to guide the development of the four planets. The oracles had free will and could gift Zlon of their choosing with the ability to transcend the limits of mortality and channel the spiritual forces of the planets they found themselves on. These were the Fighters. Their mission was to defend the continued well-being of the planets, but they also had free will, and some betrayed the original mission.

PROLOGUE | MESSAGE FROM THE ORACLE

Because they are created from spiritual energy, all life forms can manipulate the subtle energy fields linked to their musculoskeletal systems. Over time, most of the Zlon, locked in their incarnated, physical bodies, have lost and forgotten their connection to spirit. But through special rituals that draw on the power of the oracles, some Zlon can access the energy fields carried by their bodies. Once initiated through ancient and Indigenous ceremonies, they become Fighters.

Fighters possess six special powers: strength, speed, flight, soulforce manifestation, psychokinesis, and chrono-spatial manipulation. Their initiation creates a contract between each Fighter and Si-Vin. They can then channel the underlying forces of their planet, augmented by Si-Vin's infinite power, into their spiritual and energy fields. Because the ultimate source of their power is the supreme being, they also gain functional immortality. They cannot die by natural means so they have the potential to protect the natural balance of life forever.

Our story begins on Ziffea, where a war rages between the powerful corporation and a dwindling resistance. The corporation is winning due to the technologies it has developed to maintain its global domination. The resistance struggles to hold on to its last remaining stronghold. Its only chance is to locate and destroy the corporation's central processor, known as C.O.R.E.—the Central Operating Resource Engine that controls the web of technology the corporation uses to maintain its grip on Ziffea.

***

At the break of dawn, somewhere in the south of Ziffea, three women dressed in black boarded a huge triangular aircraft shaped like a bisected pyramid. The ship took off soundlessly, propelled by advanced technology, without any chemical emissions to mark its movement. The passengers, guided by holographic arrows, made their way to the bridge. There, they were greeted by a diminutive, eye-patched crew member.

The leader of the group extended her hand and gripped the crew member's forearm.

"You haven't changed, brother."

"Haven't found a reason to do so."

Another crew member, a being whose body appeared to be completely formed from metal, wires, and gears, showed the women to their seats. This being was also dressed in black. It left the bridge and returned a moment later carrying a tray with ginger tea, confectioneries, and coconut buns, which it set on a table in front of the women. Their leader nodded and produced a disc-shaped device. When she placed it on the table, a large screen in the center of the bridge lit up.

"Here is my scanned memory of communing with the oracle," she said.

A series of images unfolded on the screen. The crew members stood alongside the visitors, watching and listening in rapt attention. The images passed by in a blur of symbols and strange alien landscapes, then froze on a text almost as strange.

"On the eve of the president's speech,
The lengthy talk becomes brief;
Servants will turn and twist
And threaten two who exist;
One is a prisoner of war,
The other will come from more;
Take these two survivors,
And Si-Vin will take them higher."

"After all of these years, she still speaks in riddles," the figure with the eye patch commented. He looked toward the leader of the women. "But wait, why do we need both of them—or any more than we already have, for that matter? The seven of us should be enough. Training newcomers will take months."

"The oracle knows something we don't," she replied. "Let's not challenge fate. If there's a hidden problem, pushing ahead could be disastrous."

"Those two, whoever they are, must be special. The mercenaries will kill them if they can identify them."

"So we have to find them first."

The crew member's eye patch glimmered, scanning the oracle's message a second time.

"Did she give you any gene identifiers this time? 'The two who exist' could be anyone!"

The woman nodded once again and pulled another disc from inside her cape. "There are only two people in the world with these genetic profiles. Download this data into your eye, and we'll find them quickly." She placed the new disc on the table. The man's eye patch shone with scrolling white text, hundreds of lines of computer code.

"Wait!" he cried, now visibly sweating. "Wait. What?"

"What's the matter?" said the woman, sipping her tea.

"These calculations *cannot* be correct. These... children... they'll exceed *our* power!"

The others murmured with excitement, mixed with discomfort. The leader of the women stood up. "Not at first. They will need every resource we can muster to realize their potential."

The metal crewmember pressed some buttons on a device. The screen changed to show a room filled with books, manuals, and manuscripts.

The woman's eyes widened as she walked toward the display. "Those are... books?"

"That is the ship's new library," the metallic assistant replied. It sounded proud. "By intercepting micro and macro data waves from ancient civilizations' communication and broadcasting systems, our partners in the South enabled us to reconstitute a library from every recorded intelligent creature in the local galactic sectors. Those are precise physical replicas of tens of thousands of years of accumulated wisdom."

The "partners in the South," otherwise known as the Community, were a group of rebels who cooperated in a leaderless international network to oppose the corporation using sabotage and computer hacking and supplied the provisions that the Fighters need. Rather than using conventional weapons, they'd developed advanced machine learning models and logistical support for the fight against the oppressor. Despite the lack of a formal leader, their members gave what food and support they could, and the Community organized protests to galvanize public support against the corporate regime.

The woman's eyes began to glisten. "Glory to the ancestors," she whispered. Then she turned to face the group. "We will facilitate the Walking Ancestor ceremony, and the youths will master the six powers. The oracle has never been wrong."

As the woman and her comrades prepared to locate the two teenagers prophesied by the oracle, they knew that time was running out. The man, who had never been able to fully trust the oracles, was still apprehensive. He had stressed the dangers involved in finding and extracting these boys, never mind the difficulties of initiating and training them. He clenched his fist and spoke of those who would seek to destroy the chosen ones before they could be located. But the woman was undaunted. She laid a reassuring hand on his shoulder. They had to act now if they were to find the youths before it was too late.

As they analyzed the oracle's message, they realized that the newly elected world president might hold the key to their mission. But with less than ten hours to go before he stepped onto the stage for his inauguration, time was of the essence. They altered their flight coordinates and prepared a new course.

The leader of the women and the man with the eye patch were siblings. They knew this would be their riskiest mission yet. They could not afford to make any mistakes, but they were resolute. They had learned to work together to build a new future for their world. They had faith in their accumulated, ancestral knowledge, their painfully acquired skills, and above all, their determination to create revolutionaries who would defeat the great oppressor. As they stood together, gazing at the oracle's words on the screen, they sensed that this might be their last chance.

The woman spoke softly. "The fate of our world rests on our shoulders. We *must* succeed." With that, they set their sights on the northern continent and the battle that awaited them.

CHAPTER 1

FREEDOM SEEKER

On this fated afternoon, the sky was gray, the building was gray, and even the staff were gray. The orphanage was run by solemn artificial intelligences. The staff were all bots, metal servants running on the most advanced machine learning software. The authorities called them General Artificial Intelligence Automatons, or GAIA for short. People from the South, on the other hand, called them *mekanations.* No matter what you called them, they were more efficient, more reliable, and a lot cheaper than living assistants, admins, and guards. They never went on strike and never asked for raises. They were perfect for the job of looking after children destined only to be killing machines. But they were battery powered and require maintenance, tune-ups, and software updates—all automated as well—to stay up to date and hypervigilant.

"Next!" the cafeteria bot said.

It sounded like a living being, but it was in fact a faceless box of metal, serving only one purpose—to place food on the trays the youths carried and to signal when the next child must come forward to receive gruel into bowls as gray as everything else.

A nameless youth was shoved ahead in the assembly line. He was wearing a striped jumpsuit with metal restraints on both ankles and wrists to prevent "misbehavior." The tag on his jumpsuit read #1966.

"OK," he muttered, raising his tray before the mekkie. The bot's camera and microphone enabled facial and vocal recognition. The metal attendant dropped its ladle into a chunky gray substance glittering with finely calibrated ingredients. It moved the ladle over the boy's tray and plopped the portion of mush into his bowl. The food looked unappealing, but it was not unhealthy. All the ingredients had been selected and measured with precisely the calories and nutrients suited to 1966's needs and metabolism. If he didn't eat all of it, he wouldn't get any leisure time this evening. And that absolutely *could not* happen. Not tonight of all nights.

"Next!"

The boy was pushed forward to his assigned lunch seat, in isolation from others. Meals were always served in isolation to prevent unnecessary bonding. Yet for the boy, there was an upside. It provided a brief interval of unsupervised time when he could daydream. The downside was the digital timer in front of him, counting down how many minutes he had before the guards assembled all of the orphans in one place again. The boy ate a little faster than usual today and finished forty seconds before the five minutes were up. He was anxious about what would happen then, but he used the breathing techniques he had learned to help calm his nerves.

Today was the day he would get the hell out of this place. Today he was going to see freedom.

It hadn't been a great place to be raised. Nowhere is when you grow up in a metal box. Until recently, 1966 used to get in a lot of fights, and he had quite a few detentions on his record. He often wondered if that was exactly what the system wanted. Everyone made such a big deal about skin tones. He didn't care much about his, but the other orphans did. And they would let him know what they thought about his brown skin by leaving bruises on it. The AIs were not immune to this prejudice either; they were designed by the same people who messed up everyone's minds in the first place. Since this was an orphanage for descendants of Dark people, it looked like they almost encouraged the orphans to fight each other. He was still a youth, but he understood what was going on.

BEEP. The timer hit zero. A door opened and a guard mekkie motioned 1966 to head back to the main lobby with the other juveniles and join his category. There were several: losers, good-for-nothings, and troublemakers—the category 1966 was in. The orphans were every possible shade of beige, brown, and black. The lightest ones got the best treatment, but that didn't mean much when they were all stuck in a prison. All the youths had either been abducted at birth or lost their parents during the countless wars waged by the North to steal the natural resources of the South. Their shared misfortunes had created a sort of solidarity among some of the youths, but they had also left a chip on everyone's shoulder.

The youth were kept here and trained until they were seen as ready to serve as soldiers.

1966 had been trapped here for so long he couldn't remember his given name, though he *thought* he must have had one once. Too bad he never met the mother who would have given it to him. It was the typical story. She probably lived in the South, and an officer of Light must have taken advantage of her during some military operation. It was the only thing that could explain his red spiky hair and slightly lighter complexion that got him treated differently than his cellmates. He had to admit that some of them had it twice as bad, but that hadn't made him any happier.

As soon as they'd cut his umbilical cord, Child Removal Services took him from the hospital and flew him up north to this living hell. They trained the youths to distrust everything, but there was one script he knew must be true. Eventually, if his training worked, he would be sent right back to one of those unknown villages and continue the cycle. But something was different in him. Like a few of the other boys, 1966 had retained some spark of individuality. He sensed that his destiny was different, that he wouldn't spend the rest of his life taking orders from artificial voices and reproducing the same traumatizing abyss. He couldn't remember his date of birth, but he thought he had to be in his mid-teens. This meant he would be deployed soon. When he reached sixteen, which could be any day now, he'd be shipped off to fight in the South, and there would never be another chance to escape.

Scheduled maintenance was going to take place today for all the mekanations. This was because it was a very important day. Today, Mr. Kravan Telron, the newly "elected" president of Ziffea, would be making a major announcement during his inauguration. To make sure security would be top notch and the military on point, a maintenance operation was set to take place at all military-related facilities.

Timing was everything. There would be a very short window of opportunity, when a certain line of code would be inserted into one of the scheduled maintenance scripts and the mekanations would be temporarily destabilized before auto-resetting. If some troublemakers were aware of this and had the means, they could cause the operating system to loop the reset until some actual living creature at an off-site control center detected the abnormality. And with all eyes on preparations for Mr. Telron's announcement, that could give the orphans a few short minutes to escape.

The boys gathered together. One of them had a finger-sized viewscreen that had been snuck into the orphanage without any of the bots noticing. It was still uncompromised and unconnected to any external networks that could be eavesdropped on. 1966 had no idea how this feat had been accomplished. Someone on the outside was behind it, obviously, but who? And why? Nobody out there cared about them; he knew that. His worthlessness as anything more than a future soldier drone had been drilled into him from the day he was brought to this place. Yet the secret viewscreen was real. He'd seen it. Maybe someone out there cared about them after all.

The only thing they could do was wait for the signal. They weren't sure why or how the bots would shut down, but someone from the outside was giving instructions. The idea of there being some unknown masterminds out there was exciting, but they recognized the risks if the plan failed. They might get put into solitary—or somewhere deeper in the ground.

But just as jealousy and greed shows up whenever people get together, not everyone in the orphanage wanted everyone to be happy. Some were straight cowards, and others were willing to snitch if that meant denying a rival the chance to escape.

1966 reviewed the plan again. Whoever arranged this would send the contraband viewscreen a message with a five-second countdown. The orphan with the viewscreen would signal to the others that the message had been received, and thirty seconds later, the security systems would shut down. All the lights would go off, and the north, west, south, and east doors would all open. This would be their chance, but it would be very brief. 1966 walked up as close to the northern door as he could, keeping an eye out while trying not to draw any attention to himself.

The kid with the screen took his pick out and started combing his afro. Wait a minute. Was that the signal? It had to be, because the kid then started walking to the southern gate. In thirty seconds, they would get a chance to break out of this place. 1966's instincts told him to pick the northern door. Most were following the signaler to the southern door, while a few others were going toward the western and eastern ones. The snitches must have been active. Everyone who approached the other doors was being stopped by the bots and ordered to sit down on the floor. When the lights went off, they would be helpless.

Suddenly, right on schedule, the hall was plunged into darkness. Everyone's metal restraints clattered to the ground, sending the room into a frenzy. He heard the doors sliding open and the sounds of the bots shuffling as they formed a ring around the corralled boys. No time to hesitate. He ran northward into the darkness.

Remembering the layout of the facility was not difficult. He had been here for as long as he could remember. As he dashed down the hallways that led to the northern exit, he found all the emergency doors wide open. He couldn't hear any of the orphans following him. Was it a trap? No time to think about it. Freedom was the only option.

He flew past deactivated security cameras and inactive security bots. He dodged past the arsenal that housed the military-grade rifles the mekkies sometimes used. There was weaponry in there meant to do away with intruders and prisoners alike. It all seemed too easy, but he had to get out of here. Running, following the map in his mind, he entered the final hallway and saw the sunlight from outside in the distance. It shone on his skin and startled him. He slipped and fell to the floor, but picked himself up without hesitation and kept running toward the light. Was this too good to be true? He couldn't focus on doubts now. Only freedom was on his mind as he burst through the open doorway. He had no plan besides this. His only thought was *anywhere but here*, and so he kept running under the cover of the gray skies and polluted air.

He found a clearing, from where he could see large white buildings in the near distance. The ground was covered by large, white, metallic squares, and a labyrinth of roadways floated high above him. He marveled at how they'd hidden a torture center in the middle of a city, though he knew that military installations made up most of the fabric of Azor City.

He looked back anxiously. Surprisingly, the security cameras and automated guns still seemed to be deactivated. *"Don't think. Keep running.*" He ran and ran until he came to an overpass. He slid into the shade of the bridge and breathed heavily. His heart was practically leaping out of his chest, but all the fistfights and mandatory exercise training had primed him for this moment. In trying to turn him into the perfect foot soldier, the orphanage had created a perfect runaway.

Concealed by the shadows of the overpass, he looked back again. There was still no one behind him. He wondered if he was the only one who'd made it out. Even if he wasn't being followed, he'd need to find a crowd to blend into, at least to buy time. The police bots that patrolled the streets were very sophisticated, as the instructors in the orphanage had told them often enough. It would take just seconds for them to identify the barcode on his uniform. Being in a crowd should at least stop them from shooting him dead on the spot.

Still breathing hard, he tried to think. As his breath grew more regular, an idea came to him. He'd go where no one would expect him to go. If he could make it to Mr. Telron's inauguration, that would be perfect. No one would be looking for him at one of the most secure events in the world. And the security would be focused on protecting the president, not looking for some runaway teen.

How would he find the venue? The kid with the viewscreen would have known.

They will find you and kill you.

Your plan will never work.

SLAP. He whipped a hand against his face. Not now! This was no time for the voices. He *had* to survive. Something primal activated in him, something that wouldn't allow him to die here. It pushed him forward, his senses heightening. He saw paths that could hide him from the vehicles blurring past him on the roads. He was now acting only by instinct. He pressed on, moving only when the coast was clear, ducking for cover, sneaking through alleyways. Making his way farther and farther into the city.

Soon, he was in the midst of a crowd. He sensed that he'd reached the downtown area. Mr. Telron's event had to be somewhere around here. But seeing and navigating among all these people felt overwhelming. He started to think about how tired he was. And thirsty, so thirsty.

No time to think about that. The most important thing was to watch out for the people with helmets and visors in white. He caught a glimpse of one across the crowded street. Oh no. Had he seen 1966 too?

He dodged into a store, ignoring the automated greeting from the mindless bot, and pretended to look at the candies in the nearest aisle. They were all produced by the same company. He couldn't stand to even look at the garbage they sold to people, but hiding out here allowed him to catch his breath.

"WILL YOU BUY SOMETHING? IT IS A CRIME TO LOITER!"

He looked up at the mekkie, then through the window overlooking the street. The police bot was gone.

"Thanks, maybe next time."

"OK, WE ACCEPT THAT ANSWER."

He went out the door, turned toward downtown, and kept walking. But he was getting exhausted now. His legs grew heavy like logs, but he couldn't risk calling attention to himself by stopping or "loitering" in another store. His breathing was raw but he had to keep going. He trudged on, scarcely aware of his surroundings, too tired now even to watch for the white visors.

Then he heard the roar of a crowd, and a vast round building loomed up ahead. Was it the stadium? It had to be!

He looked up at the sky. Despite all the years of indoctrination in the orphanage, he still, deep down, had faith in something higher than the prison walls. "Thank you, Si-Vin," he said as he followed the crowds streaming into the stadium and toward the fanfares and cheers inside.

CHAPTER 2

SEARCH FOR BELONGING

Not too far away, in the same technology-dominated urban sprawl of Azor City, another boy was getting ready to attend Mr. Telron's event, but under very different circumstances.

"Hurry up, dear," a middle-aged woman called to him from downstairs.

A big smile came to his face as he yelled back, "Yes, ma'am!"

Then he looked into the mirror, and the smile disappeared. In the reflection, he saw the oversized bed in the spacious room. Everything was kept nice and clean by housebots that could be summoned at the push of a button. He looked at the mushroom-shaped cut of his permanently-straightened hair. *I don't belong here*, he thought. He'd thought that a lot lately.

His mother had a high position in one of the military agencies that "defended" the North, but although she often gushed about her victories whenever they had guests, he knew that her kill count was mostly civilians. Some of the people she lit up could have very well been his own relatives. Adopted into an elite family, molded by them into a prized chocolate possession, what was there not to like about this life? He had it all—except for the freedom to be who he really was. It was hard to be sad, but it was hard to be happy too.

He sighed, knowing that he was only going to the event for *her*. Pressing a button on the mirror caused beams of light to descend on him, generating fabric and shaping the material. Long sleeves formed around his arms, decorated with gold floral patterns. Matching pant legs followed. The three-dimensional pattern of his shoes was beamed onto his feet, perfectly coating and surrounding them. As the clothes adjusted themselves to the specifications of his waist and hips and shoulders, the feeling of resentment that had started when he looked in the mirror gripped him more tightly. He did not need such fancy clothes. They only made his classmates envy him and look for a reason to despise him. And they didn't have far to look. His dark skin was the only excuse they needed.

He ran down the stairs in an outfit that was consciously designed to be perfect, but it was still customary to ask.

"How does it look?"

"Splendid," the woman replied.

Of course she was satisfied with him and her expensive household gadgets. It was the least she could do for "someone like him," as she often told her friends. She thought of how thoroughly she had done her duty to her nation by raising such a dark-skinned child to be an outstanding citizen. She thought of how much better it was that he lived with her than with any of the other veterans, the addicts who had used up their government benefits by drowning their trauma and depression with liquor and drugs. She was proud to be different from those fools with their guilty consciences.

Even so, memories of past "freedom missions" sometimes crept into her mind. The sound of the energy cannons and the stink of charred flesh could sometimes disturb her. *What a time to be bothered by such things*, she thought. With a shudder, she pushed the terrible memories out of her mind. It was only right that Dark children were adopted by Light parents and rescued from their nonsense and primitive traditions. She was doing her part to make the world a better place by training him to be a useful citizen of the North.

The boy, she assured herself, wasn't old enough to be troubled by this. And with the right guidance, he never would be. He was still young enough to be moldable. He got great grades in school, he was exceptional in the combat classes he took as an extracurricular activity, and his awards from school filled the lobby of their house. She gazed proudly at them, all engraved with "First Place: JagJonzan" on shiny metal plaques. She worried, though, that the name didn't mean much to him. It didn't come from his biological parents, but instead from a random string of utterances from an AI language model. Still, all would be well so long as he never tried to find out about his true origins.

She was pleased when she saw him admiring his awards. He was especially proficient at boxing, and for his age, this made him a force to be reckoned with. A few demonstrations of his hands kept the bullies at bay when they tried to call him the M-word. *What a perfectly imperfect student*, she thought with a smile.

A tall, Light, and handsome mekanation approached JagJonzan. Their suits matched perfectly.

"You have great taste, son," it said.

"Thanks, pops."

"Now, show me what you got!" it shouted.

They did a bit of good-humored sparring. The robotic "father" perfectly dodged every punch the boy threw.

"Hey now, you two," the woman scolded, "don't scratch your technogarments. You'll have plenty of time to practice your routine once we get back home."

"Aww," the two of them slumped their shoulders and looked toward the imported handcrafted carpet.

She had enough money to match on the metanetworks with an ideal partner, but she had bought one instead. This digital father was programmed for childrearing, tutoring, cleaning, vehicle repair, cooking, and assault rifle operation. It was not uncommon for people to buy a digital partner rather than take their chances with actual people. It was too bothersome. It was one of the perks of coming from the North. There was freedom to do and get whatever you wanted. The only downside to a digital father was the surveillance. They were also programmed to report any broken laws or anarchistic behavior to the authorities immediately and in detail. And that function could not be modified in any way.

"OK, Jag, are you all ready to go?" the metal giant asked.

"Ready, sir!" The boy beamed.

The three left the home and entered their vehicle, and the digital father put a finger into the ignition. The coordinates for the inauguration had already been downloaded. The vehicle emitted a pleasant hum, lifted slightly from the driveway, and hovered down the street. It would only take a few minutes to arrive at their destination: the central stadium of Azor City, where Mr. Telron would deliver his first speech as world president. Jag and his mother sat in the back as the cityscape whizzed by. Skyscrapers and malls dominated the scene, yet every so often, he could make out a military installation in the distance. Vehicles zoomed past one another with inches to spare, perfectly coordinated by Central Digital Traffic Control. Some could float, others could not. Some floated above the others, a sign of high status. None of the passengers had the same complexion as Jag. He looked down at his hands.

"Mother," he asked, "how come no one looks like me?"

"What?" Her eyes grew wide, and her face reddened. Before Jag knew what was happening, he caught a swift palm to the right side of his face.

"No crimes detected," the cybernetic chaperone remarked in a robotic voice, speaking to no one in the vehicle.

Jag looked at his mother, stunned.

"You must never talk about your appearance or concern yourself with the appearance of others," she said, staring back at him with hard eyes. "How many times have I told you that? One day we'll find a way to get you bleached and that will be the end of it." She turned away and looked out the window. "Never bring this up again until then."

The boy looked down at his hands again. Through the stinging of his cheek, he muttered, "Yes ma'am."

Dejected, he went back to looking out the window. How could he have forgotten that important rule—that he could have everything in the world so long as he was willing to never remember his past or ask questions about this false identity? For the rest of the ride, he would try to change the subject to surface-level issues. That was what pleased mother. Societal media, viewscreen programming, and fashion trends were more important than his relationships with others. Much like his digital father, he was an accessory for her.

He wondered for a moment if this was how other sixteen-year-olds lived. Yet, he knew it wasn't. He also knew that after his next birthday, he would be sent for infantry training. He dreaded the idea of going to the place that had made his adopted mother what she was. He *had to* break free before this happened. Yes, one day everything would change forever.

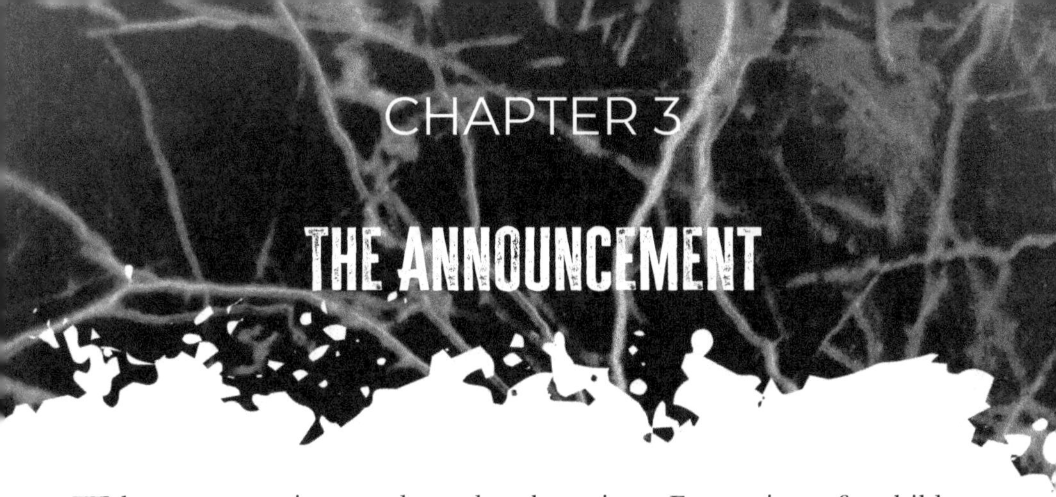

CHAPTER 3

THE ANNOUNCEMENT

There was music, crowds, and mekanations. Entertainers for children, bartenders for adults. It was a fabricated celebration, meant to showcase the nonexistent accomplishments of a politician and his billionaire friends. Sweets and junk food were being dished out to mark the historic occasion. Admission was free as well. The powers that be needed to have as many people there as possible, and they had succeeded. Tens of thousands had come, including people from all four planets. Many were dignitaries, but most were just citizens who had come for food and entertainment or from a fear of missing out on something so "historic." The state-controlled media had hyped up the event nonstop for weeks.

It was the perfect place for 1966 to avoid detection, but now that the relief of escaping the orphanage had faded, he had to make some hard choices. He was free, but now what? What was he supposed to do next?

But at least for this moment, he could relax. He leaned against a sandwich stand and rested for a moment. He breathed in a steady, deliberate rhythm and focused on slowing down and stabilizing his heart rate—he had learned at least one useful thing in his sniper weapon training classes. He had time to look around and observe the flashing lights, the laughing children, and the plushie—one tiny little kid had won a huge plush toy at one of the shooting competitions. She could barely hold the gigantic thing but was parading around the crowd with her head tilted upward. In her carefully coiffed hair, an exquisitely crafted hairpin glittered with jewels. Her dress glimmered with 3D-beamed precious silks, gold thread, and computer-generated shiny stones. As she passed 1966, she raised her prized toy toward him.

"Bleh," he said.

She stuck her tongue out and ran back to her mekkie mother, which effortlessly raised her onto its shoulder with one arm, then glared at him for a quick moment before the two fused back into the crowd of nameless revelers.

"Y'all are trash," he said to no one in particular.

He never had nice things. At the orphanage, he'd heard stories from other boys about how good kids on the outside had it and had wondered if such lives were real. Now, with a bitter taste in his mouth, he knew they were. The guys who were shipped to the orphanage when they were older had told him stories of all the shiny trinkets people outside filled their lives with. Their eyes had sparkled when they described the malls and the online shops where you could get anything you wanted, but 1966 just shook his head and wondered how people could be so greedy and shallow. There had to be more to life than just *things*? Although he'd just left a prison, he felt that he'd entered a new one—a prison of the mind rather than the body.

1966 moved through the crowd, fascinated and repelled.

All of the richest-looking people, 1966 realized, had either naturally light skin or, if you looked closely, the telltale signs of artificial skin lighteners. He watched in disgust as they gave each other fake compliments, lied about how much they liked each other, and gushed over each other's pictures of themselves on portable viewscreens.

A child with a haircut that looked like a double mushroom caught his attention. Somehow he couldn't help following him. He watched as the child's mekkie father turned and smiled at his "son."

"Wow!" it exclaimed as it pranced through the festivities. "Isn't this great?"

"Sure is," the boy responded, but to 1966, he did not sound convinced.

And indeed, Jag was still dejected by the slap he'd received a few minutes earlier. He was beginning to feel disillusioned by the whole event, though he wasn't sure why. Other young people passed by him, marveling at his computer-generated clothing, clearly envious, but he hardly noticed.

His mother looked on, pleased that her purchases were meeting her expectations. She was just as lavishly dressed as Jag, and she loved the envious eyes of the onlookers as she strolled through the crowds with her custom-built family and exchanged the usual pleasantries with other security force members. Most were also accompanied by digital partners, and a few had adopted children who looked different from them.

As they progressed toward the northernmost point of the stadium, where the podium had been erected for Mr. Telron's inauguration, Jag felt himself grow more and more uneasy. He knew that when they got home again, his mother would amuse herself by mocking and sneering at the people she had just been so friendly with. He was sure the others would all do the same. It was always like this when they went out. He wondered what they said about him behind his mother's back. Subtract his fancy appearance, and these fake friends wouldn't be smiling at him with their 3D-generated teeth, would they? Their hearts beat like his, they breathed the same air, but in their interactions, they were just like robots. He knew he couldn't speak to his mother about his concerns, so he said nothing. She could read his expression though. Smugly, she smiled at him. "This is just the way it is," she said.

He turned his head away without saying a word.

They continued on their way. Even though his digital father was programmed to bring excitement and wonder to the boy on any occasion, no smile crossed Jag's face. As they walked past the gift terminals, he crossed paths with a kid with wild, spiky red hair and a double ponytail. His clothing looked different. He was different. They locked eyes. It was as if time itself had stopped. Maybe in a past life they had been friends or family, maybe adversaries. But they both sensed in that split second that they had incarnated here, in this era and on this planet for a reason. They knew it deep in their souls.

"What are you doing?" Jag's mother called. "Keep walking!"

Time resumed, and the boys continued on their separate paths. But though they had parted ways, they felt validated. They came from different backgrounds, but for a moment they sensed a deeper affinity. Their frowns eased into smiles, if only a little bit.

The excitement in the crowd grew until it was interrupted by loud speakers blasting out patriotic music. Jag turned toward the source of the fanfare and an automated vocal announcement followed.

"PLEASE COME TO THE MAIN STAGE FOR THE ANNOUNCEMENT."

CHAPTER 3 | THE ANNOUNCEMENT

The crowd buzzed with excitement. The beginning of Mr. Telron's world presidency had been touted by the media for months as the most significant political event of the century. Jag sighed as he thought about the nonstop advertisements he had seen about the event. He was starting to think that every company in the world was working really hard to make the public like this guy. It wasn't just in Jag's imagination or even a slight coincidence..

Mr. Telron was the bland public face of something much more powerful that seemed to run the world behind the scenes. Along with other, lesser figures—the cabinet ministers, legislators, policy experts, and so on who made Ziffea look like a democracy—his role was to keep the people smiling while the interplanetary corporation ate up the planet.

"I want to thank you all for coming today," Telron began. "You all are *epic* and you all are on *fleek*!"

The crowd roared and whooped. His flour-like complexion contrasted with his fancy blue suit. Though middle-aged and conservatively dressed, Telron liked to use what he'd presumably been told was the latest slang. He probably thought this showed that he was down with the younger generation.

"My friends," he said, "all this food, fun, and entertainment has been provided by the best company in the world, All-Mark. They deserve an applause, no cap, no cap, amiright?"

All-Mark was a subsidiary of the largest, most powerful corporation in the solar system. All the big mass-market companies were. The crowd cheered anyway. They ate this stuff up. But deep down, Jag questioned it. Although they wouldn't permit his questions at the educational centers, Jag often wondered who owned the politicians? Could these special shoutouts be the result of backroom deals and royalty cheques? The businesses raked in profits, the laws allowed it, and politicians gave the appearance of being in touch with a manipulated public. The authorities wouldn't allow such a big conspiracy to go on like this, would they? No one could give him a straight answer. He looked back toward the stage.

Telron hesitated for a moment. "But there is something extra special that I want to mention tonight, *outasight*?" he resumed. Some of the suits in the back looked uneasy. The world president seemed to be straying from the script on the holographic prompter.

"I want to come clean with you, my friends. Clean as a dream. Not only do I think it would be great for us to welcome more freedom into our lives with open arms, I want to make that freedom better for *all* of us."

The suits in the back started to whisper to each other. Some of the better-dressed members of the crowd began to murmur. Grumblings occurred in the crowd. Something didn't fit with the program.

"When I say *all* of us," Telron added, "I mean every single one of us. You gotta trust!" The crowd was getting uneasy now. Jag looked past his digital father. Some of the less sophisticated models of digital parents had started to beep as they processed Mr. Telron's words for potential unorthodoxy.

But the new world president was undeterred. He'd had a bright idea, and he was going to run with it.

"That is why tomorrow," he announced, "immediately after I am formally sworn in to office, I will be having a sit down with the congresses of our constituent republics to find ways to eliminate... the color barrier!"

Now, gasps of shock and consternation rose up from the crowd. Jag watched as his mother raised hands to cover her mouth. Telron looked worried, but he pressed on.

"Too many of us have been left behind," he shouted above the rising noise of the crowd, as some the suits behind him moved forward, grim-faced. "That's why I think—"

BANG!

The shot echoed around the stadium. It was impossible to tell where it had come from. Telron staggered and grabbed at his shoulder. Then, with a look of astonishment on his broad, reddened face, he fell to the floor.

Jag's eyes widened. What was happening? An assassination? He looked toward the west block of the stadium, then toward the eastern side. Did the assassin disappear? That didn't matter anymore. Thousands of people in the packed stadium were confused, scared, and running in all directions.

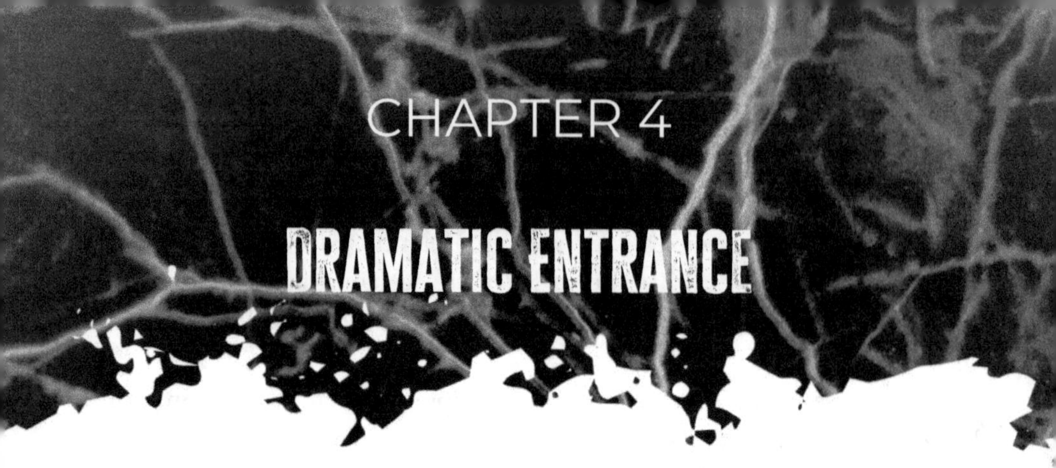

CHAPTER 4

DRAMATIC ENTRANCE

1966 watched the world's president fall with a strange mixture of dread and excitement. The crowd erupted into a frenzy. He watched drinks and rubbish hurled into the air and heard screams from all directions. People rushed past him, their eyes wide with horror, mouths open, pushing and shouting as they panicked. He didn't feel the same pressure to leave. He took a few steps forward, walking toward the stage amid the chaos, feeling oddly invulnerable.

Guardbots scrambled to shield the president from any additional fire. Everyone else rushed to leave, all at the same time. Feet stomped, hands pushed, people were trampled and crushed.

Suddenly, 1966 felt a shoulder hit him from behind and was almost thrown off of his feet. The momentum of the crowd carried him forward now. Then he saw the other kid get shoved to the ground and disappear under a junk food stand as it toppled over. The mushroom-haired boy tried to shield himself from the crushing stampede, but he was too weak. The roof smothered his body. The woman who'd been dragging him around tried to run away. She was trying to save herself, but was shoved aside by the raging crowd.

The mekanation that was following them started to glitch out. It stopped in place, rotated its head 360 degrees, and announced, "CRIMES HAVE BEEN DETECTED!" Then, it spun and rotated its hands, then its torso, and moved rapidly around the tightly packed crowd, scraping and slashing the clamoring people it smashed into.

The lady shrieked, "No! This can't be happening!" But her digital partner slammed its metal palms into her, shredding her ten-thousand-world-dollar designer outfit. The dozens of other mekanations throughout the crowd were acting the same way, spinning, rotating, and slashing at anyone in reach in a strangely coordinated manner. The bots closest to the exits locked the doors to prevent people from leaving. The only exit they left alone was behind the northern stage.

1966 recovered his balance and pushed closer to the stage. He watched the scene, unharmed and strangely calm, as if indifferent to the chaos around him. Weaving between the mekkies and their shrieking victims, he made his way toward the stage in time to see Telron helped to his feet by two mekkie bodyguards.

"Mr. Telron, are you hurt?" he heard one of the guardbots ask.

"What does it look like?" the world president shouted, pointing at a spreading bloodstain near the shoulder of his blazer. "Get me out of here!" he squealed.

The mekanations on the stage were still fully functional. They rushed together and formed a shield around Telron as the two bodyguards led him off the stage and through the exit behind. The dignitaries and other guests of honor were also led to safety.

Throughout the rest of the stadium, the chaos and panic only increased. The crowd, unable to escape, were still being cut and slashed by their once obedient helpers. 1966 looked on, neither fazed nor injured, as those bots that were still functioning properly began to locate lobbyists and advertisers safely escort them outside.

Those left behind grew desperate. The sway and force of the crowd broke the aura of safety around 1966 and knocked him to the ground. As he struggled back to his feet, a bot jumped right ahead of him. Its limbs were soaked in blood, its eyes glowing bright red.

"NUMBER 1966. CRIME COMMITTED!"

Its hands began to spin like blades in a blender as it approached.

The boy froze. They had found him. His legs felt like rubber. He knew he wouldn't have the strength to defend himself as the mekkie spun toward him.

WHAM.

Droplets of his blood sprayed through the air, and the impact of a ton of metal launched him several feet into the air. With a thud, he hit the ground and lay there, unmoving.

Helpless but not unconscious, he heard the sound of metal being twisted and torn somewhere nearby. He opened his eyes to see a diminutive figure dressed in complete black body armor whip its hand right through the center of the solid metal mekkie, dividing it into two clean halves. Then it launched itself soundlessly into the air and hovered above the crowd. He noticed that it wore a black patch where its eye should have been. A white pupil glowed at the center of the patch.

This strange being darted around the stadium, slicing through every haywire machine it could find, cutting through them with its right palm effortlessly tearing through metal like sheets of paper. Narrowly avoiding contact with any of the survivors, it chopped through the bots with the precision of a sewing machine. This ebony clad warrior worked at lightning speed, seeming to transport its body through time, smashing pieces of hard steel to fragments. In just a few moments, it disposed of every one of the berserk mekanations. Only the stationary bots remained intact at the exits.

A taller figure in a black alloy cape now leapt from the crowd and hovered in the air. From its hand came bright beams of light that homed in on the mekanations at the exits, crushing them like delicate flowers. A beam of light from its other hand blew gaping holes in the locked doors. People rushed through them to the safety of the streets outside.

The taller figure stood on thin air and called out in a female voice, "Zoticon!"

"What?" the other called back in a male baritone, sounding almost annoyed.

Those aren't mekkies. Who are they? 1966 thought to himself.

"Did you find the potentials?" said the female voice.

There was a momentary pause, then a moment later: "Found them!"

"They might not make it out of this alive." The being pointed to where the boy with the mushroom haircut was buried under the fallen snack stand. "Get that one under there. I'll bring the second one and meet you back at base."

"Affirmed."

The being in black attire darted over to 1966, who still lay where he had fallen, bloodied and gasping for air.

"Hang on, we'll take care of you," the being said as he lifted 1966 with one arm and scanned the surroundings. Twisted pieces of mekkie bodies lay everywhere, but apart from the groans and contractions of cooling metal, there was no sound or movement.

As they hovered in the air, 1966 watched his rescuer's partner descend and, with one hand, lift the large piece of metal hiding the mushroom haircut kid's battered body and whipping it to the side like it was a piece of paper. It landed several meters away with a heavy thud.

By this point, 1966 had begun to slip in and out of consciousness. Everything was moving so fast. He was being carried by something floating. What was going on? Who were these people, if they even were people? Was he going to die?

As they hovered there and his rescuer scanned the stadium for remaining threats, 1966 caught a brief glimpse of a group of the remaining survivors looking up at him. Some looked dumbfounded. Others seemed angry.

The female arrived beside them, holding the other boy in her arms.

"You're going to survive," she told him, "Just hang on."

An elderly man from the group below stumbled toward her.

"Bastard!" he screamed.

The woman turned toward him.

The old man waved a fist, "You devils! You caused this!"

More of the group joined him.

"Mutatiin!" they shouted. "Damn mutatiin!" Other taunts and slurs followed. One of the men picked up a shard of metal and threw it at her. It fell short, but the others started to look around for anything sharp and hard they could throw.

"Zoticon!" she yelled. "Time to get out of here! Now!"

"All right. Be safe."

In an instant, the four of them had disappeared. Trails of dust swirled where they had once hovered.

ŻOTICON

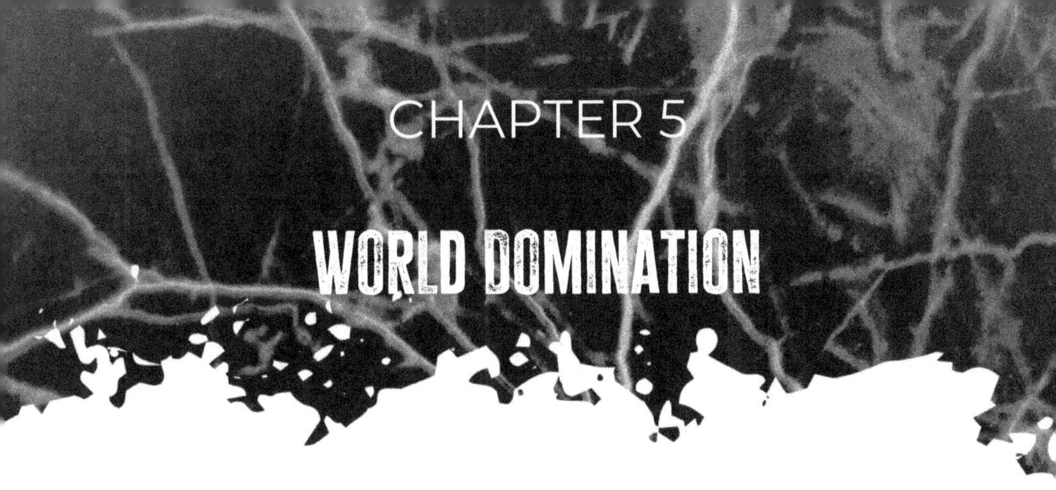

CHAPTER 5

WORLD DOMINATION

High Commander Phutais, the head of Zi-Tai corporation, sat in his throne-like office chair, resplendent in his white and gray military colors. He wore bulletproof technofabric that had been reinforced at the cellular level thanks to most of his natural flesh having been replaced with tungsten and near impenetrable alloys. A mask covered his face, revealing only his eyes. Before logging onto the scheduled conference, he turned his eyes to a viewscreen to watch the coverage of the attack on the evening news.

He was unnerved, even though the night had still gone according to plan. He wondered who were those two beings who had interfered? He wanted to see the media's take on it.

As expected, it was all over the news. Rolling coverage, of course, with presenters who almost seemed to enjoy reporting what had happened.

"Breaking news!" gushed a woman in a snug crop top that displayed her ample cleavage. "A terrible, absolutely freakin' terrible event has taken place in the capital!" Her excited style of delivery was also designed to get attention.

"Oh, you better believe it, a tragedy, a real tragedy," her male co-anchor said, trying his best to look solemn. He was dressed in a professional suit to ensure that most viewers would focus on his scantily dressed partner, but he spoke with the same excited intensity.

Beneath his mask, Phutais smiled to himself. He had made sure years ago that the "news" media was always delivered like this, as entertainment for the masses, another shallow distraction from the soulless reality of their transient lives.

The reporters' words sounded spontaneous, but they had been calculated and carefully scripted. Their looks, their dress, their makeup and hair, all of it was designed to keep the state-run media's ratings high and viewers' minds preoccupied with the bright flashing surface of things rather than thinking about causes and effects.

Behind the presenters, a giant screen looped video of the devastation, highlighting the destroyed mekanations and damaged stadium exits against a soundtrack of ominous, pounding music. After viewers had got their fill of this, the program cut away to live interviews with survivors. Every one of them stressed the horrors perpetrated by the two crazed "terrorists."

"They just showed up out of nowhere and started destroying GAIAs and killing people," one man said, his eyes glowing with excitement.

"I don't know what happened first," said a young woman, tears in her eyes, "but my digidad didn't stand a chance,"

"This lady was shooting lights out of her hands, it was wild!" enthused a teenage boy.

The feed cut out before he could finish. Phutais knew what that meant. They had to censor something. It needed to be like this. The narrative had to be controlled. Horror was good. Excitement was fine. But any possible praise for the terrorists could not be in the script. The message had to be clear and reassuring: the authorities knew best, and despite occasional outrages like this stadium attack, they would keep everything in check.

"Well, as you can hear from the survivors of this crazy, insane atrocity," the female anchor bubbled with excitement, "the mutatiin have done it again!"

Phutais shifted uneasily in his seat. That last bit sounded a little too much like congratulations. "Stick to the script," he snarled to the viewscreen.

"Uh, OK, thank you," the male newscaster nervously jumped in, straightening his back as the camera zoomed in on him. "The attackers have been identified as dark-skinned terrorists. Mr. Telron, out of the grace of his heart, wanted to welcome them into our society, but they don't deserve that. They are terrorists, and they must be found and stopped."

"Oh, of course, we all agree with that," his partner shot back, a touch of panic in her eyes. "Right, let's get some more *super* insights from the scene with our live correspondents."

CLICK.

Phutais shut the screen off, propelled his chair to a different part of his huge desk, and switched on his viewscreen console. A loading bar at the bottom of the screen, labelled MILITARY ENCRYPTION, reached 100 percent. He slammed his steel finger to the keyboard.

"Thoughts, questions?" he said to the screen as it lit up with a row of faces.

A female talking head spoke first. Under her image, the name MERIDIAN MALICIER glowed in red lettering.

As Chief Officer of Consumption, Meridian controlled Zi-Tai's goods and services sector. As usual, she wore a lab coat to suggest she had just come from working to improve one of Zi-Tai's myriad products, but Phutais knew she always carried a pistol with JUSTICE etched on the barrel, in case she needed it. A genius in business, her job was to generate profits, but to do so she also had to maintain the inflow of the raw materials that Zi-Tai needed.

"Well, we're payin' em what they're worth!" the bloated face next to hers said with a boisterous laugh. Under his image was the name HARBUSH COMISAR. He was the Supreme Security Specialist, with responsibilities for policing, monitoring the societal media and other data streams, and quelling any protests. He was still dressed in his signature heavy ivory-colored armor, which was also the official police uniform. A semitransparent protective visor covered his eyes. It doubled as a digital monitor so he could check license plates or personal ID data on the fly.

"The good news is that we now have all the justification we need for commencing our crackdown on the opposition," Phutais announced. "It will only be a matter of time before we rid the world of these terrorists."

"With all this panic, isn't now a good time to negotiate more weapons sales with Azor City's neighbors?" Meridian chimed in.

"And they'll need a bunch of security patrols too. Lemme know when we can get more voltage lasers for the police." Harbush laughed.

"Both of those are already in the plans."

"And sir, I take it y'all don't need none o' dem *big* guns like we do, huh?" Harbush asked.

"No," Phutais said smugly, "unless you have something that can kill things that are already dead."

They all laughed. Except for one.

"Telron," Phutais said. "You're on mute."

There was no reaction.

Phutais raised his voice, "Unmute yourself, you damned fool."

A familiar, bland face flickered onto the screen.

"Oh, oh, sorry about that," Telron said with a nervous chuckle. Underneath his terrified face was the name KRAVAN TELRON. He was still visibly shaken from the attack. His wound had not been serious. It had only taken a few minutes to repair using the bioskeletal nanosuture Meridian's Surgelab subsidiary had recently put on the market. Although Telron was officially a popularly elected world president who represented the voice of the entire planet, his election had been staged and carefully controlled by Zi-Tai.

"You did well today." Phutais smiled at him. "You almost made it seem as if you were *allowed* to go off script."

"Y-yes, sir," Telron stammered, "just following orders, you know."

It was clear he was more afraid of this meeting than of his staged assassination attempt. He knew perfectly well that the individuals participating in this call were directly or indirectly responsible for the deaths of millions.

Zi-Tai Inc. had started off as a modest business with good intentions. After more than a century of ceaseless, terrible warfare, the people of planet Marka had been exhausted and demoralized. Phutais, then a young, idealistic entrepreneur, took up the challenge of finding a way to secure world peace. Transactions were made, influence was gained, and over time, his company became a broker for negotiations between nations. In what seemed a benign idea at the time, a leadership class was created, carefully selected from the best and brightest Phutais could find then rigorously trained to provide selfless governance and given absolute power over the masses. This, Phutais had believed—and he had been sincere at the time—would guarantee a peaceful state of affairs that could never be challenged.

Since that time, over fifty years ago, Marka had remained under their complete control. It had been sucked dry of its resources, its environment uninhabitable outside the vast domes that supplied converted oxygen to the populace. The wars had ended and only one world power remained. It was unclear what happened to the clients who gave Zi-Tai its first big break, or to the original group of associates who'd assisted Phutais in his rise to power.

What *was* clear is that since that time, Zi-Tai—the Four-Winged Angel—had become unstoppable in its relentless pursuit of power. Zi-Tai achieved its goals through military might, political influence, cutthroat business practices, and changing the laws however they saw fit.

On Ziffea, Telron had been an ambitious minor politician dreaming of rising to the top. In Phutais and Zi-Tai, he found what he wanted. Given the outcome on Marka, this was a risky gamble. But it worked. Phutais was tempted into relocating to Ziffea, and within ten years, Telron was poised to be world president. Technological superiority had been easy to achieve. Zi-Tai's advanced AI servants were wildly popular and quickly put all competitors out of business. A loyal billionaire class was created, composed of Telron's family and friends, while all of his political enemies had unfortunate accidents. By the eve of his inauguration, the northern continent and much of the south had been absorbed, and all that was left were a few holdouts where the Community continued to resist with the help of the rebel Fighters.

All was going according to plan.

"Maiden," Phutais called out to a participant whose visual feed was pixelated and voice distorted.

"Yo," the voice replied. Underneath the image was the label MAIDEN.

"The shot you fired was perfect."

"Good. Let me know any place in the world to pick up my check, and I'll be there in five."

"I am sending you the coordinates now. Ensure that no one sees you when you collect the box. Feel free to eliminate any witnesses as usual."

"My pleasure."

"Now that the formalities are out of the way," Phutais said, "I have a question. Which of you destroyed the GAIAs? We never commissioned that. It was not part of the plan."

"Damn straight," Harbush blasted out, "*Our* boys were supposed to steal the glory."

"The media did their job, " Meridian said. "The polling data shows that animosity toward the terrorists is spiking."

"Hmph, still woulda been better for our boys to handle it," Harbush puffed as he turned his head to the side.

"Anyway, it wasn't *my* department," Meridian said.

"And you, Maiden?" Phutais asked. "Which of your contractors would know about this?" Phutais stared at the distorted visual feed with growing anger.

"None of them," Maiden replied confidently, "but send me another check like this, and I'll scour the world and eviscerate whoever it was."

"No, not yet," Phutais said cautiously. He knew she was serious. He would have to keep a close eye on her. Even Phutais knew little about Maiden, apart from the fact that she was the greatest assassin in the solar system. She was a living creature like the others at the meeting, but like Phutais, she had special powers. She could manipulate elements, travel at incredible speed, and crush whole buildings with her bare hands. Phutais knew that whoever was responsible for destroying all those bots at the stadium could do things like Maiden and himself.

"We'll save that discussion for another time," he said. The identity of the saboteurs would need to be looked into urgently, but he didn't want to say so here.

"So, do we move onto phase two?" Meridian asked.

"Phase two?" Harbush interjected, looking confused.

"Check your email attachments," Phutais sighed. "It's marked 'ethnic animus.' Contact my secretary if you need any clarifications. I'm a fan of short meetings, aren't you?"

The others laughed, though Telron still sounded a bit nervous.

"All right, then. I'm gone." Maiden's feed clicked off.

"See ya," Harbush waved just before his image left the screen.

"I'll be in touch with your secretary," Meridian said as her screen went black.

"All right, I'll have my speech writers follow the phase two instructions. But sir, please, can we dispense with the 'damned fool' talk. I am *paying* for your services, you know!" Telron said.

Phutais laughed. "Don't be so sensitive. No one in the galaxy offers what we offer. And by the way, you already signed the contract. One order of democracy will be served once we get through phase five. Again, for any other questions, talk to my secretary," he added with an edge to his voice. "I have another meeting now."

"Right, right," Telron replied. He knew better than to rock the boat. Phutais communicated the message just with his eyes, any wrong move and Telron could lose more than his contract. "Well, thank you again, Mr. Phutais."

"Don't ever use my name. I don't know where you are right now, but no one can know that we ever speak directly. Call me sir, exclusively. One day, you will earn the right for me not to call you a damned fool, but for now, this will have to do."

"O-O-OK, right, right, sorry sir, talk next ti—"

Before he could finish, Phutais slammed they keyboard and shut off the video conference. He stood up and strode to the window of the thirty-story tower in which his offices occupied the penthouse. The stars lay all above and around him. The three moons gently coated his silhouette in a soft silvery light.

He looked at a photo of the two figures in black, each holding one of the boys. He glared at the shorter of the two.

"This little punk really thinks he can fight against the future? What a clown!"

Crumpling the picture was not enough. His three-fingered hand turned bright yellow, and beads of light poured into his palm, incinerating every scrap of the photo.

"It's very simple," he said out loud. "Zi-Tai will rise and our enemies will fall."

CLICK. An autonomous vacuum cleaner appeared behind him and swallowed up every tiny burnt shard of the photo before disappearing into a hidden compartment in a floor panel.

Phutais left the conference room and passed along the hallway in long, powerful strides. Each triumphant step reminded him of the necessity for absolute victory.

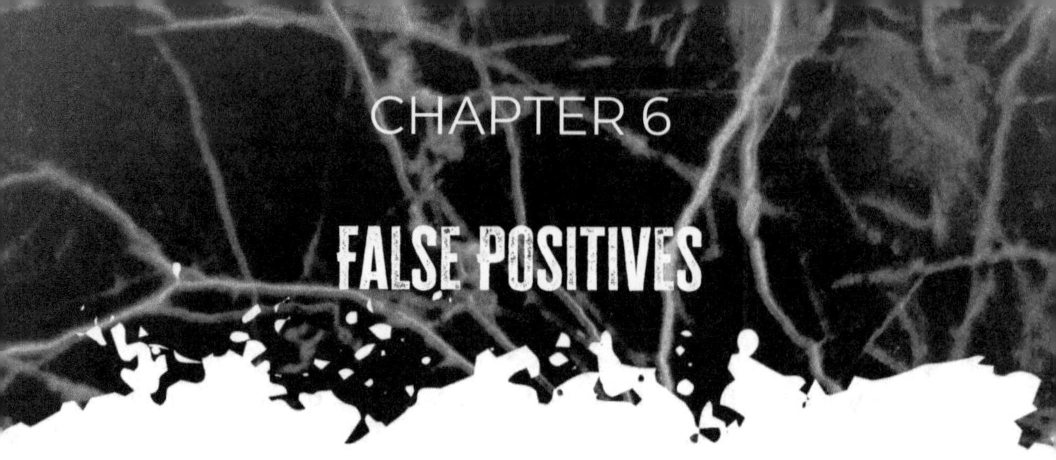

CHAPTER 6

FALSE POSITIVES

A metallic voice emerged from the surgery room.

"They are on life support. The first young man has a fractured pelvis, torn shoulder ligaments, and a torn vertebral artery. The second young man has a compacted cervical vertebrae, a skull fracture, and a collapsed lung."

"OK, send AnnRoticon in there. We need their consent to the initiation."

"Affirmed."

AnnRoticon stepped into the white-lit room, still wearing her battle uniform. She walked between the two hospital beds. Despite being a veteran Fighter, she was aghast at the bloodstains and bandaged body parts of the two youths. She looked into the viewscreen that showed Zoticon's face.

"How much longer will we wait? They might not make it if we delay any longer."

"Whenever you're ready."

AnnRoticon stretched out her arms in opposite directions, palms facing the two battered bodies.

"Hand healing touch!" she announced.

To the uninitiated, what followed would have seemed uneventful, but to the experienced eye, an astounding, otherworldly process was unfolding.

A bright purple glow emanated from the midline of her body. Swirls of light concentrated into her palms as an aura of green particles encircled the bodies of the two boys. Flows of energy penetrated their muscles, bones, and bloodstreams. Their bodies hummed softly and vibrated gently. Bones began to realign. Tendons and muscle fibers were restored and blood flow reestablished. All of the damage was undone.

AnnRoticon lowered her arms, and the light subsided.

"Rise and shine." She smiled at the boys with her eyes.

The two youths moved drowsily and shifted in their beds.

1966's eyes opened. He sat up as if he had never been injured. He looked toward the healer. She wore a headwrap and a cape that covered her body. He remembered this woman from the stadium, but a feeling of distrust came over him. He jumped from the bed but immediately fell to the floor—but not because he was weak or exhausted. His body felt completely healed, so much so that it felt unfamiliar and hard to coordinate. The woman stretched a hand out to help him up. He turned away from her and braced his elbows and forearms against the frame of the bed to rise up. He looked around the room, not trusting this strange place any more than the stranger who was speaking to him. She was a Zlon like him, but her mouth was not visible and her eyes were shaped differently. She couldn't be from Ziffea. Who was this woman?

His thoughts were interrupted by the sound of a loud yawn. Startled, he looked toward the source of it. On the other bed, 1966 saw the kid with the mushroom cut stretching his arms out. He was rubbing his eyes, scratching the back of his head and looking around the white room. Then his eyes went to AnnRoticon. "Where is this place?" the boy asked. "Is this heaven?"

Then, he looked toward 1966. "Hey, you're the kid from before!"

"Who's a kid?" 1966 shot back. "You don't look much older than me—"

SHOOSH.

They both looked toward the source of the alien noise. Two metal doors on the other side of the room had parted. A smaller person with the same polygon-shaped eyes, mouthless face, and shimmering high-tech outfit entered the room in a brisk walk. He stared at the boys for a moment, as if coming to a decision. 1966 looked nervously back and forth between the two figures. The new arrival, he remembered with a start, was the other rescuer from the stadium. What was going on here?

1966 moved to the other side of the bed to avoid being surrounded. He looked suspiciously at the short being's one robotic eye, noticing the slight buzz it made whenever the retina moved. It shifted toward him at that point, and he quickly averted his gaze.

"Let me cut to the chase," the eye-patched man said. "We are presenting you with an ultimatum."

"Ultimate ton?" 1966 said, "What's that?"

The other youth looked up now. He was almost smiling.

"Everybody knows that word," he announced. "It is the biggest and heaviest ton, not like a little one." He looked back, smugly, at 1966 and then at the man in the black body suit, who only frowned.

"Zoticon," the woman laughed softly, "they're teenagers. Let's tone down the sophistication."

"Oh, right," Zoticon said. He looked around, pacing from left to right. The eyes of the two youths followed him.

"OK, I'll make it simple," he said. "You will come with us, or you will die."

The youths stared fearfully at each other.

"Zoticon!" the woman stepped forward. "Let me handle this." She turned her mild eyes on the boys. "Hello, my name is AnnRoticon. Please take a seat and I will answer your questions."

Once they had sat back down on their respective beds, AnnRoticon explained what had taken place before the two boys were brought to her and Zoticon's headquarters.

The other youth's eyes lit up. "So you guys are like comic book heroes? How come I don't have any scratches from all that? I thought I was done for."

"Your injuries were life-threatening," she replied. "I healed you."

"Ahem. Let's not go any further than that for now," Zoticon interjected.

"This is the most I can explain to you at this point," AnnRoticon said as she nodded.

"You healed us?" asked 1966, his eyes widening.

"Yes. As an educator, I would not be able to live with myself if I didn't do all that I could to save you two."

1966 looked at her suspiciously for a moment. Then he ripped off one of his bandages. No bruises. No damage. His body looked perfectly normal despite all the dried blood on the bandage.

"Is this magic?" he asked.

"Were we kidnapped by magicians?" the other boy chimed in, grinning.

"I am starting to regret this," Zoticon said. "Now, listen to me. Either we do the procedure to make you members of our team, or we take you back where we found you. There is a very high chance the enemy will then descend on you and kill you on the spot, but that won't be our problem."

"What?" the youth said. "Why would anyone wanna kill me?"

1966 stayed silent.

"If you have no wish to join us, we can take a U-turn and give you a parachute."

"And sir, what would I use a parachute for?"

"Because," Zoticon said, "we are now 20,000 feet above the ground in our mobile base, the *Black Raven*. I can't give you any more information on the position or specifications of this aircraft unless you agree to become one of us. If I did and you refused to join us, I would have to kill both of you."

"Sounds like we don't really have a choice," 1966 said.

AnnRoticon looked annoyed. "We're so sorry about this," she said before turning to face Zoticon.

<Can I at least tell them what they'd be signing up for?>

<Sure, but if they leave and say anything to anyone, our mission will be compromised. Be very careful what you tell them until after they agree.>

"Hey, hellooo?" the mushroom haircut kid waved to them. "Why did you guys stop talking?"

"We didn't stop talking. We were communicating privately using telepathy."

"Tele-what?" interjected 1966.

"Let me explain. You were on the brink of death. I healed you using my powers. If you choose to come with us, we will teach you how to harness your own powers and use them to beat the bad guys."

"Huh." The youth pressed a finger to his chin. "So we could learn how to beat up bad guys without even having to throw hands?"

"Even more than that. You will learn how to save the world."

"That's dope," he responded. "And you can make it so we don't get hurt?"

"To heal you, all I did was accelerate your own soulforce, which has always been there," AnnRoticon replied. "And once you have been fully trained…" She trailed off, looking cautiously at Zoticon, who nodded back. "Then you will be able to self-regenerate like us and live forever."

"Live forever? Are you for real?" blurted out 1966. Then, with a suspicious look, he added, "So you guys are really, like, super ancient?"

"Mind your manners, young one." AnnRoticon wagged a finger. "But yes, you will become essentially indestructible, thanks to the enhanced mental and physical abilities you will be able to access."

"So what's the catch?" 1966 asked.

"Good question," Zoticon replied, stepping in. "The catch is that you would have to serve with us, obey orders, and fight the good fight until you perish."

"Perish?" 1966 asked.

"You don't know that word?" said the other youth, smirking at him. "It means where you go to pray."

AnnRoticon stifled a laugh. "It means dying."

The boys both looked shocked.

"So about that whole living forever thing," said 1966. "Was that a lie or what?"

AnnRoticon sighed. "Let me explain in a bit more detail."

She told them they would study under her and Zoticon. They would be instructed in how to cultivate their powers, and in return they would use those powers to help save the planet. She then related how Zi-Tai had previously technoformed the planet Marka after completely draining its material resources, along with the emotional, mental, and spiritual resources of its inhabitants. She explained how the media had disguised Zi-Tai's role in the subjugation of Marka as progress and development, so that all but a handful of dissidents knew the truth.

The two youths had been taught the history of their neighboring planet. But they had always been suspicious of the official explanation. The name of Zi-Tai had never been revealed to them before this point. Neither had they ever received any confirmation of their doubts from any other grown-ups. AnnRoticon's explanation was concise and well-paced, and it included all the relevant information except for the reason these two youths had been chosen. When 1966 asked about that, Zoticon only replied, "Confidential."

AnnRoticon cleared her throat. "Zi-Tai has been using the same plan on Ziffea that they used on Marka. It involves another very important element: a policy of Light supremacy—"

"Light supremacy, what's that about?" 1966 shot back, interrupting her.

The mushroom haircut kid cleared his throat, "It's when—"

"Stop playin', you don't even know!"

"Nah, nah, I do, I actually know this one. Mother used to talk about it all the time. It's when light complexions deserve to live and dark complexions deserve to be sent off the planet. She used to say to me each night that if it wasn't for her adopting me, I'd be on a trip to outer space!"

"So this one actually knows something after all," Zoticon said.

"Hey!"

"Outer space is a euphemistic way of saying it," Zoticon continued, ignoring the youth's sulking face. "Light supremacy means that people with light complexions are considered more deserving of life than those with darker skin tones."

"But I always wondered, aren't there light-skinned people in the South?"

"They don't count. Only certain ones living in the North are classified as Light."

"What if I wanted to self-identify as Light?"

"Doesn't matter. Even if you think you're not Dark, it's their algorithm against yours."

"But you're, like, light blue with fur! Why do you even care about this?"

"And that," replied Zoticon, "is none of your business unless you're part of our unit."

"So you're from a different planet. And you want to recruit us to save our planet?" 1966 shot back.

"Yes. Defeating Zi-Tai here will help us liberate Marka. But remember, if you join us, you will never be able to go back to being a mortal."

"Hmm." The other youth rubbed his chin. "We'd better think about this."

CHAPTER 6 I FALSE POSITIVES

1966 sat on the hospital bed. His legs dangled as he placed the side of his face into his palm. There was silence in the air for a couple of seconds as the other teen observed him.

"I've made up my mind," 1966 said. He leapt from the bed. "I'm not interested. Turn this ship around. I'll be fine on my own."

"Wait, what?" the other boy's eyes grew large.

"Oh no." AnnRoticon put her palm to her face.

"Good. Glad we got it sorted out before there are any other misunderstandings." Looking over at the corner of the room, Zoticon said, "OK, Atkon."

"Yes?" a robotic voice responded from a loudspeaker on the wall.

"Turn the ship around and get the parachutes ready."

"Are you sure?"

"Yes, I'm sure. They're false positives. I knew my scanner needed recalibrating."

"Affirmed."

Zoticon turned briskly toward the door. "We have no time for this nonsense." He glanced back at 1966, who looked back defiantly. "Get yourselves cleaned up and ready to get off of my ship."

CHAPTER 7
ULTIMATUM

The *Black Raven* glided almost silently through the somber sky and over the dark seas far below. The night was lit by the three moons that circled Ziffea. Under the cover of its spectral field and reflective camouflage, the huge aircraft was undetectable to even the most advanced conventional technologies. It was perfectly suited for covert operations.

At the insistence of AnnRoticon, both youths had been escorted to the *Raven*'s middle deck area and seated on a plush sofa. On a coffee table, she arranged juices, teas, sweets, and other treats. A large curved window gave a spectacular view of an expansive sky filled with stars and the glistening sea beneath.

1966 was uninterested and eager to leave.

"They said that if you go I gotta go too?" the other youth said.

"I don't care."

"Well, that ain't fair. You're messin' it up for the both of us."

"Not my problem."

Silence. Not a word was spoken. The only movement was the clouds that crept through the air in the distance. The youth with the mushroom cut looked at 1966. He saw a look of loneliness in his eyes—a very familiar one.

"Yo, my name's Jag. Can you at least tell me your name?"

"No."

"Why not?"

"We're not friends."

"Dayum." Jag looked away.

The pair sat quietly for a couple more minutes until AnnRoticon entered the room with a rolling table with more beverages. Someone clearly hoped that hot chocolate and sweetened condensed milk would change the youths' sour mood.

"We'll be back at the site in about thirty. You guys need anything else?"

Despite the silence that greeted her question, she hesitated before leaving. Jag looked down and dug his heels into the carpet.

"Ma'am?"

"Yes?"

"Are you sure that we'd get some kinda super powers if we stayed, but if we go back home, people will try to kill us?"

1966 sighed and fixed his eyes on a random corner of the room.

"You'll certainly have a higher chance of survival with us," AnnRoticon said, watching 1966. "But—" She paused, uncertain, and glanced at the half-open doorway. "It's not entirely safe here either."

"What? Why?"

"Zi-Tai sees us as the only obstacle between them and total world domination."

She walked toward the window and gazed out at the sea of stars in the night sky. When she turned back to the boys, her eyes had welled up.

"We are the only thing that can stop an unstoppable force. We fight against the Four-Winged Angel!"

Her words made both boys jump, though for different reasons. 1966 had heard the name before. When he had first been taken to the orphanage, the Four-Winged Angel had been whispered about by some of the older boys, usually in the dorm after lights out. 1966 had been too young to understand, but he knew the name meant something terrible.

An image of being back in that hell came to him. A couple of boys had been caught talking about the angel and were done in by a snitch. One of the mekkies dragged them out to the eastern gate, and they were never seen again. They were told to keep their mouths shut, and no one ever mentioned it again. 1966 had repressed the traumatic memory—until this very moment.

Jag had never heard of angels before, never mind a four-winged one. His mother was against any "mumbo jumbo" and lived in fear that one day he would revert to his "unruly" origins, so she had banned all mention of anything that you couldn't see, touch, or learn in the industrial education centers.

"The four-winged what?" Jag recoiled and his head nearly bounced off of his neck.

AnnRoticon put a hand to her chin. Her gaze went to the tray, knowing that she should not have disclosed that name. Not yet.

"Oh!" she quickly gathered some of the candy wrappers from the coffee table and placed them back on the tray.

Startled, Jag asked, "Is everything OK?"

"Yes," she said hesitantly, "but I may have said too much. Would you like more hot chocolate?"

"Oh, sure. Thank you ma'am."

"Y-yes. Not a problem."

She placed some things on the tray, as if trying to look busy, then shuffled out of the room. The doors closed behind her.

Jag looked at 1966. "Isn't this wild?"

"You were sounding like you knew everything, but you didn't know this?" 1966 scoffed, leaning away from him and placing his hand beside his full cup. His drink was still untouched.

"You knew about the angel?" Jag tilted toward him. "I need to know more!"

1966 leaned as far back as he could. He realized how little he actually knew and felt uneasy about it. He didn't want to lie and pretend he knew more than he really did.

"Well, if I knew more, I wouldn't tell you anyway!"

Jag sighed and turned away.

"Why're you so interested anyway?" 1966 challenged him. "We'll never see these people again."

"Bro, they saved our lives? Why are you so mad at them?"

Silence. Jag took a sip of his tea.

"You didn't know? These guys are the terrorists they talk about on the news!"

SPSHH!

Liquid sprayed out of Jag's mouth onto the elaborate, handcrafted rug on the floor. He gaped at 1966, his mouth hanging open.

"Terrorists?"

"Yeah, they taught us about these people at institution level 1! Where did you go to school. Or did you?" he sneered.

"Whoa, whoa," Jag said, jumping up and down on his seat. "Institution? So you're an orphan?"

1966 turned quickly away. The back of his hand awkwardly toppled his hot chocolate onto the coffee table.

"Ack!" he said. "See, that's why I don't want to talk to you." He took a napkin and cleaned up the mess, then stood up. "You're a privileged little brat."

"Am not!"

"Are too!"

"Take it back!"

"You're trash!"

"You're trash!"

"Grr, I'm so sick of you and this dumb place!"

"Well, I'm sick of you and your attitude!"

They sat in silence as the engine of the *Black Raven* hummed quietly. The nearly invisible aircraft floated smoothly through the sky. As it broke through the cover of the clouds again, the vast ocean far below gleamed in the window. They watched the scene as if unfolded, but their thoughts were elsewhere.

Jag looked down at the stained rug. "Where will you go back to?"

"What?"

"You're an orphan that ran away. Where are you going back to?"

1966 just looked at him. He knew that he did not have an answer to that question. Instead, he just grunted. He got up and walked toward the window, then suddenly jumped back like he'd seen a ghost.

"The hell?" he exclaimed.

"Huh?"

"Yo! I-it's coming right at us!"

On the bridge, Atkon had been tracking the mysterious object for several minutes before 1966 saw it. A surgeon, scientist and cybernetically enhanced Fighter, Atkon's consciousness was linked with a limitless connection to the *Black Raven's* information systems. They were the living computer, both literally and figuratively, of the team. Although they were also highly skilled in the use of psychokinesis and soulforce, they primarily provided support for the Fighters onboard.

A red light had appeared against the silver cascade of stars and was now growing rapidly in size. It was heading straight toward them at high speed, scattering the clouds in its wake with a screeching sound that disturbed the night sky. It couldn't be a projectile. Its trajectory was too uneven. It zigzagged as if making split-second decisions, perhaps uncertain of the exact location of the *Black Raven* behind its camouflage.

Multicolored alarm lights flashed around the room, accompanied by the wailing of a pulsing siren. A robotic voice burst out of the loudspeakers. "ALERT! ALERT! FIGHTERS TO YOUR BATTLE STATIONS. ALERT! ALERT..."

The two boys ran over to the speaker just as a blue holograph of a cybernetic being seemed to materialize below it.

"Enemy detected. Identified as level five threat! Prepare to engage. I repeat..."

The youths stared at each other.

"What do we do now?" Jag yelled.

"Man, I don't know!" 1966 shouted back at him. "I just wanna get outta here!"

As they stood there, frozen, the *Black Raven* dove back into the cover of clouds. The stars disappeared, and the approaching red light with them.

The holograph was still speaking.

"Enemy signature confirmed," it announced, and then, even more urgently, "Enemy identified as codename Death-Dweller!"

Something nearby whirred and buzzed like heavy machinery. The two teenagers cowered in fear as the lights started to flicker.

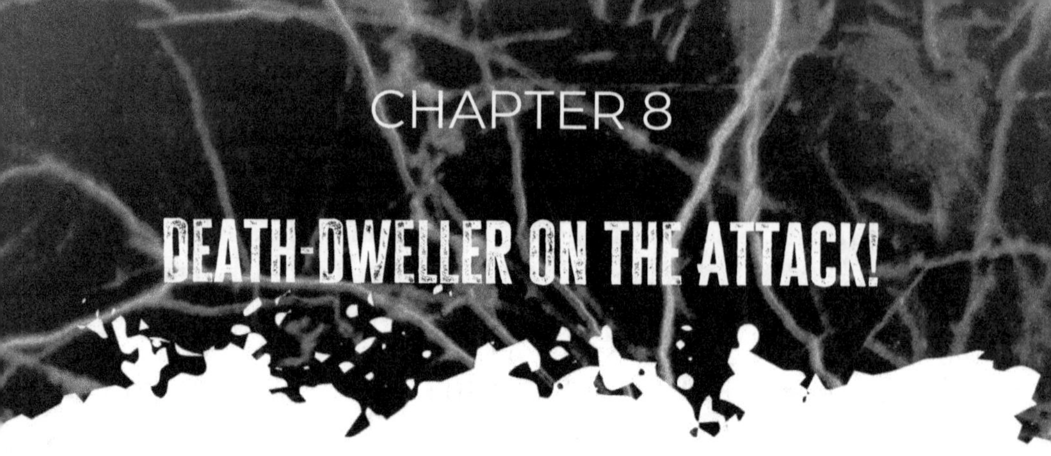

CHAPTER 8

DEATH-DWELLER ON THE ATTACK!

The doors to the bridge swooshed open. AnnRoticon ran into the chamber in a black, hooded technogarb cape and dress. The bangs that covered only one side of her forehead blended with the bluish-white color of her fur. Her eyes were furious.

"Did you say Death-Dweller ?" she called out as she stormed toward the captain.

"It's exactly who you think it is," Zoticon replied.

"Let me at him. I will send him back to his grave."

"I can't let you do that."

She froze in her tracks and stared at him. "And why not?"

"We cannot risk losing you. You are the only one who can heal."

"So will you take him on?"

"No," he replied, startling her. "Don't you see? This is a chance to kill two birds with one stone."

"You don't mean you want to send the students?"

"I do," Zoticon replied. "What better opportunity could there be to enhance their training?" He looked at the large viewscreen at the head of the bridge. Multiple cameras gave different perspectives on the veering red light in the sky. It was closing in.

"I will step in if things get out of hand."

AnnRoticon screamed in fury, slamming a fist against the console.

"My sister," he said, moving toward her. "Trust me, there will be a time and place. But if you fight him with your powers, you're also going to destroy the ship."

AnnRoticon turned her back on him.

"Fine," she said. "Then I will provide intel support for the students."

"Of course." Zoticon nodded. "Now, let's get on with this." He turned toward the front of the ship. "Atkon," he called.

"I'm on it," the familiar metallic voice replied from the bank of control terminals on the far side of the bridge. Atkon placed their alloy gauntlet on a call terminal.

"Black Mountain, engage the target," they said into the large video screen.

At once, four figures appeared, all dressed in dark technogarments. They wore jet-black battle suits that coated their skins and taut musculature from the neck down in a texture that resembled silicon but protected them like armor.

The four apprentice warriors were already in their eject hatches. One of them, with bright blond hair that rose high above his head, was identified as WILLONEO below his image on the video screen. His frame was slim and well-conditioned, like a marathon runner.

"Affirmed, I'll provide backup for BlazeCom."

A nervous-looking, stocky individual with that name displayed under his image straightened up on hearing this.

"Oh, OK, I'm on it. We ain't never fought a level five, though, right?"

"Anyting can appen, so I'll be melee support," said a dark-skinned soldier with a southwestern accent. Her hair was carefully braided, with green beads at the tip of each strand. She could have easily been mistaken for a female weightlifting champion. The name NANIMAROON appeared under her image.

"Based on Atkon's analysis, let's be careful out there," said the fourth. She wore stylish glasses that were just for show. She had an air of wisdom, a mahogany complexion, and thick cornrows and locs that came down either side of her face. The name ANANSIBLU lit up under her as she spoke.

"All right, students," AnnRoticon said into their headsets, "this is the real deal. There is an enemy Fighter out there. Remember your training, work as a team, and you'll be fine." She spoke calmly, but it was a struggle to conceal her rage and hatred at the murdering traitor she knew as Death-Dweller . Still, she couldn't risk her students getting as riled up as she was. She forced herself to sit down in a chair beside Zoticon.

They both looked into a split-screen display that was hooked up to several cameras. The cameras struggled to keep focus on the red beaming star that now lit up the clouds with a faint glow. It was very close.

Zoticon stood up and spoke into his headset.

"Let's not waste any more time! GO! GO! GO!"

Four hatches opened in front of the four defenders. They shot out and fell from the aircraft like trapeze artists, coasting through the clouds, glowing with the light of their soulforce energy. NaniMaroon and BlazeCom had hues of red, AnansiBlu and WilloNeo's bodies were coated with blue. The Fighters weaved through the sky to locate and confront the threat.

Back on the middle deck, the two youths cowered in the darkness. Through the long, curving window they watched the action unfold before them. A viewscreen clicked on below the window. Zoticon's face stared out at them.

"Aah!" Jag jumped backward.

"You two, get to the bridge. Now."

As soon as his image disappeared from the screen, luminescent arrows lit up the floor, pointing toward the door. It slid open, and more arrows appeared. They led down a long dark hallway and disappeared around a bend.

Jag jumped to the door. 1966 stayed where he was.

"Yo! What are you waiting for?"

"I go where I wanna go."

"Are you crazy?"

"Leave me alone!"

"Fine, good riddance!"

Jag ran through the doors. They stayed open for a couple of seconds then slid back shut. The arrows on the floor of the middle deck dimmed and disappeared.

Meanwhile, 1966 sulked his way back to the sofa. The outlines of dried-up slices of cake and room-temperature beverages were faintly visible in the dim, starry light from the window. His stomach growled. He looked away from the table and shook his head in dismay.

You fell for it, and now you're trapped!

1966 jumped and looked around him, startled. "Who's there?" he gasped.

His eyes, accustomed to the half-light, searched the room. It was empty. Was someone crouching in a dark corner of the dimly lit space? The eerie space started to feel like a dream. Then the voice came again.

You can't escape. You're going to die.

The voices echoed inside his head. "I hate this… I *hate* this!" he whispered back to the shadows. He shook his head so violently that tears came to his eyes. He sat in the darkness and dried his face with his sleeve.

Suddenly, the *Black Raven* burst through the clouds and more light returned to the room. He forced himself to stand up again and went back to the window. There, he watched in amazement at what looked like a moving light show. The battle was raging. And it was fierce. In the distance, colored lights bounced against each other, swirling, darting, and colliding. *It's like a video game*, he thought, then he reminded himself that this was real. There were real people flying through the air out there, and one of them wanted to kill all of the other ones and maybe come for the ship next. And that one, the red light bobbing and weaving among the rest, looked like it was winning. 1966 swallowed hard as he watched it slam into a pink light at incredible speed. The pink glimmer fizzled as it slowly fell downward.

You can't escape this by yourself.

The voice was still inside his head, but he answered it aloud.

"I don't care, I don't want this!"

He hit the window with his fist, but his hand only bounced off it.

"Ow!" he shouted, rubbing his fingers. "What is this stupid thing made of anyway?"

In the vast sky, the lights danced on. Some even brighter beams shot out from among the rest. Most seemed to miss their targets, but 1966 could now make out bodies behind the maneuvering lights. Amazed, he saw that they were being fired out of the palms of moving, flying people. Some were being deflected by glowing crimson flashes that seemed to come from the red attacker.

The lights were even brighter up close.

BlazeCom was falling from the sky. For a moment, he had no control. He looked down in terror at the cold, dark sea thousands of feet below, then caught his breath, steadied himself, and shot back up. A pink aura surrounded his body. He plunged through a bank of clouds and homed in on the target again.

"What's up with this guy?" he asked, speaking into the intercom in the collar of his suit. "Good thing I blocked that, cause I would have been done for!"

"I can't get a lock on him, he's too fast!" WilloNeo replied from somewhere above. He opened his palms, and aimed them toward the enemy. Swirling currents of mist seemed to materialize out of thin air. Like a living cannon, WilloNeo unloaded his ammunition. The shots lit up the night sky.

BlazeCom looked to his left. "Coordinate our attacks!" he saw AnansiBlu yelling. She hurled long streams of pulsing blue light into the night with the force of a hundred water cannons. One of the streams connected with the target but was swatted away by the intruder's right hand as if it were a wisp of smoke.

"Almost got him," she said. "Get in there, Nani!"

To his right, BlazeCom watched on as a flying mass of flame soared through the air toward the momentarily distracted robed figure.

"Hah!" NaniMaroon had closed on him under the cover of swirling flames and landed a punch, but Death-Dweller blocked it with his forearm, then leapt away. The flame clung to his body as if he were coated with napalm.

"Mi ketch yuh. Big Bang detonate!" she announced with a bright smile.

The target's forearm glowed with light and suddenly—*BOOM!*

The blast was large enough to demolish a small building. It produced a dull aftershock even inside the heavily armored *Black Raven* and completely obscured the scarlet menace in red smoke. NaniMaroon floated over to AnansiBlu. They gave each other daps after nodding and winking at one another.

BlazeCom gave them a sour look. WilloNeo's jaw tightened.

"Don't celebrate till we see his corpse—"

His warning was interrupted by the sound of clapping. From the red smoke, two hands emerged. They gave four more sharp, quick claps, which cleared the smoke at once, revealing a figure with beautiful lilac eyes and what appeared to be a clerical collar around his neck. He was dressed in a long, flowing, blood-red robe like a trench coat, which went down to his ankles but parted in front to show a pair of immaculate black dress pants and black designer shoes. Long, thick red hair hung down almost to his feet. He was lean but solidly built and wore a wide smile as he continued to clap.

"Well done," Death-Dweller said.

The four defenders froze, astounded. How could their enemy float there, seemingly unharmed?

"Return to battle formation," they heard AnnRoticon order through the intercoms in their collars. Her voice was urgent and resolute.

They floated toward each other. Death-Dweller gazed derisively at their diamond formation.

"Hey guys, that wasn't any way to treat a guest," he said, pretending to pout. "Now, show me where Zoticon is, and I won't have to hurt anyone's feelings."

DEATH-DWELLER

CHAPTER 9

GOT A DEATH WISH?

WilloNeo clenched his fist in response to Death-Dweller's challenge. "Hurt our feelings?"

"Just kidding, guys," the long-haired menace replied, casually flicking away the bangs over his forehead. "Show me where your invisible airplane is and maybe I'll spare your lives. Maybe."

Death-Dweller's red aura now started to intensify. Around it, a deep, black darkness started to emerge. As he focused his intent, his power appeared to grow.

WilloNeo could no longer restrain his anger. He began to float cautiously forward, loosening the formation.

"Wait deh nuh!" NaniMaroon called.

"This guy is all talk," the high-haired maverick shot back. He cracked his knuckles theatrically. "He can move fast all right, but let's see him dodge a fist full of slugs at point blank range."

Death-Dweller grinned at him. "I guess I'll have to set an example with you then."

SHOOM.

WilloNeo's eyes darted left and then right. He couldn't keep up. The red aura seemed to bounce around in multiple directions at once—too many directions to even count—as Death-Dweller buzzed around the four Fighters like hundreds of killer bees circling a hive.

While the fighting intensified, the *Black Raven* continued on its course, full speed back to Azor City and the stadium. Now on the bridge, Jag sat safely in the same room as the ship's three commanders. He huddled into himself and curled his arms around his shins, thinking.

"Estimated time of arrival: one hour," Atkon announced from their bank of terminals. Jag looked up to find Zoticon and AnnRoticon both staring at the large viewscreen. But they said nothing.

CHAPTER 9 | GOT A DEATH WISH?

Jag observed the scene and thought to himself, *What are we even supposed to do when we get there? What's gonna happen to us?*

He'd had some experience fighting in a ring—his digital father had enrolled him in boxing lessons after other boys at school started bullying him. But he had never faced a threat like the one he imagined would be waiting for him when they got back. He remembered being almost trampled to death in the stadium and could hardly understand how he was still alive. He stared at his hands, scanned his body, and wondered if this was all just one bad dream. He turned toward the woman standing at the head of the bridge, in front of a viewscreen and a dizzying array of colored knobs, buttons, levers, and unidentifiable gadgets.

He thought about his mother and about how angry she would be with him if he came back home late. He gathered up whatever courage he had and approached AnnRoticon.

"Um, Ms. AnnRoticon ...?" She looked busy, but he had to talk to her. He was sweating bullets, but he still somehow managed to walk right up to her.

"Excuse me, ma'am, it's getting late and... I..."

AnnRoticon concealed her frustration. Remote monitoring of trainees was demanding at the best of times. Any wrong move now could result in major injuries or even death, not to mention the threat Death-Dweller would pose for the ship if he located it.

She glanced toward Jag and saw the innocence in his eyes. This was a mere child wrapped up in all this! She thought of the urgency of the situation, of the terrible oppression that Zi-Tai had brought to the people of Ziffea... and to her desecrated homeland.

A rich purplish light suddenly appeared as if from nowhere and quickly surrounded her chest. The aura grew until it had surrounded her whole body, illuminating the entire area around her.

"I'm sorry. You can't call your mother now."

Between the light show and the mention of his mother, Jag nearly jumped out of his skin.

"Um, OK!" Jag replied, seemingly stunned. He went quietly back to his seat.

"Ann!" Zoticon turned to her, clearly sensing her pain. "He's searching for our energy signatures. Remember our breathing techniques."

She closed her eyes and breathed in... One, two, three... The purple aura gradually subsided. And out... One, two, three... She would not give in to the all-consuming rage of seeing that traitor's sneering face again.

Relieved, Zoticon turned back to his own viewscreen. Breathing mindfully and intently, analyzing the familiar threat, he showed no fear. He looked around the room, only now noticing that only one of the two youngsters was present.

"Wait, where's the other one?" he called to Jag.

"He... he didn't wanna come with me."

"So he's in that room by himself?"

1966 couldn't take his eyes off the dazzling duel in the sky. He had no clear idea what was happening, but he sensed that the team was in trouble. He could also see that they had skills and powers he had only ever dreamed of. Why would people so strong need him, or that spoiled brat who'd left him alone in here? It seemed unreal. He had never felt needed before. He thought of all the times he had been treated as an outcast and come to see himself the same way. Raised as an orphan, knowing he was a child of oppression contrasted with the thought that he had been chosen, treated kindly, and even offered the power to "save the planet," or whatever that meant. The dissonance filled him with both hope and confusion.

"Why would they be so nice to us if they're the terrorists?" he asked himself.

Outside, WilloNeo tried in vain to make sense of the army of after-images Death-Dweller's rapid movements had left behind. Mentally and emotionally, he was starting to feel outmatched. His three companions had scattered, each desperately trying to catch up to the threat posed by Death-Dweller.

AnnRoticon slammed her hand on the console.

"Position A, focus on defense!" she shouted into her viewscreen.

The authority in her voice snapped the four apprentice Fighters back to reality. They assumed a square formation, covering each other's backs.

Death-Dweller, seeing the change in strategy, slowed to a crawl. With hands casually by his side, he homed in on WilloNeo and came to a floating halt directly in front of him.

"Go ahead, shoot your shot," he called, smiling insolently.

"I'll kill you!" WilloNeo yelled.

"No Willo! It's a trap. Focus on defense!" AnnRoticon bellowed into the bridge's microphone.

WilloNeo raised his arm. A buckshot burst of tiny, highly pressurized water droplets shot out of his hand. Death-Dweller, still smiling, dodged and weaved between them, moving swiftly and flawlessly through the night sky.

WilloNeo's eyes widened. His jaw dropped in astonishment.

"My turn." The red-robed villain leaned to his left and instantly appeared behind WilloNeo.

BAM.

With palm clutching closed fist, he hammered an elbow into the warrior's temple with enough force to send WilloNeo tumbling toward the deep dark ocean below.

"No!" BlazeCom rushed toward the long-haired figure.

Death-Dweller's violet eyes turned toward his assailant. "You got a death wish?"

BlazeCom was frozen in place, unable to comprehend what was happening before him. Death-Dweller's long hair twisted and hardened, weaving itself into three distinct designs, each appearing to consist of steel beams durable enough to withstand the weight of a building. As suddenly as they formed, the structures shot forth toward the three remaining Fighters. BlazeCom, caught off guard, was knocked senseless, his body sent spinning. AnansiBlu narrowly escaped being battered by the second steely projectile, dodging just in time as its knife-like edges careened past her. NaniMaroon's arm was grazed while she tried to somersault backward to avoid the twisting strands of metal.

As quickly as his hair had shape-shifted, it resumed its normal form to again hang gently down to the back of Death-Dweller's knees.

"Don't let them fall, Anansi, Nani!" AnnRoticon pleaded.

"Affirmed!" the women said in unison. They turned their backs on the attacker, and heedless of their own safety, plunged down into the night to rescue their tumbling comrades.

1966 looked on in horror. His knees wobbled. His hands trembled. It had suddenly dawned on him. "They're only fighting this guy because we asked them to turn around." He fell to his knees. "Nooo!"

SHISH. The doors slid open again. Jag burst into the room.

"Yo! Captain's orders, come with me!"

"Get offa me!" 1966 swatted Jag's hand away.

"What's wrong with you?" Jag yelled. While they struggled he accidentally hit 1966 on the cheek with an open palm.

"Oh! You're about to find out now!" 1966 yelled back, jumping to his feet and tackling Jag with one of the moves they'd drilled into him at the orphanage.

They were an even match for one another as they tussled in front of the window, struggling against each other, lit by the light of the three moons.

Death-Dweller couldn't see them, but his eyebrows raised. His supernatural sensitivity to conflict and violence detected the juvenile animosity in the distance.

"Ah-ah-ah!" he exhaled, bubbling with excitement. "Feels like someone is mad at someone. In the middle of the sky?" He licked his lips. Now he knew where the *Black Raven* was.

"I love a game of hide-and-seek," he said to himself grinning now with a full set of fangs. Red light poured from his chest until it coated his limbs and extremities. An orb of crimson surrounded his body.

FOOM.

He charged straight toward the *Black Raven.*

"ALERT! ALERT! Enemy inbound!" Atkon warned over the ship's intercom.

"No, not toward us." Zoticon looked to AnnRoticon. "Toward them!"

CHAPTER 10

PLAYING HARD TO GET

CRASH!

The boys jumped, then turned to one another, terror painted on their faces.

A voice roared out of the intercom. “Emergency, emergency! Hull rupture detected. Decreasing altitude. Seal immediately!”

The door opened with a sudden whoosh. The boys watched teacups, plates, and even the charts that had been hung on the wall fly out into the depressurized hallway. They felt the sucking force of the vacuum too, but managed to grab onto their chair arms at the last second.

A floating red orb appeared at the open door. As the boys stared with a mixture of dread and fascination, it darkened and dissolved, revealing a figure dressed in a trench coat and a clerical collar, with long red hair descending almost to his waist. As the orb faded away, his feet touched the floor, and the door closed behind him.

The two boys fell back into their seats. They could only stare, frozen, as the uninvited guest walked slowly toward them, smiling.

“Really? You two aren’t even fighters.” He laughed. “Why would he go through the trouble…”

As he approached, he raised a hand toward them. A red glow emerged from his palm as his shadow moved across the shattered plates on the floor.

“Unless—” Death-Dweller didn’t get a chance to finish his sentence. He just barely blocked a right hook that appeared out of thin air. The impact of the blow pushed him back several meters, knocking him back out of the room. The boys, barely able to keep up with the speed of events, gaped with wide eyes at the two black skid marks that streaked across the floor from Death-Dweller’s shoes.

Looking in the direction of the attack, his eyes lit up with excitement. A smile beamed from side to side on his face as he yelled, "Zoticon!" Behind him, a flurry of fists materialized. The two moved through the hallway like a dance. Punches were thrown, too many to count. Zoticon's lead hand could not be seen, but he frequently stepped to the side, easily avoiding Death-Dweller's attempts to counterattack. Neither was landing any clean hits.

Zoticon was barely visible, and his feet never touched the ground. Death-Dweller was at a disadvantage, unable to keep up with the speed of his opponent. Blocking and receiving more blows to his forearm than he could dish out, he was forced to retreat, but this didn't dampen his mood. "I've missed you so much!" he jeered.

"Get out of my ship!" Zoticon shot back as he traced his target, following every movement. Finally, he forced Death-Dweller to take one step back too many, falling through one of the craters he himself had created in the ship. Zoticon didn't let up. He followed Death-Dweller through the gaps with a rapid combination of punches and parries that gave his opponent second thoughts about mocking him.

"Die already," Zoticon whispered.

BOOM.

He landed a forceful heel kick that Death-Dweller needed both hands to block, forcing him to stumble back. "Die? You and I both know that can't happen!"

BZZZZ.

The intruder's red hair lengthened again, this time forming into giant saws that tore through the hallway and slashed up and down the walls. Zoticon avoided each attack, baiting his enemy and luring him on.

"Playing hard to get?" Death-Dweller grinned. He chased after Zoticon, sawing left and right, trying to close the distance. Finally, Zoticon had to back off. He flew out through the ruptured parts of the ship, then leapt toward one of the holes the intruder had made in the hull. Death-Dweller happily pursued him outside, and the force of the wind tunnel caused by the ruptured hull sent them both flying out faster than they expected.

Atkon's voice came over the loudspeaker again. "Emergency. Emergency! Hull rupture detec—"

"I'm on it!" AnnRoticon flew from the engine room, holding a large slab of metal the length of a small minivan in one hand. She entered the room where Death-Dweller's entrance had twisted the fittings and breached the hull. Undisturbed by the force, she floated over to the hole in the floor, quickly threw the slab across it, and pointed her hand down. The edges of the slab melted and fused with the hull, sealing the breach. The sucking wind stopped at once.

"Atkon, ah weh unnu deh? Mi cyaan see unnu!" NaniMaroon called into her transceiver.

"Reducing stealth," Atkon replied. The *Black Raven's* reflective camouflage faded, making it easily visible among the clouds.

WHOOSH. Two hatches opened below, allowing the Fighters to return to the cargo compartment. AnansiBlu and NaniMaroon floated in, each carrying one of their injured, semiconscious companions. The hatches closed behind them, and the ship once again disappeared into the night sky.

Now only Zoticon and Death-Dweller faced each other in the sky. For a time, they floated there, staring at each other, motionless. Then, in an instant, they simultaneously assumed fighting stances. Death-Dweller placed one open palm ahead of himself while the other slowly caressed his clerical collar. Zoticon's fighting stance was two closed fists in an orthodox boxing stance.

"Hello again, old friend." The words emerged from a smile with teeth that glimmered like razor blades. Death-Dweller opened his arms, as if he was going to give his opponent a hug.

Zoticon dodged without breaking his stance. "You fool," he shouted, "we have no time for this."

"You put on quite a show yourself at the stadium. What a performance!" Death-Dweller sneered.

"Why are you here? You have ten seconds before I cleave you in two."

"Whoa, whoa, hold on, it's not like I fought first," Death-Dweller teased.

"Nine... Eight."

"OK, OK." Death-Dweller pouted. "You've never been much fun."

"Seven... Six."

"Fine, I'll cough it up," Death-Dweller said. "You know Zi-Tai is pushing even deeper into the South, right?"

Zoticon stopped counting. "Of course I know this."

"Well, they haven't sent me a contract yet."

"With good reason." Zoticon pointed at Death-Dweller's collar with his palm facing upward. "Why would anyone trust a priest that breaks every commandment?"

"Hey, don't be so uptight. We both have a nice body count."

"The difference is, you're proud of it."

A sinister smile crept over Death-Dweller's face. "I might not follow the rules, but I don't hide from my past, like you."

Zoticon looked off to the side. "Bastard."

"Ho ho! Nothing wrong with being born out of wedlock." Death-Dweller wagged a finger. "I never saw you as the religious type, Zotty."

"You're *annoying*. Is this all you came to tell me?"

"Well, that..." Death-Dweller smiled. "But also, if they're not looking for our help, it means they don't need our rituals."

"Really?" Zoticon seemed to be deep in thought.

Death-Dweller watched him with an amused look on his face, swirling a finger through his long hair.

"Isn't that *interesting*?" He looked toward the nearly transparent ship, then back at Zoticon. "So, other than that, I see you're back in the business of finding fresh bodies."

Zoticon instantly appeared in front of him, his fist just inches from Death-Dweller's chin. "If you touch them, you will die."

"Oh, oh, *big* words..."

They backed away from one another. "Your visit is over," announced Zoticon. "Next time you want company, just send a text to some other team in the Community instead of trying to wreck my ship."

"Send a text? I don't even own a telecommunicator. Rates are way too expensive nowadays."

Zoticon turned away from him and floated back to the ship.

Death-Dweller waved goodbye. "Say hi to sweet little Annie for me."

"You sicken me." Zoticon's body was enveloped in a dark-purple glow. He launched himself toward the ship. The speed of his movement caused ripples of force that pushed Death-Dweller back and rumpled his hair and clothing.

Death-Dweller shrugged. Muttering "tough crowd," he turned and flew in the opposite direction until his red aura was just a glimmer of light on the horizon.

CHAPTER 11

TAKING THE FIRST STEPS

"Twenty minutes to arrival." Atkon's voice rang through the hallway as AnnRoticon walked out of the recovery room and walked toward the lounge. A few pieces of debris from Death-Dweller's attack still littered the floor. Passing the guest room, she heard Zoticon's raised voice.

"What's this all about?"

AnnRoticon stopped short of entering the room, but did peek in through the small porthole beside the closed doors. She was surprised to see the youth with the mushroom haircut bowing before the commander.

"We're sorry!" he was pleading, with tears in his eyes and his face almost pressed into the floor. "You did all of that for *us*."

"Save your apologies for the apprentices," Zoticon barked back. "They were hurt only because we turned this ship around." He glanced at a corner of the room. AnnRoticon followed his eyes and saw the spiky-haired child huddled there by himself.

Zoticon motioned for them both to rise. "Get up," he said, "you'll be back in Azor City soon enough."

'No!" the youth called from the other side of the room. His face was buried into his arms and knees, hiding his tears and his pride.

"What do you mean, no?" Zoticon snapped, stepping toward him. "Get up!"

The red-haired youth got to his feet but avoided eye contact.

Zoticon took a step in front of him. "Explain yourself," he commanded.

"I don't know what to think, but I know you saved us," the child replied. Tears ran from his eyes onto his forearm. He rubbed his pride onto his sleeve. AnnRoticon continued to watch the scene unfold. She felt emotional toward this child. She did not know his origins but knew that he must have been exposed to countless fake reports about she and Zoticon being the actual "terrorists." Did he not know that Zi-Tai routinely released faked videos to further their own narrative?

From the center of the room, still prostrate, the youth with the mushroom cut blurted out into the carpet, "He saved us *twice*!"

"So, what of it?" Zoticon seemed to know what was coming, but he wanted to hear it from them.

"Why did you protect us from that crazy guy?" the spiky-haired youth turned his head.

"Because you are both fools, and neither of you would have stood a chance against him."

"You protected us even though we turned down your deal?"

"Yes, of course," Zoticon said. "I'm responsible for the safety of everyone in this ship. But that ends as soon as I drop you off. After that, you can fight people like Death-Dweller by yourself."

"What?"

"You're free to go back to your families. Whatever is left of them."

AnnRoticon, observing from outside, shook her head, *Brother, that's too rough,* she thought. T*hat approach has never worked for the others. He'll definitely need my help with them.* She continued to watch through the porthole, patiently waiting for her opportunity to intervene.

"Hey, um, sir, can you at least let me call my mom?" the youth with the mushroom haircut pleaded. "I want her opinion."

"Your mother? Was she there with you at the stadium?"

"Yes, she must be flipping out right now."

AnnRoticon gasped. She remembered that he had asked about his mother back at the bridge. Because she rescued him from the stadium and saw what happened she felt a responsibility to step in. She slowly entered the room. "I'm sorry, sweetheart," she said, moving toward him and offering a hug.

He backed away. He got up on one knee and whipped his head toward her. "Sorry? For what?"

AnnRoticon replied, "The lady you were with, she..."

"She what?"

Zoticon stepped in. "She's dead."

"Zoticon!" AnnRoticon shot him a look that could kill.

The child's dark hair hid his eyes from view. His shaking body seemed to be consumed by numbness. AnnRoticon placed a hand on his shoulder, but he scooched away. Getting up off the floor, he walked toward the sofa and sat alone. Even the spiky-haired one seemed to look at him with empathy. They all understood that neither of the boys had a home to go back to now.

The silence was broken by AnnRoticon. "Give them another chance, Zoticon!" She took a step toward the spiky-haired one, then glanced back to the dejected youth on the couch. "Come with us. We can take you in."

"We can't *force* them," Zoticon said, folding his arms. "You and I both know they have to decide for themselves."

"We're not going to leave them out in the cold, either," AnnRoticon replied, walking over to her younger brother and glaring down at him.

Zoticon sighed. "I suppose not, but it's still up to them."

1966 looked out the window. They were getting close to Azor City now. Once they got there, he knew the authorities would be looking for him. Then he would be put back in the cold, unforgiving walls of the orphanage.

He looked at Zoticon, "If we go back to the city, what will that... Zi-Tai group do?"

"The enemy will not stop," Zoticon replied, "until every last memory of you and your ancestors is annihilated."

1966 was genuinely bewildered. "But why?"

AnnRoticon clapped her hands together, insisting. "We have to explain the four wings, Zoticon."

He looked at her and nodded. "Go ahead then, but make it brief."

"I'll try." She sighed.

The four wings of Zi-Tai, AnnRoticon explained to the boys, were commerce, the military, the law, and government. Commerce related to the corporation's profit-generating activities and included its media programs, as well as machine and technological development. She told them how products and services were pushed on the public through subliminal advertising and an unchallenged monopoly. Even the societal media apps rewarded influencers for flaunting the benefits of consumerism. Of course, all the platforms were under heavy surveillance and censorship by police agencies to ensure that supply and demand was thoroughly manipulated.

"If that's true"—Jag scratched his head—"how come we never heard about this?"

"Well," AnnRoticon replied, "journalists who tried to report on this all got 'terminated' and were never heard from again. Zi-Tai is ruthless about preventing northerners from hearing any different perspectives."

Jag rubbed his face right after hearing that. 1966 guessed that that reflex meant they both must have gotten swiftly punished whenever they dared to question their superiors. *He's lucky all he got was a slap for things like that*, 1966 thought to himself. He then looked toward AnnRoticon.

"So what can you tell us about the military?"

Zi-Tai's armed forces specialized in protecting the North against hostile threats to its global hegemony, AnnRoticon explained. She told them that the South had once enjoyed a relative level of peace between the territories, thanks to the natural abundance of food, water, and other resources. However, with Zi-Tai's arrival, these resources became increasingly threatened due to their lust for power. AnnRoticon emphasized that although conflicts between the northern nations were once common, Zi-Tai overpowered any opposition and set them all in line. The deployment of GAIA technology and a bloated military force enabled them to swiftly "unify" the North and expand their influence into the South. The enemy threw loads of money toward weapons development, testing, and technological advancement, all while receiving significant funding from the puppet government.

"Are you with me so far?" AnnRoticon asked the boys.

They nodded.

"The media's job," she continued, "is to make sure the public believes there is always an unspecified threat from everywhere."

1966 recalled all the scripts they were forced to memorize back at the orphanage. "A common saying in Azor City was... *Danger is everywhere.*"

"Exactly." She raised a finger in the air. "That's why the military is *essential.*"

Jag slowly shook his head. "Well, all of this—it sounds like it's against the law!"

"I was just about to get to that," AnnRoticon replied.

Law, she explained, specifically "law and order," was really meant to provide intel to the other wings from communication networks and from on-the-ground surveillance of the population. Informally, the authorities were called the "think police" because they usually arrested or even executed people they only "thought" were going to do bad things. Usually, these were poor, darker-skinned people. When there used to be uprisings, order would routinely be restored through a combination of violent suppression and media blackouts.

"Care to share a bit about this topic?" AnnRoticon raised an eyebrow toward her comrade.

Zoticon sighed. "OK, fine," he said, crossing his arms. "Trials are quick, prisons are plenty, and orphanages are meant to brainwash undesirables into serving as the military's slave soldiers."

1966 turned his head downward quickly. He felt AnnRoticon's eyes watching him closely but sympathetically.

Zoticon looked at her. "One more wing left. Not much time."

Government, AnnRoticon resumed, more commonly referred to as "democracy," was run by a class of elites that worked in line with the other wings. Back in the old days, votes used to be counted from all the citizens. Then, the voting laws were changed—supposedly to create a more "efficient" system, but in reality so that the officials Zi-Tai wanted were elected by carefully programmed artificial intelligences. Government was now designed to feed the wants and desires of the other three wings. Flashy politicians served a role to manufacture consent from the people. The media and the government worked together on this.

1966 listened carefully. He turned toward Jag, who now sat dejected on the sofa, eyes facing the floor. He then turned to face the woman whose fist was now clenched and shaking. She addressed the both of them. "Zi-Tai won't stop until the whole planet is theirs. You both are descendants of people from the South. Fate demands that you avenge your ancestors!"

Jag's eyes opened wide.

"Ahem," Zoticon coughed, looking over to her, "I can take it from here."

"Hmph!" She crossed her arms and took a step back.

1966 gazed at the both of them. Then his eyes went to the youth on the couch. Jag looked like he was still absorbing the idea of home without parents. There was no longer such a large gap between them. Now, they were both orphans. It was really starting to sink in. He looked back at the two leaders of the Fighters.

Atkon's voice echoed through the hallways. "Ten minutes to arrival. Ready passengers for drop-off."

"Time's running out, you two. Make your decision."

1966 looked at Zoticon, noting how his uniform was almost unscathed despite the attacker's ferocious onslaught. "And if we go with you, that red wacko is going to keep showing up?"

"He might. But I will teach you how to fight back."

"Are there more flying weirdos and people in spandex?"

"It's not spandex. It's advanced technofabric. It's less likely to be incinerated by the speed of our movement."

"Why are you so sure we will be able to help?"

AnnRoticon looked uncertainly at Zoticon. He shook his head and motioned for her to remain silent, then quickly turned back to the boys.

"No more questions."

AnnRoticon folded her arms, turning away from the eye-patched commander. She walked around to get a good look at the room. Toppled furniture and damaged glassware were strewn everywhere.

"Why don't we give them a little more time to think about it?" she said to Zoticon. "Let's give them a bit of space."

"Fine. Five minutes before we bring them to the hatches. We cannot waste any more time than that."

As the two officers began walking toward the exit, 1966 thought about his options. Voices echoed in his mind. *You're not good enough* was his first thought, but another followed quickly: *If you go back, you'll be hunted and locked up.* "But if I stay with them, I'll just be hunted," he mumbled to himself.

1966 replayed the image in his mind of Zoticon protecting them. No one had ever hit someone so hard for him before. Whatever happened, he would never forget that. Rather than shame, it was pride that pushed him to return the favor this stern commander and the rest of the crew had done for him.

"Hey," 1966 called out, just as AnnRoticon and Zoticon reached the door, "I hate owing anyone anything." They stopped and turned. Jag looked over at him too.

"I've made up my mind," 1966 said, putting his hands behind his head in a relaxed pose. He looked up at a corner of the room. "I want you to teach me how to fly and beat people up."

AnnRoticon's eyes smiled and glimmered.

Zoticon laughed. "It's about much more than that," he said. "The enemy will not stop until all your people are dead."

1966 looked down at his feet.

"I… I… then…" He stuttered, searching for words. His hands balled into fists and fell to his side. "Then I want to learn to protect the people."

"A little better, but still needs work," Zoticon said. Then he turned to the other youth, "And what about you?"

Jag thought about the hospitality received from strangers. He thought about how hard people who didn't even know his name were fighting for him. Something deep, something life-changing, resonated in him.

He got up from the sofa, but his eyes did not leave his shoes. "We got nowhere else to go."

"That's not convincing enough for me." Zoticon crossed his arms and turned toward the door.

"OK, OK, OK," Jag shot back in a panic. He bowed his head and fell to the ground with a speed that banged his knees and hands against the carpeted floor and made him cry out in pain. "Please take us in!" he yelled, tears welling up in his puppy-dog eyes.

"Get up," Zoticon breathed, rolled his eyes, and turned to face him once more. Jag stood up, sniffing and wiping his nose with his sleeve. The old man walked toward him.

"From now on, your life will become practice and then executing what you have practiced. Are you truly willing to put in the work?"

"Y-yes," Jag wailed. "I want to make a difference too… for everyone."

"Are you both sure about this?" AnnRoticon demanded, sounding much sterner than before.

"Yes, ma'am." The two boys jumped up together and saluted.

"There will be no turning back," Zoticon sighed. "Literally. We already turned the ship around once, and this is getting annoying for me."

"Yes, sir!" both boys yelled, then they looked at each other. For a second, it seemed like time stopped. Jag saw something in this other youth's eyes that echoed his own feelings. The same glimmer they had seen in each other's eyes when they met at the stadium was there again. The future was uncertain, but their decision had given them a feeling of determination.

"OK, Atkon," Zoticon called into the intercom. "Return course to Sector 25."

"Affirmed. Changing course," the metallic voice responded.

Zoticon turned to his companion. "Ann, you ready for this?"

"Of course. I've *been* ready for this!" She winked.

"Then let's prepare the ceremony."

CHAPTER 12

NO GOING BACK

It wasn't going to be easy. 1966 knew that as soon as he stepped into the large, bright room. They called this the training hall. It was entirely devoted to the art of fighting. A hundred feet long and almost as many wide, with 20-foot ceilings, it was the largest chamber on the *Black Raven.* To minimize distractions, the floors, walls, and ceilings were all an even gray. There was special padding on the enclosure that allowed it to absorb most of the damage that training with immeasurable strength could cause. It was flame retardant, heat resistant, waterproof, and shock resistant, and it could withstand even a temperature level of absolute zero. Nothing less durable could have withstood the Fighters' training, all-out sparring, and initiation ceremonies.

A single sliding door controlled entry, but a reinforced synthetic window allowed anyone to watch and study.

This window was a one-way mirror. Those watching from the adjacent observation room could not be seen from inside unless an infrared light was turned on. WilloNeo and BlazeCom sat on one side of the observation room, AnansiBlu and NaniMaroon on the other.

Atkon, the mechanized instructor, stood with their hands behind their back and their legs widely spaced at the back of the room, carefully monitoring the situation.

WilloNeo looked at them with one raised eyebrow. "You know I never asked. If you're here, who's piloting the ship?"

"I am," they explained matter-of-factly. "Not only can I provide the airborne warning system support and remote piloting, I am always connected to the *Raven*'s closed circuit network."

"I guess he *is* the whole ship," BlazeCom scoffed.

WilloNeo and BlazeCom laughed at their own bad joke. Atkon didn't budge.

"Tap yuh naise, you're supposed to be learning," Nani shouted.

"Shh." WilloNeo put a finger to his mouth. "You're way too loud. Can't you be a bit more ladylike?"

BlazeCom chuckled. Anansi adjusted her glasses, then turned the page on the decorated book with a large triangle on the back that she held in her lap. "If I remember correctly," she said, "we're the ones who carried you two little puppies back to the ship."

BlazeCom stopped laughing.

"Oh yeah." Nani looked straight at him. "Uh nuh memba mi carry yuh rass ah yuh yard afta yuh get bruk up?"

The two women laughed and high-fived each other. The two men responded by jumping out of their seats and taking a few steps toward them

Nani raised her head toward them. "Kom touch a button, nuh."

Suddenly, a translucent barrier of electricity materialized between them, dividing the observation room in half.

Atkon didn't move, but said, "I hope it is clear why they asked me to chaperone you. Take a seat, young men." The two returned grudgingly to their seats, and the barrier dissolved. As it did, the training room door swooshed open to admit Jag.

1966 was still at the entrance and the two boys stood side by side. They were startled first by the sheer size of the space and then by the unfamiliar yet sweet aromas of burning incense. Jag was holding his own hands to quell his nervousness. 1966 looked more confident. Until a voice materialized in the boy's mind.

They're going to kill you here.

"No," 1966 mumbled to himself, "we're gonna be fine. We're gonna be fine."

Jag looked at him in shock. It seemed to calm his nerves to hear that, and so he also repeated, "Right, we'll be OK."

1966 was embarrassed to be caught talking to himself. That stressed him more than the upcoming ceremony. He tried to distract himself by looking around the room. At the center of the mainly empty space were two rectangular concrete-looking slabs, with a rolling table between them. A set of containers and what looked like folded clothing lay on the smaller table. They had to be things for the ceremony, 1966 decided. Zoticon and AnnRoticon were already there, moving about busily. From the rolling table, they took turns pulling long, thick robes over their bodies. The robes were decorated with intricate patterns in red, black, and green and were very different from their tech suits. They looked heavy and seemed to be made of some coarse, ancient, natural material. Neither of the boys had ever seen anything like it before.

Outstretched from the sleeve of her robe, AnnRoticon's palm gently motioned to them. "OK guys," she said brightly. "When you feel ready, come and lie on the altars."

1966 felt his heart racing. He took a slow, deep breath to calm his nerves, closed his eyes for a moment, then walked to one of the large slabs and lay down on it, hoping the others couldn't see the trembling he felt in his hands. It was slightly cold to the touch. Solidly built. He wondered how they had even got something so heavy in here. From the corner of his eye, he saw Jag climb up and lie down on the other slab. His mind started racing. He again breathed slowly and deeply, and tried to calm his thoughts. He had made his decision. He would stick with it.

"You understand there is no turning back now?" Zoticon asked. "You have already seen too much."

The boys nodded.

Zoticon walked to the front of the two altars. As AnnRoticon made her way around to the youths' feet, she spoke softly.

"The general public is totally unaware of the rituals, the rites, and the passage that you two will undergo, as we did before you, and as countless generations did before us."

AnnRoticon took a container from the rolling table. She removed its top, which she placed beside the incense. Unfamiliar aromas surrounded the youths.

From the observation room, Anansi looked on with an unblinking interest.

"Atkon," she said, hunting through the pages of her book, "there's nothing in here about the origins of this ritual."

Atkon nodded. "Correct. Your book was created on your planet. The Walking Ancestor ceremony came from *our* planet. We think it must have come from an oracle, or at least one of their disciples, but its exact origins have long since been lost." They pointed at her book. "This tradition has only been passed on orally. You will not find it in any book. We could not allow this ritual to fall into the wrong hands."

BlazeCom and WilloNeo looked bored. Nani pointed to them. "Den ah weh yuh ah do wi dem peeple inya suh?"

WilloNeo raised an eyebrow. "Whaat?"

"She said, 'Hope you are having a good day,'" Anansi told him while delicately turning more pages in her book.

WilloNeo waved her off.

"Anan, I didn't know your patois was so well developed!" Nani laughed, patting her lovingly on the shoulder.

"Can you tell I've been practicing?"

Atkon cleared their throat. "We must have silence now. Observe carefully, if you are serious about being educators."

BlazeCom and WilloNeo jeered and silently taunted the two women. Nani kissed her teeth and turned away from them, joining Anansi in watching the ceremony. As it unfolded, AnnRoticon's voice carried a gravitas that was very different from her usual friendly way of speaking. Between the ritual utterances, she hummed in deep resonant tones. The vibrations could be heard as well as felt by all those who could hear them.

1966 was clearly becoming agitated. He grew more self-conscious until he looked over and figured that Jag must also be wondering what they got themselves into. It reassured him to know he wasn't alone, but that didn't make it any less scary. Zoticon addressed the two of them. "The process you are now undertaking will change you forever. By activating your connection to the deepest levels of your consciousness, you will gain a bridge to the highest potential of all people." He raised his hand into the air and began to whisper in a language 1966 could not recognize.

While he did so, AnnRoticon continued the explanation. "It is said that many eons ago, before our planets existed, there were ancient ancestors who endured the ordeal of being captured, sold into slavery, and transported across oceans like chattel. Many died during the transit, diving into the deep waters facing a physical death. Some were voluntarily selected, but this was not suicide. They transitioned to the next realm to strengthen those who remained." She began to hum again.

Now, Zoticon spoke again. "Transitioning to the afterlife gives us the power to influence reality differently from a physical, mortal existence. But *this* ceremony empowers you to transition and remain in the physical world. It will cause you to walk the world as an ancestor. Your physical body will not know death. In exchange…" He paused and quickly lowered his hand. "If you are to die, your souls will know no peace. You will be endlessly chased by harvester spirits that will scratch, bite, and eat pieces of you for all eternity. You will never transition to the next realm."

At this, Jag swallowed so hard 1966 could hear it over AnnRoticon's humming. The only thing louder, 1966 thought, must be the sound of his own heart leaping out of his chest. Suddenly, voices whispered into his ear. *Be afraid. You should have left while you still could. You are going to die here.*

He tried to ignore them and continued with his slow, deep breathing technique, calming his panic down to a barely tolerable nervousness.

AnnRoticon, sensitive to the boys' anxiety, reduced the solemnity in her voice. "To overcome adversity, we must transcend the confines of reality. The process of your instruction will therefore involve your whole being: body, mind, heart, and soul." This time, she did not resume the humming after she finished speaking.

Zoticon raised his hand high then lowered it toward the ground, before allowing it to sweep from left to right and finally return to its original position. Seven points on his body, from the top of his head down to his tailbone, lit up with a dark-purple light. AnnRoticon's body lit up with the colors it had shone earlier, when she'd helped to heal the two youths. She stood with her hands facing them, motionless, yet braced for what would happen next.

Zoticon held out both fists in front of him. "We will now honor the past, present, and future. Repeat after me," he instructed the two youths. Instinctively, they closed their eyes. "To our ancestors…" he intoned.

"To our ancestors…" the youths repeated.

"To Si-Vin…" he pronounced.

"To Si-Vin…" they answered.

"To the generations that follow…"

"To the generations that follow…"

"I will fulfill my purpose."

"I will fulfill my purpose."

As scary as it was, 1966 felt as if he was being welcomed into a new family. It was an indescribable emotion. He was smiling, but he was also crying. Although he couldn't see Jag now, he heard him sniffling too. He felt a deep sense of relief at being accepted into something so much larger than himself. All of the running, all of the adrenaline, all of the danger of being hunted drifted away, leaving a feeling of lightness in his soul.

Zoticon threw a fist into the air and yelled to the sky, "ANKH UDJA SENEB!"

1966 opened his mouth to repeat the unknown words but was interrupted by what now emerged from the ceiling.

SHOOOM.

A swirling white vortex expanded above him, swallowing the highest parts of the room. From the center of the vortex, a stream of rainbow-colored thunderbolts repeatedly crashed against his body.

K-KRAAAK.

It happened too fast to be scary. There was no time for his brain to interpret what was happening, but from the bottom corner of his eyes, he saw AnnRoticon pushed back by the force of the impact. Even though she could float above the ground, she was struggling to remain in one place. Despite her strength, she was being thrashed around by an invisible power. Looking up, 1966 saw Zoticon levitate and struggle to keep still. Only later would 1966 learn that even a slight miscalculation at that point could have turned the whole ship into a squashed tin can…

In that moment, however, 1966 could only watch, stunned, as the rainbow-colored bolts of energy smashed into his seemingly battered body like a jackhammer. But there was no pain. Instead, he felt as if his body was being reborn. He felt his very nerve fibers changing, and something was happening to his bones too. There were too many changes to keep track of, yet there was a calmness about it. And a familiarity. As if he had done this before. Was he really becoming an ancestor while he was still alive?

The bolts shifted their focus to his extremities, then to the core of his torso, then moved upwards to his neck and head, forcing him to close his eyes. A surge of neural activity caused his whole body to convulse. The uncontrollable movements grew in intensity.

Zoticon moaned in agony, closing his own eyes but continuing to keep his fist raised as black streams of energy began to pierce through the sleeve of his forearm. He was visibly sweating, but he kept as still as he could. Ann held back from calling out his name.

Black bolts were stabbing the youths now, heightening their seizure-like convulsions and causing drops of blood to flash through the air.

Ann's heart started to beat rapidly. She looked at Zoticon. Bolts from the vortex cut holes through his forearm, turning it as black as charcoal. But, undeterred, perhaps unable to stop the otherworldly progress of the event, he kept his fist in the air. Seeing his determination but mindful of the initiates, Ann thrust her hands out ahead of her and yelled out, "Healing hand touch!"

Purple lights now covered her body. Green glimmers of light sewed up the wounds almost as fast as the black lightning opened them. Still, the strikes intensified. Even with all her power, she struggled to keep up. "Please, Si-Vin." Her voice shook. "Let them live!"

Flashes reflected from the one-way mirror, casting shadows behind the observers with the intensity of divine intervention. The bolts beat at the bodies of the children until they vibrated. And just as Ann was reaching her limit, two final bolts hit the center of the youth's foreheads. With this, the last ash of incense fell. The ceremony was over. The flashing lights began to settle. The vortex shrank and closed. 1966 and Jag lay motionless on the crumbled altars. Ann stood there, shaking, while Zoticon fell to his knees. Then she let out a sigh of relief when she saw the rise and fall of the youths' chests.

CHAPTER 13

REAWAKENING

His eyes opened to a familiar ceiling.

1966 looked drowsily around. He was lying in a bed. To his right, he saw Jag stretching and yawning, his head just barely above the sheets. This had to be the recovery room.

He thought back to the ritual. Still with his back against the warm bed, he raised his arms and hands above him. There was no pain. He had suffered no apparent damage despite what had felt like being ripped apart by a strobe light from the ceiling of that strange room. The fresh feeling that permeated his body reminded him of waking up after AnnRoticon had healed him. He used his hands to push up from the bed and get a better look around himself. Jag was rubbing the back of his head. When 1966 looked at him, the other boy returned his gaze.

"Bro, I feel like I just woke up from a thousand-year sleep."

"You're tellin' me."

"Can you get up?"

"Yeah, I think so."

The two got to their feet together, both stumbling and off balance at first. 1966 felt like he was adjusting to a different sense of gravity. There was a lightness and responsiveness to his body that he had never felt before. Looking down at himself, he could see a faint emanation of light coating his arms, his fingers and what he could see of the rest of his body in the hospital gown. He felt more solid in his body, yet lighter too. The feeling of refreshment was deep. He even felt it in the back of his eyes.

"Yo-yo-yo-yo!" Jag backed away, pointing at him.

"Wh-wh-what?" 1966 stuttered.

"Your eyes. They look just like the Fighters'!"

"Yo, yours are looking kinda different too!"

They looked around for mirrors or any other reflective surface. All they could find were the metal frames of the bed stands, which just caused their faces to bend and curve, distorting their appearance too much to see themselves accurately.

"Just take my word for it," 1966 said, looking again at the aura that surrounded him. "I guess we got changed from the inside out."

Jag also seemed to be coated in a faint glow. "Wait, does this mean we can fly too?" he said, then he jumped into the air with a force that sent him hurtling to the ceiling.

BAM.

The back of his body was jammed into the ceiling panels right beside the overhead light. And there he stayed, without falling. They both looked at each other, blinked once or twice, and burst out laughing. As they laughed, the sliding doors opened and AnnRoticon and Zoticon walked in. They were no longer wearing the heavy robes. Ann was back in her black cape with ornate designs. She carried a small bundle under each arm. Zoticon, meanwhile, wore his standard black combat uniform. His right arm was in a sling.

Ann laughed gently when she noticed Jag stuck in the ceiling. Zoticon only glared at him. "Get down from there," he barked.

But the youth's hands and legs dangled from above. He looked left and to right, unable to budge the rest of his body. "I-I can't!"

Ann laughed again, and this time 1966 joined her. Zoticon just sighed.

"Gimme a second, I'll help you down." Ann floated gracefully up to the ceiling beside Jag. She took his arm and yanked it down quickly, so that he would come free without slamming into the cement floor. Small pieces of chipped paint and damaged ceiling tiles fell from the young man's imprinted figure. She caught him in her arms. "Your first lesson in using air-stepping will be to clean up after yourself."

So AnnRoticon and Zoticon are going to be our teachers too, 1966 thought. *That could make for some interesting clashes.*

Flustered, Jag looked at Ann, "Sorry ma'am."

She winked at him as they floated downward, then hovered before touching the ground. Jag stumbled as he got his footing.

"You're both going to need a lot more space than this room has," Ann said. "Let's return to the training hall." She motioned the boys toward the door, then paused. "I almost forgot," she said, laughing. "You can't start your training in hospital gowns!" With a grin, she handed each of them one of the bundles she'd been carrying. "Here are your new uniforms. Welcome to the team."

1966 held out his arms.

PLOP.

The bundle was a lot heavier than he expected. It was a different kind of technogarment than anything at the orphanage. He scanned the sleeves and legs. The size looked perfect. *These black suits will be our uniforms now*, he thought to himself. He thought about what it meant to be a part of something larger than himself.

He looked over at Jag, who was jumping up and down with excitement. "Ayyyee!" he squealed, looking at the uniform and snapping his fingers, head bobbing, doing a two-step. Ann laughed again.

"Hurry up and get changed," Zoticon said. "We'll be waiting."

The two new recruits clumsily reacquainted themselves with walking without floating as they accompanied their teachers down the hallway toward the training room. 1966 tried to force his feet to stick to the ground by taking long, lunging steps, with his arms stretched out ahead of him. Jag was gradually getting the hang of it too, occasionally placing a hand against one of the walls to push himself back down to ground level. Ann sometimes put a hand on one or other of the youths' shoulders to keep them from drifting off like helium balloons.

"You both survived the transformation," Zoticon said. "You should be proud."

"Wait, what? You mean we could have died?" said a shocked 1966.

"Yes, of course," he replied. "If it wasn't for AnnRoticon, there is a chance you wouldn't have made it."

"You would have let us die?" 1966 asked, turning away to conceal the resentment that filled his eyes.

His disappointment was not lost on Ann, though. <*Zoticon,*> she said, communicating telepathically so the youths wouldn't hear, <*why do you have to be like that?*>

<*Like what?*> he responded, pretending to be puzzled.

Ann sighed and turned back to the initiates. "Look, you both did amazing," she told them. "And I wouldn't have let a thing happen to you."

"Thank you, ma'am," Jag said.

"Zoticon would like to say the same," she added, "but he's still working on it."

"Mr. Zoticon," Jag asked, "what happened to your arm?"

Zoticon had been clutching his right forearm, which was in a cast. The hand and elbow that poked out from the ends looked charred. Caught off guard by the concern in Jag's voice, Zoticon appeared ready to give a harsh response, but he hesitated, then continued walking ahead of the others.

After an awkward silence, Ann said, "That was from the ceremony."

"Can't Ms. AnnRoticon heal your arm like she healed us?" Jag called to him.

"No," Zoticon replied with his chin in the air.

Jag couldn't keep his eyes off the injured arm. It looked in bad shape. Had it also been beaten down by the lightning bolts during the ceremony? They had told him that Fighters could transcend the physical limits of reality, but it seemed there were still forces that could hurt them.

"Anyway"—Zoticon looked at the cast—"It will heal by itself in a few days. That's another advantage of being a walking ancestor."

"And of working together as a team, right?" Ann winked at him.

"Hmph," Zoticon retorted, still walking ahead of them. He entered the training room and surveyed it. He nodded in approval. All the debris from the ceremony had been cleared away.

"Wow, who cleaned up in here so fast?" Jag asked.

"How long were we out cold?" 1966 looked at the elder Fighters with suspicion.

"It only took an hour for the other students to get this place sparkling again," Ann replied as she welcomed them into the room. "You'll meet your teammates and get your share of chores soon enough, but there is one more test."

"Ah… I hate tests." 1966 dug his fingers into his scalp and rolled his eyes.

"We need to see what elements you have," Zoticon explained.

"Elements?"

"Correct. You saw how some of us have auras?"

The boys looked at each other and nodded.

"Well, now you have auras too, even if they are still faint. They come with the territory, and before we can proceed, we need to see what type yours are."

"How do we do that?" asked Jag.

"AnnRoticon will lead the way."

The youths turned to their female teacher. She explained that everyone had inner gifts they could be trained to use. Their initiation had unlocked these gifts. Through practice, cultivation, and meditation, they would now strengthen and develop them. By working in unity, as a cohesive team, they would exceed their previous limitations. "But before all of that," she said, "you need to take a seat and practice breathwork with me."

"Breathwhat?" said Jag, growing even more confused.

"You will experience it firsthand. We will start with something we call Black Meditation."

She directed the youths to set up cushions and mats in a circle. Zoticon then lay on one of the mats while the two boys sat, supported by the cushions, facing Ann. The female elder sat in a cross-legged position on one of the other mats. She led the process with instructions, guidance, and grace. At the orphanage, 1966 had done exercises that resembled breathwork for combat training, but never before had he practiced with others for peace.

Soon they were all breathing in unison. Ann's guided meditation led them to visualize a connection to the air that entered and left their lungs. Out of the corner of his eye, 1966 noticed Jag's breathing had calmed down and become very regular. 1966 turned inward, noticing tingly sensations in his hands and feet, neck and back, and each time he exhaled, his nervous system settled into a feeling of safety. His feet felt nestled against the ground. His lungs carried air back and forth in a steady, calming flow. Never before had he felt so settled in his own body. Had it not been for his teacher's soothing voice, it might have felt scary, but when he brought his attention back to his breath, his spinal column felt aligned and connected. In fact, his whole body felt interconnected. He visualized the clouds that surrounded the ship, then the seas and the land below, and finally the entire planet.

"And in those times when you may doubt the body or the mind, remember that the planet, that all of nature, breathes with you."

They took a moment to sit in silence. 1966 noticed the calmness of his breath, at times visualizing the planet, and settling into the depths of his consciousness. He experienced a subtle wave of lightness traveling through him, replenishing his body, mind, and spirit.

"Now rise," Ann said. She stood up from the floor. The boys followed suit, getting up from their cushions while Zoticon changed his posture, so that he now sat in a cross-legged position. He sat there, still, eyes closed, holding space during the next stages of the process as the elder continued her instructions. "Place your hands together in front of you," she said.

The boys did as directed and held that position for a few moments. After a while, she said, "Now draw them apart, close your eyes, and feel the energy in the gap between your hands."

It was an indescribable feeling, something like an invisible rotation that moved between their hands and fingers, then along the vertical axis of their bodies. Something about Ann's presence and the resonance from Zoticon's continued meditation accelerated the spinning of the two youths' vital energy centers.

"Now," Ann said, raising her palms above her head, "show us your souls!"

"Our *what*?" asked a startled 1966, opening his eyes and raising one eyebrow. He looked at Jag, perplexed. A glimmer of navy-blue light had appeared on the mushroom haircut kid's brow.

"I can do it!" Jag exclaimed. From between his outspread hands, a liquid substance materialized in thin air, then thickened and darkened into a mass of black energy the size of a stone.

BOP.

It fell to the ground and bounced a few times before settling as a bouncy dark blob.

"Uh, did I do it?"

1966 gave him a smug smile and closed his eyes. "I bet I can do it too, but better than *that*!"

A warm dark red glow began to appear in the middle of his forehead. In between his hands emerged a small flicker of flame. Wanting to show up his classmate, he forced the flame to expand, tightening his muscles and intensifying the strained expression on his face. Suddenly, the fire jumped to his right arm. He opened his eyes to see the whole length of his arm engulfed in flames. Terrified, he leapt up and down and began to run around the room, trying to beat down the flames with his other hand. "It's hot, it's hot!"

Jag laughed. "Yoo, now *that* is lit!"

Unamused, 1966 shouted back, "Nah, man, I can't put it out!"

"Stop, drop, and roll!" Jag hollered at him.

1966 fell to the floor and rolled over and over, but the flame would not go out. Zoticon opened his eyes, rushed over to him, lifted him up with one hand, and slapped him in the face, all in one smooth motion.

"Ow! Hey!"

The fire went out, leaving burns all over the ground and marks on the sleeve of his technogarment. 1966 rubbed his sore cheek with his other hand, avoiding eye contact with anyone.

"We just gave you this uniform," Zoticon scolded, pointing at the slightly scuffed sleeve. "And you've already marked it up."

1966 was going to respond but seeing Zoticon's eyes caused him to hesitate.

"You and I both know why that happened," he added. "Your focus was impure."

1966 broke eye contact and looked down at the floor. Shame swelled up within him. "I... I'm sorry."

Ann shot a fierce look toward Zoticon.

"Ehrm, well..." he said, readjusting his collar and looking for a way to reduce the stinging pain he had left on his student's face. "Well, good accountability for your actions."

Ann rolled her eyes.

"Ahem," Zoticon said, clearing his throat and changing the subject. "Will we be giving these two codenames? We can't use their government names."

Jag jumped up and down, nearly slipping on the black liquid on the floor at his feet. "Yes!" he exclaimed.

Zoticon went over to him, looked down at his feet and then at his face. "Your codename is now BlackBlob," he announced.

"Blagblub?"

"Black. Blob," the commander repeated more slowly.

"What?" 1966 laughed. "Is that really what we're going to call you from now on?"

The newly designated BlackBlob looked down at the dark substance at his feet. It quickly evaporated, as if it had never been there. "It sounds weird," he muttered. Then he asked more loudly, "Can't I get a name that sounds trendier?" He paused. "Like 'Invincible Death Weapon'?"

Zoticon turned around. "No." He walked over to 1966 again and looked him up and down. "And you..." He paused, thinking for a moment. 1966 was still rubbing at his singed sleeve. "Your name is..." Zoticon continued to ponder. "Yes, you will be FireArm."

"What? FireArm?" the youth exclaimed in surprise.

"Correct," Zoticon affirmed. "It will be better than referring to you as..." He straightened himself up, "a string of numbers from an orphanage."

"I guess..." the newly named FireArm muttered.

BlackBlob snickered.

"Then it is settled." Zoticon crossed his arms, looking smug. "Atkon will register your call signs in the system."

Ann's face was in her palm. Glancing over to her, Zoticon grew self-conscious and cleared his throat.

He walked to each initiate in turn and gave them a fist bump, which they awkwardly accepted.

"Welcome to Black Mountain," he said.

"Black Mountain?" FireArm asked.

"Yes," Ann replied. "This is the name of our movement."

"Under this name, we fight until the world's oppressor falls," Zoticon said with resolve. "Understood?"

"Yes, sir!" FireArm and BlackBlob said in unison.

"First, we train, and then..." He pressed his fist against his heart. "We *win* this war."

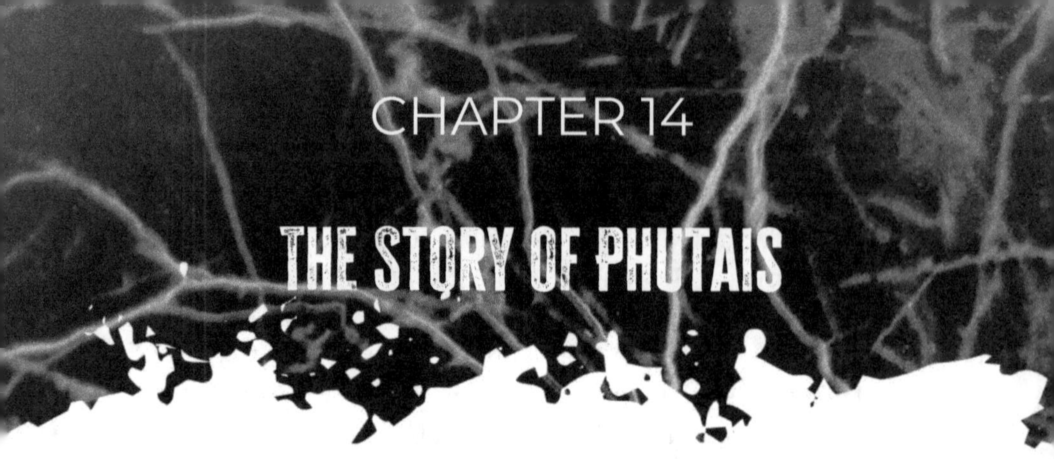

CHAPTER 14

THE STORY OF PHUTAIS

Phutais looked out from the penthouse balcony of his thirty-story high rise. Behind him, three figures lay on a family-sized bed.

"Leave."

The three ladies smiled in unison and clicked the Accept Payment buttons on their portable devices. His gaze never left the sky. Ziffea's three moons shone down on his half-naked body.

The ladies of the night thanked him for the transaction, then took turns going to the mirror and pressing some buttons on it. The lasers that shot out of it removed their lingerie while simultaneously weaving new 3D printed outfits onto their figures. No one would ask any questions when they saw three officials leaving a military installation after a midnight consultation at the High Commander's office. They passed through the door in single file, leaving Phutais alone in the suite.

"Beautiful. What a beautiful night," the tall, toned high commander said to himself.

Against the backdrop of moons and stars, he took a moment to reminisce about Zi-Tai's evolution. He reviewed the challenges and almost unbroken string of victories that had led the corporation he founded to the present moment.

He thought about the conquest of his home planet, Marka. He remembered how the conflict among different governments, corporations, and paramilitary forces led to unceasing warfare, unending bloodshed, and battles for power and control of resources. Zi-Tai had been just another of the players at first, but under Phutais, its focus on AI—general artificial intelligence automatons and data-driven solutions based on statistical models—had proved decisive. After much research and testing, advanced technology was used to accurately predict which policies would unite the war-weary people of Marka and shape public opinion to accept corporate rule under a single all-encompassing provider of goods and services. Of course, the only possible choice had to be Zi-Tai.

Phutais had been a voracious reader as a youth. Nothing made him feel more enthralled than being alone with a book that could teach him something. He recalled with pride how he had quietly mastered so many different disciplines while still only a teenager. He had been raised in a wealthy family that had bred generations of fierce and heartless billionaires. His parents had inherited untold wealth, but to clean up their image as out-of-touch elitists, they had become philanthropists. They were also nationalists, however—patriots who flew the flag of their country high atop the roofs of their mansions and believed that only their homeland had the power to bring peace and prosperity to Marka. They used their wealth to secretly influence geopolitical events, but though their schemes often resulted in violence—coups, oppression, civil wars—they convinced themselves that the ends justified the means. They wanted to create a perfect world, and in their son, the perfect heir. They raised Phutais to be a force for change in the world, and he became just that—but not in the way they intended.

Against their wishes, young Phutais spent a lot of his time tutoring less privileged students in underfunded schools outside of their district. His parents reluctantly permitted this because it coincided with their philanthropic image, but they did not hide their dismay at the idea of their "golden boy" spending time with poor children at publicly funded schools. Contact with people from backgrounds so different from his own taught Phutais things that his segregated schools never could. He built relationships with students, staff, and volunteers. Then, one dark day, the unexpected happened. A politically radicalized shooter invaded one of the schools where Phutais tutored, somehow evaded the metal detectors, and began firing indiscriminately.

TAK TAK TAK TAK TAK.

The intruder's uniform had been emblazoned with the same flag that flew above Phutais's childhood home, but his weapon didn't discriminate. The security forces apprehended the suspect without incident, but only after a large number of students and staff had been killed. The shooter would have been released, until the authorities found out that a member of the elite was also harmed in the attack. His sentence was then rushed through, and he was executed within days. Phutais was that member of the elite. He narrowly avoided death, but his body was ravaged. His face and ligaments were torn apart, he sustained serious head injuries, and he fell into a coma. The doctors suggested what seemed to his parents an unreasonably short time limit before they would have to pull the plug. He had seventy-eight hours left. The time was ticking.

Phutais's mother was named Victorie. She and her husband, Forte, rushed to the hospital. Victorie clutched her pearls as they entered the elevator, while Forte glanced at his wrist timer. She knew he was probably missing an important meeting for this inconvenience, just like she was. But this was an obligation. The elevator doors opened, and they strode into the room where their son lay unconscious. Doctors and nurses were present, but the parents brushed past them.

"Can he hear us?" Victorie asked one of them.

"Not as far as we can tell," the lead neurologist replied.

"What a fool!" Forte sneered. "How could he inconvenience us like this?"

As disappointed as they were in their son, the parents knew they would not be able to conceive another child. Determined to revive and heal Phutais at any cost, they mobilized their unlimited funds and an army of researchers to scour the metanetworks for solutions. Anything to save their investment in the boy.

Eventually, their search narrowed down to a handful of pioneering medical scientists in distant countries. They flew them in, all expenses paid, only to be told by one surgeon after another that though they might be able to repair the damaged parts of his body with experimental procedures, skin grafts, and cybernetic prosthetics, his brain would never recover.

When the last of them had delivered the same verdict, Victorie, tears streaming down her face, still would not admit defeat. "Doctor, there *has* to be a way," she insisted.

"We will pay any price you ask," said Forte.

The dark-skinned scientist put a hand to his heart. "I'm sorry, there is truly nothing I can do."

"Can't you fix this? We are running out of time..." Victorie implored.

"Even the most advanced *modern* medicine cannot treat these kinds of injuries." There was an emphasis to the word *modern* that made Victorie's husband press on.

"So… is there anything that's *not* modern medicine that could revive him?"

The doctor made sure no other staff were around. Then he whispered something to the desperate parents. He had once heard murmurs among the Indigenous people of his homeland that might bring a faint glimmer of hope. Their legends spoke of a secret society whose practitioners lived forever and could be brought back from the brink of death.

Phutais's parents were materialists through and through, but their desperation overrode their skepticism. Against the advice of everyone in their close circle of friends and associates, they decided to go for it. Their researchers hunted for instances of inexplicable events. News articles and scientific papers relating to the materialization of matter or elemental forces were scoured. They called every expert detective and specialist they could find, attempting to differentiate between charlatans and the real deal, if one even existed. It took their intel teams nearly two full days to cross-reference and fact-check all the claims they found online. Subordinates of Phutais's parents flew private jets to remote locations to interview locals and scout rural areas, trying to gather whatever information they could.

Twenty-four hours before the hospital's deadline, they heard some seemingly reliable reports about a woman in a remote community, said to be an "ancient mother" who had walked the planet before life existed on it. The research described ceremonies that ancient peoples believed would create a contract with a creator known as Si-Vin, ceremonies that conferred immortality on those chosen to protect the planet. The most detailed report described how, after initiation, beings that were once living could be prevented from transitioning to the spiritual realm even after the physical separation of their body and mind. They could then transcend the confines of our perceived reality, alter their environments, and live as immortals. It sounded insane, but there was no time to waste.

"Honey, are you sure about this?" Victorie asked one last time.

"Damn it!" Forte's fist hit the hospital bed. "Do you have any better ideas?"

"It's just that... that primitive lifestyle..."

"I know, I can't stand it either, but at least it's one of our territories."

Their animosity toward the inhabitants of that region needed to be set aside. They had no other options, and time was of the essence. They would wager it all to save their son.

Forte bribed the hospital managers extravagantly to ensure the secret, safe transport of his comatose son to the remote southern island. Under cover of night, hours before the fatal deadline, a private jet carried Phutais, his father, and a security team to the island. Victorie was unwilling to set foot in that "wretched country."

From the island's small airstrip, Forte, the security team, and the medical staff drove many miles to a region of hills and caves. Locals there guided them to the exact location. Inside one of the caves, lit only by candlelight, sat a dark-skinned woman. She wore a heavy, white, hooded robe coated with an armored fabric that looked more advanced than anything he'd seen in his own countries. As sticks of incense burned in every corner of the cave, she stirred pots and used a mortar and pestle to beat herbs into mush. A heavy slab of stone lay in the center of the cave.

"Woman," Forte called as he ran ahead of the security detail and approached this mysterious being, "are you the one they call Destinn'd?"

She looked at him with eyes that lit up even under the darkness of her hood. Her gaze had a weight to it that he could not fathom. >*Child. Why else would you come to this place?*<

Her words echoed soundlessly in his consciousness. She was not speaking with her mouth, but her words instantly silenced the trivial mental chatter of everyone within the cave. Forte froze in place. Beads of sweat rolled down his forehead. He knew at once that this was no mortal being. Ignoring him, she continued her preparations.

The medical staff seemingly heard her words too. They cautiously brought Phutais forward. Destinn'd looked up and gestured for them to put the bandaged, unconscious body on the altar and remove the ventilator and intravenous tube. They looked at Forte in alarm, but when he nodded, they reluctantly did as the woman had directed.

She brought her herbs to a table beside the slab where the youth rested. Looking down at the body, she held one hand above him and began to speak soundlessly again, beaming her words into their minds—words they could not ignore. >*A contract can be made with Si-Vin to save his life,*< she said, and then paused before continuing. >*In return you must promise to do all that you can to bring peace to the planet.*<

He nodded his head rapidly, muttering, "I-I promise!" Never before had he felt such fear.

At once, an ancient incantation reverberated in his mind. >*ANKH UDJA SENEB!*<

In an instant, a large white vortex spun itself into existence from the ceiling, swallowing up the stalactites that hung there. The security detail and medical staff were all too stunned to react.

Forte watched in terror as his son's body was struck with multiple kaleidoscopic lightning bolts that shredded his hospital gown and seemed to tear his body up even more than the initial injuries. Forte's heart was pounding. What was happening? Was this a mistake? He now feared for his own life. He gripped his chest and tears rolled down his eyes, but like all the others in that cave, he found himself frozen in place as the bolts of energy slammed through every cell of the youth's body.

As suddenly as the storm had begun, the bolts retreated into the vortex, which then dissolved into the ceiling. Phutais' body lay naked except for a few shreds of his hospital gown on the crumbled altar. Countless droplets of blood decorated the floor. Forte stared at the old woman with horror.

Her voice once again projected itself into his consciousness. >*The ceremony was a success,*< she intoned. >*He will begin to recover fully after the next full moon.*<

Forte looked up to the ceiling and then toward his son. Her words seemed impossible to believe, but how could he doubt her after all this? He watched in a mixture of hope and disbelief as Destinn'd calmly walked back to her medicinal herbs and pressed two fingers against an incense stick, putting out the red ember. >*Remember your promise,*< he heard inside his head. >*Now leave our land. And never return.*<

The medical staff anxiously examined their equipment. To their amazement, none of it was damaged despite the fragments of stone that lay all around the boy's still unconscious body. They lifted him back onto the gurney and checked his vital signs. They informed Forte that Phutais appeared to be stabilizing. His neurological activity was normalizing. Some kind of miracle seemed to have happened.

There were no other formalities, no goodbyes. They left the cave without another glance at the old woman. Forte made every one of his attendants promise to never speak a word of what they had witnessed. He made it clear that anyone who disobeyed him would find themselves in a coffin. They knew better than to question whether he would keep his word.

Phutais was readmitted to the hospital. True to the old woman's word, when the next new moon rose in the night sky, he recovered from his coma. The doctors, who knew nothing about the ceremony, were astounded by the sudden transformation. His eyes opened on his parents, with all their closest aides behind them.

"Father." His first word brought tears to his parents' eyes.

"My son," breathed the old man. The only other thing he could say was, "You're alive."

Phutais sat up in bed, moving his three-fingered prosthetics as if it were second nature. He did not resent the loss of his limbs or their metal replacements. He felt a lightness in the core of his body. He felt as if he could live forever.

"Mother," he whispered.

"Yes, my son?"

"I know what happened. I heard her voice. What of the sorceress? We must repay her."

"Oh..." Victorie hesitated.

"What is it?" He stared at her uneasily.

Forte stepped forward. "We... uh... made a decision that that whole island was prime real estate."

"But I heard her!" Phutais shouted. "You thought I was unconscious, but I *heard* her!" He rubbed his head in frustration and could sense metal touching metal. "She said we must protect it!"

"Protect *what*?" his father replied. "Plants and trees and wild animals? Listen, the treaties mean nothing. There are profitable minerals under that land."

Phutais looked around the room. Everyone was smiling at him. Was there no one else who shared his regret, his anger? "Mother? Did you agree to this too?"

Victorie looked at him sternly. "Dear, your head must still be recovering. You must have been teaching too many of those undesirables. Have you lost interest in commercial real estate?"

Phutais looked back at his father. "But she saved my life!"

"Of course. But she was outsmarted. Now she can find some other cave to crawl into."

Everyone in the room erupted in laughter—except for Phutais. He was silent. He realized that his parents could not understand his objections. He guessed what they were thinking.

Why couldn't he laugh at the stupid old woman's misfortune, like everyone else?

Just because he had been brought back to life by that witch?

What was he learning at those schools?

He read them like an open book. They were predictable. They wanted him to be the same, and he hated them for it. Phutais put his parents out of his mind and started to consider what had just happened to him. He thought about his life's purpose. Had he been brought back to life for this? Just to take others' land and make money from it? A contract had been made with a god he didn't believe in, but a stranger, through that god, had brought him back to life without asking for money, only for her people to be left in peace. What was his life worth if that promise was broken? Were they all on the side of evil here? Something snapped in his mind, and he burst into a fit of laughter. In fact, he laughed louder than all of the others. He leapt from the bed, and his metal feet shattered the linoleum. His father panicked. "What's going on? What are you—"

"Disappear," he responded. In an instant, his hand was on Forte's forehead. In the next instant, his father's body was crumpled inside the hospital wall. Blood dripped from the cracks he had made there.

Phutais looked at the aides, who stood still as if frozen in time.

His mother shrieked.

"Disappear!" he said to her as his left hand touched her forehead. In a split second, Victorie's entire body had been pushed into the floor. Pieces of cartilage could be heard squishing alongside the sound of her pulverized bones.

The aides stood there, still frozen but now shaking. The smell of their soiled garments mixed with the metallic smell of blood. Phutais gazed at the cowards. "All of you," he shouted, his body glowing now with a dazzling white light, "you are what's wrong with the world!"

In a flash, the blazing halo that surrounded his body had burnt everyone in the room to cinders. It was blinding, like seeing a sun up close. But he could see through it. He saw the enormous flash that consumed the whole hospital. He was able to materialize his intention into a force that crushed concrete, metal, and bones into bits. He floated into the air as he saw everything around him instantly vaporize. Where the hospital had been, there was now a smoking crater. No one had survived except him.

And no one could save the world except him, he realized. He would fulfill the promise of the one who brought him back, but on an even larger scale. He would find a way to end *all* of the wars. As the only heir to his family's vast fortune, he had the resources to finish that project right now, within his lifetime. He would make it so that there were no longer people who had to fear their land being taken. He would forge a solution that would destroy all competition and create permanent world peace. He would complete what his small-minded parents would never have been able to do.

Phutais now had almost limitless funds. He learned from the surviving associates and staff that faking one's own death was not as expensive as he had thought. He also learned that it was relatively inexpensive to rid the world of any of the witnesses to his transformation. He would be able to continue the work of his family without any opposition or suspicion. He worked and studied incessantly. He organized research teams that gave him knowledge of medicine and access to experimental laboratories. He funded early-stage robot helpers.

A few months later, and after many late nights of experimenting, he found himself in one of his laboratories. Surrounded by chemical solutions, computers and test kits, Phutais held up a vial. "Computer, what does this one do?" he demanded.

The machine analyzed data charts and projected an identical, three-dimensional image of the vial onto the screen.

BEEP.

From the speakers came a voice. "Solution #9890. Amphetamine type. Allows employees and soldiers to engage in long work shifts without fatigue."

"Good." He raised another vial. "And this one?"

BEEP.

"Solution #8765. Antidepressant type. Allows for partygoers to experience euphoria while suppressing emotions of fear, shame, or doubt."

"Hmm." He filled two separate syringes with the solutions, then addressed the screen again. "Any dangerous side effects from mixing and matching?"

BEEP.

"Negative."

"Well then." He put the syringes into a belt across his chest. "Looks like we have a party."

His experiments with chemicals taught him how to suppress his emotions through intellect and will. After mastering his natural instincts, he sought mastery of the natural world. He hired the best and brightest collaborators using a simple rule: hire slow, fire fast. He met crime lords, but some of them were too cutthroat and had to die. He met oligarchs, but some of them were too greedy. Dead men told no tales. This earned him many enemies, but also a reputation that made few foolish enough to admit their opposition. Anyone who did would never be seen again.

His meetings were famously short. He had no time to play games. "Your first assignment is to stage a coup," he might say to a startled face on a viewscreen. Or: "Crush Sector #236236 and funnel resources to Sector #632146. You have ten days."

Then he would hit the keyboard and end the call. *BANG.*

His practices attracted like-minded individuals who enjoyed doing his bidding. They would prove their allegiance by flattening economies, bankrupting business rivals, and disappearing the major stakeholders of his competitors. His power grew. He learned how to make shadow organizations that spread his puppet governments across the continents. This paved the way to mold the monopolistic corporations he acquired over time into one vast clandestine entity. Zi-Tai became the guardian angel of the world. It was anywhere, everywhere, and everything.

Of course, his enemies did not go down without a fight. Assassination attempts were aplenty, and they drove Phutais into complete obscurity even as many of his highly paid doubles lost their lives.

He learned not to fear death by natural means. He no longer grew sick or frail through age. His prosthetics from the surgery were refined and remolded to compensate for the body parts and facial features that had not regenerated after the ceremony. A permanent mask was affixed to his face. Food and water were unnecessary. But his thirst for power grew.

His indestructible body and his capacity to demolish entire buildings at will made his enemies cower in fear. But this still wasn't enough for him. He had to control the narrative too. With the revenue from his endless corporate acquisitions, he soon had almost total control over the means of production. The media prayed to the gods of advertising, and Zi-Tai answered. He cut off the top of each pyramid, gradually installing his pawns into every position of influence. Electronic device commercials endorsed either products that Zi-Tai subsidiaries controlled or markets that were completely manipulated by its shadow corporations. Independent news outlets collapsed or were absorbed. Talking points even mildly critical of the "new generation" were removed from scripts—and just like that, Zi-Tai controlled the voice of the nation.

Having achieved total control of the media, he knew that the police, the courts, the universities and think tanks, and the politicians would soon fall into line. The dominoes fell one after another.

With his growing control of media narratives, he learned early on that if you repeat something often enough and on enough mainstream outlets, it will be accepted as true no matter how contrary to common sense. By manipulating these different institutions, he was in a position to *create* common sense whenever he wanted to.

Even Phutais himself was surprised how fully and quickly the whole planet fell into line. It took nearly a century to cover most of Marka's roadways, walkways, and open spaces with gray platforms that served the dual function of connecting everyone to metanetworks and providing wireless charging stations for millions of early-stage GAIA units.

Food was artificially mass-produced so that there was no more of a concern about food shortages. AIs made decisions about how best to distribute it, as well as shelter and finances. The algorithms were biased toward people of Light. It was just a mere coincidence that they were designed by staff members who shared the same skin complexion as Phutais and his ancestors. But this was not a major issue; news articles always reassured the public and assuaged their concerns while driving their fear toward the foreigners.

Laws were designed to eliminate any possibility of protest, and the military imposed quarterly forced migrations to "preserve the peace." Darker-skinned people who wanted the benefits of being around people of Light—and could afford the high cost—paid for genetic bleaching. AI models predicted that this would encourage "diversity" and prevent "marginalization." While initially, there were protests and even a few uprisings, the policies of Light supremacy were already so dominant in public discourse and dissent was so effectively discouraged that any serious attempt to resist was tracked and eliminated both professionally and personally.

In the end, Phutais succeeded in doing what none of his long family dynasty had done before him. He created world peace. It took him 90 years, the equivalent of three generations, but he learned from his mistakes and realized he could accomplish the same goal in even shorter times in the three other inhabited planets in the solar system. All the GAIA calculations and statistical analyses indicated that it would take only another 30 years to achieve complete interplanetary peace.

Planet Ziffea was his next target. Phutais was now ten years into the same project, and the monopolies and media control were falling into place. Telron's inauguration now provided a public face for Zi-Tai's behind-the-scenes manipulations. Phutais knew that the doctrine of Light supremacy would be the most significant accelerator. His experience on Marka showed that visual identifiers of power and privilege were the easiest way to divide the opposition and control public opinion. Making the world love a precious minority and despise all other groups ensured an atmosphere of fear, confusion, and mistrust. This made it easier for all of them to be controlled. The politics would favor it, the cops would enforce it, and the people's distractions would leave no space for opposition to take root. Phutais was in absolute charge of the military. All he needed was for none of the other wings of the Four-Winged Angel to fail.

He never had found or eliminated that old woman, but surprisingly, she didn't stop his rise to power either. He had been brought back to life and killed his own parents. Maybe the sorceress had expected that outcome? What if she wanted all of this to happen? Phutais pondered on this as he stared out at the stars and watched the multitudes of Icarus Unit drones patrolling high above and around his penthouse suite. They only rarely blocked his view of his home planet as they buzzed around like moths. In his mind, they complemented the sky. All was right in the world, and the angel was in its heaven.

"What a beautiful night," he said to himself again.

HIGH COMMANDER PHUTAIS

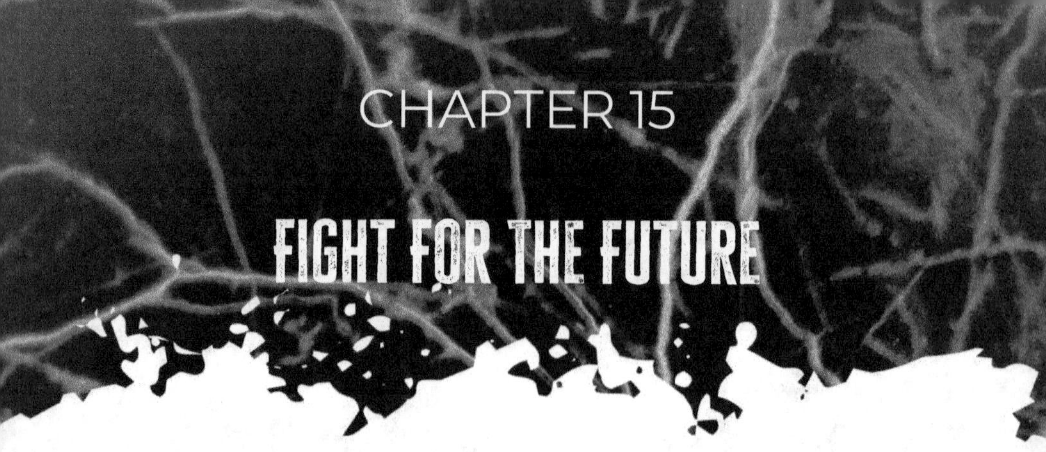

CHAPTER 15

FIGHT FOR THE FUTURE

1966 woke up, his heart racing. He was back in the lunchroom of the orphanage.

Why am I here?

He looked around. Sweat dripped from his forehead.

No!

He panicked. "This isn't right!" he screamed.

He was surrounded by mekkies with flashlights. They had recaptured him. Behind them, he could see the betrayers, the abusers, the other prisoners mocking him. Taunting him.

Why did you trust them?

I knew I couldn't trust them!

You're good for nothing!

They planned this all along.

CLANK.

The mekkies began to strap him down with metal bracelets chained to the wall.

The first rule is, don't trust anyone. So why do I keep letting it happen?

He thrashed against the chains, but he couldn't move.

NO!

He woke up. Beads of sweat fell from his forehead. Around him, he heard only the soft hum of the *Black Raven* in flight. He looked around and saw the bed cover on the ground. The bed seemed to have moved a couple of meters from where it had been when he'd gone to sleep. "Another nightmare," he whispered to himself. "I'm not there anymore. I'm not *that* anymore."

He looked down at his chest. The label *1966* was gone. He was FireArm now. He was out of that hellhole. He would never go back. So why was he still seeing it in his dreams?

To reassure himself, he got out of bed and walked around his room. This wasn't a windowless cell. This place was different. They gave him an outfit for sleeping in, a proper bed, and a large room of his own with a window to the outside. And not just any window to the outside. Clouds. Stars. He was flying high above the world. He looked back at his disheveled bed and the rest of the furniture. A desk with his own computer, a mirror, a viewscreen, and a large digital clock on the wall. Through a door beside the desk was his own private bathroom.

FireArm knew the ship was large and that he'd only seen a small part of it so far. And yet it was invisible to anyone outside. It might have flown over Azor City, maybe right over the orphanage, during his childhood years there. Five minutes to eight. He and Jag had been given an extra hour of rest due to their transformations the night before. His stomach gurgled. That ritual was no joke. He would need to fill his belly before they could start this first day of training. And what was *that* gonna be like?

The sliding doors closed behind him. He looked left and right down the large hallway and yawned as he tried to remember where Ann had said the cafeteria was. She called it the mess hall, which had made him laugh. Had she said it was near the ceremony room or the engine room? And where was the engine room anyway? He wasn't even sure he could find his way back to the ceremony room.

As he stood there uncertain, BlackBlob appeared through the neighboring sliding door, also yawning and barely awake. They walked drowsily together down the halls, following the large luminescent arrows that beeped and lit up on the floor ahead of them. The text on them read, "THIS WAY." There must be sensors everywhere. This was standard in all buildings in the city, but FireArm grew suspicious. Why did they need them here? Maybe this place wasn't all that different from the orphanage, after all. Had he just exchanged one prison for another?

As he walked down the corridor with his new comrade, BlackBlob was thinking what a relief it was to know that his movements would no longer be logged into government databases and every late arrival at school deducted from his social ranking score.

With more yawns and droopy eyes, they followed the arrows to the dining area. Zoticon, AnnRoticon, Atkon, and the rest of the crew were already there.

BlackBlob tried to keep his eyelids from falling as Atkon introduced each of the team members by name. “Good morning, everyone,” FireArm said, covering his mouth as he yawned yet again.

“G-g-good morning!” BlackBlob said more perkily when he met AnansiBlu and NaniMaroon, trying his best to appear fully awake. WilloNeo and BlazeCom seemed bored. They only glanced and looked away when they were introduced, then avoided further eye contact with the new recruits.

When BlackBlob extended his hand to shake Willo’s, Blaze swatted it away.

SLAP.

“Ow!”

“Don’t touch us till we say so,” WilloNeo explained with a chuckle.

“What the…?” BlackBlob staggered backward. That swat, he realized, had come while Zoticon and Ann were busy talking with Anansi and Nani. He got the sense that FireArm also noticed this, but none of them said anything. Memories of school bullies played through his mind. They were showing who was alpha. He had no interest in befriending them.

Ann turned to face them. “OK, are you boys ready to eat?”

FireArm nodded as BlackBlob rubbed his stinging hand and gave his best side-eye to the two older boys. “Sure,” he replied, less eagerly than he would have a few minutes before.

“And gentlemen,” Ann asked, “will you be joining them for the orientation?”

WilloNeo gave her a smile detached from any emotion. To BlackBlob, it seemed like his mouth was filled with thousands of little fangs.

“Thank you, Miss Ann, but BlazeCom and I will be working on our assignments.”

“OK, great,” she replied. BlackBlob breathed a sigh of relief.

The new recruits sat at the table with Anansi and Nani. Atkon stood by, fiddling with a miniature device of some kind. They showed it to Zoticon and Ann, who were at a separate table, planning the agenda.

The spread on the table was a sight to behold. FireArm's eyes widened. BlackBlob was hit with fragrances and flavors that filled the air. Fried dumplings and bakes were piled up on one large plate. On another, codfish had been cooked down with caramelized onions, salt, pimento, thyme, and a variety of garlic seasonings. There was a small bowl of hot pepper sauce for anyone daring to add spice to their life, and beside it, a plateful of fried plantain glistened with a perfect brown crisp around its edges. Nearby, chickpeas, tofu, broccoli, and red onions swam in a mouth-watering tomato soup in a large bowl. The vapors of the different dishes swirled and mixed deliciously in the air.

Never before had either of them seen such colors, smells, and fragrances. In Azor City, seasoning was seen as at worst unnecessary and at best secondary to factory-based "sources of nutrition." These amazing provisions could not have been more different from the bland "beige" meals back home.

Nani beamed with pride, soaking in their obvious surprise and delight about her cooking skills.

"Mmm..." Anansi tilted her head toward the chef and with a hand on her waist said, "Blessings for the food!"

The others repeated the invocation.

"Now, eat, eat, eat!" She grinned.

Nani's eyes shone with a sincerity that washed away the bad aftertaste of BlackBlob's interaction with WilloNeo. She didn't hold back on the helpings either, heaping plates in front of the two new recruits until, laughing, they had to beg her to stop. BlackBlob and FireArm could feel their tastebuds preparing for a life-changing experience when she laid the heaped plates in front of them and said, "Welcome to Black Mountain!"

Anansi split one of the fried dumplings, and they watched as she placed the seasoned fish into the opened fried flour, creating what looked like a small sandwich. Nani circled the table, pouring small glasses of soursop juice for each of them.

"We're teachers in training for Black Mountain South," she laughed.

"South?" BlackBlob said as he alternated between showing interest and shoving as many dumplings into his mouth as he could.

"Yeh man! We're from Ann's squad. We focus on training new Fighters and providing support while Zoticon focuses on direct attack and defense."

Nani and Anansi shared their origins. As young girls, they spent much of their childhood behind the walls of detention centers. Before Zi-Tai had touched down in Ziffea and started to "unify" the North, the warring nations regularly exchanged artillery fire and dropped bombs on one another. Millions of civilians were displaced due to the never-ending disputes for territory and resources. Being refugees at a young age, the girls were abducted from their families and transferred to these state-run centers. Although there were fewer mekanations back then, there was no less cruelty.

While in bondage, they met their teacher, AnnRoticon, who had a special interest in prison abolition and a particular passion for demolition. This unique combination played a crucial role in liberation missions, where she flew as many captives as possible back to the South. Touched by her unwavering determination, and inspired by their shared commitment, she initiated them into Black Mountain South. Over the years, they dedicated themselves to unlearning the lessons from the North and delving into the realms of love, family, and the forgotten histories of their people. As the sole survivors of Black Mountain South's third contingent, they stood strong.

BlackBlob held onto every word, nodding excitedly even when it wasn't really needed. FireArm paid attention too, but thoughts of WilloNeo, BlazeCom, and that slap spun around in his mind. There was something off about those two, but he didn't want to voice it. He wasn't an alpha, he was still a nobody, he wouldn't be understood. He played around with his food and gave one-word responses when he felt he had to.

After the meal, Atkon gave them the tour of the ship, complete with long lists of specifications for the aircraft, layouts for the rooms, and even algorithms for the communications protocols. The two youths fought back their tiredness, which had only grown thanks to their full bellies. Walking off the calories, they eventually made their way to the ship's library. They gaped at the long aisles filled with paperbacks, hardcovers, and photocopied manuscripts. FireArm stared wide-eyed at these relics of the past. Never having seen a "book" that hadn't been uploaded into a computer, he asked Atkon how to turn them on. The group erupted in laughter.

"Here," Nani said, grabbing a book from the counter beside her. The black cover read *The Autobiography of Malcolm X*. She explained that it was a 3D-printed reproduction from a far distant past. "You turn it on like this." She grinned and opened it to the first page. He looked at her as if she was from a different planet. "An den yuh tun each page," she said, handing it to him.

"Ok, I get it," he replied, feeling foolish. He set the book back down on the counter and moved away from Nani.

"Sorry, I didn't mean—"

"Nah, it's cool, don't worry about it." FireArm shrugged off her apology.

Meanwhile, BlackBlob was bouncing around, looking excitedly at shelf upon shelf of books. "I've never *seen* a real one either," he said. "But why do you have so many?"

Atkon hovered down the aisle. "This is a repository of wisdom from long-extinct intelligent beings from several galaxies." They selected a few books. "Many of these texts were banned at one time or the other. Wisdom is dangerous to tyrants."

Ann floated up to them. "Your first assignment is to choose one book for pleasure. We will select the rest for your education."

Zoticon returned with a stack of books. With a thud, he set them on a table in front of the two youths. As they picked them up, read the covers, then flipped through the pages, getting used to the strange sensation, he explained that these books contained all the background information and theories needed for the Black Mountain training course. "Black Mountain," he concluded, "is the vanguard for the revolution."

FireArm looked at him intently. BlackBlob raised his eyes from one of the books.

Zoticon pressed a closed fist to his heart. "Our purpose is to *fight* for the future."

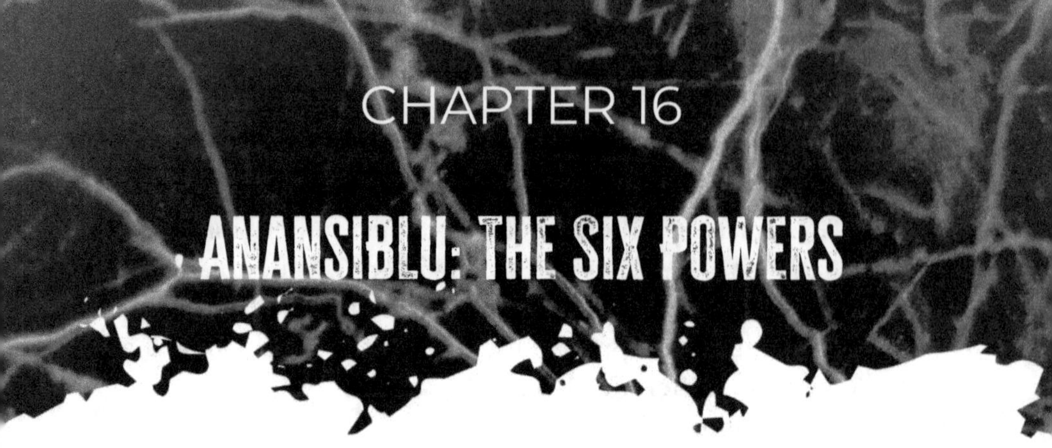

CHAPTER 16

ANANSIBLU: THE SIX POWERS

BlackBlob passed a door that was slightly open. He heard voices and music that had once been all too familiar. A shiver ran up his spine.

"This is Mr. Puffer."

"And I am Ms. Clean."

"And this is BOX News. Thank you for tuning in today."

"It has been hyper extra good to see you! Come back tomorrow for more good truth!"

BlackBlob had not heard those voices since news nights at home, when his digital father tore him away from his video games to listen to BOX's summaries of the "Official Truths." Its manufacture of consent, as Zoticon called it, was prohibited viewing on the *Black Raven*.

Intrigued, he leaned in and peeked through the gap. WilloNeo and BlazeCom were huddled over a miniature viewscreen. An assortment of other devices and wires lay around, likely to prevent detection by the *Black Raven*'s sensors. A number of unidentifiable but pungent-smelling bottles reflected light from the viewscreen in the otherwise dark room. The screen had switched to a stream of rapid-fire commercials for products meant to make viewers feel a sense of lack or a need for shiny objects. It saddened him, reminding him that his mother used to sit through stuff like this all the time.

WilloNeo reached for one of the bottles, blocking BlackBlob's view of the screen. Still, he heard a burst of familiar, fervent music, followed by another voice intoning the slogan, "Get the truth from BOX News daily. Your only guarantee of peace and prosperity."

He watched as WilloNeo and BlazeCom turned to each other and nodded. Puzzled, he tiptoed away from the door. When he was far enough from it, he broke into a jog. He was going to be late for the scheduled orientation in the training hall.

The expansive space and all-white decor of the training hall would take some time to get used to. As he entered, embarrassed about being late, he saw FireArm and gave him a fist bump. At the center of the room, Anansi floated cross-legged, two meters above the floor. She was reading from a thick book and did not look up.

BlackBlob was taken aback.

"What the—?"

"Yeah, she's been like that since I came in a couple minutes ago. It's like she doesn't even know we're here. Where have *you* been?"

"Uhh, let's just say I took a wrong turn..."

"I get that, this place is huge—"

"SHH!"

Startled, the boys looked up. Anansi was staring straight at them, her index finger pressed to her mouth. Finally she spoke. "Come. Take your seats. Right next to me."

Her eyes returned to the book as the boys looked for chairs. There were none. The room was empty, except for Anansi silently floating in the middle.

More silence. BlackBlob looked around the room, searching for a hidden closet where chairs might be kept. FireArm stared at Anansi. She turned a page in her book.

"Umm... We got a problem," ventured BlackBlob at last.

"And what is that?"

"There are no chairs in this room."

"And why is that a *problem*? Aren't you Fighters now?"

BlackBlob and FireArm looked at each other.

"You mean Zoticon hasn't told you about the metaphysical correlates of your powers yet?"

"The meta wha...?"

Anansi sighed and glided toward them, still cross-legged. "Well then," she said with a smile while adjusting her glasses, "I'll have to teach you two the basics."

She held the large book up in front of them. "Look at this emblem."

"Yo!" BlackBlob's eyes opened wide. "It's the same design as on Atkon's suit!"

"Correct." Anansi nodded. "This is the emblem for Black Mountain. It includes the triangle shape of the *Black Raven*, the circle of the planet we protect, its three moons, and our six powers."

The two youths studied it intensely.

"See anything you recognize?"

"I feel like I've seen this part before," FireArm said, pointing at the black symbol in the middle.

"Really?" Anansi wore a coy smile now. "Where did you see it? While reading about Galaxy Zone 780, right?"

"Yeah, there was something about Ko… matic science?"

"Kemetic science," Anansi corrected.

"That's it!"

Anansi pointed toward the center of the emblem. "The emblem in the middle represents the eternal cycle of rebirth. This refers to the fact that we can exist forever, unlike uninitiated Zlon."

"Is it true that we can't die?"

"Two things can take us out." She handed the book to BlackBlob, then turned to her left and threw a punch. A wave of ice formed and created several frozen columns of thorns in the middle of the room. "Some soulforce attacks," she explained, "are so strong that they can rip molecules apart. That's why Atkon's body is encased in metal. They had some tough battles back on planet Marka."

BlackBlob peered through the pages of the book. There were countless pages filled with combat arts postures, incantations, and historical documents. "So other Fighters are our own worst nightmares," he said as he turned more pages.

"Right. But there's nothing to stop Zi-Tai from researching some other way to annihilate us. That's why, at all costs, we have to avoid being captured and studied."

FireArm moved over to BlackBlob and flipped the cover of the book to get a good look at it. "What about the other symbols?"

Anansi smiled and adjusted her glasses. The columns of ice vanished. "Let's start from the left and go in the direction of the moons so we end at the top. Each of you will demonstrate what you know about each of the six powers."

Anansi pointed to the first image on the left. "See the flame over the water and the moon behind it? This is called soulforce. It represents the ability of Black Mountain to channel and use the natural elements for the betterment of the planet."

BlackBlob asked, "Um, ma'am, what does *elements* mean?"

Anansi smiled. "I'm glad you asked. They are the fundamental substances that constitute all matter."

BlackBlob blinked. Then he blinked again. Anansi remained silent.

"Ma'am, I have no idea what that means!" BlackBlob confessed.

Anansi raised her shoulders and looked at his classmate. "Hey, FireArm! Call upon the element of fire!"

"Yes ma'am!"

He put his arms out ahead of him. He flexed his muscles until his hands trembled. "Urghhhh!"

Anansi went over to him. "Don't strain! It's not about your physical muscle. It comes from here." She pushed a finger into the center of his chest so hard he stumbled back.

"OK, got it!" He remembered the initiation ceremony and focused his intention. A little candle appeared between his hands, and then a flame rapidly spread up the rest of his arm and over his shoulder.

"Whoa, whoa, whoa!" Getting ready to stop, drop, and roll, he dived toward the floor. But before he touched it, Anansi leapt in front of him and grabbed him by the collar, leaving his legs dangling in the air. "Hey! Look at me," she demanded.

The fire dissolved. "What the—?"

"It disappears if you lose focus. Always stay focused in battle." She placed him back on the ground while he stared at his arms, resolving to remember that important message.

Anansi pointed toward the symbol at the bottom left. "See this thing that looks like a fast-forward or rewind symbol? This is called *acceleration*. It signifies the ability to move through space without regular physical limitations." She turned to FireArm's companion. "BlackBlob, you're up."

He started to focus using the technique Anansi had explained. "Right…"

Before he could finish his sentence, he slammed into the wall—and bounced off onto his rear end. Anansi floated over to him.

"Looks like we're going to need more practice."

She moved her finger to the image at the bottom of the diagram. "This is a fist. It signifies both incredible strength and the ability to defend against physical forces. It's the reason why you didn't get smashed to bits running full speed into the wall just now."

"Heh, oh, right." BlackBlob scratched his head and laughed nervously.

She moved her finger to the bottom right. "This is a figure with wings and an arrowhead pointed upward. This represents what we call *air-stepping*. It enables us to resist the gravitational force of the planet and walk on air. Anywhere!"

She looked at her eager students. "FireArm!"

"Right!" He tried to do a backflip but instead found himself flying upward at an intense speed. His back slammed into the ceiling and bounced off, sending him straight toward the floor, face first. Just before he hit, Anansi gracefully caught him and settled him gently on his feet. "Right," she said, adjusting her glasses. "For the sake of the walls and ceilings of the *Raven*, you're both on cleaning duty for the next few weeks."

She moved her finger to the right of the diagram. "This is an image of a figure breaking through a wall. It represents chrono-spatial manipulation."

Her students raised their eyebrows. No words were spoken. Moments passed. Finally, Anansi cleared her throat. "This refers to the ability to defy laws that govern reality and to change the natural course of things."

FireArm looked at the symbol intensely. "Chrono—what? What does that even mean?"

BlackBlob tilted his head to the side. "Isn't everything on this list already about changing reality?"

Anansi laughed. "Yes, you're right, but this one relates to time, space, and alternate dimensions. I can't tell you more than that. Nani and I are still studying it."

"Hmm..." FireArm and BlackBlob peered at the symbol, still mystified but more interested than ever.

Anansi pointed at the last icon. "This one on top depicts an open eye with an arrow pointing upward through it. This symbol represents psychokinesis, the ability to move things with our mind."

"Psychic stuff!" said BlackBlob eagerly. "In video-programs, don't they call it tilapia... or telepa-see—?"

Anansi smiled. "Close. But this is more than just *telepathy* or telekinesis. Our intention can change or increase the effect of any of the other powers."

She looked at FireArm. "Want to know why your soulforce only covers your arm?"

"Why?"

"Watch this." Anansi raised her right hand in the air.

SHEEEK!

BlackBlob and FireArm jumped. She had fired a huge icicle from her palm. It split four ways and hit all four corners of the room instantaneously. "Where our mind goes, our spirit follows," she said, placing her hand back on the book. The icicles dissolved into the air. "With time and practice, you will learn to hit objects outside your reach. Remember this: aim *past* your opponent!" She raised her fist in front of the two of them. They stared at her and nodded with looks of determination.

"When we combine our mental energy with our soulforce," Anansi continued, "we can direct the elements outward and easily take out moving targets, no matter how big or how fast they are. And if we focus our minds on the shape of the spiritual energy, the trajectory it travels, and the exact scale of damage, we can launch devastating projectiles from kilometers away."

She pointed two fingers toward her own head and raised her other hand between FireArm and BlackBlob. "When combined with air-stepping, psychokinesis can carry objects or even people to safety." They both rose slightly off the ground.

"Yo!"

"Whoa, what the—"

They started waving their hands and trying to grab the air around them.

"Focus on the core of the planet. Repel it with the parts of your body that face the ground."

After some adjustment, they stilled. Anansi let her hand fall to her side. "Good. Now you're getting the hang of it." Her glasses glistened in the light.

BlackBlob scratched the back of his head. "Hmm… I hope so!"

"There's a lot to this stuff." FireArm rubbed his chin.

"These are the six powers," she said. "We can use them infinitely. Except we have to honor the contract."

"What contract?" FireArm asked.

"The initiation." Anansi took the book and returned to her cross-legged position, floating in the air.

"Zoticon did it for you, and AnnRoticon did it for us. As long as we are fighting to protect the world, Si-Vin grants us the ability to defeat our enemies."

FireArm attempted to sit in the air and fell on his tailbone. "Ow!"

BlackBlob materialized a ball of energy that fell a meter ahead of him and splattered on the ground like a water balloon. "This is a lot harder than it sounds!"

FireArm rubbed his lower back as he got up. "This is going to take some getting used to."

BlackBlob reflected on what he had seen earlier. The bottles, the video program, the gap in WilloNeo's door. He looked at his teacher. "Ma'am, what if we stop this training?"

Anansi floated over to them with a serious look. "Two things to keep in check. Vicarious trauma and a lack of purpose." The two youths looked at her intensely. "If you stop training, and if you stop living with purpose, your mental force will degrade and will literally eat at your soul. Seriously."

FireArm swallowed hard.

"After battles, we recommend participating in ceremonies to process our victories and losses together as a group. Otherwise"—she placed a hand on her chest—"your heart will harden."

BlackBlob looked at her with eyes like headlights.

"Taking care of each other, eating food for the soul, and cleansing the spirit lets the powers know that you honor them. Then they will protect you."

Silently, BlackBlob resolved to look out for his teammates. He looked at FireArm. "Yo."

"What's up?"

"Let's train."

"Cool, let's go."

Anansi floated back to the center of the room and looked at them with a smile. She opened the book and turned to one of her bookmarks. "You'll be fine as long as you look out for each other."

BlackBlob wondered about WilloNeo and BlazeCom again. He wondered if he should tell someone. He also wondered if they needed anyone to help them.

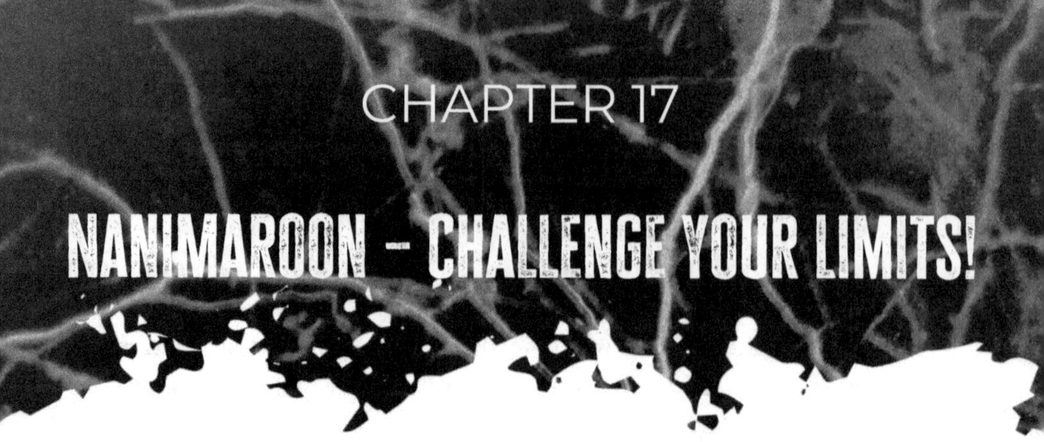

CHAPTER 17

NANIMAROON – CHALLENGE YOUR LIMITS!

NaniMaroon stood in the center of the brightly lit training room and waved at the two boys as they waited hesitantly by the door. The memo stated that she would be providing physical training. They didn't know what that meant, but she seemed suited for the job. Her fierce muscles were wrapped in a black, yellow, and green body suit. FireArm realized this must have been the technogarment Zoticon had been talking about. It looked sleek, metallic, and impenetrable.

Nani cracked her knuckles and walked slowly toward them. "Your first task," she announced when they were a meter or so in front of her, "is to avoid being hit."

"By what?" BlackBlob hesitantly asked.

"By me," she said.

SHOOM.

Even with her build, she moved with the speed of a hummingbird's wings, bolting from left to right, visible for an instant in one space before continuing her dance in another. The two youths could not move. They were defenseless, ambushed by a single person.

"You've gotta be kidding," BlackBlob exclaimed.

BAP.

"Yuh too slu man!" An open palm landed on the side of his shoulder, pushing him back a couple of feet.

"Ow!" He clutched his arm as Nani continued to bounce around the arena.

"You can't say 'ow' during a real battle, you know!"

FireArm tried to move out of the way of the teacher's onslaught. "Does that mean he's disqualified?"

"Nuo, wi jus ah staaht!" Nani's right palm pushed forcefully at the left side of his ribcage.

BAP.

"Oof!" FireArm stumbled backward. Nani darted from left to right. He tried to match her speed but failed repeatedly. He tried to charge forward, but a chop to the back of his knee sent him sprawling to the floor.

"Ahhh!" He clutched the back of his head as he fell.

"If we were fighting for real," she yelled as she moved through the air, "you would all be burnt to a crisp by now!"

BlackBlob tried to leap backward but lost his footing on the landing. Nani appeared right in front of him. "Nice try," she said before she jabbed a finger into his sternum. He fell on his rear.

"Ow, I mean... Augh," BlackBlob sputtered. "I surrender!"

"Time's up!" Nani slowed her pace and touched the ground with one foot in front of her downed opponents. They were still panting loudly, trying to catch their breath and regain their senses.

"You need more cardio," she announced, pointing at BlackBlob. "You need more protein," she added, waving a finger at FireArm.

"But how are we supposed to even dodge something we can't see?" FireArm grumbled.

She winked at them. "With practice."

The physical training involved more than just dodging punches. Even though the students had been unable to dodge any of Nani's attacks, their bodies were learning. She knew, too, that they would have to fight enemies whose skills exceeded what she could provide. If they couldn't outmatch her, they had no hope of outmatching Death-Dweller. And if they couldn't fight Death-Dweller, they would never be able to defeat the army of Zi-Tai.

Before they learned the more advanced skills they were going to need, she realized, they had to get stronger. She would pursue that goal relentlessly.

After some recovery time, she sent them to the weight room. Benches, cable machines, skipping ropes, ellipticals—everything needed to tone and refine the body was there.

BlackBlob recalled some of these from his boxing training. But some of the machines seemed to defy common sense.

"What's that one?" FireArm pointed at a large black ball the size of a small family flying vehicle.

"Oh that?" Nani replied. "That's a force ball. It works with some magnets and computers. It gets heavier each time you use it."

BlackBlob pointed at another. "Yo, Fire, this one's called a treadmill."

"Bruh, I know what a treadmill is."

Nani walked over to it. "Well, actually, that's not a treadmill," she said. "That's a gravity walker. Your feet get heavier the longer you run on it."

They both looked at each other. FireArm laughed. "Is there anything that's not *extreme* here?"

Nani smiled. "I know all this might look intimidating now." She placed her left palm on top of her right bicep and bent her elbow. "But follow our training and you'll be unstoppable."

She pushed them to their limits that first day. She knew they were still depleted from the beatdown in the training room, but they had to be pushed.

The schedule was tight. FireArm worked on the InfinityBall. He rapped his fists repeatedly against the weighted sack that floated in midair, allowing him to hit it from any direction. BlackBlob jogged on the gravity walker, struggling not to float away by accident, stopping every couple of moments to land before returning to as steady a gait as he could manage. After warming up, they tried the force ball, then moved on to bench presses, dumbbells, slabs of iron, and other devices for building muscle mass. Nani pushed them hard to challenge their limits, but also taught them to pace themselves.

"Our muscles aren't like uninitiated folks'," she said to FireArm, who she was spotting as he bench pressed cylindrical gravity weights. She continued, "The more we train, the stronger we get. And there's no ceiling to our power!" She cackled with excitement.

As they worked out, Nani yelled at, encouraged, and laughed with them. FireArm noticed that though she was demanding, she still took their limitations into account and never pushed them too far. He looked toward his classmate. He saw that BlackBlob also pushed on diligently. FireArm figured that they both hoped to one day match the speed and trajectory of their teacher's fists. Drenched in sweat, the boys finally went off to shower.

Nani smiled to herself as they left the weight room. She looked on with pride. *Man! Dem gud! They did better than any of us did on our first day! These two will make the difference.* She thought to herself.

A new confidence surged in her. She watched the two return from their showers, laughing and joking with each other. She saw that their shared hard work was creating a bond between them. A new rapport had developed in only a few hours of facing challenges together. *Just as Auntie Ann and Uncle Zee predicted,* she thought.

"All right, guys, one more sparring session before we call it a day." She pointed to boxing gloves and headgear on a white altar on one side of the room. "But this time, you go up against each other."

Judging from how he picked them up, FireArm looked like he had never seen gloves and headgear in real life. Still he seemed eager to learn how to put his fists to good use. BlackBlob didn't need any directions. He wove the hand wrap around his fingers like it was second nature. Nani had not asked any of them about their fighting history yet. But by looking at them she could tell they both had experience.

She needed to see how well they could already fight before planning her training regime. "Okay, warm up first. Stretch, bend, do whatever you need to do." She glanced at the clock on her portable viewscreen. "You'll start in five minutes."

FireArm scanned his opponent while they warmed up. BlackBlob was shadow boxing. His fancy footwork and peekaboo style of defense couldn't be an accident. He looked like he had been coached and had practiced moving in a coordinated way for years. FireArm thought back to his close-quarters combat training, but what dominated his mind were the street fights in the hallways, when mekkies sometimes let the kids run loose. He threw some punches and kicks in a wild but fierce combination. He was ready for a fight.

"Round one. Fight!"

The two pairs of gloves touched. FireArm jumped straight in with a roundhouse that caught BlackBlob off guard, but it was easily avoided. BlackBlob fought more carefully than he had during their little scrap the day before. He looked like he was in his element.

Left hook. PAF. Right jab. PAF. Right jab. PAF!

All his jabs connected, but only with FireArm's gloves or forearms.

BlackBlob himself, meanwhile, managed to protect his vital areas, and the wild movements of his legs prevented any blows from touching his face. FireArm threw his fists in all kinds of directions, and while some connected, most missed. BlackBlob bobbed, dodged and wove his way out of any critical situation. Floating like a butterfly, he backed up and gained distance. FireArm threw some awkward combinations that might have downed an amateur, but not someone with BlackBlob's prior training.

FireArm started to get frustrated. His footwork became sloppy. BlackBlob kept his fists close, only throwing jabs when necessary to tempt FireArm into recklessness. The bait worked.

BOOM.

Each hasty miscalculation was punished by a body blow from BlackBlob.

BOOM.

FireArm tried to ignore the pain, but his punches got more and more predictable.

BOOM. BOOM.

His legs began to tremble. He was losing mobility. BlackBlob used his right foot to propel himself past one flailing glove and landed a mighty uppercut that knocked FireArm into the air.

BANG.

Then there was darkness.

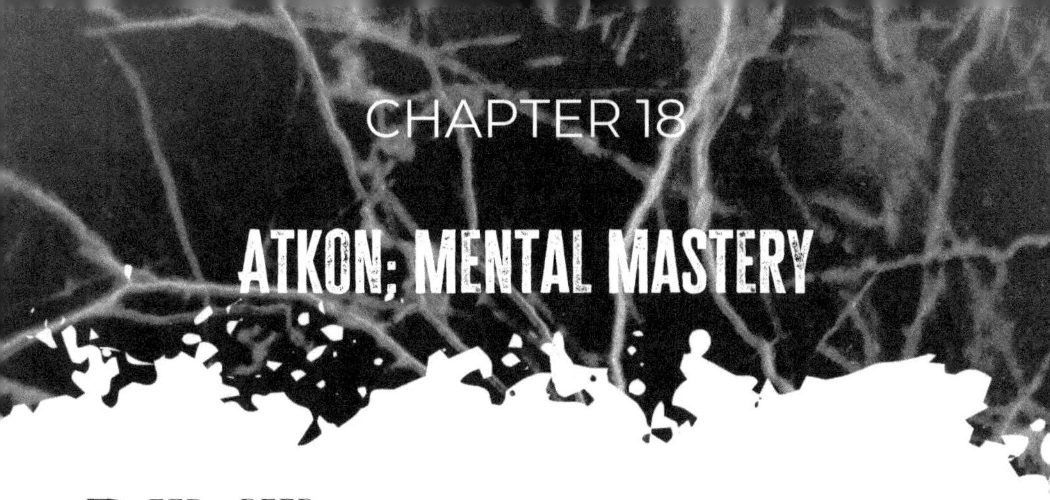

CHAPTER 18

ATKON: MENTAL MASTERY

BEEP... BEEP.

The sound of the heart rate monitor woke him up.

FireArm rubbed his face and stared up at the familiar ceiling of the recovery room. His whole body was sore. Never before had he received such a beatdown. He hadn't been ambushed. He hadn't been tricked. It was a fair fight between men, with no loser. Everyone wanted him to be there. *I made the right decision being here,* he thought to himself with a smile.

The days went by. Anansi managed the administrative side of things. The students were regularly grilled on their memorization of key texts, their knowledge of communications protocols, and their understanding of martial arts principles. Nani continued supervising their strength and physical training and taught them not only how to land punches but how to take them. They sparred regularly, with a focus on building their strengths and minimizing their weaknesses.

The next module of instruction related to their minds. But when they reported to the library for the first lesson, to their surprise, they found Atkon waiting for them instead of Anansi.

"Greetings, new recruits," they said in familiar metallic tones.

"Yo, Atkon!" BlackBlob replied with a wave. Atkon nodded to them as they entered the library.

"Hey, Mr. Atkon?" FireArm asked.

They laughed. "No need to use Mr. or any other titles. Just Atkon is fine."

"OK, cool," FireArm replied. "No disrespect, but how come you're teaching the mind training and not AnansiBlu?"

"Wow, that *is* disrespect!" BlackBlob interjected, widening his eyes.

"Bro, stop it," FireArm replied.

"No offence taken," Atkon replied with a laugh. "Anansi is busy training at the bridge. And I personally had an interest in teaching you both."

"Really?" BlackBlob replied, startled.

"Mental mastery is more than just intellect and, ahem"—they pretended to cough—"and… not gonna lie, I am best suited for this task."

In that moment, the youths knew they were in good hands and that it was safe to speak with their commanding officer. They nodded, and their teacher continued. "Because of my prosthetics, my physical strength is limited. In exchange, my psychokinetic training was more intensive than that of the others. The result is that my mental ability is two hundred percent more effective than most other Fighters."

Their teacher pointed toward their heads. "Not only can I listen and speak into the minds of others, I can even be a channel to help Fighters speak into the minds of other Fighters, so long as they are a set distance away from me."

"What?" BlackBlob backed away slowly. "You mean you can read our minds?"

Atkon laughed. "Only if you direct your intention to speak to me. Then, I can broadcast to you."

"And umm…" Sensing an opening, FireArm pushed on. "So how did you get all mekkie-like? Aren't we supposed to be indestructible?"

They closed their fist. "There are some soulforce attacks that even we cannot recover from." A glimmer appeared in their eyes. "I will teach you all that I know so that what happened to me never happens to either of you."

Atkon floated to the back of the room and returned with an armload of books. These books, Atkon said, explained the recorded history of Ziffea and the hypothesized processes that had created it. They explained that history progressed in cycles. There were ebbs and flows, of course, but generally civilizations were created, became more and more sophisticated, reached their peaks, and ended. Some of the books, Atkon told them, described civilizations and species that had been extinguished eons ago. They mentioned the Fishpeople of Galaxy Zone 207, the Arcturians of 536, the Hillfighters of 670, and the ancient, long-extinct humans of Galaxy Zone 780. The sectors were related to the galactic coordinates where intelligent life had been detected.

FireArm was especially interested in what Atkon told them about the humans.

"Why did they fight so much more than everyone else?" he asked. "Why did they do that to each other?"

"We cannot know for sure," Atkon replied, putting a finger to the base of their metal face. "None of them are around to tell us."

Humans were a forgotten race, they explained. But they were still of interest because Zi-Tai appeared to follow some of their tendencies. This was an example of why Black Mountain sought to study the past. They knew their enemies did the same as well. But not all of what they read about humans represented the worst of the species. They discovered, for instance, a very different worldview that appeared to originate from a location on ancient Earth called *The Congo*.

"There are four key states," Atkon read as they sat atop a bookcase, legs dangling from above. "Birth, prime, death, and ancestorhood. Then we repeat."

They spoke about the implications of this cycle and how it applied to all walks of life. All things were created and then ended, and all events could also be predicted if one understood their initiating force.

"Spooky. Telling the future?" BlackBlob wiggled his fingers. "You mean like psychics?"

"Kind of like that," said Atkon "Although we don't know how Si-Vin created the world through synchronicity. We are not here by coincidence. Simultaneous things can happen at the same time or as a consequence of what precedes them."

Atkon went on to discuss how training a Fighter's mind could enable them to read the synchronicities. By doing so, they could direct the manifestation and manipulate the velocity of soulforce attacks. They could even expand their energy fields to protect themselves and others against any type of damage.

"Mind is one of the most important of our modules," Atkon concluded. "Even if you are weak physically, what you do with your mind can more than make up for it."

Atkon then led the students to the meditation room, a smaller space dimly lit with candles. Here and there incense burned. Geometrical shapes of various sizes and weights were arranged on the floor at the back of the room. Here, Atkon poured fever grass tea into two cups. "Welcome to the meditation room," they said, offering each of them to the new trainees.

FireArm looked around the room. As his eyes adjusted to the half-light, he noticed what looked like ancient charms, energy crystals, and spiritual artifacts that must have come from many different cultures. A few of them, he somehow sensed, looked like they came from Galaxy Zone 780.

Atkon instructed them to take blue mats and cushions from a shelf and arrange themselves as comfortably as they could in the middle of the room. FireArm took some pillows to assist his posture. BlackBlob selected a bigger, thicker mat from the bottom shelf. Their teacher reminded them to return whatever they used in this room to exactly where they took it from when they were done. They were always to leave the room just as they found it. Ancient paintings and ornate designs of spiritual figures covered the walls. This was a room for both prayer and meditation, which Atkon described as the same thing, depending on the intention.

FireArm and BlackBlob sat in silence. No glowing lights emerged, no superpowers. BlackBlob soon became restless and had to be reminded by their teacher to wait for the synchronicity. FireArm, who had spent many years in isolation, was slightly more comfortable. Feeling alone with his thoughts was scary sometimes, but they could also soothe him. In the orphanage, he had often had to keep still while letting his mind roam freely. In this environment and with Atkon's guidance, he started to feel comfort in his mind,

Atkon taught them to breathe using what they called the guided planet meditation. This, they said, would let them ground themselves in the present moment. That sounded easy in theory, but in practice it was challenging. FireArm noticed his mind jumped from thought to thought, memory to memory—anything that offered more interest than this dark room. But Atkon stressed the need for self-compassion. He told FireArm to non-judgmentally return to the present moment any time he noticed his mind straying from it. The two youths had previously thought that meditation meant emptying the mind, but this was different.

Atkon's guidance made it easier, but BlackBlob still needed reminders. Atkon gently redirected his thoughts back to his breath, when necessary. "Practice observing the mind rather than mastering it."

In addition to physical training, they integrated Black Meditation with Atkon into their routine. FireArm practiced the technique more than BlackBlob. He hoped it could eliminate the negative voices in his head, which always taunted him in challenging situations. Sometimes, that motivation seemed to backfire and cause the negative thoughts to flare up more intensely than before. He would then remind himself of Atkon's teachings and ground himself. He tried as best he could to stop being afraid of the voices, but this only made them scarier. It was a struggle, but seeing BlackBlob was struggling with it too gave him something to smile about. He felt reassured that they were both confronting their thoughts.

Weeks went by. Gradually, the youths became more skilled in their meditative practices. Their meditations stretched from five minutes to 30 minutes and then to hours. And one day, the progression to the next level that Atkon had promised finally took place. Atkon had welcomed them with tea, as usual, and they had sat down cross-legged on their meditation mats, as always. Outwardly, little had changed about them, but Atkon could sense that they now had what it took to level up.

"This time, I want you to focus your minds on the seven shapes in front of you." They gestured toward a row of geometrical models arranged in line on a table near the opposite wall. On the left, the row started with a small, clear quartz tetrahedron. To the right were six incrementally more complex and heavier shapes. The seventh was a black tourmaline decahedron. It looked solid, heavy, and nearly immovable.

"FireArm," Atkon said, "I want you to move the object on the left without touching it." An order like that would have perplexed them at the beginning, but they had been conditioning their minds for precisely this type of work for weeks now.

FireArm closed his eyes and called up an image of the nearly translucent tetrahedron. Frustrated, he returned to his breathing. He tried to remember steps, procedures, anything to help himself out and became distracted. Without judging himself, he returned to his breath and waited. Moments after, a feeling of lightness and appreciation began to grow in him. This felt pleasant, but he knew he had to return to his breath. He thought of the cycle. Birth. Peak. Death. Ancestorhood. He returned to his breath. The cycle re-entered his awareness. He sat with it. He observed it. He observed a timelessness. Unsure how much time had passed, he opened his eyes and focused on one corner of the quartz tetrahedron.

T-TAP.

The tetrahedron spun, flipped over, and landed on another of its equidistant sides.

"I did it!" he exclaimed.

"SHHH." BlackBlob and Atkon both hushed him.

"Sorry, guys," he smiled, closing his eyes and returning to his meditation.

He returned to his breath. He acknowledged his victory and then returned to his breath. He expressed gratitude and then returned to his breath. He observed his mind and then returned to his breath.

ATKON

CHAPTER 19

HEAL YOUR TRAUMA

The fleet of senior students, led by Zoticon and flanked by interns, formed a V-shape in the sky beneath the *Black Raven*. Their auras left streams of pulsing colors behind them as they cruised over the forested, mountainous terrain below. Suddenly, they veered sharply to starboard and plunged recklessly toward the sheer side of the highest mountain in the range.

FireArm and BlackBlob gasped as the fleet on the viewscreen seemed to disappear into the mountainside.

"What the—"

"Language, FireArm!" said AnnRoticon sharp, yet motherly.

"But they just *disappeared*!" FireArm cried.

"Right into the side of a *mountain*!" BlackBlob chimed in.

"You didn't see the entrance," said Ann, "but I'm not surprised. It's well hidden by the trees."

"Entrance to what?" the boys demanded together.

"See the trees?" Ann replied. "We are now over the southern continents." She pointed to a map at the corner of the screen. "This is an underground Zi-Tai extraction facility. They take the minerals out, export them and process them in the North, and then sell finished products back to the locals at a higher price. Meanwhile, their extraction process poisons the local flora and fauna."

"Well that's..." BlackBlob searched for the right words. "That's unfair!"

"Right. And Zi-Tai's puppet governments run by the world president won't lift a finger to stop this." She gestured to another camera. "But *we* can."

FireArm and BlackBlob watched the viewscreen intently. They weren't qualified to fight yet, so there was a lot they could learn from seeing others do the work. Cloaked pyramid-shaped drones fed camera footage directly into the *Black Raven*'s ultrafast intranetworks. Because Atkon was directly connected to these feeds, they could transfer them securely through a lossless connection with almost zero lag.

FireArm marveled at how fast the Fighters flew in such a well-coordinated formation, and wondered how long it would take before he could do so too.

Ann saw him staring in awe. "You'll both be able to fly like that," she said. "In time, and with practice."

FireArm had his doubts about that, but he wanted desperately to do well. He wondered what it would be like to fly at a speed that matched the *Black Raven*'s. He wondered what it would feel like to fight to save the world.

"Come." Ann clapped her hands together. "Time to move on to the next phase of your training."

"Aww," BlackBlob moaned, "can't we watch them for a few more minutes?"

"It will be available on replay. You can study it on your personal computers during your leisure time. Right now, you've got work to do."

"OK, Auntie Ann." BlackBlob dragged himself away from the screen. FireArm smiled a little uneasily at the word *Auntie*. It somehow sounded natural even though they weren't related. He'd been amazed at how quickly the team had come to seem like family, but he still felt some reluctance about it. The occasional laughs most of the crew gave him were always welcome, though.

Ann escorted them to a room they had not been in before. It looked like the training room, but it was much smaller. The ceilings were not as high, and in the center, three chairs were arranged facing each other in a triangular pattern.

"Welcome to the healing circle," Ann said.

Scents of sage lingered in the air, which seemed to have a palpable weight to it, an inexplicable heavy feeling that was not oppressive. FireArm felt a strange feeling of déjà vu. He saw that BlackBlob also looked confused yet curious. FireArm felt apprehensive. He wondered if it was the smell of the herbs.

"W-what are we going to do here?" he asked.

There was something about this room that made him wary. The heavy atmosphere triggered a sudden, vivid memory of being locked up in the orphanage "discipline chamber" for defending himself against one of the bullies. The mekkies had beaten a false confession out of him. Everything was always his fault. But what was the connection between that and this mysterious room? He was trembling to the point where it must have been visible.

Ann looked at him with gentle eyes. "We are going to heal your suffering here," she said, then she welcomed them to their seats.

FireArm froze. His breathing techniques weren't working; he had no breath to work with. He felt his survival instinct kicking in. His body seemed to be shutting down even as a heavy weight grew in the pit of his stomach. He couldn't have moved even if he'd wanted to.

BlackBlob noticed. "Bro, you good?"

"Uhh, yeah I'm straight," FireArm lied.

BlackBlob frowned at the obvious lie.

Ann took a seat and looked over at FireArm. In a soft voice, she said, "We're both here for you, just let me know what you need."

Her words were gentle and non-judgmental. With the patience of a master meditator, she was willing to wait an eternity in silence. No one here would *force* him to respond like he'd had to at the institution. Even if he *knew* this intellectually, his body still trembled. He perceived this place as a mortal threat. Fear gripped his throat.

"I'm not sharing anything about my past," he announced.

"You don't have to," said Ann. "You could only share what you are comfortable sharing."

"Really?"

"That's right; this isn't like how they do it in the movies."

She wasn't laughing at him, he thought. *She was trying to lighten the mood.* That told him there must at least be some degree of safety here.

You're never safe. You're a terrorist.

That familiar voice was back. He tried to fend off his negative thoughts.

It seemed like BlackBlob sensed his teammate's discomfort. He perked up as if he realized that sharing vulnerabilities was not FireArm's strong suit. "I'll go first," he said.

"Great," replied Ann, relieved. "Let's review our grounding exercises."

FireArm hesitantly approached his seat and slowly lowered himself onto it. Gently, Auntie Ann nodded her head toward them both. FireArm knew this was a place of sharing, and though he felt unable to share at this moment, he did not want to compromise BlackBlob's training.

Gradually, the elder guided the students to breathe in a comfortable rhythm. After some hesitation, FireArm also felt his mind recentering on the task at hand.

"We have been working together for some time now," Ann said gently. "Now I want to take a moment to explain why we must heal our suffering and recover from our past."

CLICK.

Large pixelated images began to appear on the walls. Not just images, FireArm realized, but movies from a first-person perspective. Startled, he looked to his sides and then above. A series of different scenes flashed over the ceiling, the walls, and even the floor. They were immersed in them.

FireArm's eyes grew wide with fascination as the brief clips all around him merged into one another. The only thing that even stayed the same color was their white seats. FireArm didn't recognize the faces that came and went as the clips continued, but many of them looked like they came from a different planet. What *was* recognizable was the fear and horror and pain on them. They were being fired on by strange weapons. Terrible injuries and dead bodies seemed to be everywhere.

"This…" He looked at Ann. "This is *your* mind?"

"Yes," she responded. Her expression was accepting. Undisturbed by the collage of dreadful images that played across her face, cast from the projections like light on stained glass. "This is a visual representation of the horrors that I have witnessed," she explained, "and that I healed from."

"What?" BlackBlob was stumped. "But… but *how*?"

She pulled something from under her seat that resembled a golden, metal, coil-like device inside a see-through capsule. It was lined with buttons at the top. Ann explained that these controlled the contents of the imagery. "Atkon used his infinite knowledge to design this room to heal from our pasts." She held up the golden coil. "This device allows us to remotely control the procedure."

"Why would we need to do something like this?" FireArm asked defensively.

She looked at him with certainty. "Because your past has conditioned you to be distrustful of the process."

She clicked a button. The imagery faded, and the room returned to its original state. Ann studied the boys intently for a moment. They stared back, wondering what was coming next.

"There's something I want to ask you," she said at last. "What's your read on Willo and Blaze?"

FireArm flinched but said nothing.

"What about them?" BlackBlob asked.

Ann spoke solemnly. "They are the only ones to have never set foot in this room. Not once."

FireArm didn't like being put on the spot, but the question forced him to reflect on their first encounter with the two older Fighters. He saw BlackBlob quickly rub his hand. FireArm guessed that he must also be remembering how it felt after they smacked it away when he tried to introduce himself.

"We added this module as part of the orientation for new trainees because of vicarious traumatization."

"Vicarious traumati—What's that?" BlackBlob rubbed his chin.

"Terrible or painful things you witness can get imprinted onto your spirit." She placed a hand by her heart. "To grow stronger, you have to unburden yourself from the pain you carry with you."

FireArm reflected on this for a moment. "But they still can fight," he said. "They're still in Black Mountain."

"That's true," Ann replied. "But the enemy is not only out there." She pointed to her head "It's also up here."

Suddenly, the sensation FireArm had felt in his gut when he entered the room was back. He did his best to control his breathing, trying to keep the discomfort from overwhelming him.

"What I am telling you is this," Annsaid, watching him carefully. "Being a member of Black Mountain means you will fight. A lot. People will die. People you care for will die."

She hesitated for a moment before continuing. "Those images were people from my homeland, people I couldn't save. They were people whose deaths weighed on my conscience."

FireArm realized that they must have seen dozens if not hundreds of different faces. He noticed that despite all the pain those faces represented, Ann was still a teacher, a healer, and a parental figure for them. *What a badass,* he thought.

"The motto of Black Mountain is: defeat the enemy wherever he appears." She pressed a fist to her chest. "The only way to do that is first to defeat the enemy within yourself. Before we change the world, we must change ourselves."

She pressed another button on her device. New images flooded the room, but this time in much higher resolution and from multiple angles and perspectives. Startled, FireArm realized that this was the battle whose beginning they had seen before they came into the room. They watched as explosions leveled the extraction site from the inside out. The target seemed to be destroyed, but then a distress signal called for more backup. They saw Zoticon slicing through giant metal machines, his right arm coated with a purple destructive aura that elegantly passed through steel with precision. Anansi hurled large columns of ice, crushing enemy artillery in the distance. Nani tagged metal vehicles, then disappeared into the tree line. Seconds later, explosions ripped the vehicles apart. WilloNeo and BlazeCom managed the smaller threats. They tore through sheets of metal with their bare hands, dodging fire from drones and returning it when necessary. They fought with ferocity, but their progress was slow compared to their female counterparts, who zipped past them, hitting everything they missed.

"These men have been working with Zoticon for some time now. They have accumulated sorrows, regrets, and guilt. That makes the difference between a soldier and a legend."

"What makes you think I have problems like that?" FireArm stood up, his heart racing. The heavy feeling in his gut was spreading through his body now.

"Your eyes," said Ann calmly.

"What about them?!" FireArm was yelling now.

"You stopped trusting others a long time ago."

He got up, knocking his chair to the floor.

"You don't know nothing about me!" he stormed out of the room.

"Fire, come back!" BlackBlob called after him, to no avail.

In the hallway, FireArm shed tears by himself. He'd thought he was doing so well, but he'd failed yet again.

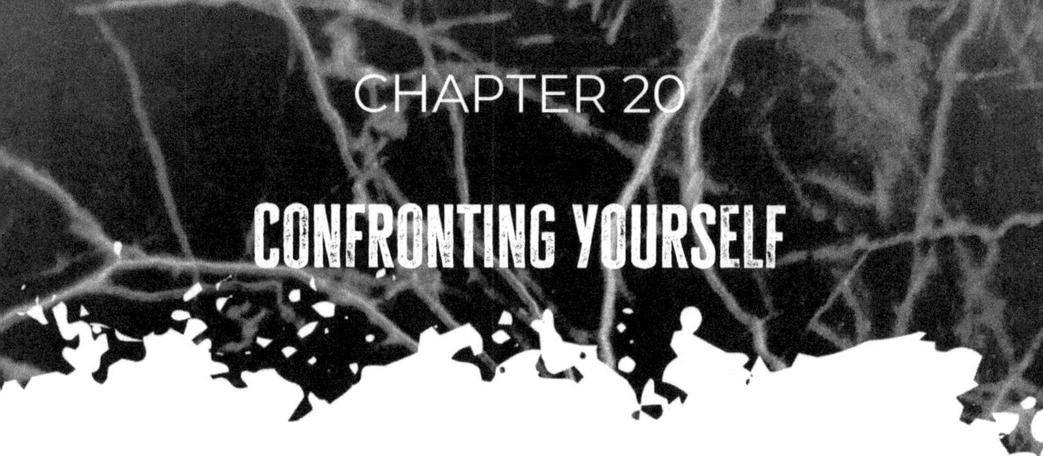

CHAPTER 20

CONFRONTING YOURSELF

BlackBlob leapt up.

"Can I go and talk to him?"

"No, give him time." Ann wanted to give FireArm the time to process. She knew how hard it was to witness and confront one's deepest emotions. Her look was one of determination, not of negligence. "The best way *you* can help him is to show him that you can heal."

"All facts." BlackBlob couldn't fight that logic. "I hope he'll be all right, though."

"He will."

The two returned to their meditation, grounding themselves, being aware of the present moment. Still concerned for his partner, BlackBlob took some time to achieve his focus. When he nervously voiced this concern to Ann, she reassured him, letting him know that if he felt he needed to stop at any time, he should simply inform her. She pointed to the device under his seat. He reached down and found it. "Okay, I'm ready," he told her. "…I think."

She nodded. "Good. Press the button at the top, and the system will calibrate to your thoughts."

CLICK.

Scenes from his past filled the room from floor to ceiling. Familiar faces appeared one after another. Some made him clench his teeth. Others brought relief. This was manageable until an image of getting slapped by Mother filled the ceiling above him. His heart sped up.

"Would you like us to return to the breathing techniques?" Ann asked, sensing the seriousness of his distress.

"Y-yes," he replied through tears.

His breathing was labored at first, but as they breathed together, he returned to a place of safety. As he centered his focus again, the room grew dark.

"Good," said Ann. "It's overwhelming at first, isn't it? Let's start with just one specific target."

"OK," he said, but his voice was trembling.

"You got this. We'll deal with this together."

He nodded and continued breathing at a relaxed pace.

"So, what would you like to work on first?"

"Can it be anything?"

"It sure can."

"For real?"

"Yes, of course."

"Hmm..." He searched for the right words. "I'm afraid of doing the wrong thing."

"OK, let's focus on the belief underneath that. If it is true that you are afraid of doing the wrong thing, what does that mean about you as a person?"

"Oh..."

BlackBlob searched deep down inside for the answer. "It would mean, I don't know, that I'm a coward?"

SHOOM.

The room lit up with countless images. Some of the people in them were recognizable. Others were blurred. Multiple images of his mother scolding him shot to the ceiling. Images of school bullies looking down at him covered the walls. The disdainful faces of an endless stream of strangers scrolled across the floor. There were also strange images of people in hooded cloaks and pointed hats, screaming and wagging fingers at him. Ann took special notice of these masked figures.

"Return to the breath."

The images gradually faded and dissolved.

"Who were those people with the pointy white hats?" Auntie Ann asked.

"My teachers in school," he replied. "They kept saying I was a troublemaker."

"And were you a troublemaker?"

"No!" BlackBlob shot back. "I always did everything they said, but they called me the… the M-word."

"That's terrible." Ann knew the relentless nature of the enemy's ambition, but what would teachers gain by attacking children?

BlackBlob leaned back. "Are you OK, Auntie Ann?"

She noticed indigo soulforce energy gathering in her fist. "Oh… Yes, I'm good." She shook her hand and took a deep breath. Her spirit energy returned to its normal state.

"Sorry about that," she said. "Would you like to heal from that abuse?"

"I don't know if anything will change, but OK."

"All right." She leaned back in her chair. "First, I would like for you to imagine something that makes you feel good."

CLICK.

Bright flashes of pink and neon-green images lit up the ceiling. Faces of pop idols, lollipops, and candy, accompanied by cheerful, catchy music, filled the room. His eyes brightened and laugh lines appeared at their corners. Dimples formed around his bright smile. Then he remembered Ann was in the room. He touched his face and fidgeted with the controller.

"Uh, hey!" he said, pointing at the walls, "didn't you say this stuff would be confidential?"

Ann couldn't stifle her giggles. "Yes, of course, press the right button on your device."

The room returned to a neutral gray. "Phew!"

"Ahem." She coughed. "There really is no judgment—"

"Yeah right!"

Ann laughed. "OK, sorry, but the lollipops had me cracking up."

"Who doesn't like lollipops?"

"True, true… You can put them back on. I won't laugh. Promise!"

"Yeah, let me enjoy *my* process, Auntie Ann."

The room lit up again and the joy returned to BlackBlob's face.

"OK, so what's next?" he called out as he bobbed his head to the music.

"We challenge your fears of fighting the oppressor."

"Using lollipops?"

"Not just lollipops. Look." She pointed at his chest. He looked down to see a soft blue aura forming around his solar plexus.

"What is that?"

"It's the good feeling that comes from noticing what you love."

"It feels great!"

"Now we will use that good feeling you have generated within yourself to heal your past."

Ann guided him through a process that involved focusing on the good feelings that the positive imagery created and contrasting those with the stresses of the negative imagery. Minutes went by while she cued him to bring up thoughts from his consciousness. The room lit up with the white-hooded men, and then with images of his favorite musicians. The face of his scolding mother appeared, followed by bright images of baby animals wearing miniature hats. Each time the positive images came up, the negative images that followed felt less daunting. The images of his teachers stopped wagging their fingers at him. Images of cherry-flavored lollipops appeared on the walls as the intimidating figures diminished, until they dissipated altogether. The room returned to darkness as BlackBlob's breathing became more regular.

"Good. What happens now when you think about that belief that you're a coward?"

The room stayed dark.

He thought about it. His eyes searched the corners of the room. "Wow. Nothing."

"Place your hands like this." Ann put her left hand near her right shoulder and her right hand near her left shoulder. BlackBlob did the same. As his forearms crossed over his heart, Auntie Ann said, "Now accept this."

"OK."

WHOOSH.

He felt a sudden surge of positive energy around his body. The light-blue hue now surrounded him.

"I feel lighter, like I just dropped a few pounds."

"We are not finished."

"This is dope!"

Ann let her arms fall into her lap, and BlackBlob followed suit. The negative energy that had weighed him down was gone. When, at Ann's suggestion, he tried to revisit the negative belief, only faint, blurry images flickered here and there in the room.

"In place of the limiting belief, we need an expanding belief. If you could choose anything, what would you like to believe about yourself?"

He paused momentarily. "I want to believe..." BlackBlob looked around the room. "...that I'm *brave*."

Immediately, images of frenzied men carrying torches burst onto the walls. BlackBlob shuddered. "Return to your center," Ann quickly commanded. His breathing went back to normal. The images faded.

"The same thing that helped you clear the negative energy," AnnRoticon said, "will now help you internalize the belief that you are brave."

He straightened up. "So does that mean..."

"Yes?"

"Lollipops?"

"Yes!"

BlackBlob's smile lit up his face. Over and over again, they repeated the same pattern as before, alternating between images of the feared stimulus and the cue for feelings of joy and excitement until the room fell—and stayed—dark. Then, they crossed their forearms over their hearts once more.

"Is 'I am brave' still the belief you wish you accept?" Auntie Ann asked.

BlackBlob reviewed the past few months. He had been strengthening his body and learning deeper techniques of meditation while floating on an invisible ship with a group of people who wanted to save the world. He thought about how much work he had done—and how much help he had received—to this point. Those negative messages might have hurt his feelings, but they never dug deep enough to touch his soul. Tears filled his eyes.

"Yes, I accept this. I *am* brave. I'm here, after all!"

BlackBlob grinned with a full set of teeth as a new confidence surged through him. The bluish haze floated around his body.

WHOOSH.

The force of his aura made his clothing ripple and shook his hair from left to right and back again.

Ann looked on proudly. "Congratulations," she said. "You have completed your first target."

BlackBlob felt a rush of euphoria. An image of the person he had now become hugging his younger self spread across the wall. On that day, he learned how to rescue himself.

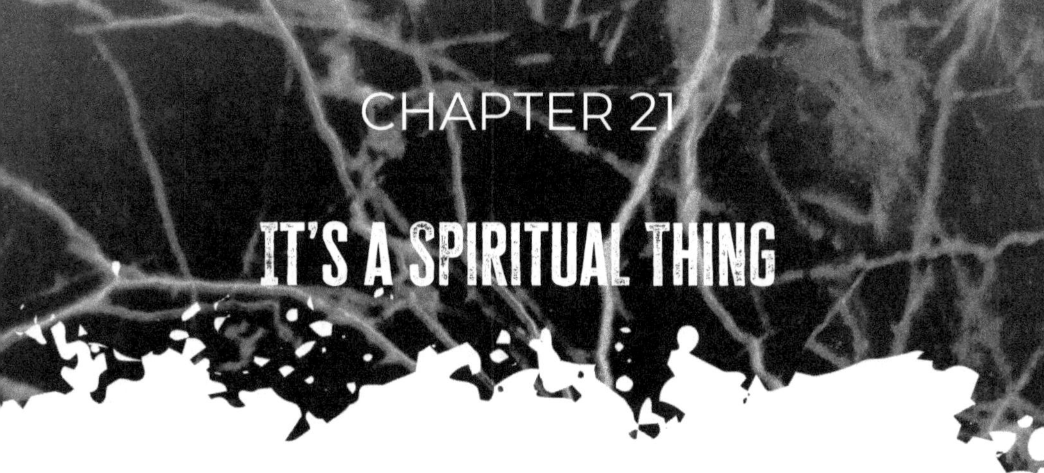

CHAPTER 21

IT'S A SPIRITUAL THING

SHEEEE!

BlackBlob ran into FireArm's quarters. "Bro, it's like I lifted a huge weight off my shoulders!"

"For the hundredth time, leave me alone!"

Despite BlackBlob's obvious excitement, FireArm was not convinced. He lay in his bed looking up at the ceiling with crossed arms. Not only was the idea of talking about his trauma scary, but the fear of losing his trauma was even worse. Who would he be if he started trusting everybody and anybody? No, it was out of the question.

"Well, Auntie Ann said not to force you," BlackBlob said, looking resigned.

"Good, leave me alone."

"I can't do *that*, though."

FireArm turned his head away from his friend and stared out the window. He had been sulking in his quarters since last night. Hearing BlackBlob fidgeting, he looked up at him again.

"Man, you're still here? What are you waiting for?"

"Bro! Aren't you excited?" BlackBlob lit up.

"For what?"

"Today we start working with our *elements*."

"The elements? Like shooting fire out of my hands?"

BlackBlob smiled. "Yeah, they're gonna teach you how *not* to stop, drop, and roll during an actual fight."

FireArm remembered his first failed attempt at using his powers. "Aaah." He turned his head back into his pillow.

"OK, fine. Zoticon warned us about kicking people when they're down."

BlackBlob thought for a moment. "I know the lessons after physical training are optional, but if you join me in this, I might just give you a rematch."

FireArm's eyes lit up. He hadn't forgotten the uppercut that had knocked him out many months before. He had never had a chance to pay BlackBlob back for that one. It reminded him of his decision to stay in Black Mountain. With newfound energy, he lifted his head from the pillow.

"Heh." He smiled. "You just got lucky."

"Oh, did I?" Suddenly, BlackBlob started shadow boxing, feet leaping from spot to spot, throwing jabs left and right. Then, an uppercut.

"Remember that combination that did you in?" BlackBlob sneered.

"Look, if you want me to get serious next time"—FireArm got to his feet—"don't say I didn't warn you."

"He's back on his feet! It's a miracle!" BlackBlob cheered, stretching his hands out and waving them like an overjoyed announcer at a boxing match. "All right, now you can finally get outta here. Let me get dressed and then we'll get this thing started."

On the bridge, Zoticon stood beside Atkon with his back to the door, studying the latest video feeds. They showed plumes of smoke billowing between the trees. Heaps of scrap metal lay over destroyed metal platforms.

SHEEEE.

The sliding doors opened. The four Fighters who had been on the sortie entered. They formed into a line on one side of the room, facing Zoticon on the other. Keeping his back to them, eyes still fixed on the viewscreen, he stepped to the side and motioned them forward.

"I want you to take a very careful look at this," he told them. "What do you notice?"

Nani rubbed her chin. Willo's eyes scanned the images. Blaze looked at the four quadrants, which each showed a different angle on the scene.

Anansi raised her hand. "I think I know," she said. "It's the number in the corner."

Zoticon turned around to face them.

"And what does that number signify?"

"It indicates that *ten* trees were knocked down during our mission."

"And do you know by whom?"

She scratched her head. "Couldn't have been me. I wasn't in that area."

Blaze and Willo glanced at each other. Willo adjusted his collar. Sweat dripped from his hairline. "I … I mean, ah, it could have been any of us in the heat of battle."

Nani glared him. "Cyaan bi tu sure bout dat... The leaves would be burned from my flames."

Anansi gave Willo the side-eye. "We were the only two water elementals on the mission."

Nani snickered.

Zoticon took a step forward, his head in the air and his eyes cast down.

"No one but Black Mountain as a whole was responsible."

They all hung their heads.

"We are supposed to prevent climate change, not contribute to it. Even if it were just one tree, they control the news. They are just waiting for our missed shots to end up hitting civilians."

"Understood, sir." Willo gave a fabricated smile and nodded quickly. "We'll do better next time, sir."

Zoticon turned quickly toward him and looked him up and down.

"Remember your purpose. Stop slacking on your training. You're all dismissed."

Willo swallowed hard. Blaze put his hands behind his back, trying to hide his fidgeting fingers.

The Fighters saluted, turned, and walked out in single file. Zoticon watched, deep in thought, as the entrance closed behind them.

"Welcome." Ann was tending to the plants in the room when BlackBlob walked in. In one hand, she held a metal watering can; with the other, she stroked the leaves of the plants. His eyes widened as he took in the view around him. It was the same room they used for emotion training, but the images on the walls could hardly have been more different. The whole room was lit up with a near infinite view of clouds, the sun burning brightly above them.

"What *is* this?"

"*This* is the perspective of the *Black Raven*. The clouds below, the sky above. It is a live view from the visual feed, from the drone sensors around Zoticon's aircraft."

Patches of white flew past. The sun was so bright and realistic that BlackBlob held a hand over his eyes.

FireArm was out in the hallway. He heard the voices of BlackBlob and AnnRoticon and felt slightly nervous. *I don't want to let them down*, he thought to himself. He took a few short moments to practice his breathing. His mind became quiet. His heart rate went back to normal. *OK, I got this. I could do this.* He reassured himself as he approached the entrance.

Even with his preparations he was startled. Upon entering the room he was surrounded by the endless horizon of clouds, the blueness of the sky, and Si-Vin's blazing sun soaring in the heavens.

"This room is... outside?" he asked.

This unobstructed view was greater than that through any window. For someone who had spent so much of his life locked indoors, the view high above the clouds was disorienting. But it was also thrilling. He remembered how, in the orphanage, he had lain in bed after the lights-out order, staring at the blank, dark ceiling and wondering what it would be like to escape up into the sky. At those moments, the longing for space and freedom had caused almost physical pain

"That's right," Ann answered. "Isn't it wonderful?"

"Auntie Ann," BlackBlob said, "I keep forgetting to ask you, but where are we flying to? Feels like we've been in the air forever."

"We are flying to one of the last remote areas that hasn't been wrecked by the wildfires and floods and other disasters that Zi-Tai's reckless ambition has brought this planet."

The scenery in the room looked like a painting. Clouds appeared like brush strokes, dancing on the horizon, replacing the pattern of the room itself. Ann poured water into a lush green tub of mixed flowers. Soft scents and spiritual energy surrounded her. Her breathing got slower and more drawn out. Finally, she turned away from the imagery and walked gracefully to her seat among the three still arranged in the center of the room.

"Ready for today's assignment?"

"Yes ma'am!" BlackBlob shot back.

FireArm only nodded. He thought about their progress so far. Their bodies were toned, refined by their determination and consistent practice. Lifting iron and training with NaniMaroon had pushed their physical capacities to the point where they could crush large boulders with their fingers. Under Anansi's direction, they had turned countless pages through long days and nights and sharpened their abilities to think critically and remember the lost histories of their people. Through Atkon's psychokinetic training, they had acquired the power to bend reality and move objects with their minds. He recalled BlackBlob saying that he had confronted the ghosts of his past. The next activity would challenge more of their preconceived notions and their sense of possibilities.

Ann raised her right arm. A swirling light formed a few inches from her palm, then floating particles of darkness appeared. The light coalesced from her body and focused itself into a single point, forming what appeared to be a dark indigo orb. It produced shockwaves that rippled through her technogarment and shook the chairs under them. Then, suddenly, it vanished.

"You will both learn to harness the power of the soul."

"Eeeeehhh?" BlackBlob almost fell out of his seat.

FireArm wiped the sweat from his forehead and asked, "Auntie Ann, how in the world are we supposed to do that?"

"It is the inevitable culmination of this phase of your training," she replied. She then stood up with her back toward her students, facing the clouds on the back wall. "When we commune with the ancestors, not just those who walked and breathed like us, but the plants, the animals, the insects, when we make a promise to protect the cycle of life, nature lends us a hand."

"Auntie Ann, with, um, all due respect, I nearly thought you were about to blow up the whole ship," BlackBlob confessed.

She turned quickly. Her eyes were sharp. "We *need* that kind of conviction from you."

FireArm looked toward the clouds. Images of the red-clad invader coursed through his mind. The speed with which he'd moved. The power to strike down opponents. The ability to fly through the air like a rocket and rupture solid sheets of metal like they were paper. He thought of the Black Mountain emblem and the six powers that Anansi had showed them during the orientation. It was making sense now. How else could they defeat that kind of power without bending the rules of reality?

"So how will we commune with the ancestors?"

"You will put yourselves in nature."

"How, um, what...?"

She reached under the chair.

CLICK.

The tiles of the room darkened and then shifted to images of a field. Blades of grass danced in the wind, blue sky filled the ceiling, and a lighthouse towered above an endless ocean. The scent of salt water wafted through the air. Waves brushed against the shore, and gulls keened in the distance.

"This is virtual reality?"

"All of reality is holographic, to a degree. To help put your mind there, we've designed these process rooms."

"It feels very real."

"Start with your imagination, and then you will learn to bring it to reality like we can. BlackBlob, you will begin."

She clicked another button. Large bullseyes appeared between each of the five plants.

"Commune with the power of the ocean, focus on the need to change the world, and hit each bullseye with your soulforce."

ANNROTICON

CHAPTER 22

SETTING THINGS IN PLACE

Bursting suddenly though cloud cover, the *Black Raven* plunged toward the remote headland below, braked and hovered for a moment, then landed softly only a few meters from the water. A well-concealed door at the rear of the craft slid open, and FireArm and BlackBlob sprang out eagerly onto the sand. After months without touching solid ground, the boys longed to feel the sand under their toes and breathe fresh, cool air again.

Sweat. Tears. Meditation. Learning.

Over the previous months, the two youths had progressed at an unprecedented level. The guidance of their elders had been crucial, but there also seemed to be something special about these two recruits. Almost from the start, FireArm's punches had burst through punching bags. BlackBlob had conjured blue masses of pressurized water from midair. They became skillful Fighters, sparring in midair while soaring alongside their hidden aircraft.

Now they were ready for their spiritual training, but this required a more natural environment. Thus, the *Black Raven*, for the first time in many months, had landed at one of the secret locations thus far untouched by Zi-Tai—somewhere the Fighters could still feel safe.

The spiritual training module maximized the destructive potential of close and ranged attacks, but it could only be mastered after the physical and psychokinetic powers had been sufficiently developed. It was distinct from the other abilities, in that it involved communing with nature. Although virtual reality had served an important role thus far, to progress further, the two young men needed to feel the soil beneath their feet, reach their arms around solid trees, and swim in waters untouched by the pollution that was encroaching on much of the world. These were things that everyone had taken for granted before Zi-Tai came along, but they were rare now. The boys had to experience them to understand what they were fighting for. Experiences of the mind, body, and spirit would foster a much deeper meditation.

And so the training continued, and the new recruits grew stronger. Still, Zoticon held back on any celebration. The young men had trained well and sparred well, even better than he had anticipated, but they had never been in the crosshairs of murderous intent, never seen firsthand what this war was all about. They did not understand yet that Zi-Tai was willing to sacrifice anyone and anything, even the planet itself, to achieve its goals.

"They need more training," AnnRoticon said as she watched the two sitting cross-legged in a field of tall grass.

"We don't have time," Zoticon replied sharply.

"But FireArm did not complete the emotion training."

"He'll be fine. He'll learn it on the battlefield," Zoticon shot back. "Just like I did," he added after a pause.

"Oh, brother. That's not reassuring."

They spoke in low tones, but their words could be overheard if someone were stealthy enough. BlazeCom had been crouching behind some of the lush foliage while suppressing his energy field. If anyone found him, he'd have told them he was just meditating. But actually, his intention was set on eavesdropping. His assignment was to listen in and get some dirt on someone, anyone, really. He was satisfied, and now it was time to report back.

Trained as an assassin, his aura was undetectable, and his feet made no sound as he retreated. He quickly entered the *Black Raven*, and sped through the hallways, jumping past the lobby and into the living quarters of the senior fighters.

Blaze reflected on his past. A decade ago, he and Willo had become orphaned soldiers when an unknown renegade Fighter invaded their base in the South and murdered their teacher. This forced them to learn on their feet and navigate the shadows in order to survive. Luckily, Zoticon found them and took them under his wing. It wouldn't have been too pretty if the Fighter mercenaries had captured them, and even worse if Zi-Tai had gotten a hold of them.

Black Mountain provided a refuge from the hostile world, but even as new recruits themselves, they witnessed relentless violence. All their predecessors were killed in action. They stood as the lone survivors of Black Mountain North's third contingent, realizing that no true refuge could be found in a world full of suffering. Being a part of the team had always been a matter of survival.

That's why he and Willo couldn't stand the new recruits. It was so frustrating that all of their hard work was ignored just so Zoticon and AnnRoticon could focus on their new pets. *Those kids weren't so special, they brought this onto themselves,* he thought. Blaze knew his accomplice would welcome some dirt on them. He stepped briskly into Willo's private quarters, fell on one knee, and delivered the news.

"What?"

Willo's feet left the desk they had been resting on and planted themselves on the ground right in front of Blaze's hands. Willo had always been the elder of the two, and his face was distorted with rage.

Blaze continued, "T-that's what they said, I think."

"I hate that spiky-haired one. Let's give 'em a real initiation!"

"Heh… OK, boss."

Blaze smiled weakly and went back to his own quarters down the hallway. Willo's teeth formed into daggers. *Finally,* he thought, *a change in the monotony.*

Hours later, FireArm lay on his back, enjoying the sunshine. Dark shades protected his eyes from the huge bright sun that blazed overhead. The heat baked itself into every cell in his body. He sighed happily at the sensation.

SPLASH.

Off to his right, he could see BlackBlob playing in the waves—flying high into the air then cannonballing off an invisible jumping board, shaking the water out of his big, floppy head of hair, then again flying high into the air. "Cannonball!" he yelled as he dove back into the waves.

FireArm looked to his left and watched Nani tending the barbecue. "Di burger dem dun!" she shouted, swaying her hips and grinning.

A Fighter barbecue needed no propane tanks. From her left hand, she radiated an intense heat that kept the grill at an ideal temperature for each item. The patties were baking. The seasoned poultry sizzled. A pot of boiling corn bubbled. The mouth-watering aromas rose and mingled around the ocean paradise. Her right hand alternated between changing the music from the large speakers behind her and flipping the burgers with a spatula.

"Daahlin, send me one of those corns once they're done, would you?" Anansi called. She sat a little closer to the water, with an ice-cold fruit beverage in one hand and her latest, enthralling book in the other. As she chilled under a giant umbrella made of ice crystals, her feet occasionally dipped into the waves of a receding tide. Her seat was a comfy block of soulforce-generated ice that lifted her above a small collection of seashells and fossils gathered from the ancient sand of that unspoiled beach.

FireArm turned his head and faced the horizon. He sighed happily. Gazing at the waves in the distance, he reviewed his training. *Let me try something out,* he thought to himself. He sat up and extended a thumb and index finger from a closed fist. These he pointed at an empty can of soda he had seen WilloNeo drop onto the otherwise pristine beach on his way back to the *Black Raven*. It was several hundred meters away, but his mind's eye could even read the small print on the can.

"Focus," he told himself.

His eyes closed. His breathing slowed. He visualized the type of impact he wanted. He listened to the sounds of the waves and the wind in the trees. He felt the heat that surrounded him bouncing off the white sand. Then his eyes opened.

CRACK!

A pellet of blazing heat emerged from his finger, and in a split second, it homed in on the center of the can and vaporized it.

"Gotcha!"

He grinned and blew the remaining flame from the tip of his finger, twisting his wrist in the air before cocking it back into the side of his swimming trunks.

"Hey, sharpshooter!" BlackBlob yelled from the waters. "Come and cool off in the waves!"

FireArm lay back down, adjusted his shades, and then, resting his hands behind his head, called back, "Maybe later. I'm good over here!"

As he was getting ready for a quick nap, a shadow fell across his face.

"Glad to see you're enjoying yourselves."

"Auntie Ann!"

At the sound of FireArm's startled voice, all four Fighters looked toward her. None of them had detected her presence.

"You're all late for the mission briefing," she announced with a stern look, glancing sharply at BlackBlob as he emerged from the water, his big mushroom hairdo dripping wet. "And for your first mission, at that."

She looked at Anansi and Nani. They tried as best they could to avoid eye contact. "You all need to set an example. I'm surprised you would both be late."

"Sorry, Auntie," said Anansi. "The time on the agenda must have been wrong," she added sheepishly.

Ann clapped her hands. "Wrap up the party, and back in the *Raven*, let's go!" She turned and left.

Nani looked at Anansi. "Ah hu chienj di taim fi di briifin pon di ajenda?"

"There's a zero percent chance I would ever be late."

"Mi nuo dat... Ah bet mi kno who ah mess wid it..."

Suddenly, a loud beeping erupted from the trees behind them. It was the *Black Raven*'s enemy detection sensor.

"Oh no!" shouted Anansi. "Everyone, back to the ship and prepare for take-off. Now!"

Moments later, the *Raven* was in the air, cloaking shield on, safely out of range of the Zi-Tai patrol. No one had been too surprised when the alarm went off. The *Black Raven* always had to be ready to move at a moment's notice. Sanctuaries like the beach were few and far between, and Zi-Tai was aggressively colonizing the few remaining free zones. And because the *Raven* was such a huge ship, it had to be airborne and cloaked as often as possible.

Moments later, the team assembled on the bridge. WilloNeo and BlazeCom were already in line.

"Took you long enough," WilloNeo scoffed at Anansi. BlazeCom snickered after Nani kissed her teeth back at them. All of them wore nearly identical technogarments, except that the men wore the red, black, and green colors of Black Mountain North, while the women wore the South squad's yellow, black, and green. Laser-printed, crafted from rare, cloned materials printed, their technogarments were the first line of defense for the onslaught that awaited them. Skin-tight, impact-resistant uniforms with matching gauntlets and boots that were much more than uniforms, these outfits protected their wearers from most percussive injuries, and even low-impact explosions. For photon projectiles, warheads, and high-impact detonations, the Fighters would need to rely on a combination of mental fortitude, soulforce, and the will of the ancestors.

FireArm and BlackBlob ran in moments later, adjusting their suits and catching their breath.

Nani raised an eyebrow toward them.

"Unnuh luuk shaap, een!" She winked.

BlackBlob thanked her nervously, scratching the top of his head, while FireArm nodded and kept his eyes on the main viewscreen. This was their first mission, and he didn't want to disappoint the team.

Zoticon and Ann stood on either side of the screen. Between them was a three-dimensional graphic showing the topography of the area. Atkon was typing away at a keyboard at the side of the room. Each keystroke altered the data on the screen. The mission targets were highlighted in bright green.

Zoticon squinted, looking at the new recruits.

"You're late," he said, "We only touch down for training and to fill up on supplies from the locals, not for tanning."

"Sorry, sir, won't happen again," FireArm said, looking sincerely and resolutely at his teacher.

WilloNeo murmured something quietly to BlazeCom.

AnnRoticon's eyes seemed to be searing right through Zoticon. It looked like he changed his mind about driving the point any further. "Well…" He coughed and adjusted his collar. "Let's get on with it then."

The objective was sabotage. The goal: to clip the commercial wing of Zi-Tai. Without revenue, it would lose its competitive edge and its influence against any of the last remaining businesses. The Four-Winged Angel's lifeblood was mineral extraction. Only Zi-Tai had the technological capacity to drill deep into the planet's crust and collect otherwise unreachable precious minerals. Access to these materials allowed them to fully dominate the supply and the profits. The two main extraction sites on the planet generated trillions of world-dollars on a quarterly basis. Something had to be done about them, but they were heavily guarded. If only one was attacked, security around the second would be stepped up to an unprecedented level. Both had to be taken out simultaneously.

The mission was to completely disable the two main extraction sites. Their cranes, drills, and heavy machinery would not be the only targets; destroying these would only temporarily set Zi-Tai back in their plans for global domination. Instead, the huge, deep mines themselves had to be rendered unusable. Despite its technological advantage, Zi-Tai had taken years to carefully set up this arrangement. Until Black Mountain could locate the enemy's headquarters, destroy the C.O.R.E. and finish Zi-Tai for good, buying more time with sabotage missions like these would have to do.

The team was split into two squadrons. On the screen, under the big red capital letters saying SQUADRON 1 appeared the faces of drowsy-eyed BlazeCom and battle-scarred WilloNeo. FireArm's picture, looking way too serious, came on next.

"Hey I know that guy!"

"Yo, stop it, Blob!"

Under big blue letters spelling out SQUADRON 2, AnansiBlu's wise glasses and locs appeared next, quickly followed by NaniMaroon's strong yet cheerful smile. BlackBlob's photo was the only one where his eyes had drifted off to the side.

"C'mon man, didn't you see where the camera was?"

"Bro, shut up!"

Giggles echoed around the room.

"Is there a problem?" demanded Zoticon.

The two youths straightened their backs.

"Ahem." Nani stepped forward. "When do we begin?"

"I appreciate that eagerness," Zoticon replied. "The operation will commence the instant *Black Raven* arrives at these specific coordinates." The map on the screen zoomed in on the destination.

"We are currently flying toward zone 6236," Atkon said, stepping forward. "From there, both squads will proceed by self-propelled flight to their respective target locations."

"Affirmed!" Nani announced.

She then stepped back in line and winked at the two newest members of the team. BlackBlob exhaled in relief as Zoticon briefed the Fighters on the details.

Through all of this, WilloNeo and BlazeCom just looked downward. FireArm kept a wary eye on his two senior colleagues. Had they specifically asked for him to be included in their team? He felt a mysterious tension in his gut.

Ann watched the new recruits with concern. At the end of the briefing, she told them, "This will give both of you the combat experience you need while letting you be around more experienced Fighters."

WilloNeo stepped forward. "Do we have permission to use lethal force?" All eyes went toward him. The air in the room seemed to freeze.

"Well," Atkon said as they continued to type on the keyboard and the screen zoomed in more closely on the map, "based on the Community's intel, there should not be any life signals. It will hopefully stay that way for the next hour."

"Damn it," WilloNeo said under this breath, his teeth shining brightly. Anansi stared at him with a sharp look. He returned her gaze, licking his lips. BlazeCom hummed approvingly. FireArm just looked on, more wary of his teammates than ever.

"Is there a problem?" Ann asked.

"N-no, ma'am! Just a joke, heh."

"If you compromise another mission, there will be consequences for you, Willo."

"Oh, heh, no… no worries, ma'am!"

BlazeCom chuckled.

FireArm watched them with a sick feeling forming somewhere under his solar plexus.

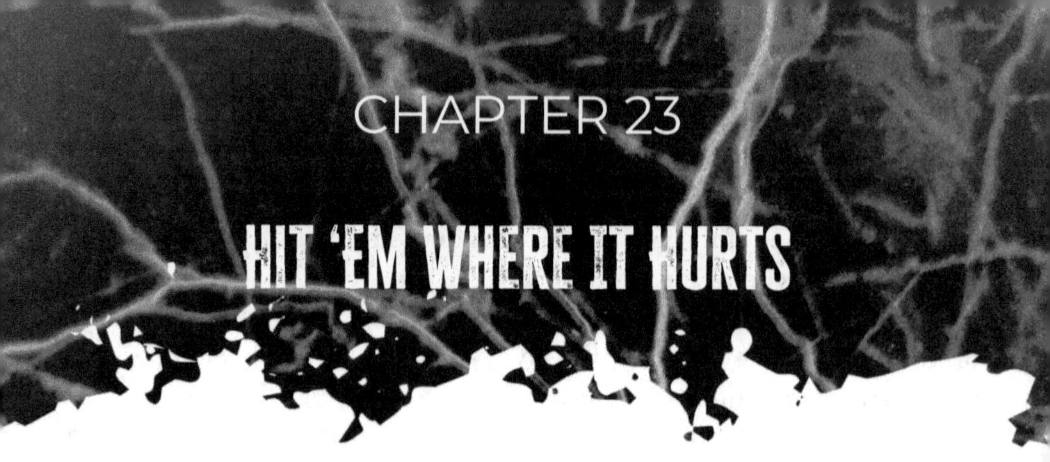

CHAPTER 23

HIT 'EM WHERE IT HURTS

Dark gray clouds puffed out of the chimneys. The mining site housed a single large cone that stretched 200 meters into the sky. This allowed for a subterranean drill that could reach deep into the planet, scooping out rare materials and delivering profits to its greedy sponsors. Surrounding the drill were refineries and depots that could initiate the process of transforming the raw materials into marketable products. Some of these were inadvertently toxic to those who consumed them; the rarest were made into jewelry for the few who could afford it. All generated huge profits for Zi-Tai.

The hatches opened before the two squadrons. "Commence the mission," Atkon's voice echoed through the ship.

SHOOM.

Six bursts of light shot out of the invisible aircraft. Three headed west and three east. They flew past clouds and over water, their speed throwing droplets of water high into the air. Above the dark ocean, they burst through the midnight sky with the three moons high above them. Zooming toward their destination, their speed and trajectories were well planned. Exactly two kilometers before reaching their targets, they decreased their speed to reduce the risk of detection and carefully watched the new lines of code that Atkon sent to black boxes carried by Anansi and WilloNeo.

"Ready." Atkon paused for a few moments, then said, "Go."

CLICK.

Both team leaders pushed a button on their devices. At their respective targets, hundreds of mekanations busily at work suddenly stopped and slumped. Thousands of levers and pulleys ground to a halt. The towering drills piercing into the heart of the planet gradually slowed their descent and stopped. Most important, the cameras and motion sensors that dotted the landscape and controlled entry lost power.

A digital timer showing 30:00:00 appeared in bright red on the bridge of the *Black Raven*. Zoticon and AnnRoticon stood facing it. "Cut the connection," ordered Zoticon. "Proceed with the objective."

The broadcast link between the *Black Raven* and the two squadrons severed. They could not be certain that there were no backups for the enemy's detection systems. Radio silence would prevent any unplanned drone patrols from linking communications generated by the squadrons to the cloaked aircraft. From this point on, the Fighters were on their own. The red numbers reflecting onto Zoticon's eye patch started to change. The countdown had begun.

The squadrons descended onto their targets. Flying rapidly over the ground, still in tight formation, they brushed past roads, streetlamps, terminals, and metanetwork cables. No metal guards or lasers or gunshots met them at the entrance. They flew past the front gates and entered the complex. Both squadrons touched down just as the digital timer burst through the numbers 28:30:45. Time was of the essence.

Squadron 1 reached the walls at the drilling site. Under WilloNeo's instruction, FireArm and BlazeCom placed small gray boxes onto two consoles.

CLICK.

Pressing the buttons on the devices caused the main gates of the site to open. A series of large materials transporters, filled to the brim with precious materials, rushed at full speed through the exits.

"Where are those going?" FireArm asked BlazeCom.

"The cleanup crew will pick them up before we wreck the place."

FireArm raised his eyebrows. That must be members of the Community they'd been talking about. How many non-combatants were on their side? Everything seemed so well organized. The transport vehicles were speeding off into the distance, powered by unknown lines of code. Their engines hummed as they drove off, pilotless, toward the horizon.

WilloNeo floated down in front of his two fellow Fighters. "All right! Let's tear this place up. Save the tower for me."

SHOOM.

He shot up into the sky like a rocket and spun through the atmosphere, aiming for the highest point of the drill. FireArm sped through the air toward the buildings that stored emergency reinforcements. They could switch back on at any moment. No time to waste. His legs flew through the air, slashing pieces of metal and wire like twigs snapping under tornadoes. His hands, though covered with gauntlets, came alive with the dark flames of his soul and rampaged through hundreds of mekanations as if they were toy soldiers, melting them into scrap metal on contact. His punches lit up the rooms, crushing metal and turning mekkie faces inside out. They reminded him of the solemn faces of the orphanage guards. He grinned as the wide swings of his burning fists cut through the remaining robotics and left the storeroom charred and ruined.

He flew out of the room and bolted through the air, heading west to the refinery. He reflected on the first enemies he had defeated. The thrill of his emotions was inseparable from the fear and adrenaline of crushing his oppressors. "Always wanted to do that!" he shouted out loud.

As he soared through the air, he saw WilloNeo firing what looked like bright blue shotgun pellets through his forearms, punching holes through the tower as he descended from its highest point. Mist-like sparkles ripped through the metal structures. WilloNeo descended quickly, firing an endless barrage of pellets with the rhythm of a turbine.

To his right, FireArm saw BlazeCom racing through structures coated in a coral-colored orb. Covering his body in his soulforce energy, he collapsed columns and walls and everything else in his path. His robust frame became a battering ram that blasted through concrete, steel, and electronic equipment like a stick of dynamite to a house of matches

FireArm marveled for a moment at the demolition squad the three of them had become, then he refocused on his assignment. He dove through the ceiling of a gray building and found more of his lifeless targets. His limbs moved with precision. In seconds, hundreds more metal dolls were crushed or melted.

But then—

"NO! PLEASE!"

He turned to see a man cowering underneath him, trying to protect himself with a wrench. FireArm's red hue lessened and disappeared. Why was there a living being here? He flew out of the room, blowing pieces of scrap metal and debris behind him. Driving up through the air with urgency, he sought out his squadron leader. WilloNeo was still working on the tower.

"WilloNeo! WilloNeo!" FireArm stopped a short distance below him.

"What is it?"

"There's someone down there! Maybe an engineer working on the night shift?"

"Good," WilloNeo said, flying right up to FireArm's face. "Kill him."

"What?"

"No survivors. Kill him."

"N-no, we can't. He's not a combatant."

WilloNeo now towered over his subordinate.

"Are you disobeying your commander's orders?"

FireArm backed away and braced for a fight. "You're not the commander."

"Wrong. I'm your senior officer. Do you know the punishment for insubordination?"

FireArm thought about the orphanage. He thought about punishments. His heart began to beat against his chest. "I don't care, it's not right!"

WilloNeo hesitated, then called out below him. BlazeCom shot up from the ground. Before FireArm could turn around, the other Fighter's arms had him into an impenetrable headlock.

"W-what the—"

"Now, let's see. What building did you just fly out of…?"

WilloNeo put the side of his hand to his forehead, forming a visor-like shape with his fingers, and scanned the site below.

"Oh." He pointed. "There!"

"No!" FireArm tried to wriggle free, but he could not escape BlazeCom's iron grip.

From Willo's hand shot a powerful beam of energy that tore through the air and homed in on the engineer, or whoever it was. There was a blinding flash of blue as the terrified civilian disappeared under the weight of the collapsing building. The impact of the blast shook the ground and left a mist of particles that dissipated into the air. FireArm looked on as pieces of metal and shattered glass tumbled and scattered around the place he had flown out of only moments before.

Everything started to get hazy. FireArm thrashed and thrashed and thrashed against BlazeCom's grip. Then, everything around him went black.

CHAPTER 24

NO SNITCHING

BEEP.

The timer went to 00:00:00. Viewscreen and audio feed reinitialized. Low glimmers of light descended to the *Black Raven*'s recuperation point, where it hovered now at a low altitude. As the two teams re-entered the ship, the hatches closed, and the craft accelerated once again into the clouds, disappearing into the sky.

The boombox was turned on and bass-heavy music blasted from it. Hands were clapping. Feet were stomping. Anansi and Nani congratulated their squadron. "Gwaaan man!" they shouted together.

BlackBlob moved and shifted his feet, popping and locking, shifting with the rhythm of the beat. They all jumped with the excitement of the moment.

"He can throw hands *and* he can dance!" Nani shouted out, moving and swaying with fluidity while Anansi bobbed her head in approval. Then three others entered the docking area. Anansi did a double take, then abruptly stopped the music.

There was a grumbling complaint. "Good, turn that crap off."

"Who's tryna kill vibes?" BlackBlob looked in the direction of the raspy voice, and his jaw dropped.

Behind WilloNeo and BlazeCom, both of whose uniforms were tattered and ruined, was FireArm, limping with disheveled hair and dark bruises on his face.

"Whoa, whoa, whoa, what happened?"

"Nothing." BlazeCom turned to BlackBlob, then shot his gaze back at FireArm. "Right?"

FireArm looked away from them. He lumbered over to the sink, filled his hands with soap, and washed the dirt from his face, brushing the soot from his hair and hands. He cleaned himself up, went to the mirror, pressed a button, and changed outfits.

Nani's cut-eye toward WilloNeo almost drew blood. Silence gripped the room like stale air. She looked back at FireArm. "Well," she said uneasily, "what's important is you got back in one piece, right?"

She went over to him and stretched out her arm to put a gentle hand on his shoulder. He shifted rapidly through the air to avoid her, then turned and walked off toward the debriefing room. The door closed behind him. The rest of the team washed up, changed outfits, and followed him in silence.

The six Fighters lined up, standing at ease, in front of the two commanders. The light from the viewscreen cast shadows behind them. Together, they watched the footage from the aerial drones on a split screen. The two mining sites had been completely leveled. Remnants of the large conical structures were scattered, thousands of pieces of the demolished drills strewn across the shattered landscape, and all the large structures melted, burned, and nearly unrecognizable. It would take months if not years to restore either site to any semblance of functionality.

Floating several meters above the floor, Zoticon and Atkon studied graphs and statistical analyses on handheld calculators and bright screens.

Then AnnRoticon spoke. Her tone was serious. "Why are you injured?"

"W-well, Ms. A-Ann..." Willo began, stuttering and fidgeting. Blaze looked like he was sweating bullets. FireArm turned his head away from all of them.

"Answer me. What is this?"

Her tone was authoritative. Changing their outfits couldn't hide the effects of the fight from her. As a healer, she detected injuries without needing to see them. They knew her intuition could penetrate into their intentions. She was, after all, one of the top initiators and instructors on the planet.

"We, um, got into a fight," FireArm said, his gaze never leaving the floor.

"What?" She moved quickly in front of him. "How did that happen?"

"It's simple," he replied, "I... I didn't follow orders."

"You *caused* this?" She stared at him in disbelief. "How could you be solely responsible for injuries that your seniors also sustained?"

"We got caught in the line of fire because of me."

A dark smile flitted across WilloNeo's face. BlazeCom gave a stifled sigh of relief.

"So because of you, all of you sustained damage?"

"Enough, AnnRoticon." Zoticon said, floating down to them, his alloy-coated boots gently tapping the floor. He looked at FireArm without expression, then tilted his head toward WilloNeo and BlazeCom, scanning their injuries with his metal eye. Then, turning back to FireArm, he asked softly, "What is the meaning of this?"

"I told you already, I messed up."

"Watch your tone," the commander warned. "And look us in the eye."

AnnRoticon's gaze weighed once more on her sibling's head.

Zoticon sighed, "We're not your enemy, FireArm."

The youth reluctantly turned his head toward him. They shared a long, searching look into each other's eyes. FireArm sensed a moment of sincerity before Zoticon turned and floated back up to his original position. "Atkon, give them a rundown of the results so far."

Another set of metal boots descended and touched the ground.

"We have been calculating the result of your efforts," Atkon announced. "Zi-Tai will face a loss of several trillion world-dollars over the next few months because of your work." They typed something on the luminescent keys of his handheld device and put a finger onto a holographic blue square that floated above it. The Fighters looked toward the main viewscreen as the graphs from Atkon's device scrolled across it.

"Both squadrons," Atkon continued, "also succeeded in securing the materials for the Community. They have been successfully picked up and are already being redistributed through our underground channels." On the screen in big blue letters was the message "PICK UP OK."

Pie charts showed a bright green portion labelled "90%" and other smaller divisions. A legend showed a detailed breakdown of the distribution.

"Our Indigenous partners will benefit greatly from this. Although the government treaties will still prevent them from reacquiring their land, at least our hackers in the Community will be able to wire financial support straight to their bank accounts."

"Mi glad fi hear dat!" Nani pumped her fist into the air.

"That's what we like to see." Anansi wiped her glasses with a napkin. She looked toward BlackBlob and FireArm. "You guys should be proud."

BlackBlob gave her a muted smile. His eyes went toward FireArm, who appeared to be carefully studying the smaller divisions on the pie charts.

Zoticon looked at FireArm and BlackBlob. "Do either of you have any questions after your first mission?"

"Someone died tonight." FireArm blurted out.

Zoticon stiffened. "Explain! Now!"

Blaze and Willo's muscles tightened. Beads of sweat rolled down their foreheads. Zoticon swooped through the air. He hovered before the two of them, looking at them at eye level. "Is there a reason why your subordinate volunteered this information and not you?"

"Uh, uh, we were waiting till after the briefing!" Blaze coughed out the words.

"Who ended him?"

"FireArm did!"

Zoticon's eyes fell on the spiky-haired youth. He then returned to Blaze.

"Did you identify the victim?"

"No, it's because—"

"Foolishness!"

Blaze hung his head down.

"FireArm."

"Yes."

"What did the individual look like?"

"I, I couldn't see him, it was too dark."

"How did he die—"

"The building collapsed on him," WilloNeo interrupted.

FireArm's heart was racing. *I need to tell the truth,* he thought to himself. *I need to say something! I need to do something!*

No one will believe you, said the voice in his head.

But—

Nobody likes a snitch.

He wanted to stop the voice, but he was ambushed by his self-doubt. He felt isolated, even though he was in a room with others, with his comrades. He swallowed up his feelings and said nothing.

Zoticon floated in front of Willo. He stared at him deeply, until Willo's eyes twitched and made him look down at the floor. Zoticon turned away to face the screen once more.

AnnRoticon looked disdainfully at the three of them and shrugged. "We will have to see how the news covers it tomorrow."

A heavy silence descended once again.

"The news?" BlackBlob broke the silence. "Why does that matter?"

"If it was a Dark person," she said, "they'll emphasize the financial costs, and if the person was Light, they'll play the terrorism card."

Zoticon fixed his attention on the graphs and numerical data. "You're all dismissed," he barked.

The six Fighters left the bridge. BlackBlob watched FireArm. His friend's eyes never left the carpet. He was still limping, but he refused BlackBlob's offer to help him. They all parted silently and went back to their quarters.

At the bridge, the three commanders studied the data together. The large projection screen alternated between charts, computer code, and images of the devastation.

Ann looked at Zoticon. "FireArm was only pretending to limp."

"Saw that." His mechanical eye buzzed toward her.

"But Blaze and Willo were beaten up pretty bad."

"Saw that too. He took on two Fighters without even having started the emotion training." He looked toward her with a raised eyebrow. "What did I tell you?"

"Right on that one." Ann closed her eyes and raised her hands. "So I guess you agree that the oracle's decision to pick those two up was right?"

"Hmph." He looked back to the screen. "Time will tell."

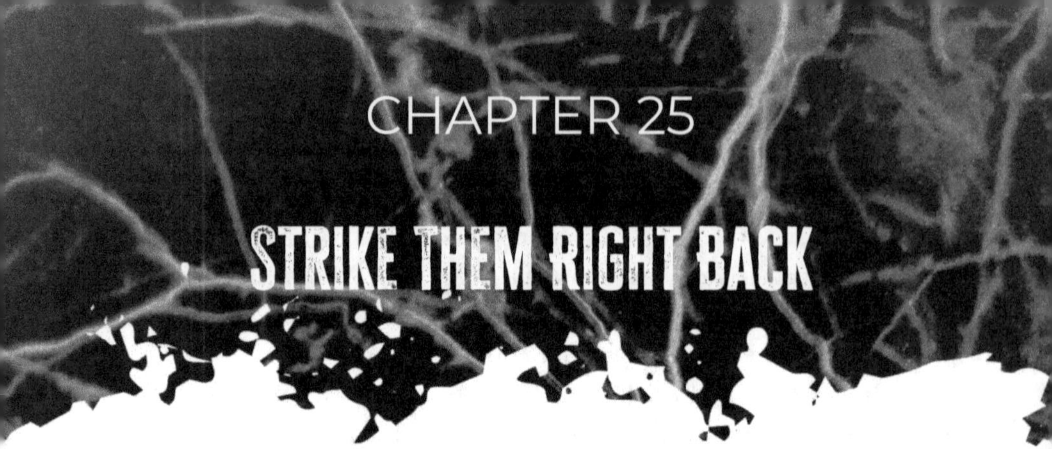

CHAPTER 25

STRIKE THEM RIGHT BACK

In a black room, a viewscreen turned on. Dramatic music played. Sounds of trumpets leading armies into battle, somber melodies, and sounds of urgency and drama, all accompanied by three-dimensional graphics in bright colors and striking shapes. Then the shapes came together to form the words "BREAKING NEWS." An image of the dead engineer's face flashed onto the screen.

"We interrupt our regularly scheduled broadcast to report on a terrorist attack." The look on the newscaster's eyes was one of dread.

"Yesterday evening, cowardly terrorist attacks on the Highgrave 1 and Highgrave 2 extraction sites were repelled with minimum damage to the facilities, which however will be offline until further notice. This may cause some temporary shortages of fuel and other products throughout the North." She paused and stared at her notes, then looked up. Was there fear in her eyes?

"It, ahem, remains unclear how the terrorists were able to penetrate the facility's, er, impregnable defenses. Assistance from inside is strongly suspected. The authorities will leave no stone unturned until the traitor is identified, apprehended, and punished!"

Even with all the excitement, her tone was unusually serious. Helicopter footage showed the devastation from all angles. Graphs of the levels of stock in All-Mark, Surgelab among others, showed green arrows turn to red slopes. The graphics were accompanied by blinking lights, alarm bells, and sirens.

Phutais slammed his keyboard, and the screen shut off. Pieces of the keyboard fell to the floor but were instantly vacuumed up by an automated mini-maid that disappeared back into the wall almost as quickly as it had wheeled itself out.

The green MILITARY ENCRYPTION bar lengthened until it reached 100%. Suddenly, another screen appeared, with four familiar faces. "Listen closely," Phutais said, his eyes on Meridian's. "I don't want to see any more of that footage being broadcasted. We need to shut down all mention of any major breach of security or serious damage!" He slammed the table. Meridian's face grew pale.

"Y-yes, sir! Of course."

"We will need to recoup our losses. So I've decided we now have an excuse to increase costs to the consumer, expand deeper into the South, and seize more territory." There were vigorous nods of agreement all round, though a couple of the members adjusted themselves in their seats and exchanged nervous glances with one another.

"Thoughts?" Phutais asked. "Questions?"

Harbush was in his heavy ivory-colored police uniform. He was always in that same uniform. Did he ever take it off? Who could say? Bush's visor was down, but this could not conceal the rage in his eyes. "Who the *hell* caused this?" he asked.

Telron fumbled over his desk. Pages of documents flew above his head. "I-I've never seen anything like this before," he mumbled.

"If necessary, I-I'll go and shoot them myself!" declared Meridian, and she waved her pistol in the air, her hand trembling with anger.

Some of the others might have been exaggerating their anger for show, but Meridian, he knew, was perfectly serious. Commerce was her responsibility, and she always took anything that could interfere with her market manipulations as a personal attack. She carried that pistol all the time. She probably even slept beside it.

"The people who did this will pay," Phutais declared, tapping strongly against the desk in front of him. He looked toward a distorted silhouette on his viewscreen audience. "Maiden?"

"Yes." Her voice was distorted too. No speech recognition software would ever be able to identify her. The metallic audio effect echoed softly.

"Look into your black book and find me some of the best you've got."

"I'll make some calls." Her name and image disappeared from the screen.

"Harbush."

"Sir."

"Beef up security around other key installations. Scan all the metanetworks the Darks use for any recent suspicious transactions."

"I'm on it."

Harbush said before his image faded from the screen.

"Telron."

"Y-y-yes, sir?"

"My associates will send you a script for your upcoming speech. Download the file marked Replacement Conspiracy, and use the rhetoric about 'Light brothers' as an example."

"O-OK. Great!" the small man replied. "Brilliant as usual, sir!"

Phutais ignored him completely. "Meridian?"

Her hair was disheveled and her movements jerky. Bullets were slipping in and out of cartridges as she frantically loaded her sixth pistol.

"Meridian!"

"Oh—sir!" She placed her weapon on top of a pile of laser rifles and other weaponry.

"We've managed to keep these raids under wraps until now. Explain to me how this got on the news!"

"Sir, until now the disruptions have been minimal. We've always been able to cover things up one way or another, but this one just did too much damage. You can't hide an attack that thousands of people are going to feel the effects of."

"Damn them, Meridian! They're targeting our lifeblood, and you're not doing a thing about it."

"They..." She swallowed hard and looked away, trembling.

Phutais glared at her. "Well? What is it?"

Meridian turned to him again. Her eyes were wide with fear. "They... appear to have... special powers, sir. Our defenses can't cope."

Phutais looked at her silently and let her continue.

Meridian closed her fist to stop the trembling. "Last week, they destroyed an energy plant. But get this, there was no meltdown or any fissure leakages to the surrounding environment. It's as if they care about the people. They try not to harm anyone."

"They must be fools. If they aren't driven by profit, then what's their motive?" He took a moment to think about it. *There had to be a pattern somewhere,* he thought. Then he nodded to the screen. "Pull up the data from your subordinates."

Together they reviewed a number of graphs and charts. They pored over pictures of crushed pipes, chimneys, and processing facilities. Occasionally, they switched back to the worldwide network of informal news sites. The official stations had gotten the message to ignore the raid, but the thousands of wannabe media stars who broadcasted from their living rooms and basements were proving much harder to shut down. So far, at least, the coverage was dominated by amateur pundits framing corporations as the victim and focusing on the plight of the business world while denouncing the "terrorists" as vicious enemies of the people.

Before-and-after images of the sites showed billows of smoke, then debris-littered fields and dilapidated buildings.

Phutais raised his head suddenly. "I know where they will attack next."

"How? Each of my plants on each continent got hit in the past month."

"Are you talking back to me?"

Meridian swallowed hard. "No sir!"

"Good. You will increase GAIA security in four locations. And you will increase research spending for Initiative Five. Understood?"

"Y-yes, sir!"

"Initiative Five, sir?"

Startled, Phutais saw an image on the left side of his viewscreen and barked, "What are you still doing here, Telron?" He glared at the red-faced politician. "You should have signed off ten minutes ago when I told you to download that file."

"I'm... sorry, sir. But what is this Initiative—"

"It's top secret and above your paygrade. If you so much as mention the name to anyone, I will decapitate you and turn your head into a vase," he added.

"Yessir! Of course, sir! I—"

"This meeting is over!"

Phutais slammed his desk. Shards of his computer bounced across the desk. The faces of Telron and Meridian faded to blips. The office was now silent. Phutais stared off into the distance. The name MAIDEN blinked on the screen.

"What now?"

The viewscreen opened to show the heavily pixelated silhouette of the speaker. "We can commission one member from Landross's organization," the distorted voice suggested.

Phutais looked again at the viewscreen showing the devastation from the previous night's attack.

"Will just one be sufficient?"

"If it is not, they will return the deposit at no charge," Maiden responded.

"What is his threat level?"

"Threat level three. But he is a three-for-one deal."

"I don't know what that means."

"You will not regret it. He will be more than enough."

"Hmph." Phutais turned his head. "Fine, I will confirm his deployment in a matter of minutes."

"Good. Call me." Her voice and image disappeared.

Phutais lifted himself from his chair and walked out onto the balcony. In the distance, uncountable drones flew and fluttered like schools of fish, some of them in V-shaped patterns speeding along the morning sky. Some were armed with energy weapons, others with explosives. All of them flew with a gentle hum as they swarmed through the sky like insects.

He went to a recliner chair and turned on the news on a miniature device. Telron was giving a speech. He looked distinguished and well put together. His makeup artists and dressers had outdone themselves. Behind him, the white-and-blue flag of the northern continent undulated slowly. The bottom right corner showed a woman who moved her hands in graceful, well-defined ways to translate his words for the audibly impaired.

"My fellow Ziffeans," Mr. Telron began, "we have wolves in sheep's clothing among us." His manner was very different from what it had been during the meeting with his masters. He was poised and fluent. Polling numbers were trending in his favor. Political unrest was being manufactured in countries where criticism of Zi-Tai was rampant. Being berated momentarily was a worthwhile cost for the adulation of billions and the reward of being the public face of the invincible corporation.

"It's the Darks. They are responsible. They cannot be trusted. They took away your safety." He was following Phutais' script word for word. "But they cannot take away our super freedom!"

The crowd cheered. Flags with blue and white emblems flapped and waved. Fists were thrown into the air and patriotic slogans drowned out the somber atmosphere of the engineer's vigil.

CHAPTER 26

CONSEQUENCES

Cruising through the air, invisible in the darkening sky, the *Black Raven* soared through thick clouds, undetectable even as parts of its hull glistened in the rays of the setting sun. In his quarters, FireArm stood by the window alone. The days since the raid had been focused on workouts, meditation, and spiritual renewal. FireArm had walked by the emotion training room each day without so much as turning toward it.

His injuries had healed quickly. *I guess this is the life of a "walking ancestor,"* he thought to himself. He knew he should have been excited, even ecstatic, to have such powers, but he could not shake the memory of the innocent man WilloNeo had callously killed. No, not killed. Murdered. And FireArm had done nothing. Said nothing.

The sliding doors opened. BlackBlob and Nani entered. Anansi came in behind them, wheeling a double-decker tray that carried silverware, beverages, and richly aromatic fragrances from the southern hemisphere. FireArm turned and stared at them. "I never asked for any of this."

"Well, we just happened to prepare it anyway," replied BlackBlob, as he got busy setting FireArm's small table.

"We just like good food," Nani added, placing napkins from the tray onto the table.

"Coincidences happen," Anansi said. She put plates on the table beside the napkins and cutlery.

FireArm sighed and looked back at the window. The three visitors opened up food containers, pots, and baking pans. Whiffs of ginger, turmeric, cumin, and other spices filled the air. The redolence of jerk chicken spices, thyme, rice, and kidney beans, with a hint of coconut milk, filled the room. Fresh salads, steamed vegetables, and smoked tofu lined one side of the table.

"You meat eaters can stay on your side of the table."

"Aww, why you gotta be like that, Anansi?" BlackBlob laughed.

"You think they would let us hurt nature in here? Atkon gets us only the finest cuts from cellular agriculture! Gimme sum ah di kari, weh mi mek widdout nuh ressipi," Nani said, raising her head in the air. Laughter filled the room.

FireArm was too distracted by the aromas to keep looking at the sky. He turned and gazed at the colors and textures of all the varied dishes.

"Hey FireArm, you ever try roti?" Nani asked. "I made it myself." He took a step forward, curious. Playfully, she thrust a plate with a large flatbread stuffed with seasoned split peas and filled with curry chicken in front of his mouth.

"What's this?"

"You know that huge library? We found a bunch of recipes!"

FireArm turned his gaze back to the clouds. "I'm not hungry." The sound of his stomach growling betrayed his words.

"Ah lie yuh ah tell, tek di fuud nuh!"

"Come on and join us, FireArm." Anansi poured a glass of fruit juice in front of the empty place mat. BlackBlob got busy filling his plate, chewing, and drinking, almost all at once.

FireArm lifted his shoulders. "Aiight… Fine," he sighed.

Nani handed a plate to him and sauntered back to take her place at the table. FireArm hesitantly made his way there too and set his plate down. The other three welcomed him with clapping hands, clinking glasses, and words of encouragement.

"Unnuh see," exclaimed Nani, bouncing in her chair, "the quickest way to a man's heart really is through his stomach!"

"Don't mind her," Anansi said with a laugh. "Eat. Eat. The food's getting cold."

They ate together, shared laughs together, and though it took a moment for FireArm to warm up to them, he welcomed their consideration. Anansi and Nani laughed as they watched the two youths try to wash away the burning onslaught of scotch bonnet peppers. They drank beverages scented with sorrel and with ginger while Nani tried to describe why spicy food was the best food. Laughs echoed around the table, and the playful atmosphere lightened the young man's heart, even if only temporarily. BlackBlob licked his plate clean after emptying the last food container. Nani went to Anansi's tray and placed a set of incense sticks on the table, lighting them by snapping her fingers.

After they took turns washing and drying the dishes, they sat together again. They each took time to share compliments and advice with one another.

"So first of all," Anansi began, "great work out there, you two."

"Well, hey, thanks!" BlackBlob responded.

"We know it hasn't been so easy with all of the training, but we wanted to hear your feedback. How are you guys feeling about being in Black Mountain?"

"Well," BlackBlob said, putting a finger to his chin, "did you and Nani butter us up with this food just to score points with us?"

Nani and Anansi laughed, while FireArm remained silent.

"Nah, I'm kidding, just kidding," he continued, "Thanks for making it easier for us to be part of the team. I mean, between Nani's bone-crushing training and your brain-crushing reading assignments, I'm starting to get the hang of this whole Fighter thing!"

"Unnuh see!" Nani proudly exclaimed. "I told you guys you would get stronger!"

"Glad to hear that." Anansi adjusted her glasses. "And you, Mr. Strong and Silent—"

FireArm couldn't even hear the rest of her question. He knew his turn was coming up next. They wanted him to share what he was thinking. But his mind was flooded. His heart started to race. Not again, he thought to himself.

Stop snitching.

His jaw was clenching now.

You're too weak.

The voices were as relentless as ever. But something was different this time. He felt the presence of kindness, the smell of the incense sticks, the aftertaste of warm spices. There was a momentary opening. He could bring himself to the present. The voices receded. He had to say something before he again convinced himself not to.

He blurted out, "I couldn't protect that man!"

He pressed his knuckles into his hair and lunged forward in his chair. It had taken him everything to say it. Now, he would have to bear the consequences. He tried to hold back his emotions but tears betrayed him. He wiped them away with his sleeve.

In that moment, all of the others knew how hard it had been for him. Nani gave him an encouraging look. "Tek yuh time, youtman."

But he didn't say anything else. The ship's propulsion system hummed continuously in the background. A gentle rhythm that could be felt as well as heard, it resonated under their feet.

Anansi sat back in her chair with her fingers crossed between each other. "We sit with it together."

They sat then in silence. Moments passed. Smoke from the lit edges of myrrh rose, twisted, and dissolved around them. FireArm's tears disappeared too. BlackBlob looked toward him. "We gotchu, bro," he said.

"NO!"

BlackBlob was startled by this, but Anansi nodded for FireArm to continue.

"You don't get it," he said, looking around the table. "You just—" He stopped, wary of the eyes that looked back at him. "None of you do."

Anansi leaned forward in her chair. "FireArm, let me ask you a question. How long do you think Nani and I have been at this?"

FireArm looked them up and down. He had often wondered how old they were. "I dunno, like ten years or something?"

Nani could not contain her laughter, but Anansi lkept a measured smile.

"That's cute. Multiply that by three."

Nani twisted her head. "Wha mek yuh affi be so precise?"

FireArm looked at BlackBlob. His jaw had dropped too.

"Nani," Anansi sighed, "we need to be real with them."

Nani brushed imaginary dirt off her shoulder. "Fine. Mek dem know seh Black nuh crack."

"Well, yes, that's one way of putting it," Anansi replied. She held back her laughter and explained, "Fighters stay at their physical peak forever. As long as they take care of themselves."

"S-so what?" FireArm tried to shake off his disbelief. "What does that have to do with anything?"

BlackBlob's jaw still gaped. Anansi stretched out her arms. "This is how we take care of each other," she said.

Nani waved a purple box in front of FireArm's face. "You think I seasoned that meat and stole incense sticks from Auntie Ann just for fun?"

Anansi added, "If anyone on this ship knows what you've been through, it's us."

Nani cracked open a cold one. "Win ar looz… mek wi selibriet laif."

The words hit FireArm like a brick. He stopped to think as shivers ran up and down his spine. Could he learn to accept himself one day? Would he ever celebrate his own life? His teachers seemed to think so. And in that moment, he felt they had no reason to lie. A small glimmer of a hope awakened in him.

After that, the group wound up their meeting. They loaded the dishes and utensils onto the tray, clearing the space just as the incense stick dropped its last piece of ash. BlackBlob looked at his comrade. "We're all just glad you came back in one piece, bro."

BLACKBLOB

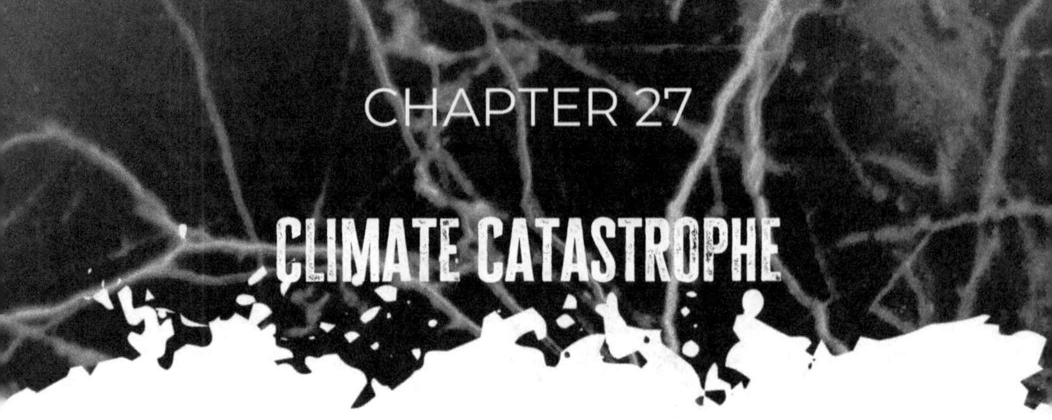

CHAPTER 27

CLIMATE CATASTROPHE

Glistening in the sunlight, the *Raven* flew high above the mountains. Below it lay the pure blue waters of lakes and the lush green forests and grasslands of the largest of the southern continents. There was a world of a difference from the sterile metal planes of the North. Still largely unconnected to the metanetwork, the remoter areas of the South could still provide sanctuaries where the Fighters could rest and load up on provisions.

In the North, thick metal sheets called motherboards covered every open space except the designated agrozones. Together with the metallic gray streets and sidewalks and the wired-up office towers and apartment blocks, they formed an unbroken aggregation of wireless surveillance, low-latency connections, and data transmission, all for a populace that had become totally dependent on them—just as Zi-Tai wanted. Very little could be grown in such a totally mechanized environment. The North relied for its food almost entirely on its power to make the South grow and sell it for cheap. If that power could be disrupted, it would be game over for the Four-Winged Angel of Zi-Tai. This was the core of the Fighters' plan.

The *Black Raven* flew a predetermined course generated by supporters from the Community throughout the region. It zigzagged through aerial landmarks and coordinates to cross safely into the southern hemisphere and avoid detection from the assembly of military bases that lay along the North-South border.

Aromas of mint tea wafted through the bridge. "There are a lot more bases here than I remember," AnnRoticon said, setting her cup down.

Beside her, Atkon was busy punching numbers into a never-ending spreadsheet. "Reports from the Community indicate that northern surveillance is being ramped up," they announced. "They're planning something."

Zoticon floated down from the ceiling holding a miniature device that tracked the trajectory of the *Raven*. "They are expecting us."

The three leaders had spent the past few days in almost constant communication with their southern allies. After the sabotage missions in the North, they now needed to focus on the North's ongoing expansion into the South and ultimately break the power of the North altogether.

AnnRoticon studied her video screen notes with one hand while sipping tea with the other. Images of wasted, bare trees and deforested land scrolled across the screen. Near the border, vast areas of the South were being cleared of wildlife and foliage to make way for motherboards. Tears welled in her eyes as she watched video of Zi-Tai's bulldozers clearing flowers, trees, and homes, but she had to stand up when she came upon one clip that she found especially alarming.

"Computer!" she called out.

"READY," replied a digitized voice.

"Analyze the level of water toxicity caused by the mission target."

"ANALYZING."

The main viewscreen lit up to show a grid map of the landscape, with a circle around a large structure almost three kilometers wide. It appeared to be a dam, and it had cut a huge wound into the landscape, dividing a river in half with its lifeless metal. The water on either side of the dam was morbidly discolored. Familiar sheets of metal slabs had fully colonized the once heavily wooded areas that surrounded the dam. Mekanations were working busily, driving vehicles and operating machinery that sorted goods into various buildings and silos along the banks of the river. Factories billowed smoke into the air, while slaughterhouse vents sprayed rancid particles down into the surrounding soil and neighboring bodies of water.

The screen lit up with charts showing percentages and indications of thresholds being exceeded. Warning signs with skulls and crossbones flashed.

"I have never seen such a high level of toxicity around a new site before," Zoticon said, floating beside her. "Not sure what's worse, the threat to the environment or the toxic seafood delivered back to the supermarkets."

Atkon stopped typing and glanced over at the two commanders. "Our sources tell us that this is only the prototype. They are planning to replicate and distribute this model throughout the South."

Ann gazed at the pollution numbers in horror. "This is terrible beyond anything we've ever seen," she lamented. "They are poisoning the whole population!"

Zoticon clenched his fist. "We'll put an end to this before the sun rises!"

Time passed and the three moons rose in the sky. Darkness covered the land. Black Mountain was ready for the mission.

Six Fighters looked at the viewscreen in the briefing room. Screenshots of pipes, concrete, and tainted provisions scrolled down one side of the screen. Numerical data was continuously updated on the left. Zoticon accompanied the horrifying images and stats with further information and instructions. "Are we all clear on the objective?" he asked.

BlackBlob raised his fist. "Yes *sir*, they're all about to get this work!"

A whispered voice added, mockingly. "Oh yeah, they're *so* gonna get that work!"

BlackBlob turned sharply to his left. WilloNeo grinned back at him. BlazeCom snickered while BlackBlob lowered his head as well as his fist. The room grew tense.

Suddenly, FireArm's right arm spontaneously burst into flames. He thrust it in front of WilloNeo's pale face. "You got something to say?"

"FireArm! WilloNeo," Ann scolded. "This mission is important. When it's over, I will mandate both of you to complete emotion training."

FireArm inhaled and exhaled quickly. He nodded at Ann. Then he kissed his teeth toward WilloNeo, blowing out the flames that covered his wrist. The veteran Fighter exchanged glances of smugness with BlazeCom. It seemed as if their rank protected them, though only up to a point. BlackBlob nodded thanks at FireArm, but the young man didn't see the gesture. He was busy looking outside the window once more.

Turning away from the viewscreen, Zoticon looked with concern at the team. "The two squadrons will advance to the center of the structure and branch out from there to clear the western and eastern wings of the dam. We expect the most security near the shorelines that connect to the transportation routes. With the element of surprise, our attack will likely destabilize them, and they won't expect two threats at once.

"We must destroy this prototype," he added, "but keep in mind that it has a large surface area, and they have stepped up security recently. So play it smart and, above all"—he looked carefully at BlazeCom and WilloNeo—"work together as a team."

The two veterans looked at him but said nothing in response.

Meanwhile, Ann turned to face BlackBlob and FireArm. Her eyes flashed as she spoke. "You are going in with the same squadrons as last time. Follow the plan and use all your skills." Then, she turned to address the whole team. "Stay alert, look out for one another, and defeat the enemy!"

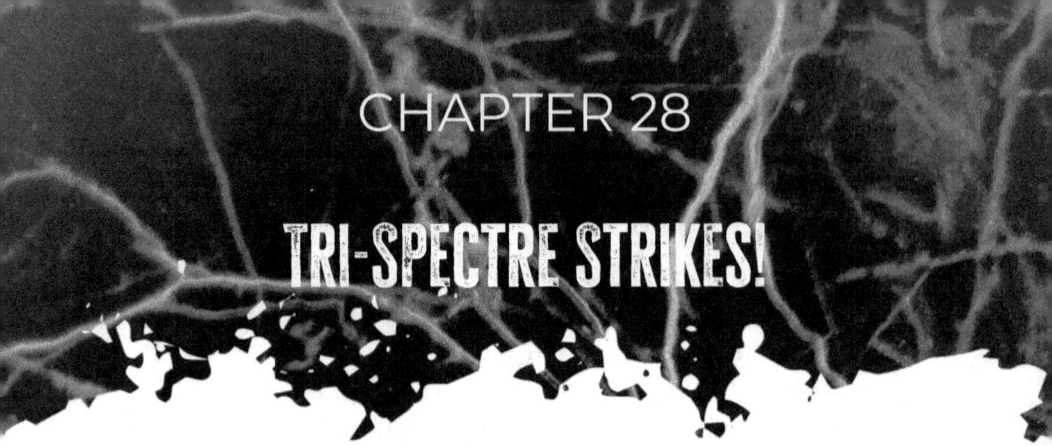

CHAPTER 28

TRI-SPECTRE STRIKES!

Under the cloak of night, the three moons floated in the sky, watching their planet. The *Raven* descended, gliding, through the clouds and then accelerated toward the drop zone. The six Fighters in their dark black technogarments floated free of the ship before descending rapidly toward the enemy structures. The cloaking devices in their suits reflected their surroundings and reduced the chance of being intercepted by enemy fire. Back in the *Raven*, a digital countdown appeared on the bridge's main viewscreen and reflected off Zoticon's black, metal eye. 29:50:67. Connections were cut, and the soldiers were on their own.

SHOOM.

The Fighters swooped toward the target. They dove toward the center of the structure in tight formation. Red and blue lights shot across the horizon until, unexpectedly, a wide, cyan pillar of light materialized in the sky, obstructing any direct path to the factory.

"Who the hell is that?" WilloNeo yelled into his transmitter.

"Raatid cup man, luuk pan 'im!" Nani exclaimed.

A figure emerged from the pillar of light, ripping it open. As it reformed around him, a gigantic, blinding orb of electricity surrounded his floating body. Shrouded within this force of destructive energy was a giant figure, his armor plated with ivory and gold. His face was covered by a metal mask in the form of an upward pointing triangle. In the center of the forehead was a shining diamond. His chest was protected by a massive breastplate that glistened in the moonlight. On each shoulder were large pauldrons that extended like heavy, protective shells. He floated toward his adversaries at a measured pace, armor gleaming ominously in the silvery light of the three moons. Then he spoke.

"Welcome to the party. Allow me to see you out." The voice was suave and mocking.

"Dude is looking like he lives at the gym!" BlackBlob said.

"Oh no. Slow your descent everyone," Anansi cautioned, "we might need backup."

"Bunch of cowards!" WilloNeo yelled. "Always wanting mommy to come bail you out."

Anansi ignored him. "Do not engage before knowing his threat—" She was interrupted by a blast of blue energy flying past her.

"I'm a senior officer too! C'mon, Blaze, he'll be slow in all that armor. Let's just dive past him. We got a mission to accomplish!"

WilloNeo and BlazeCom accelerated toward the intruder, feinting to his left and then banking to the right. A surge of light burst from the beast of a man. Bright, roaring electrical lights bounced and danced around his body. "Ya won't get past *me*, lads!" he bellowed, as if they were opponents in a game.

Large orbs of light traveled from his hands, but the two Fighters easily evaded them, continuing their descent.

KA-KOOM.

The balls of energy blew up behind them like a storm of fireworks. They were not meant to be lethal, but they lit up the sky like flares in the night. Blaze and Willo kept pressing on, keeping a focus on their mission. Until they detected something up ahead.

BURRRRRRR

From below came the metal sound of cranking. As they approached the target, a barrage of ground-to-air artillery rushed up to meet them. Volleys of hot lead tore through the air.

TAKTAKTAKTAK

The two had almost reached the target, dodging and deflecting the volleys of projectiles with tremendous skill. But as Anansi and Nani watched, they saw their companions surrounded by an ever-increasing stream of volatile ordinance until they could no longer even be seen amid the explosions. High above them, the huge armored intruder floated, seemingly unconcerned.

Nani looked toward the squadron leader. " Mi ah get sum bad fiiling 'bout dis, yuh nuo," she said.

Anansi checked a device on the left gauntlet of her technogarment. "Our comms are jammed. I'll have to head back to get the *Raven*'s attention. Destroy that artillery and maintain the offensive, but do not engage the unidentified threat until we get confirmation."

"Affirmed." BlackBlob saluted and descended toward the artillery. Anansi shot off in the opposite direction.

"Oh no, you don't," the white-armored stranger warned, placing two fingers from his right hand at his head and pointing two fingers from his left hand toward the retreating officer. A teal flash emerged from one of the clouds and smashed into Anansi's shoulder, shattering the right sleeve of her technogarment. Sparks and blue embers flashed as she gripped her shoulder.

"Anansi!" BlackBlob yelled.

"It will heal, focus on the mission!" Dazed from the impact, she continued accelerating, though now more slowly. Nani wiped away a tear, then took a deep, slow breath. As she exhaled, her body was enveloped in a searing blaze of heat. "Shi ah guh bi arite. But mi cyaan seh di seim ting fi di likkle tin man!"

"Little? Ain't nothin little about me, you kitten." The intruder laughed. He flew full force toward Nani, who met the large ball of lightning with a flaming aura of rage.

BAPBAPBAPBAP

The two exchanged a flurry of strikes. Nani moved past the large hulking fists thrown by the knight in heavy armor. He made no attempt to dodge hers. Leaping over his haymakers, she landed a heel on the back of his neck. He did not budge.

"Mi raataid!"

Nani focused on outboxing her opponent, landing some combinations and retreating outside of his reach while Anansi continued on her flight path. BlackBlob could not take his eyes away from the uncountable exchange of hands, palms, and fists. It looked like a duel to the death. He itched to help but remembered what Anansi had said about not engaging. He looked helplessly over at his comrade.

FireArm was also mesmerized. He was amazed that Nani could hold her own against this armored giant whose fists were twice the size of hers. Looking down at the dam, he glimpsed BlazeCom and WilloNeo through a fleeting break in the barrage of missiles. They looked stuck, as if searching desperately for an opening to enable them to move in on their objective. A new volley of missiles chased them. They swooped, dodged, and shifted out of harm's way, but FireArm thought some of the projectiles were beginning to graze them as they streaked through the air to avoid direct hits.

They're gonna die.

"What?"

You heard me.

The voices were back. FireArm hit his palms against his forehead.

"FireArm!" BlackBlob flew over to him. "What's the matter with you?"

"Argh!" FireArm shook himself out of his trance.

"Yo, you good? We're on a mission!"

"Right, right, I know."

"What's the matter with you? Look, Nani's laying hands on that punk-ass. Let's take out the AA guns before they target us next."

"OK, you're right."

"Damn straight I am!"

FireArm and BlackBlob focused their soulforce into their palms. Surges of spiritual currents encircled their hands and grew intensely bright. This drew the attention of the towering intruder.

"What the bloody h—"

SLAM.

While the giant knight was distracted, Nani landed a fierce, flaming dropkick to the back of his head. It destabilized him for a moment, and he lost his balance in the air.

"Do it!" Nani yelled at them.

SH-SHOOM.

The two radiant Fighters descended groundward and soared past BlazeCom and WilloNeo. Then they split apart to draw the fire of the weaponry below. BlackBlob headed westward, FireArm to the east. They juked and swerved and vaulted themselves across the sky like comets, while the ammunition from below followed them like a distant tail. The two Fighters hurdled closer and closer to the dam until it was in range.

Nani watched with excitement from above. "Now!" she screamed.

Still streaking across the sky, they aimed their palms toward the dam. Using the guided force of their extrasensory training, they launched their charged-up spiritual energy like heat-seeking missiles toward their multiple targets.

The explosions stretched across the river. Pieces of wreckage careened high into the sky. Even at the tremendous speeds at which the two Fighters crossed the sky, their blasts homed in precisely on their targets, devastating the automated weaponry, leaving craters in their wake, and preventing any chance of a counteroffensive.

No more bullets were fired. The sky grew quiet.

CHAPTER 29

LOSS OF LIFE

The heavy armored enemy stood firmly on thin air, towering over all others in the night sky. He scanned the devastation below. Fires, rubble, and scrap metal were scattered across the dam. His eyes blazed with hatred. But it was the swirling storm of electricity that formed around his body, and the lightning flashes and wind it generated, that drew all eyes to him. The Fighters looked on with fear but also determination.

WilloNeo and BlazeCom nose-dived toward the wreckage of the dam. Now that there were no automated defenses, they could descend without endangering the mission. They sped down toward their target, then leveled and prepared for landing, pushing their feet ahead to allow for contact with the ground. Not far behind them, a bright light careened toward them. Blaze turned his head. "He's too fas—"

Before they could take evasive action, two huge gauntlets reached out from behind and grabbed their ankles. White-armored arms swung them through the air like dolls. They whirled and flailed helplessly before smashing into the concrete pavement.

BAM.

Their opponent looked down at them with a condescending smirk. Willo was planted in the ground inches beneath the rubble. Blaze squirmed on the surface, scrambling to regain his balance.

"Now, keep still or I'll get mad."

Above their opponent a flaming mass was descending quickly.

"Oh, you'd like some more?"

He bent his knees, pushed off the ground, and drove into the sky toward the meteoric blaze. Nani's entire body was coated in a fierce heat. The two forces were on the verge of colliding with each other when at the last minute she changed course.

"I'll be right back for you!" shouted Nani as she avoided a direct collision, veered past the enemy, and moments later, landed gracefully next to BlazeCom and WilloNeo. The enemy did not pursue her; he only watched the flames dissipate around her. Nani then pulled a barely conscious Willo out of the rubble and helped Blaze to his feet.

"How many more times do we gotta rescue you two?" she smirked, before looking up at FireArm and BlackBlob. "Get them to safety." Blazing once more, she launched herself back at the armored threat.

"Affirmed!" they responded.

As she flew upward to confront the enemy, FireArm and BlackBlob descended toward the dam. As they approached it, their comms signal came back on. "Enemy detected and identified as a level three threat," said Atkon's voice.

FireArm watched the struggle above from a distance. The hulking figure was slugging it out with Nani. Her punches inflicted no damage on her opponent's ivory-and-gold armor, and his speed continually increased. She struggled to dodge the rain of blows from his massive fists. Using both forearms at the same time, she was forced to block rather than attack.

FireArm watched in alarm as Nani struggled to defend against the tyranny of her opponent's fists. He wasn't letting up. "This guy's only a level three?" he said into his transceiver.

"Enemy signature confirmed," came the reply. "Enemy identified as codename Tri-Spectre."

Sticking to Nani's orders, FireArm forced himself to look away from the duel and fly toward the dam. His feet touched the ground. Demolished motherboards and anti-air weaponry were strewn everywhere. He walked straight over to WilloNeo… and gave him a back hand to the face that knocked the veteran Fighter back on the ground.

BAM.

Instantly, BlazeCom went on alert. He turned to face FireArm, and they glared at each other. BlackBlob descended staring in shock at his friend. "Bro, what are you doing?"

"That was for last time."

WilloNeo coughed up blood. "Last time?"

FireArm's face tightened.

"How dare you call any of us cowards?"

The veteran laughed. "It's because you *are* one."

"We're fighting to protect you, what are you talking about?"

"I didn't ask you to protect me, you amateur."

"How can you call me—"

Their confrontation was interrupted by the voice of AnnRoticon. "Fighters, changing mission objective. Provide support for NaniMaroon and prepare for extraction."

"Extraction?"

"Yes, Anansi will return to ensure you all make it out of there."

FireArm couldn't bring himself to respond. His eyes were on the still-dazed WilloNeo, who was struggling to get up, and on BlazeCom, who continued to stagger from the encounter with the enemy. A feeling of disgust settled in his stomach at seeing them in such a sad state. He turned his eyes away to meet the sky. "Affirmed, backing up NaniMaroon."

"Be careful."

FireArm leapt into the air, and a wave of fire carried him toward the dueling pair at a dazzling pace.

BlackBlob looked at the two injured Fighters. "You guys going to be all right?" he asked.

"Are *you guys* going to be all right?" BlazeCom repeated back to him, imitating and exaggerating the younger man's voice. WilloNeo laughed out loud even though he was still spitting blood.

BlackBlob got a heavy feeling in his gut, but seeing FireArm rush to defend Nani inspired him and restored his focus. "I guess it's not our job to save everyone," he replied, then he turned his gaze upward and shot into the sky like a bullet from a gun.

BlazeCom and WilloNeo were alone in the wreckage of the dam. Willo looked around carefully. There was no immediate danger and the enemy was distracted. "Let's at least take out some more of this dam. We can still finish the mission before nerd-girl comes back."

"R-Right, boss."

They blasted projectiles of elemental energy into the structure. Towers began to fall like dominoes. Blaze, covered in a ball of flame, stomped and collided into walls, knocking them over. The platforms supporting the entire dam looked as if they were about to give way.

Although Tri-Spectre was fighting ferociously, this did not escape his sharp blue eyes. Nani had been losing ground. Unable to land any direct hits, she now backed away, hurling volleys of flame at him that he easily swatted away. Desperate now, she coated her hand in a sheet of flame, stepped in while he was still distracted by her last volleys, and planted the flame on him. "Big Bang Detonate!" she shouted, leaping away.

The force of the explosion shook the whole area. Pieces of white armor tumbled down toward the river. After the smoke had cleared, Tri-Spectre's left shoulder pauldron was nowhere to be seen. He covered the vulnerable spot with his right gauntlet, but now he was encircled by three airborne fighters, covering his exit routes.

"He's vulnerable to soulforce now!" BlackBlob yelled.

"Let's end this!" Nani charged up a powerful attack in both of her hands. FireArm focused his intention into his right arm, while BlackBlob's hands both began to shine with a blue aura. Tri-Spectre was not looking at any of them. Instead, his attention was focused downward. Without warning, he nose-dived toward the dam.

"Now!" Nani yelled.

The three of them fired powerful bursts of light that homed in on Tri-Spectre as he made his descent. *BAM.* He twitched and maintained course. *BAM.* He shifted and maintained course. *BOOM.* A cloud of smoke covered him, but he maintained course. Large fragments of armor fell into the river. He continued, unaffected, and landed on the dam with an impact that cracked the platform and shook the steel banisters. As the smoke cleared, he looked unbothered, though his heavy armor was gone. He stood calmly in a black velvet outfit that expanded around his toned figure. A clerical collar was now visible beneath his triangular mask, which was still unscathed. WilloNeo stared at him, shocked. "His collar? Is he with Death-Dweller?"

Tri-Spectre stood there silently, looking deep into Willo's eyes. The Fighter stared back at the eight feet of burgeoning animosity. "I-I'm not afraid of you," he said, though his legs shook and his fists refused to stay clenched.

A turquoise beam of light rose from Tri-Spectre's spine. His body shook from the surging current of electricity, amplified by the diamond in the center of his forehead. From his back emerged two sets of appendages. Another set of arm-like extensions arose from the left side of his body, and yet another from the right. The four appendages waved in a flailing electrical current and maneuvered like independent extra arms.

"Nothin' personal. Just business," he quipped. Then he released a rapid set of strikes from his new arms, pumping and extending them like pistons.

CRACK. CRACK. CRACK.

Each hit struck like lightning.

CRACK. CRACK. CRACK.

The arms made of volatile spiritual energy repeatedly pounded against WilloNeo's flesh, beating the technogarment into pieces, tearing through cartilage, and covering the platform with the crimson color of carnage.

Blaze witnessed the butchering up close. His pupils dilated and his hands shook. Unable to respond, he looked on in shock, but it was too late to stop it. It was one-sided and over in a matter of seconds.

CRACK!

TRI-SPECTRE

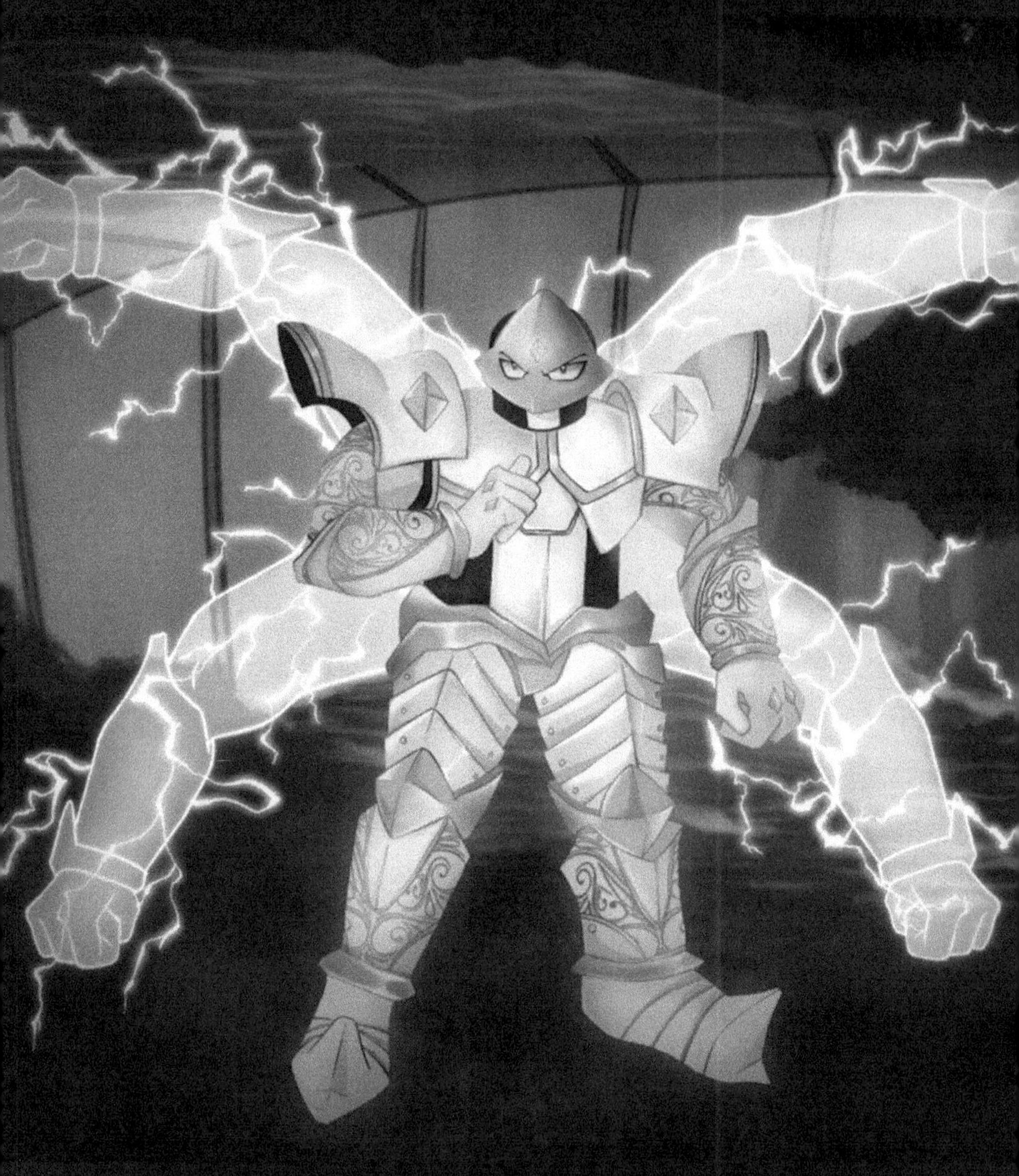

CHAPTER 30

THE FOUR-WINGED COMMANDER

"ALERT. ALERT!"

A red light blinked on the viewscreen, brightening the dark room every few seconds.

"What now?" Phutais said to himself. He pulled out his phone and looked at the caller name: BUSH.

He slammed a finger into the phone, then raised the device to the side of his head. "Speak," he commanded.

"Sir!" The voice was frantic. "The enemy is at Mandevillage Dam!"

"Oh?"

"It's crazy. They're saying these people are running in midair, shootin' lasers or somethin'."

"Why didn't you eliminate them before they reached the dam?"

"We didn't see them. It's like they came out of thin air."

Phutais stopped himself from slamming the phone into particles of dust. "Foolishness!" he bellowed. "What is the status of your forces?"

"They tore them all up in seconds!"

Phutais held out the phone and stared at it with a filthy look. "So you've failed?"

Harbush swallowed loud enough to hear on the line. "Uh no, no, it's not like that, I uh..."

"Where is the enemy now?"

"They're still there. They're sluggin' it out with some other flying nut in shining armor. Is he with us?"

Phutais hesitated. Maiden had long maintained contact with Fighter mercenaries—who better to protect against enemies of the same sort? But Phutais had intentionally kept the other wings of Zi-Tai from learning this. It would complicate things if anyone other than the two of them knew.

"Don't concern yourself with that. Monitor and intercept any communications. Either they die there or you trace them and we kill them later."

"Y-yes, sir. Acknowledged!"

Phutais crushed the phone in his hand and threw the pieces under his table. He sat in the dark room, the light from the large viewscreen casting a long shadow behind him. On the screen, he could see the status of each wing of the organization: commercial activities, military operations, political process, and security forces. He had eyes on them at all times.

"Hmph." He nodded toward the political wing and it enlarged on the screen, displaying a hidden camera view of a nervous man in a business suit checking his phone. He was in the middle of a tea break with government lobbyists and other political figureheads. Suddenly, he grew nervous, placing his hand by his breast pocket. He interrupted the conversation he was having and exited the room, nearly tripping over a chair. The camera turned off. Phutais waited a moment before tapping three times on the desk. A phone began to ring from one of the cabinets to his left. He picked it up and jabbed a finger into it. "You're three seconds late. Speak."

"I-I'm s-so sorry," Telron stuttered, struggling to catch his breath. *He must have sprinted into one of his secure and soundproof secret service vehicles,* Phutais thought. No eyes or ears could witness this call. "S-sir? You summoned me?"

"I want an update on the southern expansion. Now."

"Y-yes, I was just speaking about that actually, you see, things aren't exactly as they, er, ought to be, you know?"

"Cut to the chase."

"Well, we have some members in the North who are a little… hesitant to accept more motherboards."

"Fine. Send me a list. I'll have Harbush increase crime in those regions. That will convince them. What about the South?"

"Oh." Telron was taken aback. "Well, on the upside, I'm pleased to say that our contracts for additional building and development are being negotiated—"

"But?"

"Oh! But, but a couple of the foreign leaders are starting to push back about our expansion. They're trying to rally together."

"Have you read speech number 145 yet?"

"Umm, yes, yes I have, and they're still upset with us."

"You fool. Who is *us*? Remember, if you mention our conversations to anyone, you won't even have a grave to rest in."

Phutais could hear Telron's teeth chattering.

"Y-yes, OK sir. Got it, sir!"

"Read speech number 146 at your next press briefing. If that doesn't appease them, we will have an excuse to take their land by force and that will be that."

"Yes, yes, I agree, sir, I can positively—"

Phutais crushed the phone in his hand and threw the debris under his desk.

He glanced at the digital clock on his desktop. There was time for one more call. He nodded toward the box at the top right of the screen.

An image appeared of a woman hastily leaving the backstage set of a news studio. She nimbly dodged television cameras, lights, and crates, and made her way to a secluded area outside, in the rain. She pressed a button on her glasses and a drone flying above her head descended quickly to prevent any of the precipitation from touching her pristine hair, makeup, or surgically perfect face. She pressed another button on the other side of her glasses. The camera shut off.

A flip phone from a cabinet on Phutais's right started to ring. He whipped it open and cracked its screen with his other hand before raising it to his head. "Speak."

"Sir," Meridian panted, still out of breath, "we have some updates."

"State them."

"We still don't have any identifying information on the terrorists, but we found out who has been stealing our money from the metanetworks—"

He slammed his hand on the desk. Chips of paint flew up from the impact.

"Whose money?"

The sound of a rapid heartbeat could be heard through the phone.

"Y-yes, sorry, sorry, sir. Your money, of course. Your money!"

"And don't forget that."

Trying to redirect his rage and calm the mood, Meridian stumbled over her words. “Um, uh, how about we focus on who did it?”

“Tell me, then.”

“We analyzed the code that was injected into some of the digital workers. We now know how they controlled our trucks. Some of the code was very professional, but some of it was amateurish—”

“Get to the point. Give me a name.”

“Oh, sorry, right! They call themselves the Community.”

“What kind of foolish name is that?”

“Right? Probably a bunch of kids in their parents’ basements. They have been trying for some time to inject code to short-circuit city blocks while destabilizing our news networks.”

“So they caused the blackouts that affected the Child Removal Service buildings?”

“Could be. Indie news outlets are starting to mock our technology, running stories about unplanned power outages on societal media. There must be a conspiracy.”

“They are all terrorists. Shadowban all societal media accounts that violate our expectations. I’ll have Telron issue a decree to make having anything to do with this ‘Community’ illegal. Harbush can arrange for extraditions.”

“Right!”

Phutais looked at the clock. “I have an appointment,” he growled before grinding the phone into little bits. Since Maiden’s contractor was confronting the enemy, there was no need to summon her yet. As he got up from his desk, little machines scampered underneath it, scooping up bits of microchips and cellphone covers before returning into the walls to disintegrate them.

He walked slowly and decisively to the door. “All right, Maiden, let’s see what a level three threat can do.” The door slammed shut behind him.

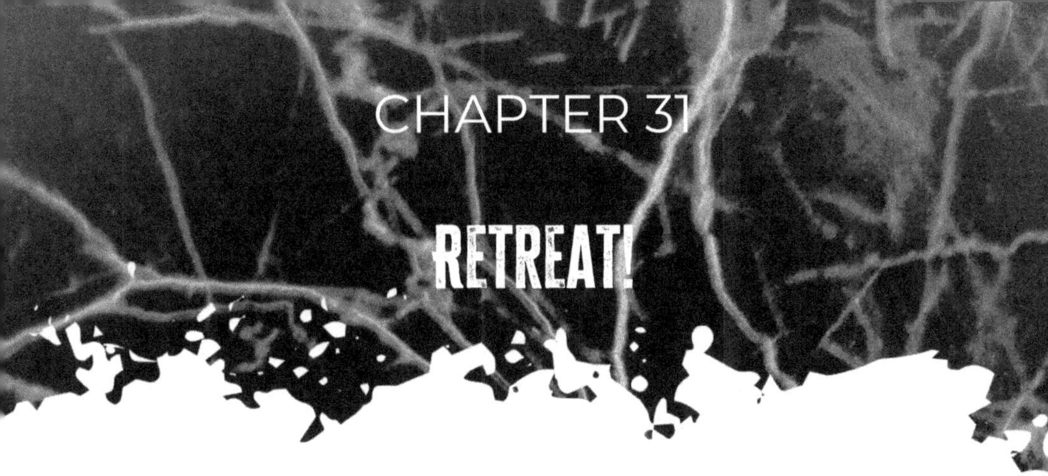

CHAPTER 31

RETREAT!

"It can't be."

BlazeCom's legs buckled beneath him, and he fell to his knees. Seeing the crumpled body of WilloNeo left his face pale and his gaze vacant.

AnnRoticon's voice blared into his transceiver. "Get out of there. Now! Retreat! Retreat!"

The bulky intruder turned his gaze to the trembling Fighter. Blaze couldn't move his body. He couldn't even feel his body. He could hear his commander's pleas but he was imprisoned by fear. He could only stare at the gigantic shadow that loomed over him. The only light came from the four colossal arms of pulsating energy raised above the center of his skull. Tri-Spectre brought those arms behind his back, readying their crushing descent on his helpless victim.

FireArm couldn't take his eyes off the scene.

Good. He should die, and then we all die together.

Die? Who deserves to die? he asked himself. He felt contempt toward that voice.

He looked around. BlackBlob and Nani were also staring at the scene in horror. The voices usually bothered him, but this time was different. They had targeted his comrades. He and BlackBlob had already almost died. Maybe Nani too. *After all of our training,* he thought, *who says we need to die here? Those are not my thoughts. I would never think this. I reject them!*

He mustered all the strength that he could to break free of his shock. Physically, he could not move. Mentally, he gathered his focus. Something deep inside of him, something eternal, something that had no words and no form activated these remembered words: "We're just glad you came back in one piece, bro."

He shook off his fear. His eyes blazed with determination. Nani stared at him, alarmed.

"Fire!" she called, "what are you—" But it was too late.

Time slowed to a stop. FireArm's body shifted through space. He instantaneously appeared behind BlazeCom and lifted him under his armpits. In a split second, and in one motion, they moved through space and time and appeared beside BlackBlob and Nani. Time returned to normal and Tri-Spectre's fists came crashing down, splitting the platform in half. Though most of the dam stayed intact, a large portion of it came tumbling down, dragging debris, wreckage, and various canisters and barrels into the water below. Nothing on the platform escaped. Even WilloNeo's remains fell through the crevices and disappeared. Tri-Spectre floated in midair above the wreckage, looking at FireArm. Their eyes met. They stared at each other for a moment.

To BlackBlob and Nani, it seemed as if FireArm and BlazeCom had materialized beside them out of nowhere.

"Yo wha—?"

"How did you—?"

Before they could finish, AnnRoticon's voice rang out again. "The threat is still active! Get out of there now!"

BlazeCom was still in shock, unresponsive. He gazed blankly back at the wreckage in the river, as if searching for his comrade. Nani slapped him in the face.

"Can you move?"

"Y-yes..."

"So let's go!"

SHOOM.

The five of them bolted through the air at high speed. Flying in the direction of the ship, FireArm turned his head to look back at the site of the battle. Tri-Spectre flashed brightly and then vanished from the site as if he had never been there. They continued their flight over communications towers and the labyrinth of rivers and foliage that sprawled through the region. The Fighters did not speak a word to each other on the journey back to the *Raven.* The three moons cast their silent reflections in the dark waters below them.

Minutes later, the Fighters entered the hatches. In the loading area, Anansi welcomed them with a look of relief on her face. BlazeCom stood there for a while as if lost, then found a chair and sat down, still in his battle suit, stained with concrete and ash. There was no eye contact. No warm welcomes. Not a word was exchanged.

FireArm glanced over at BlazeCom but quickly looked away before their eyes had a chance to meet.

Why did I even save him? *How* did I even save him? he wondered.

He washed his hands and face and left the room without speaking to anyone. He went straight to his quarters, buried his face into his pillow, and turned off the light. Minutes turned into hours in the faint illumination of the night sky.

His thoughts raced through many topics: the distant image of Willo's devastated body falling into the water, the look that Tri-Spectre gave him as if his prey had been stolen, the voices in his mind, and the last slap he gave Willo before he disappeared forever.

Regret overwhelmed him. He grabbed his pillow and threw it so hard against the floor that it bounced up almost to the ceiling before falling once more. A familiar self-loathing came over him.

DING.

"Yo!" the muffled voice of BlackBlob called from the other side of the door.

"No visitors!"

"Bro… You can't do this. In the books, it's called disobedience to particular order."

"I don't care. I don't want to talk."

"It's an order from the commanders. You wanna get yourself court-martialed?"

"Since when did we become a regular army?" FireArm shot back with a sneer, though he was starting to become nervous.

"Bro, we have to be just as disciplined as the other side. You *know* this!"

FireArm did not reply. He knew that was true, but hoped that if he kept silent, they'd just go away.

"Zoticon told us to come get you. We can't head back without you, Fire," BlackBlob said tensely.

Images of the meals, the incense, and the feelings of support flashed through FireArm's mind. These were people who fought alongside him. These were people who cared for him! They really wanted him to be here. Sighing to himself, he got out of bed and opened the sliding doors. Anansi, Nani, and BlackBlob stood there with muted smiles.

"Let's go, soldier." Anansi turned and led the way.

"Don't worry, Fire," said BlackBlob, "We won't tell anyone you refused a direct order." He looked at Anansi and Nani. "Am I right?" They nodded.

Zoticon stood in the center of the briefing room with his hands behind his back. Atkon typed away at a handheld computer, projecting images onto a large viewscreen behind them, which bore a huge, blinking numerical display saying 15:35:03.

The four soldiers entered and lined up in front of their commander. Zoticon turned to the viewscreen. "Who here knows what these numbers signify?"

There was silence among them.

"Atkon, explain it to them."

"Countdown discontinues once we have broken radio silence or if the *Raven* detects a communications signal intercept from the enemy forces."

A sense of unease filled the room. Anansi took a step forward. "It can't be. They knew we would target the dam?"

"Not only that, but the structure is still standing."

Nani took a step forward. "We were nearly overpowered by the enemy. Why weren't we briefed about the threat level?"

"No." Zoticon turned to face her. "The question is, why couldn't you beat a mere level three?"

Anansi and Nani stepped back into line.

"Atkon, give us a status report," Zoticon said.

"WilloNeo's body could not be retrieved. BlazeCom is currently in a state of psychological shock. AnnRoticon is working with him as we speak. His damage is more to his spirit than his physical body. She will not be able to help him recover for a few days."

BlackBlob stepped forward. "We're sorry—"

Zoticon raised a hand and turned to face the viewscreen. "*Sorry* can't raise the dead. You failed the mission, and you're all dismissed."

His words landed with finality. They left the room in single file.

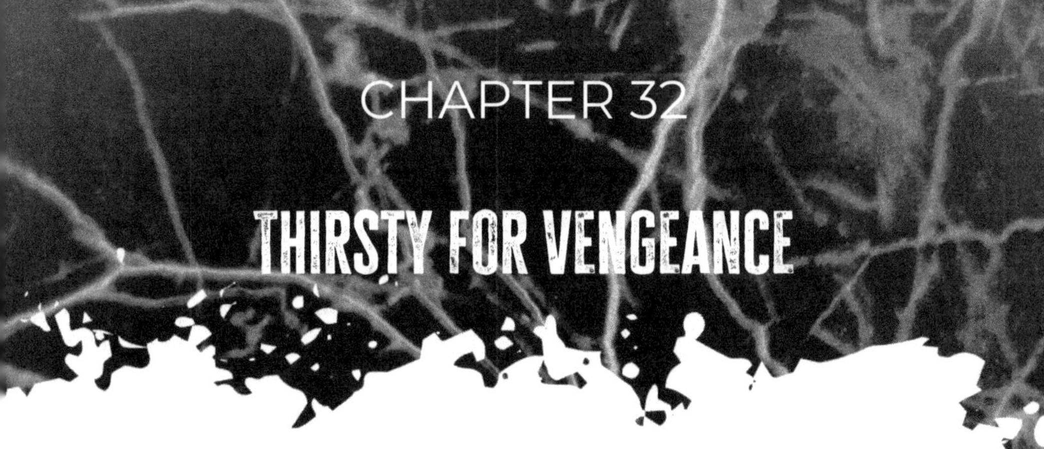

CHAPTER 32

THIRSTY FOR VENGEANCE

Phutais placed one of his hands on the banister of his penthouse balcony. The stars shone above him. Inside the penthouse, blankets and covers were strewn across the floor and draped over the edges of the family-sized mattress. Empty bottles of liquor and potent chemical substances littered the floor. A towel around his waist, he looked up at the moonlight. "Leave," he said.

Four dazed bodies emerged from underneath the comforters. Some of them quietly yawned and stretched as they lifted themselves up from the bed. They collected their belongings and lined up before the host of the party, smiling in unison after he clicked the *Accept Payment* buttons on their portable devices. One of the young men said, "Thank you, we—
"

SMACK.

The slap was so rapid it seemed as if Phutais had not even moved. "You must be new. Do not speak unless you are spoken to."

The youth rubbed his bruised face, and all four of them bowed their heads in apology. They hastily got dressed, fixed their hair, and touched up their makeup. As soon as the door shut behind them, out from the floorboards and walls crawled dozens of small mini-maids. In a moment, they had cleaned and tidied up the room as if nothing had happened. They gathered the bottles, poured the remaining contents down the sink, picked up the cutlery, and moved everything out of sight. The room was back in pristine condition.

Phutais paid no attention to them. Instead, he faced the skyline, where droves of Icarus drones and aerial security forces patrolled the area, buzzing quietly as they flew past his balcony. There were so many of them that they blocked the view of the moons. It would take minutes before all of them passed.

"What a beautiful night."

Phutais walked back into the bedroom and pressed a code on the mirror to print on his outfit for the next meeting. After that, he entered the briefing room and sat in his office chair in the darkness. It automatically slid into position at the head of the long table. He slammed a remote on the table with his right hand, and a large viewscreen appeared before him.

The official news program was beginning. Right on time. The sound of trumpets and a parade of computer-generated images brought layers of suspense, fear, and anxiety for anyone with a nervous system.

"Good evening and welcome to the Official News program." The middle-aged newscaster was visibly sweating. She shuffled through the notes on her desk. "On this evening, the biggest news to report is… the championship finals between the Azor City Authorities and the King City Dominators!"

"Good, distract them with sports," Phutais said toward the screen.

The camera cut away to athletes, cheerleaders, and an endless slew of corporate sponsors. Now aware of the increased monitoring of societal media, Phutais decided to check what was being posted on blogs and especially the most popular one of all, BOX News.

Excitement was in the air. Mr. Puffer and Miss Clean, BOX's most popular influencers, were chatting about the latest developments.

"A terrorist attack took place at the southern sector of a fishery in the outskirts of Mandevillage."

"This is uber sensational terrible!" Miss Clean said. She flailed her arms dramatically.

"That's right, Miss Clean, it seems as if they are starting to attack our neighbors to the south."

"They're disgusting. I *hate* them!"

"We all do, including our viewers. Just take a look at the polling numbers." Big green bar graphs appeared on the screen showing 98% disapproval with 2% undecided.

"Wow, that's extra magnificent—"

Phutais shattered the remote and the screen immediately shut off. Pieces of furniture tumbled to the ground beneath him, only to be swallowed up by the cleaners that scampered beneath the table. The briefing screen's edges lit up. The center of the screen blinked and illuminated the room. The bar loaded to 100% and his four guests appeared.

"Well, you all saw what was on BOX News this time. Give me updates. Now."

Maiden's distorted voice came through the speaker. "I'll make a few calls," she said before her pixelated image disappeared from the screen.

Harbush cleared his throat and pushed his chest out. "Well, *our* forces picked up on some suspicious transmissions around the site."

"Oh?"

"Yessir, but we could only find out where the damn things were sent and where the damn things were received."

Meridian perked up. "We know they were at the dam, but where were they connecting to?"

"I'm getting to that," Harbush snarled. "The problem is the signal ended up where there was nothing in the area but mountains."

"What? How?"

"We didn't see no caves or nothin'."

"Were the coordinates for longitude and latitude consistent on each pass?"

"Try again in a language that I can understand, lady."

Meridian sighed. "OK, thick skull, did it go bing-bing-bing at the same location?"

"Oh, uhh I didn't check for tha—"

Phutais slammed his hand on the desk, shaking the monitor and even the legs of the desk. "This conversation is wasting my time," he snapped. "Just share whatever your staff shared with you."

"Y-yes, sir!" The viewscreen changed perspectives. Harbush's screen enlarged to show a topographic map depicting points of contact between the fishery and the mountain range. Multiple lines ran from it to the mountains, over parts of the lakes and over the plains.

Phutais studied the lines on the screen, his brow furrowing in concentration. "Our drone patrols did detect some aberrations in cloud formations. But what caused them?"

"M-maybe they're ghosts?" Telron ventured. All heads turned toward him. He covered his mouth.

There was silence. Everyone seemingly waited for Phutais's damnation. "No," he said at last. "The fool might be right."

Telron grinned like a hopeful child.

"They used to say that even a broken clock is right twice a day," Phutais announced. The world president sank right back into his chair. Phutais pointed toward the map. "Why haven't you decrypted the messages yet?"

Harbush scratched his head.

"Here, let *me* scan the data," Meridian said, holding a handheld device toward her screen. A blue light flashed to signal something was being scanned and analyzed. A moment later, she gasped. "We can't decrypt it. It's not from Ziffea!"

"Which planet, then?" Phutais demanded impatiently. "The Dusidians wouldn't dare mess with my plans. And the only things on Ziak are trees and sewage."

"Quite right, sir. No, the scanner indicates Marka."

"Well, now," Phutais replied, rubbing the tip of his mask. "Fascinating. In that case, the technology for concealing the location of their base must also be Markan. We will have to completely rewire our algorithms."

Meridian looked at Harbush. "Hey, thick head, send my team the coordinates of the signals. We'll narrow down the possible locations in no time."

"Will do, Miss Brainiac. Make sure to get out of the books and get some sunlight once in a while."

"Excuse me? Are you and your officers smoking all the drugs you're confiscating?"

Phutais slammed his keyboard. "This meeting is over. Coordinate with each other, but not on any more of my time."

"Affirmative."

"Acknowledged."

"Ah—OK, sir!"

The three screens shut off, but the fourth lit up again. A familiar pixelated face and distorted voice re-emerged.

"Argh, what n—Oh, it's you."

"Yo. Still looking for prisoners for Initiative Five?"

"Of course I am. Did you find something?"

"No question about that," Maiden replied. "It seems that Tri-Spectre found a fish in the ocean."

CHAPTER 33

UNDERSTANDING

BlazeCom walked down the empty corridor. Lonely. Slowly. One step ahead of the other. For days, he had wandered aimlessly. He toured the Raven's hallways alone and unmotivated. He had stopped training, he was barely eating, and he only showered when Ann brought it to his attention.

As Blaze passed the open door of the training room, he almost collided with FireArm. They stared at each other for a moment, standing in silence. Then, FireArm silently stepped around the empty shell of a man that his teammate had become and left Blaze standing listlessly by the door as it slid shut.

Inside the training room, FireArm went straight to the gravity ball and lifted it higher than he ever had before. He went to the gravity walker and moved faster than he ever had before, but something still bothered him. "How did I save him?" He rapped his fists against the speed ball. "More like, *why* did I save him?"

These questions had followed him like a shadow ever since the failed mission. They occupied his mind like an unwanted guest. He had been trained to move quickly, but never as fast as he did the night Willo died.

Good riddance.

The image of Willo's broken body flashed vividly across his mind. Will having this voice make me more like him? he wondered fearfully. He shook his head. "I can't let it consume me. I've gotta go rest."

His mind grew silent, as if it were waiting for him to stop fighting with it. He washed up, headed to his quarters, and opened one of the ancient books he had found in the *Black Raven*'s library. The cover said *The Fire Next Time.*

While reading through the pages, he could hear whispers, giggles, and the clinking sounds of pots and pans. He knew it must be his teammates wheeling a tray of deliciousness toward his quarters. He had been expecting a gesture like this, and he smiled. *They thought they could surprise me with all that whispering?* he thought. He wanted to beat them to it. Before his visitors could press the bell, FireArm waved a hand at the door, which slid open to reveal the three startled faces of his visitors. "Where's the food at?!" he hollered at the top of his voice.

The unexpected roar made them jump. They had to react quickly to steady themselves and keep the steaming food from tumbling all over the hallway. BlackBlob dived to catch a bowl, Anansi used her psychokinetic powers to keep the cover from flying off the Dutch pot, and Nani gripped the handle of her wheeled tray to stop it from spinning out of control down the hallway.

"Nice circus act," FireArm said more quietly, grinning and welcoming them in.

A big pot of white rice glistened as Anansi removed the cover. Warm, enticing vapors poured out from it. She set the cover down right next to large silver pot of *Ital* stew peas. Smells of pimento, paprika, thyme, ginger, and garlic seasoned the pressure-cooked sea of kidney beans, carrots, and dumplings. Scents of sauteed onions, sweet potatoes, and broccoli filled the air.

"Wait. Where's the meat?" FireArm asked, serving himself a large cup of rice that left condensation around its perimeter as it landed on his plate.

Nani kissed her teeth and looked at Anansi. "Miss Healthy told the doctor on me."

Anansi rolled her eyes. "Oh please," she said. "Atkon said cholesterol and diabetes runs in our families. You can go a day without eating a former living creature, surely."

"Yuh chat tu much! I told you it's made in a lab! And it's his lab! And aren't we're Walking Ancestors? Anyway, shush, mek mi nyam mi bickle in peace."

FireArm looked over at BlackBlob. He was quiet despite all of the excitement. It's like he was just *there*, staring silently at the food. "Hey, bro." There was no response. "You good?" FireArm asked.

BlackBlob looked up with an unusually sober look on his face. "Let's pray before we eat."

Three pairs of eyes turned toward him. "Sure," they all replied.

BlackBlob took out a small black book from his back pocket. The cover was beaten up, and the pages were worn. From pages he had marked, he read through the Ceremony of Gratitude prayer. They gave thanks for the food, expressed their gratitude to the plants, animals, and people who had sacrificed their lives and efforts for the meal. In so doing, they expressed their gratitude for their physical, spiritual, and mental health.

"All thanks due to our creator."

"*Asé*," Anansi and Nani said in unison.

The food now carried a subtle glow nearly imperceptible to the eye. The flavors seemed to have an extra special seasoning. The food was blessed. They paused for a moment and then they ate until their bellies were full. It was quieter at the table, but no less enjoyable. When they were done, they rose together. They took turns passing plates and cutlery to each other so that they could be soaped, rinsed, and placed on the drying rack.

"I never asked but," FireArm looked over to Anansi, "where're you all are getting this food from?"

"We have a pretty large fridge and freezer for our supplies, you know," said Anansi.

Nani smiled. "And the meats and seasonings are from donations that Black Mountain gets from our partners in the South."

FireArm placed a plate onto the rack. "Donations?"

Nani used a rag to wipe the table. "We couldn't do this without a community behind us. Didn't Zoticon give you his fancy speech about being the 'vanguard' of the revolution?"

"Yeah, I remember something like that."

"Not everyone can fight the system by throwing fire out of their hands."

FireArm gave a half smile. "Well, I guess that's true." He picked up another plate with one hand and illuminated it with the other, drying every last particle of water on it.

"OK, now you just showing off." Nani giggled.

Anansi watched BlackBlob gently remove a purple box from the bottom rack of the tray. He set mats on the floor in a circle. She smiled at him. "Look at you go, *someone* has been taking notes."

BlackBlob said nothing but lit the incense with a torch lighter from his pocket. The blue flame hovered next to the tip. The orange incense stick let loose a swirl of smoke and a soothing fragrance for the soul. BlackBlob inhaled the aroma and exhaled slowly, "Yeah," he said, "something like that."

They cleaned up, put the food away, and began their meditation. Breathing in and breathing out. Breathing in and breathing out.

After a few moments of synchronized inhalations and exhalations, they each slowly settled into the rhythms of their own comfort. There was a further moment of silence, and then BlackBlob began. "I invited Blaze, but he didn't wanna come. Still, we gotta talk about Willo." He looked at Anansi. "Didn't you all say we could live forever?"

Anansi adjusted her glasses. "Well, kind of," she replied softly.

"So then how did he die?"

For a moment, there was silence. BlackBlob watched the ash falling from the incense stick. *With all of our powers, we couldn't save him,* he thought. Tears formed in his eyes. This caught the attention of Nani. "I'll try not to be harsh," she tried to cushion her words, "Ah wha do unnuh man? Dem stop dem training so wha yuh expec? Everybody haffi dead some time, ah suh di ting set—OW!" She was unsuccessful. Anansi must have thought Nani did enough "cushioning." Her elbow pressed against Nani's ribs.

"Well, then." Anansi cleared her throat. "Let's say it in a different way. He was up against a really powerful enemy, and he let his own physical and spiritual powers wane."

BlackBlob moved forward in his seat. "But it's like Zoticon said. How can we expect to win if we can't beat a level three?"

The words must have struck a chord. Nani grew emotional, likely reminded of her previous reprimand from the commander. "Bwoy, mi sorry fi him yuh nuh. But wi cyaan bring 'im back. So wha wi agguh do?"

"Aw, daahlin…" Anansi spoke softly and moved over to comfort her. Even FireArm looked sympathetic. For a moment the only sound in the room was Nani's quiet sniffling. Finally she spoke again. "Thanks, Anan," she said, gently touching her friend's hand.

"No matter what happens, we'll defeat the enemy," Anansi said.

BlackBlob looked at them, nodded to them but he still wasn't satisfied with the answer. He turned to FireArm. "Also, since when can you just disappear? We never practiced no magic trick like that before!"

"Disappear?"

"Yeah. You were up in the sky, then the next second you were down there with Blaze, and then the next you were with us. We never saw you move!"

FireArm looked down at his hands. "I… I don't know."

All eyes were on FireArm now. He could feel the pressure. The voices in his head murmured indecipherably. He started to fidget. "Don't lie," Anansi told him.

He looked up at her almost panicking. "I'm *not* lying." He didn't know what else to say.

She pointed toward him. "You used Zoticon's technique."

"Zoticon's technique?" His back straightened.

"Remember when he fought Death-Dweller? He saved you guys."

"Yeah." He hesitated. "Well, I really don't know how I did it, I just did it."

"Hmm." Anansi scrunched up her forehead, put her glasses back on, and looked him in the eye.

What's up with her? he wondered. *Is she reading my mind or hearing my thoughts?*

"You'll have to ask him," she said.

He was startled. *Would that old guy really help? He hasn't been very convincing since I've been here,* FireArm thought to himself. But as he pondered what Anansi had said, his doubts were challenged by the look of hope in all the eyes around him. It was clear that his teammates believed in him. Why shouldn't he believe in himself? A final piece of ash fell into the soft pile that had been accumulating. With that, the incense breathed its last breath of myrrh before dissipating into the air.

FIREARM

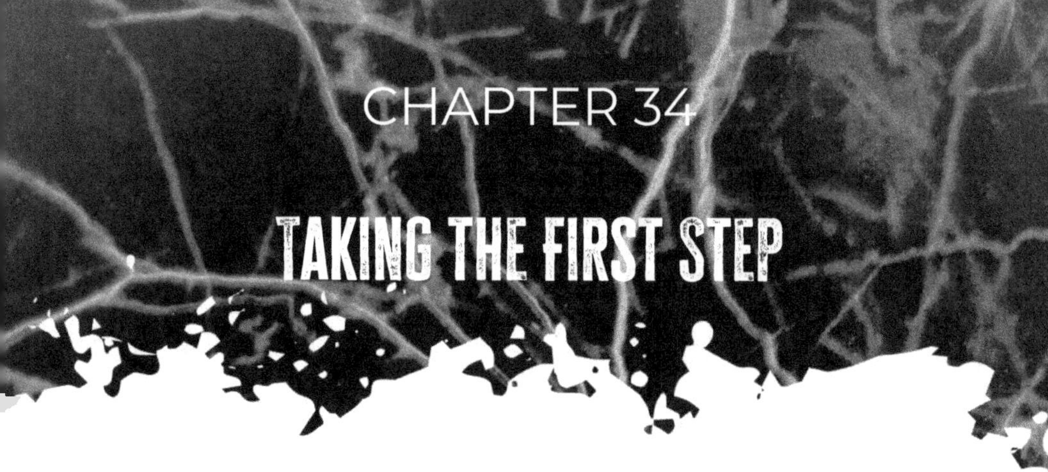

CHAPTER 34

TAKING THE FIRST STEP

The sound of footsteps echoed through the hallways. On the main viewscreen, the three commanders watched as the five humbled Fighters walked, heads held down, back to their quarters. Ann looked at Zoticon. "That wasn't the right move,"

"Don't you get it?" he snapped back. "They tracked our exact location. Now Zi-Tai can strike us at any time!"

"You're not thinking about their morale. They know the mission failed. What's the use of making *them* feel like failures?"

He thought about it, then looked toward Atkon, who shook their head disapprovingly. "She's right. You could have toned it down a bit."

Zoticon looked back toward his sister. She only crossed her arms. "Fine," he said. "I admit it. I was frustrated. Let's go blow off some steam."

The two siblings left the bridge and walked toward the gym. After warming up on the recumbent bike and skipping rope, they entered the training hall. The large white room seemed to welcome them in—it had always been a refuge from stress. They changed into their training uniforms, then stood several meters apart, facing each other in the middle of the room. A timer appeared on a large holographic viewscreen that projected itself along the whole length of the room. Right below it, a countdown appeared on the screen. The two of them waited, looking at each other. Until it went to zero.

"Go!" Zoticon called.

They sped toward each other and engaged. Zoticon's slightly shorter height and reach put him at a disadvantage, but Ann made no concessions for this. She pressured him with lightning-fast kicks, forcing him to lean back and throw his weight onto his right leg. He tried to propel himself back into the action by throwing split-second jabs that were easily parried by his opponent's gloves. Then Ann switched tactics, with some forceful strikes to break his defense. When he threw his arms up, she moved in with a wide left, but Zoticon used the momentum from his arms to lift his entire body and swing his feet in a backward somersault. He was aiming for Ann's face, but she half turned and absorbed the impact with her left arm. She then backed off, but additional somersaults from Zoticon brought them face-to-face again.

"Remember when the master teacher taught us this one?" said Ann. She shook her left hand, and a surge of purple energy lit up seven points on her body. She stretched her arms out in front of her with one palm facing up and the other down.

FOOOM.

She assumed a fierce battle stance. Her fighting aura covered her body in a swirl of lilac glimmers that pulsated and whirled around her.

"Nice. But what about this one?" Zoticon laughed and readied himself. He placed his right foot behind him with the ankle slightly raised and his left foot ahead. His hands pressed together in a prayer gesture and then separated. When he turned his palms downward, a dark surge of violet encircled him from the ground up. Through his body and around it, flickers of darkness emerged and subsided.

"So, you want to pull out all the stops, too? Come!" As she uttered the words, they both disappeared from view.

BAP. BAP. BAP. BAP. BAP.

The rapid-fire thumps of weighted gloves on protective gear echoed through the hallways outside. In a matter of seconds, hundreds of thudding contacts between fists and forearms, heels and knees, palms and knuckles echoed. Swirls of color blinked in and out of sight like a strobe light.

BAP. BAP. BAP. BAP. BAP.

Currents of wind stirred up in the room. Their swirling movements, their deadly dance formed miniature cyclones around the spinning exchange of blows. The impacts caused tremors. Vibrations traveled through the walls. The heavy doors to the training area shook like rustling leaves. Punches were repelled, kicks were deflected, blows were blocked, until—-

BEEEP. The timer read 10 minutes.

The storm instantly subsided. The sparring partners reappeared, floating meters above the ground. Zoticon's forearm protected him from a last knee to the face, while Ann's palm blocked his final punch before it would have connected with her ribcage. They stayed there for a moment, separated, and touched down on the floor again. As they walked toward the exit, Ann said, "You need more practice."

"I'd say I'm not bad for a centenarian."

"You're the younger one, so you don't get to say that!"

They left the gym laughing.

A couple of days after BlackBlob led the prayer in FireArm's quarters, the two Fighters sat in the library, talking in whispers. Even though they were alone, whispering seemed best for what they wanted to discuss.

"Bro"—BlackBlob leaned in—"this fighting against Zi-Tai thing is serious."

"I hear you, man," FireArm responded.

"What did we get ourselves into?"

Before FireArm could respond, the library doors slid open with a hiss. The boys swung round to find Ann and Zoticon staring at them from the threshold. FireArm snatched a pen from the table and bent over his notebook. BlackBlob pretended to be reading a book—upside down.

"It's OK. At ease, it's not a mission briefing," Zoticon said.

"Wow!" BlackBlob blurted out.

"Shhh!" FireArm held a finger up his mouth and tried to look stern, but his smile betrayed him. "It's a library, keep it down."

Continuing on their errand, Ann and Zoticon went straight to the aisle where the manuals were kept.

BlackBlob nudged his classmate. "You know what? Now's the perfect chance."

"For what?" FireArm hissed back.

"Ask him how to do that magician disappear thing."

"I don't know what to call it either, but he won't like *that* name."

"Just do it."

"Stop it!"

"Shhh, it's a library!"

Ann floated over to them carrying a pile of books. "Young men," she said in a pleasant tone, "what's going on?"

FireArm grabbed a random book from BlackBlob's pile and raised it in front of his face. Then he noticed he was holding the same book that had fascinated him once before.

"C'mon, bro," BlackBlob urged.

Before FireArm could reply, Zoticon floated in front of them with arms crossed and chin slightly raised. "That's the book I'm looking for," he told FireArm. "Hand it over."

Startled, BlackBlob quickly pried the book from FireArm's hands and handed it to Zoticon with two outstretched arms. Zoticon took it without a word and turned to leave, but Ann grabbed him by the shoulders, picked him up, and turned him around to face FireArm again.

"Fine," he sighed. "So I see you have an interest in Galaxy Zone 780."

"I guess."

"What made you choose *The Wretched of the Earth*?"

FireArm eyed the book sideways, "No disrespect, but I thought you were looking for a *manual*?

"It *is* a manual. In a sense. Many revolutionaries have referenced it through the ages precisely *because* of its value as a manual."

"A manual about what?" BlackBlob asked. "It reads like, I dunno, a philosophy book?"

Zoticon's eyes softened. "It's that too. But in the process, it explains how peoples who have been colonized can take the first step toward freeing themselves." He paused and looked at each of the boys in turn, then added, "By freeing their minds."

BlackBlob glanced at FireArm, as if expecting him to say something, but Zoticon wasn't finished. "So answer the question," he went on. "What made you choose *The Wretched of the Earth*?"

FireArm looked down at the table. "I wanted to know why they were so effed up."

"The colonizers or the colonized?"

"The humans. I'm trying to learn where these problems all started."

"You will find that their species was very primitive and cyclical. There was conflict on their planet even before they started writing books about it."

FireArm got up out of his seat and looked straight at Zoticon. "So then, what's the purpose? Why even keep stuff like this if the conflicts will just keep happening?"

Zoticon slammed the book on the table. "Because one day someone like *you* might pick it up and change the world."

Not another word was spoken. For a long moment, FireArm just stared at him, and Zoticon stared back. The silence continued. Zoticon's words had landed with a weight that could be felt through the walls. It took a moment for FireArm to regain his composure.

"Teach me the invisible magic man technique," he blurted.

Ann raised an eyebrow.

Zoticon shook his head. "The what?"

BlackBlob's palm slapped against his own face so hard that the sound reverberated against the table. "You know," he mumbled, "the disappearing attack through time thing."

"Ah." Zoticon rubbed his chin. "You mean the time-stop-act-then-time-stop technique?"

BlackBlob looked on with disbelief, "No that can't be right," he said. "That can't possibly be what it's *called*."

"Why not?" Zoticon asked. "What's wrong with that?"

"Oh, uh, well, never mind. OK, sure, it's a great name."

"So how do we learn it?" FireArm asked, his eyes brightening.

"Have you completed the emotion training?"

FireArm recalled all the times he had walked past that special training room without entering. "No," he said. "Sorry."

"What?" He turned to Ann instead of replying to FireArm. < *You know, there's such a thing as being too nice,*> he said telepathically while sighing out loud.

"Ahem," she coughed loudly, then responded telepathically, *<Little brother, remember your speech about learning while in the battlefield? This is where it got us.>*

Now Zoticon coughed as well. FireArm and BlackBlob watched the two elders take turns coughing and just blinked while observing them.

Zoticon sighed again. "All right." He turned back to FireArm. "The first step will be the hardest."

FireArm looked intently at his elders. Zoticon swiftly pointed a finger at FireArm's heart. "You will need to confront your trauma," he warned.

FireArm's heart started racing, but before those inner voices could overwhelm him again, he felt BlackBlob's warm hand on his shoulder. He turned toward his comrade.

"Bro, you're long overdue," BlackBlob said. "It worked for me. Trust me, it will work for you too."

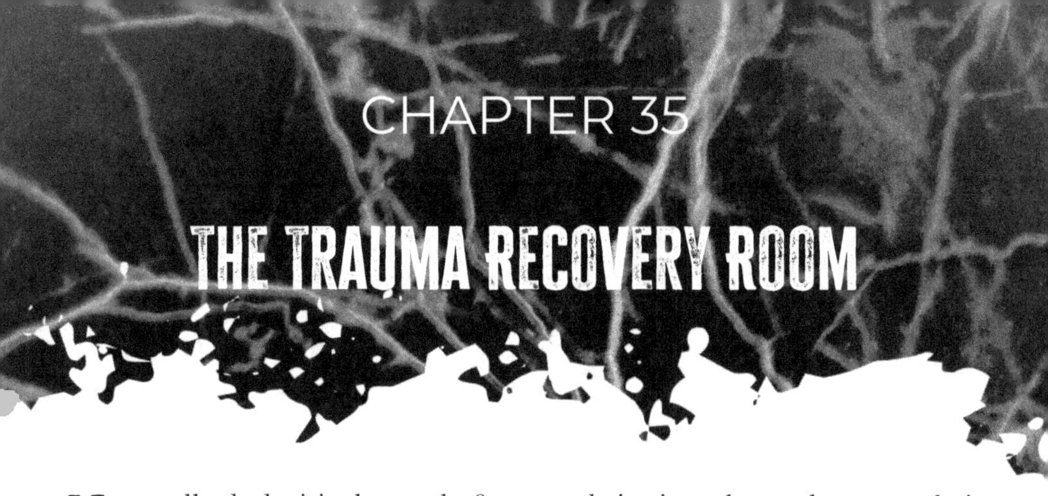

CHAPTER 35

THE TRAUMA RECOVERY ROOM

He walked decisively, each footstep bringing them closer to their destination. Zoticon led the two youths through the halls of the *Black Raven*—where they would meet their next challenge. FireArm ground his teeth and gazed at the floor. BlackBlob watched him for a moment, then turned back to Zoticon. "Hey, Uncle Zot," he asked, "didn't we just pass the therapy room a few turns back?"

"Correct." Zoticon nodded. "But neither of you have ever set foot in *this* one." Their teacher glanced to his right and waved his arm toward a blank area of the wall. A bell-like sound seemed to flow out of it. The two boys stared in shock as a hidden panel opened in the wall to reveal a small, dimly lit chamber.

Zoticon led them in. Three chairs had been arranged in the center of the room, pointing toward each other, to form an equilateral triangle. Beneath the seat of each chair was an attached compartment.

"This room was the last one created and inspired by Jegna, our master teacher," Zoticon told them. "Recognizing that Black Mountain is naturally drawn toward conflict and struggle, he designed the other training rooms to maximize their potential at battle. This room, however, serves another, more challenging purpose."

He directed FireArm to the chair on the left and BlackBlob to the one opposite. He waited silently until they had settled in, then sat down, still without a word, in the third chair. After composing himself for a moment as the young men stared anxiously at him, Zoticon explained, "Many Fighters are reluctant to sit in rooms like these because of their pride and fear of losing their egos. Blaze and Willo chose never to sit in this room, or any other, and I never forced them to. We once believed that it was a greater obligation to defeat the devils we can see rather than face our own inner demons."

"Beneath each of your seats," he continued, "is a remote control with a coil inside it. The coil represents the never-ending cycle of our lives. It is attached magnetically to the underside of the seat. Reach under your seats now and take your remotes."

Looking across at each other, the boys reached down, found the devices, and pulled them loose. They appeared to be featureless, transparent rectangles. A thick gold structure in the shape of a double helix hovered inside each.

"The consequence of failing to deal with those inner demons is that our hearts grow heavy after our battles. We experience battle fatigue from the shock and the struggle. We become traumatized by witnessing or surviving the violence of our enemies."

Zoticon reached below his seat and placed one hand over his own remote. "This room," he said, "which you were kept from knowing about until you had experienced that violence yourselves, is about confronting the trauma of violence, specifically."

The walls progressively darkened. The ceiling became charcoal, the walls obsidian. Not until everything was black did Zoticon speak again. "To optimize our potential, the first one we rescue must be ourselves. When we heal our inner child, we can then heal the children of the next generation."

An image of a child appeared at the far end of the room. His face, arms, and legs were black. It looked like a miniature Zoticon, with curly fur and without the electronic eye patch. A second figure appeared beside him—a black teenage version of Ann—and held his hand. A background emerged. They were seated by a lake, but the colors were unusual. The sky was green, the water purple.

"Their industries choked the trees to death," Zoticon explained. "Pollutants that reacted to atmosphere and water molecules made the air poisonous and the water toxic."

Crowds of people were now moving across the landscape of the walls. Forced migrations due to endless wars and territorial disputes had led hundreds of millions of this planet's peoples to seek refuge in foreign lands. His people, Zoticon told them, had been among them. Sharing a common language and culture over years of continual displacement, they constructed improvised cities called "camps."

The two youths watched as the images on the walls began to shift. They saw camps that stretched far into the distance, filled with structures whose architecture was both ancient and complex. On the horizon was a large pyramid, with billowing clouds of red smoke rising from the bombs that had decimated its exterior. Large mega-drills pierced through the dirt. Laborers carried crates into trucks at gunpoint. The goods, Zoticon explained, were delivered to lavish mega-cities on the other side of the planet. These vast cities, he added, were also responsible for the contaminants that had spoiled the air and water

"What you are seeing," Zoticon said, "is what they did to *us*."

They watched as protests erupted in the images on the walls. People who looked like older versions of Zoticon and AnnRoticon gathered up the children. Some of them broke the chains around their companions. Others hurled stones or blocks of cement at armored security forces.

In response, aerial vehicles flew at supersonic speeds overhead, unleashing rounds of ammunition into the residential structures before retreating into the distance. Towers tumbled into flames in the background. Black helicopters fired wherever the sounds of screaming inhabitants could be heard. Large bomber planes dropped huge canisters over towns and villages.

Tears streamed from BlackBlob's eyes as he watched explosions and hot red liquid cover the otherwise lush landscapes. "They took *everything* from you."

As the two looked on, armies of bulldozers, steamrollers, and other, unrecognizable vehicles swept away vast expanses of trees, hills, and rocks. Behind them came other vehicles that laid tracks, driving metal boards and silver motherboards into the ground. The wires, antennas, and other connective material were covered with thick layers of metals formed into streets and sidewalks. FireArm clenched his teeth as the once green landscape disappeared under sheets of gray. Industries were built, and thick clouds of smoke changed the sky to the color of ink. Images of the two children appeared on the walls. They stood there, shivering. Draped in blankets, huddled around fires while flakes of charcoal and snow littered the ground. After a while, they began to trudge onward through the storm and found refuge in cities with large, heat-retaining glass domes.

Zoticon pressed a button and the screen returned to black. "They *nearly* took everything from us. But they could never take away our souls."

FireArm stared at the elder and felt a deep guilt. He had never thought about what Zoticon had sacrificed to get to this point. How much suffering had he witnessed? How many people had he lost? Did they really lose everyone they knew in their village? Was this what Black Mountain was trying to prevent on Ziffea?

He thought about his own trauma. Never had he ever experienced that scale of violence at the orphanage. Right: the orphanage. That's what he was in this room to share about, right? His head felt disconnected from his body. His guilt shifted into a deep shame, clutching his throat and silencing his motivation to speak.

No, don't do it. As that familiar, fearful voice entered his consciousness from below, a rumbling started in his stomach and heart.

Run away, a voice from above ordered with an almost divine authority.

A voice from behind him seemed to breathe down his back. *You're a coward.*

He put his palms on his forehead and pushed his head down to his knees. BlackBlob nearly jumped out of his chair toward his friend, but Zoticon motioned for him to stay seated.

"We are here with you," Zoticon assured FireArm.

"You got this, bro!" BlackBlob piped up.

The voices in FireArm's head subsided, but the stressful feelings remained. Tears welled up in his eyes. He swallowed. "But it hurts so much," he moaned.

"I know," Zoticon said. "I understand. But remember your breath." All three of them inhaled and exhaled, the two boys following Zoticon's rhythm before settling into their own.

"Are you ready?"

FireArm let out a deep breath. "Ready as I'll ever be."

"OK, let's use Ann's technique. Think of something that pleases you and press that button."

"What?"

BlackBlob chimed in. "Just make sure it's nothing too, uh, specific, because it will come up on the screen."

Zoticon looked at him skeptically. “Well, yes,” he said. “Try to avoid anything we would have a strong judgment about.”

“Hmm. OK.”

FireArm pressed a button on his remote. The screens lit up with bright colors. Waterfalls and forests lined the walls. Rivers and valleys appeared on the floor beneath them. Above them was a bright sun. The images were so vivid they conjured up feelings of nostalgia he had never experienced. A feeling of peace swelled deep in his soul.

“Good. Now let’s stay here for a moment.”

Zoticon crossed his arms, his fists raised to his shoulders. The students followed suit. A gentle luminescence enveloped and coated them. FireArm noticed feelings of freshness that raised the small hairs on his arms.

“Thank you for this.”

“This is not it. This is the anchor. Whenever you get swept back to the sea of emotions, remember you can feel this.”

FireArm took a deep breath. “Got it.”

The colors faded.

“Ready to get started?”

“Yes.”

“What is the limiting belief we need to work on?”

“Limiting belief? What’s that?”

“Something you always say to yourself that blocks your progress.”

“Hmm… OK. I can’t trust.”

“And why do you think that is?” Zoticon asked.

“I… I’m not sure,” FireArm hesitantly replied, but in fact, he knew very well. Facing the reason was the problem.

Zoticon said nothing, only fixed his searching gaze on the youth.

FireArm felt the tension in the room. They were waiting for him. Pressured to respond, he blurted out, “I don’t want to think about it!”

The ceiling turned dark gray. Concrete walls surrounded the three. The walls and floor were illuminated yet completely blank, devoid of any faults, lacking vitality. A lifeless existence. The ceiling transformed into a fence that obstructed the dark sky. Artificial lights that shone throughout the night hid every single star. An image of a child being forced face down onto the ground by other, bigger children appeared and reappeared. Hands covered the child’s mouth. Elbows were forced into his shoulders.

Clothes were ripped from his shoulders. Knees were pressed into his back.

The room began spinning. The ceiling became the floor. The walls began to turn inside out. Mucus dripped from the ceilings, pouring out from the crevices in the walls, and wretched shrieks rang out, along with the repetitive chant of "Mutatiin! Mutatiin! Mutatiin!"

BlackBlob tried to contain his nausea. He looked urgently at FireArm, but his friend was also struggling to compose himself.

"OK, now contain it," Zoticon said.

"How? How?" FireArm was frantic.

"Focus. Breathe. Put it in a box and send it out of your consciousness."

FireArm looked at Zoticon doubtfully, but there was no other choice. He had to do something, or he would drive himself mad with the spinning scenes from his mind's eye. He mustered all of his strength to focus his attention on his breath. He thought of his psychokinetic training and concentrated on protecting his spirit and his mind. It took some time, but he was getting there. The thoughts grinded to a halt, his breathing stabilized, and he could sense his body again. He could feel again.

Suddenly, thick silver lines overlaid themselves over the images. They crossed and intersected over the walls, ceiling, and floor, forming the frame of a cube. The violent movies froze. The images stopped multiplying. Time and space shifted, and the content of the memories shrank in size and then disappeared.

The room shifted around the three Fighters, alternating between scenes of torture and scenes of nature. The night gradually turned into day. The attackers disappeared one by one, while the nature scenes maintained their bright colors. The gray walls dissipated, and bright sunshine shone down onto the young man, replenishing his spirit.

After each round of the process, the suffering subsided faster. A faint red glow formed around FireArm's chest. The walls now showed an older, adult version of FireArm, burning with a calm but controlled flame, holding the hand of his younger self. The tense atmosphere in the room diminished. FireArm felt his breathing calm down.

"Good." Zoticon's eyes shone with determination. "Now, what is the *new* belief you want to believe about yourself?"

FireArm took a moment to reflect. Something was different now. He wasn't on edge. Scanning the walls of the room, his eyes met Zoticon's. This was an authority figure who actually wanted him to heal. His eyes scanned once more until they met BlackBlob's. A youth who shared much in common with him, who had gone to such lengths to support him. The first kid he met that had never betrayed him. Not once. Was this trust? He looked at his palms, thinking of all the effort he had gone through to get to this point. Tears once again formed around his eyes, but this was a different emotion. This was a new emotion.

"I *can* trust. I can trust my people. I can trust the *universe*!"

"*Asé*," Zoticon replied. "Cross your arms in front of your chest once more, like me."

FireArm and BlackBlob followed his instructions.

"Now," Zoticon continued, "contain the stress once more. Send it away."

The outline of the cube returned. It vacuumed up all the remaining pain of FireArm's trauma before disappearing once more into a corner of the room, never to be seen again.

"Good," said Zoticon. "Now *affirm* what you want to believe in."

FireArm took a breath, then released it. "I can trust the universe!"

The entire room seemed to shift rapidly. The images made it look like the Fighters were launched high into the air. The ceiling twirled into a wallpaper of stars that lit up the night sky. The three moons of Ziffea hovered above them before receding into the horizon. The colors of a sunrise glimmered out in the distance, sending out a blissful warmth. FireArm's aura became more visible. A feeling of wholesomeness fell over everyone in the room as the solar system gently rotated around them. The galaxy was in harmony. The universe was at peace.

"Good." Zoticon looked around the room for a moment, watching shooting stars and other astral phenomena. "Looks like you did it."

It was like a weight had been lifted off of FireArm's shoulders. His expression grew light. He closed his eyes. He now found it easier to breathe. His shirt was wet from tears, but his smile sparkled in the faint light. He opened his eyes. "I couldn't have done it without you guys."

Like a prisoner stepping out into the sunshine after years of solitary confinement, he appreciated freedom more than anyone else could know.

CHAPTER 36

THE GHOST OF WILLONEO

BlazeCom sat in his room with the lights out. He liked the dark, felt safe in it. Sometimes he sat, sometimes he lay on the floor, but he was always motionless, in silence, only stirring to get a drink from his personal stash or to study the few photos he had of himself and Willo together.

Days passed, and FireArm and BlackBlob confronted numerous traumas. While they continued to maintain their physical training and engage in mental and spiritual practices, their focus shifted toward healing from their past. The brightness in their eyes inspired the whole team, motivating Anansi and Nani to resume their emotion training. The ship became a center for growth, with the leadership now encouraging it. As the group developed mastery over the elemental forces, a new level of confidence emerged, except for Blaze, who seemed to lag behind.

After all of the insults, the mocking and taunting, he had no reason to believe they would ever accept him. Looking outside the window, he would see them air-stepping, flying, and racing past the *Raven*. Sometimes, they would disappear into the clouds and reappear in different locations like unidentified flying objects, shimmering under the moonlight.

He saw their bright flames and he cowered, craving darkness, fearing that their brightness would cause his own candle to dim. HIs resentment started to take on a life of its own. His spiritual energy grew more and more corrupted. From his training, he knew that isolation and brooding always had this effect, but he could not stop the tormenting thoughts that assailed him during the days and especially at night.

"I wish we could meet again and show these dirty wretches who's boss one more time." He said it to no one in particular, but he felt that his dead friend heard him. He wondered how much longer they would keep him in Black Mountain if he just stopped showing up to meetings. His dismal spiritual energy wrapped itself around him. His soulforce fluctuated and faded into an echo of what it was meant to be. He became lost in his own suffering.

BEEEP. The kettle screeched. The water poured from it into the very cups they had seen when they first came onto this ship. Now, a month after their first entry into Zoticon's trauma room, they reflected on the progress of their emotion training.

"I don't get it, though," FireArm said over a cup of ginger tea. "Why would trauma healing have anything to do with his magician technique?"

BlackBlob leaned over the counter of the cafeteria. "No idea. He never explained *that*, did he?"

They sat in silence for a while, each lost in his own thoughts. Then, as if reading each other's minds, they rose together, and after giving each other daps, headed silently to their separate quarters.

FireArm washed up and got ready for bed. For a while, he sat on the edge of the bed looking at the night sky. The voices were no longer as loud or as scary. Something had healed in him, though he couldn't put a finger on what. Some of what he had healed may have been ancestral, trauma from people he hadn't even met. He thought of a mother he never knew. He thought of her attacker. He realized that he could now think such thoughts without a surge of fear, confusion, and especially self-persecution. His mind was clearer and more reliable. Tomorrow, he would finally tell Zoticon about the voices and what they had said. For now, he deserved a hard-earned rest.

He looked out the window one last time. Something caught his eye, then disappeared. What was that? It didn't look like a star. No distant planets should have been visible from here, and why would another planet be crimson anyway? It couldn't be that important. It must have been his imagination.

And so he decided to go to bed. There was another day of training ahead of him. He looked forward to becoming a better Fighter for his team.

He had almost fallen asleep when a blinking red warning light flashed in the corner of the room, followed quickly by sirens in the hallway. Atkon's voice shot through the speakers. "ALERT! ALERT!"

FireArm jumped to his mirror and pressed a button. A laser 3D-printed his battle garment onto his body.

Atkon's voice continued to echo through the hallways. "Multiple enemy aircraft detected."

"Multiple?" FireArm said to himself.

"Multiple enemies detected. Unknown threat level."

"What?" FireArm shook his head. "Never heard *that* before."

"Enemy detected and identified as a level five threat."

"Whoa, OK, time to get serious!"

The doors opened, and BlackBlob ran through in his battle uniform, so quickly he had to slide to stop himself from hitting the far wall. "Bro, are you ready for this?"

"Bet. Let's go!"

The two of them flew as fast as they could through the hallway and into the briefing room. There they saw Anansi and Nani, suited up and ready for battle in the back of the room. Zoticon and Atkon were monitoring the main viewscreens at the head of the bridge. As the youths entered, Atkon announced, "Enemy signature confirmed. Enemy identified as codename Death-Dweller." They looked at each other.

"Oh, it's *that* guy again!"

"This ain't gonna be easy..."

Anansi and Nani had been stretching and shadowboxing in preparation for the forthcoming fight, but when they heard the enemy's name, they stopped at once and turned to the main viewscreen. The enemy craft were still too distant for a visual feed, but the radar screen indicated four fast-moving targets out on patrol. The one leading the way produced a single high-intensity energy reading.

Zoticon turned toward them. "Good, everyone's here— No. Where is BlazeCom?"

AnnRoticon entered the room. "He is still refusing to come out. It's no use. We have to fight without him."

"Let me drag him out of there!" Nani rolled up her sleeve.

"No, his spirit energy is too low. He wouldn't last a second against Death-Dweller."

Zoticon looked closely at the radar signatures. His metal eye beeped and clicked as it analyzed the signals. "Atkon," he called, "zoom in on the energy signatures in that cluster."

"Affirmed," replied Atkon typing furiously on a wireless device. On the viewscreen, numerical data scrolled rapidly. It was nearly indecipherable, but Atkon drew a sharp breath when they saw it. "Impossible!" they declared. "It can't be!"

"What? Tell us!" Zoticon ordered impatiently.

"I need to announce this through the system. Black Mountain signature confirmed. Fighter identified as codename... *WilloNeo*!"

The room was silent. Not a word was spoken.

FireArm couldn't contain himself. "Did he betray us?" Involuntarily he tightened his fists until his aura started to spread over his arms. "How could he—?"

"FireArm!" Zoticon appeared before him so quickly that FireArm had to jump back. His red aura faded. "Stop it!" demanded Zoticon. "Did you forget how he found you last time?"

"Oh, right. Sorry."

Zoticon turned away quickly and floated toward the still scrolling list of numerical data. Atkon manipulated the screen to highlight some sections and cross-reference them to other series of data on a separate video screen on the main console. "Something's not right about his energy signature. It's been doctored."

Zoticon turned toward him. "What do you mean, *doctored*?"

"I am detecting machine code line injections that intersect with his spiritual energy. His is like mine, but inferior, unsophisticated, unstable."

Zoticon's eyes stared at the floor for a moment, then he turned to AnnRoticon, who was clenching a shaking fist. Her nails had been cutting into her palms ever since Death-Dweller's name appeared on the screen. Zoticon looked over at the rest of the Fighters. "WilloNeo has been compromised."

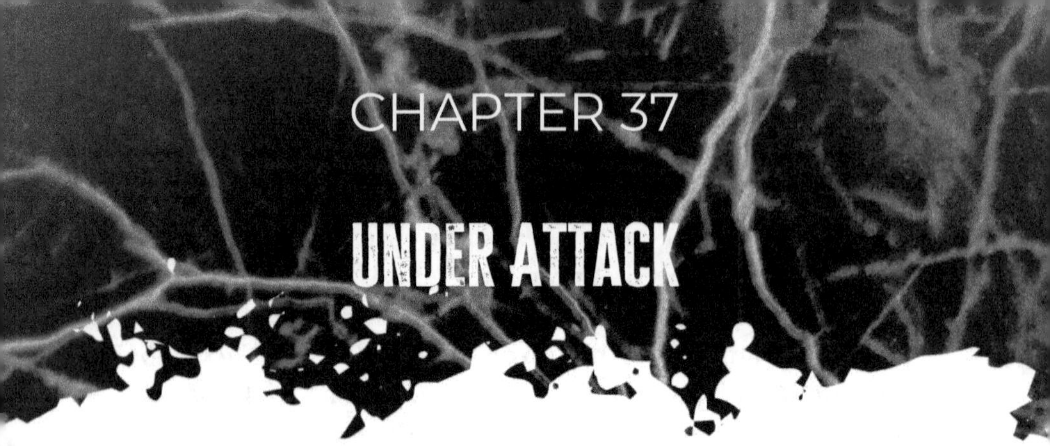

CHAPTER 37

UNDER ATTACK

BlazeCom looked toward the window. Could it be? Could Atkon be right? Was Willo really out there with Death-Dweller? He barely had enough strength to lift his head from the pillow, let alone look out the window. He tried to get up, put his hand in the wrong place, missed the bed frame, and fell out of the bed. Slowly, he crawled toward the window, his eyes alternating between the holographic image of Atkon and the visual prompt announcing that the enemy was in the vicinity. Why hadn't they launched an attack yet? Why wasn't there a prompt for the hatches opening or closing?

The enemy must not have detected them yet. If Willo really was alive, he would never see him again if they passed without detecting the ship. He had lost so many friends over his long, long life. But losing *him*? He could not bear that in his heart.

"WILLONEO!" he cried with all his might. His aura grew and brightened. From his body, flames shot through the room, engulfing the furniture, the carpet, and the walls. Out from his extremities spewed a sorrowful, bitter fire. Its brightness lit up the clouds outside his window and shone high above the ocean, for those with eyes to see it.

Far off in the dark sky, Death-Dweller grimaced, his fangs shining in the moonlight. "Ah-ah-ah!" Racing through the stratosphere, he spoke into his transceiver. "I found our little *playmates* again. Follow me!"

"Acknowledged," a robotic voice responded.

The crimson orb took a sharp ninety-degree turn and sped toward the *Black Raven* as the unmanned aerial vehicles in the convoy scrambled to catch up. Together, they carried more than enough weaponry to shred even the multi-reinforced hull of the *Raven*, behind which a fresh round of alarms instantly erupted. "Incoming! Enemies inbound!"

"Fighters, get to the hatches!" barked Zoticon. The rest of the crew flew to their prearranged positions like iron filings drawn to magnets—they had practiced this uncountable times—but Death-Dweller was splitting the clouds with the speed of his approach. He was already almost on them when the Fighters arrived at their battle stations. Before anyone could react, he had brought his face to the window of BlazeCom's burning room.

Blaze's eyes dilated with shock, terror fighting with hope in his spirit energy, staring aghast at the overwhelming aura of an enemy who already defeated him. He backed clumsily over to the bed and cowered there. The flames subsided, leaving burn marks and charred debris around him.

Death-Dweller gave him a look of scorn. "What a shame," he said to himself as the winds coursed through the air. His aura expanded, protecting him from the powerful currents as he coasted, parallel to the *Raven*, effortlessly keeping up with it.

Some distance below, from one side of the vast ship, four hatches opened. The Fighters shot up through the air in their black battle suits, ready to meet the enemy. Anansi took the lead and advanced to confront the large ball of swirling energy alongside the ship. Death-Dweller yawned. The other three Fighters followed closely behind in formation. FireArm looked to his right, at Blaze's room. He thought about the first time Death-Dweller had showed up. He had felt helpless then. Would it be different this time?

FireArm concentrated a mass of flaming energy into his fist. His eyes were focused on the enemy.

"My, my, haven't you grown?" Death-Dweller said, his eyes filled with joy and intrigue. "And that's your little playmate, too! Last time I saw you guys, you were having a tea party and munching on cookies! You really think you could fight me?"

BlackBlob's right arm charged a current of blue energy by his side. "Yeah, we've matured in one whole year. Can't say the same for you!"

Death-Dweller howled with exaggerated laughter. "I think you're right. Just seems like everyone's becoming an immortal around here! It's not a sin to stay young at heart, right?"

FireArm grew frustrated. "You're a Fighter. You have powers like us. Why work with Zi-Tai when they want to destroy your own world?"

"Simple. When was the last time Zoticon gave you a paycheck?"

Nani, the first of the other Fighters to catch up with FireArm, barked, "Shut yah mout, bwoy! But ah wha yuh a do yah?"

"Now if I told you *that*, it wouldn't be fun, would it?" He tilted his head to the right and looked beyond the four Fighters. Anansi followed his gaze. "Oh no!" she exclaimed, staring at the heavily armed aircraft in the distance. They were gaining rapidly on the *Raven*.

"They have a lock on us. Enemy missiles inbound!" Atkon's voice blared through their transceivers.

Next came AnnRoticon's. "That's enough to take out the *Raven*! Squad two, take out the sentinels. Squad one, prevent any damage to the ship!"

Death-Dweller listened in on his transceiver. He started waving to his opponents. "Well, I guess that's my cue. Nice knowing you!" His bright orb quickly dissipated, and a tailwind shot him past the fighters into the distance, far behind the *Raven*.

AnnRoticon yelled again. "Forget him! Take out those missiles!"

BlackBlob and FireArm sped toward the rear of the ship. A dozen missiles raced after them. FireArm called to BlackBlob through his transceiver, "Blob, you ready?"

"Say less!"

They separated. From their hands, volleys of bright rays connected with the missiles, impaling them with bright currents of energy and exploding just before they got out of range. An instant later, the enemy ships flew past them in hot pursuit of the *Raven*, beating out continuous rounds of ammunition from their turrets.

Meanwhile, Anansi and Nani flew to opposite sides of the *Raven*'s stern. They widened their auras to astronomically sized globes that formed into two large, protective bubbles. Anansi brought forth a large crystalized iceberg. The enemy's ammunition punctured the massive cluster of ice but stopped short of leaving from the other end before falling toward the ocean. Nani shot out a blazing sheet of magma cast an immense wall before her. The bullets instantly dissolved.

Anansi and Nani leapt toward both wings of the *Black Raven*. Anansi readied her aim, getting down on one knee and placing two fists ahead of herself. Nani gave herself a running start and then jumped in the direction of the enemy aircraft, blasting off with arms spread wide, covered with a blaze of energy that shone through the dark sky.

Anansi adjusted her glasses. She aimed her fists toward one of the sentinels, so far from the Raven that it was barely visible to the naked eye. She softly whispered, “Absolute zero.”

A faint blue light surrounded the aircraft, gradually encrusting it with a frost that covered the windshield. Streams of ice spread across the entire chassis and enveloped its surface. The aircraft appeared to stall, but not before being skewered by a multitude of large sheets of ice that punctured the engine and left it inoperable. It tumbled from the sky.

Nani flew toward the unmanned aerial vehicle at an incredible speed. The craft tried to correct its course, but it was too late. Before closing in, she curled into a ball and then whipped her limbs out as fast as possible, keeping them extended. The aircraft shattered into four separate pieces, then burst into flames. Nani flew through the cloud of acrid smoke and looped around to meet the *Raven*. There should have been one enemy craft still unaccounted for. But where was it? She scanned the sky. Was it cloaked? No. There it was, in the distance.

The craft was shaped like a large rocket and had six hatches on its sides. It must have been holding back for some reason, but now it was barreling down on the *Raven*! She watched it accelerate. It had no intention of slowing down. It was heading straight for the ship…

“It’s on a suicide mission!”

BLAZECOM

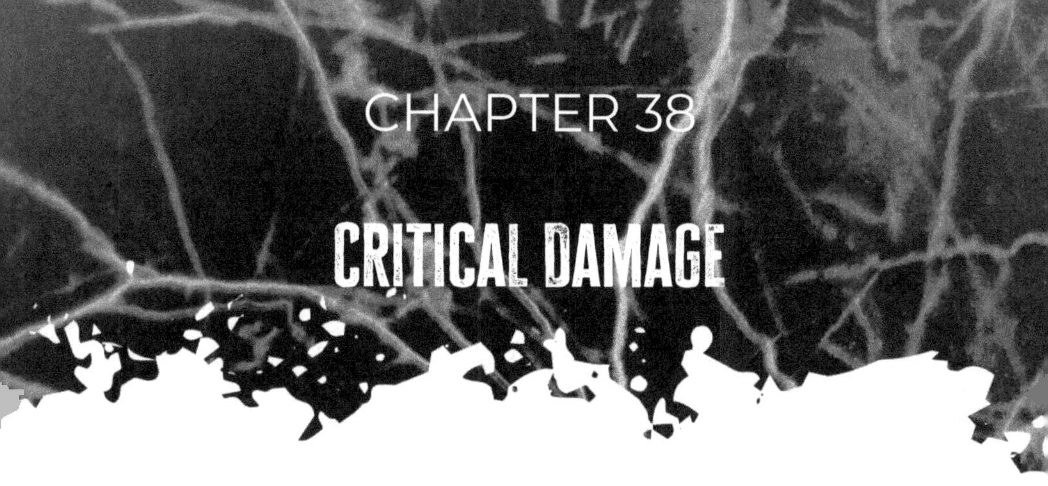

CHAPTER 38

CRITICAL DAMAGE

On the bridge, AnnRoticon stared in horror at the enemy craft as it closed in on the *Black Raven*. At its current speed, the impact would tear the *Raven* apart.

Only two Fighters were close enough to have a chance of intercepting it in time.

"FireArm! BlackBlo—"

"We're on it, Auntie!"

BlackBlob raced to intercept the remaining enemy aircraft. He charged both of his fists with blue currents and launched volleys of large dark orbs that materialized in front of him. They scrambled and headed in the direction of the incoming threat. Several meters away, FireArm swooped down through the sky in the direction of the threat. A blazing heat materialized around his biceps, flames rose from his shoulders, and he fired them toward the aircraft.

"DO IT!"

Together they unleashed a barrage of energy bursts through the air. BlackBlob spread his arms out wide and unleashed a stream of intense spiritual energy in the enemy's direction. FireArm aimed his fists ahead of himself, pulled them back, and then unleashed an endless series of swinging punches. Each swing threw searingly hot, crescent-shaped blades of energy that homed in and darted toward the enemy.

"GO-GO-GO-GO!" Ann leapt out of her chair, cheering and punching the air.

The bombardment of lethal projectiles converged on the enemy. From one of the aircraft's hatches, a figure flew out and sped ahead of it. The azure light that surrounded this mysterious individual expanded like a fog of surging energy to form something like a parasol ahead of the rocket. The projectiles exploded harmlessly against it, and the aircraft sped past the two Fighters toward the *Raven*.

BlackBlob put his hand in front of his mouth. "You've gotta be kidding me."

"We've gotta stop it!"

"Leave it to us!" Nani yelled as she jumped to the rear of the Raven's port side. At the same time, Anansi flew to starboard. Together, they expanded their auras into a large protective sheet to shield the base from impact.

Atkon's voice came over the transceivers again. "Rocket inbound. Brace for impact."

Zoticon looked at AnnRoticon. "If it doesn't cook us," he said, "we kill *anything* that comes out of it."

"Agreed."

"3…2…1—"

The protective shield ahead of the rocket disappeared. From its nose cone, six large white cylinders emerged and surrounded the *Raven* on all sides. The main body of the rocket collided with the barriers of ice and blazing heat that Anansi and Nani had thrown, just in time, around their mother ship. Nevertheless, the impact rocked and shook the inside of the ship. Zoticon, AnnRoticon, and Atkon were all floating well above the floor, but they still struggled to keep their balance as computer equipment and unsecured portable devices bounced and crashed all around them. Outside, Anansi and Nani were tossed from their positions by the impact but kept their balance and maintained their speed.

"Daahlin, you alright?"

"Yeh man, mi good!"

As they flew back over the top of the *Raven*, a blue surge of fury shot toward them through the smoke of the explosion.

"It's Willo!"

"Mek him come."

FireArm and BlackBlob had watched the encounter from a distance, but seeing the Raven surrounded, they had to act now. "Come on!" shouted FireArm as he plunged toward the ship with BlackBlob in hot pursuit.

WilloNeo dove through the air toward the *Raven*. A white visor that encircled his skull covered both of his eyes. His arms, legs, and torso were entirely covered in a sleek, white body suit, but the face and pointy hair were unmistakably his. As he made contact with the top of the aircraft, he assumed a combat posture. Without hesitation, he charged toward Anansi and Nani. They braced themselves and prepared to counter his attack, but he stopped abruptly, then veered away.

"W'happen man? Ah fraid yuh fraid?" Nani yelled.

"No, something else is up with him," said Anansi.

As WilloNeo glided backward with his arms crossed, the six cylinders that had emerged from his ship before it exploded split open. Identical figures flew out of each cylinder. They wore blue visors over their right eyes and were dressed like Willo, but their faces and hands were translucent and boneless, yet solidly formed. Their visible eyes still had the distinctive sharp look of a Fighter, but they were devoid of life, resembling the mekanations of Azor City. Each of them moved with the coordinated precision of advanced artificial intelligence units. They were perfect duplicates of one another, with the word "INITIATIVE" printed in large letters on each of their rear collars. As Anansi and Nani watched, these clones floated toward Willo, forming lines of three on either side of him. They took up their leader's battle posture—legs spread, fists clenched, elbows by their sides—seemingly awaiting their next instructions.

"Willo!" yelled FireArm as he and BlackBlob caught up with the ship.

Willo jerked his head 180 degrees to look behind him. He stared blankly into FireArm's eyes for a moment, then his neck clicked and rotated back into place. "Hydron-3 and Hydron-4. Attack," he commanded softly.

"Preparing to engage," the automaton in the rear-left position replied and turned around.

"Preparing to engage," said the one in the rear-right.

"Willo, stop this!" FireArm called out as the two clones turned and began to advance. They moved slowly and deliberately, as if analyzing the threat level that FireArm and BlackBlob posed.

"Why are you doing this?" FireArm shouted at Willo, dodging a barrage of shotgun-like pellets of blue energy from Hydron-3.

BlackBlob charged a beam in his hand and prepared to launch it at FireArm's attacker, but at the last minute, he had to dodge to his left to avoid a strike from the open palm of Hydron-4, which had sneaked up on him while he was distracted. The force of its swipe left strands of hair dancing in the air. He dodged and weaved to avoid the clone's rapid series of follow-up blows.

"Look, I don't even know you like that. Give me some space!" BlackBlob yelled, firing a counter blast from his palm.

BOOM.

The attackers' forearms blocked it, but smoke rose from the point of contact. "Direct hit! You're gonna need some repairs after that."

As the smoke cleared, BlackBlob saw that blast had detached the Hydron's arms. He watched the sleeves of its uniform float into the air. But almost at once, it spun around in a circle, and just as quickly as its hands had been blown off, it sprouted new ones and resumed its fighting stance.

"Um, we're in trouble, guys," BlackBlob called out to the others.

"Call them off, WilloNeo!" Anansi screamed through the wind.

Willo only nodded toward her and said, "Hydron-5 and -6, attack."

Two of the lifeless soldiers now charged toward Anansi and Nani. Nani defended with a flurry of blazing kicks and her enemy blocked the force of the attack. Its arms were instantly blown off, and almost as instantly the attacker spun in a circle and resprouted them. Covering the back of her comrade, Anansi shot a stream of icicles from her hand that skewered the other Hydron, knocking off its right arm and both of its legs. Once more, its limbs were shattered, and once again, the clone simply twisted in midair, and the limbs regenerated.

"Willo, what's the meaning of this?" Anansi exclaimed.

Willo answered by pointing his hand at the stern of the ship and instantly blowing a hole through it. "Hydron-1 and -2, follow me," he ordered.

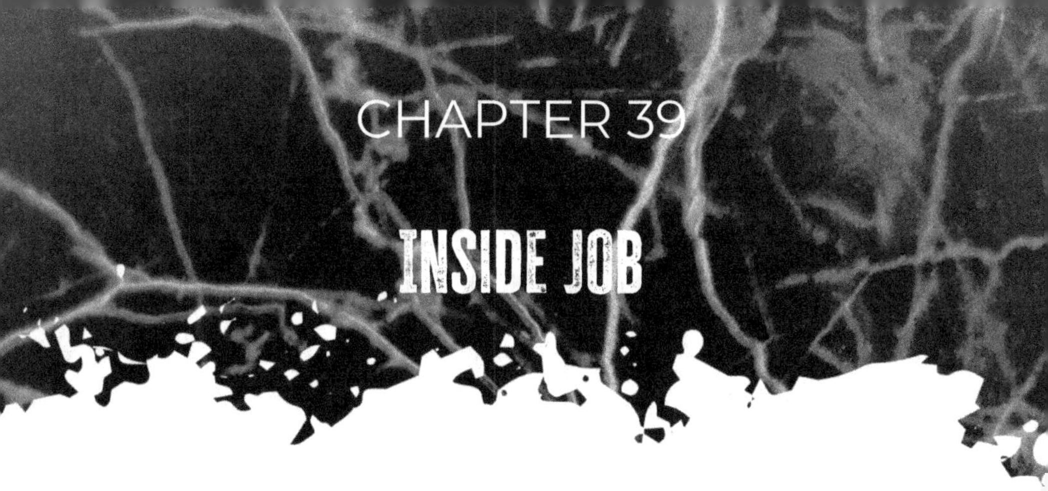

CHAPTER 39

INSIDE JOB

WilloNeo sped through the ruptured ceiling alongside the Hydrons. AnnRoticon faced them in the center of the hallway. She flung her arms out as Willo's feet touched the floor in front of her. Neither said a word, at first. Willo looked into her eyes, then scanned the hallway as if searching for something.

"Willo, you cannot go any farther!"

"I don't have to."

He raised his right arm and pointed his thumb behind him. Then he pointed a finger beyond AnnRoticon. "Hydron-1, engine room. Hydron-2, bridge."

The two henchmen fell to the floor. AnnRoticon stared at the collapsed figures, perplexed, as bubbles began to form on their faces and hands. Blue vapor rose from their mouths as they each melted into pools of viscous liquid. As AnnRoticon watched, alarmed yet astonished, one of the pools dispersed itself across the tiles. It moved like metal drawn to a magnet, darting past AnnRoticon's right foot and gliding down the hallway behind her. The other pool expanded and spread itself out, reducing its density almost to the point of becoming invisible.

"What in Si-Vin's name?" AnnRoticon yelled into her suit's intercom. "It's crawling under the tiles and soaking through the floor. He's sending something to the engine room!" She leapt past Willo so swiftly that his spiky hair trembled in her wake.

Outside the *Black Raven*, the battle continued. FireArm dodged blast after blast.

BAM.

Innumerable pellets of spiritual energy shot from the hands of his emotionless opponent.

BAM.

FireArm dodged again, but this time he saw an opening. He swooped low, sped under the Hydron, and connected with a roundhouse kick that sliced its body in half. Its pelvis and legs dissolved into the wind, but the clone just stared at him as if nothing had happened, then spread its arms out and spun around.

SPLISH!

New legs and lower body parts sprouted from its torso. "What the—?"

Before FireArm could get the next word out, the Hydron again began firing seemingly endless waves of projectiles in his direction.

Meanwhile, BlackBlob struggled against his own indestructible enemy. They exchanged fire below the rear of the *Raven*, taking turns evading each other's attacks. Reading the rhythm of his opponent, BlackBlob focused his mind on his next attack. "Take this!" he yelled, firing a buckshot of focused energy from his hands that perforated the Hydron. He fired three more rounds and decimated the physical body of his opponent. Pieces of the clone's wrists, ankles, and chest detached from its body and shattered into droplets in the wind. Undisturbed, the Hydron gazed coolly back at BlackBlob, then spun in a circle again.

SPLISH!

Regenerated parts sprouted out from its torso, fibers reconnected, and BlackBlob's enemy reconstituted itself as if it had never been hit. "He came back from *that*?" BlackBlob yelled.

"Burning him up doesn't work either!" FireArm yelled back, lunging away in the nick of time to avoid a swipe from his own indestructible enemy. "Anansi," he called out breathlessly, "what do we do *now*?"

There was no answer. Anansi and her comrade were fully engaged fighting and dodging their own attackers, leaping back and forth across the top of the *Raven* in desperate attempts to help each other. Nani managed a running dropkick that knocked one of the Hydrons off its perch atop the *Raven*. Then, she burst into a flame and chased after it. At the same time, Anansi unleashed a spinning whirlwind kick that cut through the other Hydron's neck and abdomen, leaving jagged tears and detached limbs that plummeted and dissipated behind the ship. The decapitated head floated on its own in midair before spinning around and regenerating the rest of its body. It was as good as new.

Anansi stared in horror as the now intact enemy lunged toward her again. She felt at her wits' end. "Atkon," she called out, desperate for help, "anything in the Community databases about this?"

In the bridge, the liquid enemy reformed and assumed the same battle stance as WilloNeo. It prepared to fire at the *Raven*'s control panels.

BZZZZT.

From Atkon's right hand, a devastating surge of lightning bolts propelled themselves into the enemy, dissolving it into a pool of liquid again. With their left hand, Atkon furiously typed on their keyboard while studying the data it delivered to the main viewscreen. Once again, the pool of liquid quickly reconstituted itself. Atkon waited for it to regenerate before firing another liquifying electrical charge into it.

"We have no data on these enemies," they announced through the intercom, even as they nonchalantly fired yet another powerful surge of electrical current into the clone, "but never mind that, traces of their liquid forms are leeching into the *Raven* and damaging its structural integrity. They're trying to destroy it from the inside!"

The situation was drastic. Yet out in the hallways of the Raven, Willo walked with emotionless strides, searching for his own target. He walked past the rooms where he had spent so much of his time, but he felt no nostalgia. No sentiment whatsoever, except—

He turned to look to his left, on the verge of entering a room, when someone appeared at the other end of the corridor.

"WilloNeo, what have you done?"

He had no time to react. Zoticon leaned forward and lifted his right heel from the ground as if starting to walk, then disappeared and instantly reappeared directly in front of Willo to deliver a crushing blow to his former student's solar plexus. The force of the impact pushed Willo down the hallway and into the air. He slammed into the ceiling, then broke his fall with his face, coughing up blood. He used his forearms to raise himself from the floor as he watched the pieces of his fractured visor drop into the blood-stained carpet.

By now, AnnRoticon had reached the engine room in the stern of the *Raven*. The light from the energy generator that powered the ship's anti-gravity crystal cast a shadow on a mass of liquid that appeared to be evaporating and dissipating. "AnnRoticon here," she transmitted to Atkon. "The enemy has... self-destructed?"

Atkon was still typing away on their keyboard, but they no longer had to keep liquifying the constantly regenerating Hydron. "Something's changed," they replied. "It is no longer regenerating. The bridge is secure."

In the battle outside, the four Fighters were finally seeing their opponents disintegrate into particles without regenerating. FireArm was the first to successfully destroy one of the clones. He punched through his opponent as it turned to mist, and this time it did not reconstitute. "Target down," he announced. "Entering the Raven to engage WilloNeo!"

He bolted past his teammates, who were now making short work of their own attackers, and flew into the ruptured aircraft. He darted through the hallways and quickly found Zoticon looking down at Willo. Their former teammate was struggling to stand up. The elder towered over him unmoving, as if waiting.

Behind Willo's cracked visor, FireArm saw tears. "Willo!" he called out.

"Hold your position," Zoticon commanded, thrusting out his palm. Still coughing blood, Willo steadied himself on his knees, then used the handrail along the wall to pull himself back to his feet .

"Are you out of your damn mind?" Zoticon yelled. "You have brought the enemy to our base."

Willo stumbled backward, holding his left arm and dragging the left side of his body. "Why?" he replied, spitting out another mouthful of blood.

Zoticon walked slowly toward him. "What do you mean *why*?"

Willo slid one foot forward now. "Why do you want to *replace* us?"

Zoticon stopped. "What madness do you speak of?" A movement in the corner of his eye made him glance to his left. Through an open door, he saw Blaze crawling toward him on the floor. Willo's partner gripped the carpet between his knuckles and lunged weakly at Zoticon, who backstepped out of the way.

"Don't hurt him!" Blaze moaned, then he fell helplessly to the floor again. "WilloNeo!" he cried. He turned his head to get a glimpse of his comrade and crawled toward him. Condensation and a sickly blue energy surrounded him. "What happened to you?"

"Blaze," Willo replied, "you left me behind."

"What? No! Never!" Tears fell from Blaze's eyes.

"Zoticon," said Willo, "you could have saved me. You *would* have saved FireArm."

Zoticon stared sternly back at him. "You have been compromised."

At the other end of the hallway, FireArm impatiently obeyed his commander's order to stay where he was. He heard some fast movement nearby. Turning to his left he saw BlackBlob approaching. There was an urgency in his eyes. "Hey! What are you waiting for? Where's Willo?"

"Zoticon said to wait—"

"Since when do *you* listen to anybody? C'mon!"

"Right!"

FireArm led the way. "Willo! Zi-Tai is controlling you. Fight it off!"

Willo turned his head. The tears continued to drop from his eyes, but with a twisted smirk, he replied, "You little mutatiin. I never wanted to see *you* again."

FireArm stiffened. BlackBlob charged up a dense mass of dark energy in his palm.

"You traitor," BlackBlob shouted at the frail figure. "Weren't we supposed to be a family?"

"I told you to stand down!" Zoticon yelled.

BlackBlob and FireArm both fell back, though the latter by only a single step.

Zoticon whipped his head toward Willo again. "How dare you use that filthy word on my ship!"

Blaze looked down at the carpet. His tears continued to fall, further drenching the rug beneath him. He crawled on the floor toward his friend. "Willo. I always followed you. We fought side by side for years. I did everything you asked."

FireArm noticed droplets of what looked like water drifting toward Willo. A voice echoed in his mind. *Something isn't right. Be careful.*

Blaze had reached Willo's feet. "Why would you ever say I would leave you behind."

His old companion fell to the floor on one knee. Looking Blaze straight in the eye, point blank, he whispered, "Because I would have done the same to you."

A swirl of liquid rose from the ground and enveloped the two of them in a white-and-blue storm of energy.

"I told you to get back!" Zoticon snapped.

Even as he spoke, Atkon's urgent voice came from the speakers. "Large concentration of unknown energy detected—"

FireArm leapt toward BlackBlob. "We've gotta get ou—"

The sound of the explosion that followed carried for miles over the waters of the flooded coastal regions of the ravaged planet.

WILLONEO

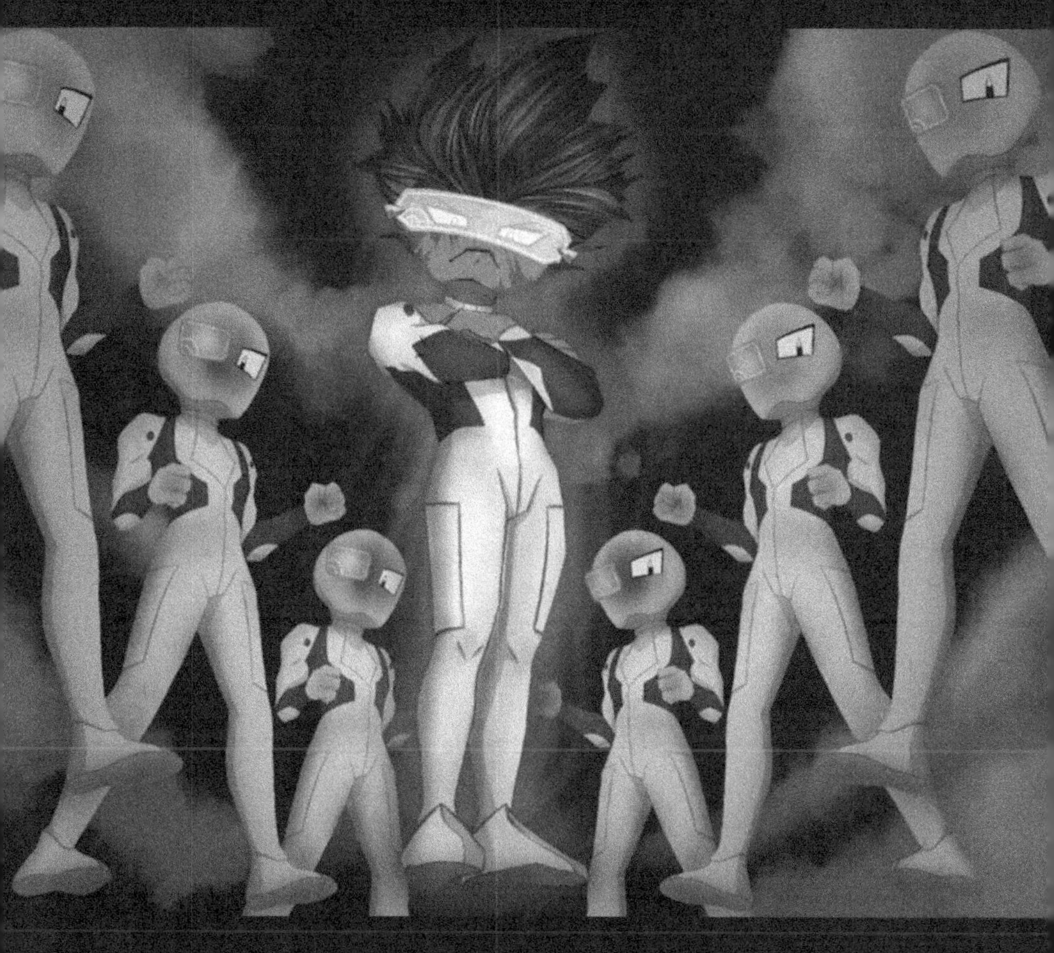

CHAPTER 40

SURVIVAL

"Wake up. C'mon!"

FireArm's eyes opened slowly. He saw someone shaking him by the collar, trying to wake him up. Was that Blob? His vision was blurry, but he managed to make out a familiar face. He couldn't focus or orient himself to his body. The sound of water was all around him. Everything seemed to be rocking and swaying.

"Hey everyone, he's awake!"

Once his senses fully returned, FireArm looked around. He was startled. He saw waves through a porthole. Were they on the water? He scanned the area. OK, he was on one of the recovery room mattresses, but there was no ceiling and only two walls. The rest of the *Raven* was missing. Parts of it were floating nearby on the dark water. Larger ones were bobbing in the water farther off. He scanned the area once more and saw Anansi and Nani on a platform.

"Praise Si-Vin," Anansi said, waving at him, "you made it!"

"Ah, yuh wake up? Mi tink yuh did dead!" Nani winked at him.

"Nani? Come on, you can't say that!" Anansi turned to her and they laughed. He tried to sit up, but his back and legs felt too heavy. The best he could do was raise his head. It was dark. The stars shone above them, and the water was black. Blacker than the night. They were surrounded by it. The sound of waves and wind reminded him of those virtual visits to the beach during his spiritual energy training. But never had he been in the middle of the ocean. Everything felt dreamy—until the pungent odor shocked his senses and made him scrunch up his face.

"Bleh," he exclaimed, turning back toward BlackBlob. "Yo, I thought the ocean was supposed to smell like salt. Why's it stinking like that?"

"Yo, that's the smell of big business," BlackBlob replied as he looked out over the waves. "Anansi was just telling me how Zi-Tai wrecked the oceans, the whole planet, like, a long time ago."

Looking at the water was both a relief and a source of heartache. The sheer expansiveness of the ocean was something he had only read about. But this ocean was dying. He imagined that there were very few marine animals that could survive these microplastic infested waters. Even those that did survive could only have done so by diving so deep they wouldn't get sucked into things like that mega-dam they'd attacked a few months back.

"What about Zoticon and Auntie Ann?" he asked.

"They're chillin' over there. They're trying to help Atkon save some files. Stink water isn't the best place for storage drives."

"I hear that. But wait, does that mean… Is the *Raven* done for?"

"Yo, it's *well* done. This bird won't be flying again."

FireArm looked at his hands. Both had burn marks that extended up along his arms. "What about Blaze? Willo?"

BlackBlob looked out at the ocean. "Don't know what kind of crazy weaponry Zi-Tai has," he said, "but that explosion ripped them both to shreds."

"Damn."

FireArm looked up at the sky. It was brightening. A new day was rising. He wondered how intense a hatred had to be burning in the enemy to use Willo that way. If that could happen to Willo, what would have happened to him if he had been captured during that fight with Tri-Spectre?

A great sadness came over him. "Man, is there anything that made it?"

"Not really. The explosion was right above the engine room. Atkon had to make a crash landing."

"Wow. They got us good."

"We're lucky that some of the rooms could handle the shock, but not all of them could float on water."

"What about the library?"

"Heh, only you would ask something like that."

"Well, what about it?"

"That's finished, bro."

The idea of losing such a vast repository of knowledge—the accumulated wisdom of thousands of years and hundreds of planets—shook him to the core. All of that recovered material, now lost forever. He struggled to get up from the bed. "I wanna go check—AHH!"

"Nah, you're not going nowhere. Doctor's orders."

A sharp pain had shot through his back. Whatever caused that explosion had been designed to take out more than just the ship. He looked at BlackBlob.

"Take some time to chill," his friend told him. "We'll keep watch in case they send anyone else."

Exhaustion overcame him. He closed his eyes and sunk into a dream. At first, it was calm on the ocean. Then the voices of his allies grew distant. Panic began to ambush him. He was paralyzed. He couldn't move. Suddenly, figures dressed in white surrounded him. Their faces were revealed. It was Zoticon, AnnRoticon and the others, but something was different. They were laughing like demons! Were they brainwashed by Zi-Tai too? All he could see was the white of their eyes. Their auras were corrupted. Their spirits were compromised. He was crippled and could do nothing as the Fighters circled him.

They surrounded his bed, pointing at him. "It's all your fault!"

Now FireArm was falling into a deep ocean crevice, sinking deeper and deeper into the dark, cold water. He was being suffocated by the poisons that clogged his lungs and blocked his airways. The ghosts of Willo and Blaze were gathering all of the youths in the orphanage. They all stood there, taunting him, teasing him. Then everyone started beating him. Fists, boots, and blunt objects clubbed at him.

FireArm struggled and struggled. As he wrestled in the darkness, he saw an image of his younger self in his cell, but he was not alone. Someone else was there. Who had protected this young child before, in the past? he wondered. Who was it who had held out a hand for him? A wall of fire rose up in front of him. Blaze's rotting carcass crept up from behind and grabbed him. From the front, the burning skeleton of Willo approached. It punched the two of them until its wrist broke off and its ribcage caved in.

FireArm's heart thumped in his chest. He felt like it was about to explode, and he began to panic. Then he remembered his breath training. Without judgment, his mind returned to his breath. He breathed in and breathed out, and realized that the toxic water could not harm him. He remembered he was a Fighter. He remembered the words "I can trust the universe."

He said those words. Again and again. The voices of the past grew silent, and the sound of his breath, though meager and unforced, claimed dominance over his consciousness. He remembered that no flame burned hotter than his spirit. As he breathed, he walked through the wall of flame unharmed. He saw the younger version of himself being cared for by an older version of himself. He walked toward them, but as he approached, they turned to face him. The older version of himself looked back with a smile of approval. He wore a black baggy suit with ripped-off sleeves and red-hot fangs that extended from its shoulders and from the leg openings of the pants. The younger child was dressed in pajamas with cartoon fire emblems for feet. The child played with a small black bisected pyramid and smiled with pride at him. They spoke to him in unison.

Don't give up. Even if the world can't see it, we have always seen you as whole.

He opened his eyes. Tears ran down his face. He had witnessed his pain without running from it. Rather than suppressing the voices, he was learning to acknowledge them and respond, to see them as parts of a greater whole. He quietly sobbed through streaming tears so as not to disturb those who rested around him.

Between stifled sniffles he looked around him. Anansi, Nani, and BlackBlob all sat in meditation around his mattress, protecting him even in his sleep. He turned and saw the light of a computer monitor illuminating Zoticon, AnnRoticon, and Atkon, who were scouting and planning for the new day—still focused, ever unrelenting, determined to keep them all alive. He embraced his feelings of gratitude. He *could* help others, and others could help him. Fearlessly, he closed his eyes and whispered to himself, "Defeat the enemy wherever he appears."

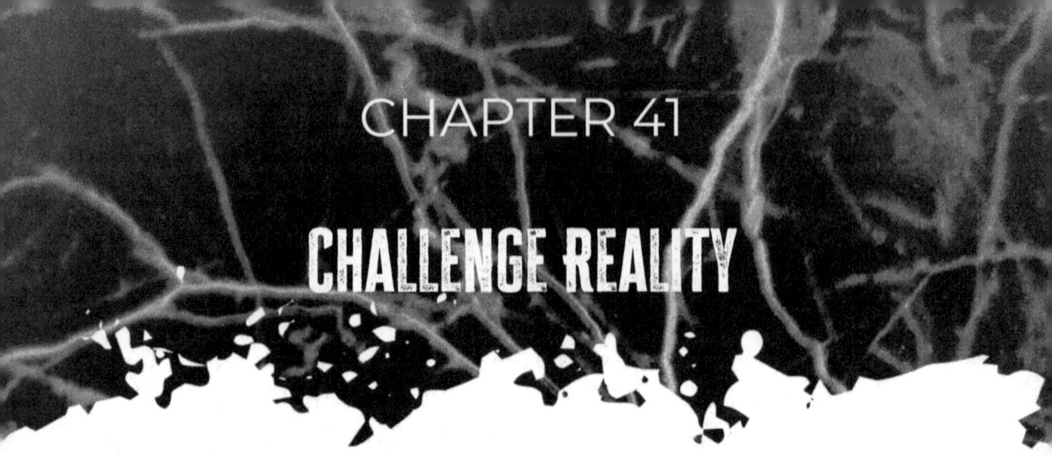

CHAPTER 41

CHALLENGE REALITY

FireArm opened his eyes again. He no longer felt the rocking of the ocean. He was on land once again, the sun rising bright behind him. His eyes scanned the area. They had set up camp on a long, wide beach. He could tell it was somewhere on the southern continent because of the palm trees. They were in the South, but not too far from the border. It would have been a paradise were it not for the beach's toxic waters and the grayish sand from the degraded coral and underwater mechanical waste.

The intervening weeks had been difficult. FireArm's injuries had been more serious than he'd realized. But after they reached the relative safety of the island, there had been time and space to focus on the healing powers Ann had taught him. Yesterday, he had been able to stand on his feet unaided for the first time and do a basic mental and physical workout. From this point on, FireArm knew, his recovery would be quick.

At his feet, he saw Ann holding a hand out above his body, which enveloped him in green energy that after a few moments gently dissipated. "Rise and shine."

"Thank you, Auntie Ann."

"I'll be back in a minute." Before she turned, he caught a glimpse of the sadness in her eyes. They had made it out in one piece, but the *Black Raven* was lost and two members of the team had died. No, they were murdered. It would take some time before Black Mountain would return to normal.

He watched the elder float over to Zoticon and Atkon, who were looking at a cracked computer screen powered by a spare battery found among the wreckage. Atkon was typing away, while Zoticon planned and coordinated strategies.

FireArm looked in the other direction. BlackBlob sat under a tree eating a mango. He called out to him. "Yo."

"What's good?" said BlackBlob, and he took a bite of the sweet fruit, splashing juice all over his face.

"Wait a minute. How come I'm the only one who got all burnt up?"

"Well, he didn't say anything to me about it." BlackBlob scratched the side of his cheek. "But I think Uncle Zee knew something was up."

"That's why he told us to stay back." FireArm looked down at the ground.

"That's right. No one else was in the hallway except us. We were closest to the blast and..." BlackBlob hesitated, then wiped his face with his sleeve. "You saved me, bro."

"What?"

"I think you used that secret magician peekaboo technique from the old man."

"Really?" FireArm was startled and quickly rose from the mattress. "I don't remember—Ah!"

"Yo, take it easy."

"I know, you said that like a hundred times already."

"Listen..." BlackBlob came over now and kneeled on one knee beside the bed. "I didn't even see it coming. At the last minute, you picked me up out of there. So it looks like I owe you one." He gave FireArm a fist bump.

"Ow!"

"Oh yeah, you're injured! You gotta take it easy, bro!"

FireArm sighed.

"Aiight, I'm being serious. I'm gonna pay you back one day. After we strike back."

"Strike back?"

"You heard me. We ain't letting them get away with that."

BAM.

The sound of fierce, repeated strikes interrupted them. FireArm turned in alarm. In the direction of the sounds of fighting and movement, he could make out Anansi and Nani practicing. Anansi wore regular boxing gloves, while Nani wore punch mitts to catch her partner's jabs and hooks. The punches came out at a machine gun rate. Drops of sweat hit the dirt beneath them as they moved and dodged and spun through the air.

"Wow, looks like *they're* not playing around."

"Yeah man!"

The two women moved gracefully as well as fiercely. Closed fists hit Nani's protective gear, and playful taunts, encouragement, and laughter rang out across the sand. Their speed increased, kicking up dirt and swaying bushes and branches as Anansi practiced her rehearsed combinations.

"But their clothes. They look different."

"Yeah, our technogarments couldn't last through that battle, and down here in the South, they don't have the technofabric mirrors we had up North. So we have to use something called *cot-ton* for clothes."

"No technogarments? Did we go back in time or something?"

"Well, we're just far enough south to be outside the clutches of Zi-Tai. The old man called it 'out of the reach of modernity,' or something like that."

"Not sure I understand any of that."

"Yup, makes two of us."

Atkon floated over to the bed.

BEEP.

They passed what looked like a camera over FireArm's body. The other side of the device showed the youth's musculoskeletal structure on a green screen.

BEEP.

"Good work, FireArm. You can be confident of a full recovery now."

"Thank you, Dr. Atkon."

"No, no. No need for honorifics." They held the device a few feet above FireArm's upper body and dragged it past the top of his head. "All I did was study to get that title. Anything I learned can be learned by you."

BEEP.

"The initial damage you sustained was from WilloNeo's energy signature." Atkon paused and frowned before adding, "But there was something else too. Something completely unknown to our databases."

FireArm slowly got up from the table and stretched his arms. "Is that why Willo and Blaze…?"

"Precisely. They could not survive at the epicenter of whatever it was that caused that explosion."

Atkon started to walk away. BlackBlob put a hand out in his direction. "Doctor—I mean, Atkon?"

"Yes?" They stopped and turned to face him.

"Those terrible things Willo was saying…" His fist clenched. "Was that because he was brainwashed, or was that him talking all of that by himself?"

Atkon took a moment to think. "Let me ask you both, young men. From your training, what do you think Zoticon would say?"

BlackBlob stiffened his posture and put his hands behind his back. "Oh—He is a casualty of our great war!"

FireArm too straightened his back and put his hands behind his back. "Uh—Everything is irrelevant!"

All three of them were still laughing when Zoticon suddenly appeared right behind Atkon. "You're all wrong. I'd say: believe what you will."

They all jumped. Atkon nearly dropped their handheld device.

"Sir!" BlackBlob nearly jumped out of his skin.

"Yes! I was meaning to check in with you," Atkon said, looking uncharacteristically nervous. They showed Zoticon the readout on their device, and the two of them peered over it for a moment.

"So, it is as we suspected," said Zoticon.

"Precisely."

"Zi-Tai has developed weaponry that can destroy even a fully initiated Fighter's genetic and molecular material. But how?"

"Anti-matter weaponry?"

"It was only split-second decision that allowed any of us to survive. And the ability to challenge reality."

Zoticon moved in to stand directly over FireArm. "You're alive," he said, as if announcing this for the first time.

"Yes, that's what it looks like."

Zoticon turned to face BlackBlob. "He saved you by using the time-stop-act-then-time-stop technique."

"Yup, that's what I told him. But uh, not in those words though."

Zoticon thought for a moment. "Why didn't you just use the technique yourself? That's what I did."

"Oh... uh." BlackBlob scratched his head.

"What? Can't you use it yourself?"

"No, sorry." He held his head down.

Zoticon looked at FireArm. "Teach him how to use it."

"I wish I cou—"

"What?"

"Everything happened so fast, I'm not sure how I did it."

Zoticon rubbed his chin. "So you have no idea *how* to use it, but you managed to save two Fighters with it."

"Yeah, I guess." FireArm looked down again.

"It's obvious then," said Zoticon. "You are only suppressing your suffering rather than healing it."

FireArm thought about this. "I don't think it's something that can be healed."

"That's the problem," replied Zoticon. "You *think* that you are broken." The youth looked up at him again. "But I do not."

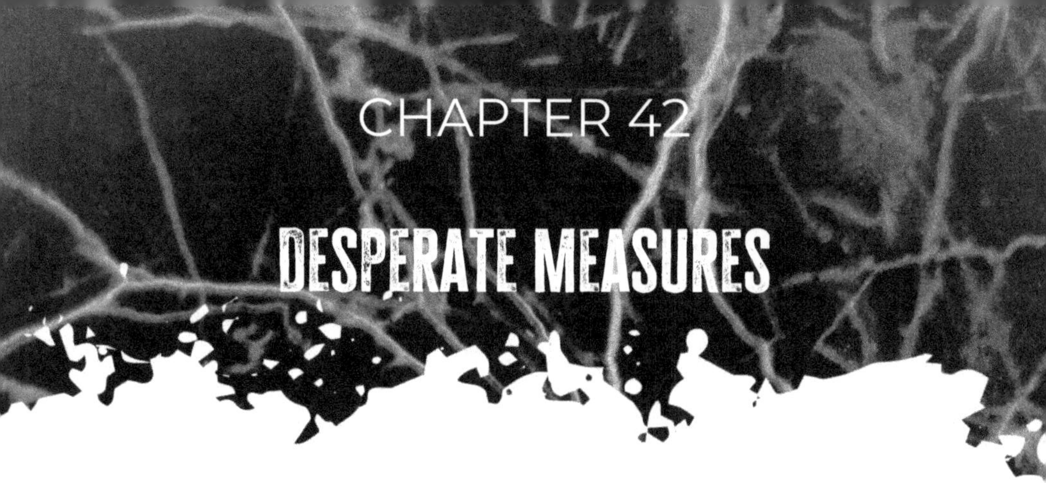

CHAPTER 42

DESPERATE MEASURES

Phutais rested under the moonlight, cradling an empty glass. The crowd of guests had left the room and shut the door behind them.

He held up a portable device. The light at the top was blinking rapidly. The ringtone played an anthem called *The United North*, with trumpets blasting out a melody of triumph. He put the device to his ear. "Why did you call this phone?" He listened as the person on the other side spoke. "The ship was destroyed but you didn't check for bodies?"

He wanted to slam the balcony into fragments and only stopped himself by remembering the mechanized soldiers walking on the streets below. He couldn't bear the idea of shards of broken glass falling from this place and allowing outsiders to question his composure. He retreated to the inside of the suite and strode through the darkness, listening to the rest of the story. "Did the Hydrons record any visual data?" he demanded.

The answer made him slam the keyboard on his desk so hard that bits of it flew and scattered throughout the room. A viewscreen came on in front of him, lighting up the room. It was a visual feed from six different cameras and perspectives. Each showed different glimpses of the *Black Raven*, but the images were fuzzy and full of glitchy squares that obscured most of the data except the flight coordinates and the date and time of recording.

"Wait, pause it there!" Phutais shouted. The video froze as a dark figure was about to smash a fist into the camera. One of the other videos showed the scrambled face of a woman and a flash of light. He looked closely at their eyes. "They're all mutatiin," he said with contempt.

He ordered the feed to resume. More blurry images unrolled on the screen. Some parts were more visible than others, but most of it was so patchy and distorted that it offered little useful information. "How could they disrupt our visuals like that?" Phutais raged. "Where did these people even get this technology from?"

He gave up and switched to a file marked TESTSUBJECT #05. This video was a little less scrambled. It showed the subject's entry into the *Raven* clearly enough, but that was followed by high levels of visual distortion and jumbled images. Yet he caught brief glimpses of a figure dressed in black who kept fading into the scrambled mess of the rest of the video. "That looks like the one who attacked the inauguration!"

The video proceeded and skipped along to an image of a smaller person at the far end of a large hallway. As soon as this figure started to come into focus, the camera spun upward, then displayed a shot of the floor tiles below before fading into darkness. The words VIDEO FEED END appeared on the screen.

"That other one was there too! Could it *be*?"

He thought for a moment about the conquest of planet Marka. It had happened decades ago. The only people who would have such bleached complexions were refugees from the pyramids and camps. It was part of the plan of Light supremacy to genetically bleach and forcibly sterilize the Dark population, limiting their numbers and removing any historical trace of their people. No Ziffean could look like that. The genetic bleaching initiative had yet to begin. Without a doubt, these were two of the remaining survivors of Marka's great world wars.

"All right, Meridian, I'll call you back," Phutais muttered into the device, then he slammed it into the keyboard, breaking both of them into several pieces. He stared at the scattered pieces. "You will lose again. We will break your spirit as many times as it takes." He gazed at the frozen image of the Fighters on the screen as if pondering something, then his expression suddenly changed and he blurted out, "Time to start Operation Light-lash."

He went to his desk, took another phone from one of the drawers, and pressed an autodial button on it. While waiting for the phone to connect, he looked at replays of the different individuals repeatedly shaking and spinning the camera as they struck it with their hands and feet or blasted it with blinding lights.

"Harbush. The resistance is increasing. Change the laws again. We will punish *all* of them. Put a curfew on the whole lot of those people of darkness. Discourage any show of support for terrorists, flag all posts on societal media, and criminalize any protest…" He stopped to listen to his subordinate. Then interrupted him. "What? You have already done most of that? Do the rest then!" He smashed that phone to pieces and brought out yet another.

"Telron. Tell the public that we will no longer teach Critical Light Studies in the North, and sign an executive order at once that forbids teachers in all parts of the South that we control from teaching history. If there is any pushback, we will ban even more books, fire more teachers, and even defund libraries if we have to…" He paused for a moment. Then yelled. "Well, what are you waiting for? Do it!"

He hurled the device at the wall in a fury. It broke it into several pieces that tumbled onto the floorboards. He nearly ripped off the handle of the drawer that held even more phones. He pressed a button on a new device a little more gently and waited for it to connect.

"Meridian. Ensure that all major news networks talk about the danger of alien immigrants and the need to strengthen our borders. Insert anxiety-provoking subtexts anytime someone with dark skin is mentioned for any reason…" He listened for a few seconds and then talked over her. "Ahh, atta girl. Now, repeat those messages nonstop. Oh, and do not show or even talk about any crimes committed by people of Light. Do it now!"

He slammed the phone against his other hand so hard that the device broke into fragments. He looked around the room. Debris from broken phones and keyboards was everywhere. The light from the monitor continued to shine onto him. Over and over, the same video played. He gazed at it, studying it as if mesmerized, until the silence was broken by the prompt INCOMING CALL flashing on the screen.

"What?" Phutais yelled loudly at it. Big letters marked MAIDEN blinked on the screen.

A familiar, dark, pixelated silhouette appeared on the camera. "What are you doing?" the distorted voice asked.

"Do you know who you just called? What do you mean, what am I doing?"

"You ordered Light-lash to commence on Ziffea? Are you out of your mind?"

"Were you listening? I asked, do you know who you are speaking to?"

"You will be forcing us to stay in the shadows."

"It's a worthy sacrifice. We do not need any of your *voodoo* right now."

"It is suicide. You cannot beat them without our help."

"Death-Dweller left before the end of the mission. We don't need your kind of help."

"You're making a mistake."

"Wrong again. We do this because we cannot risk another mistake. We will attack the morale and the spirit of the people, push them to the brink, and cut off the lifeblood of the terrorists."

"They will come for *you* now that you took one of theirs."

"And then I will finish the rest of them. Happy? This conversation is over!"

Phutais leapt into the air and delivered a powerful heel kick splitting the viewscreen and the entire desk in half. Fragments of marble littered the floor.

He glared at the bits and pieces that surrounded him. "Such shoddy workmanship," he said.

CHAPTER 43

THE TIME FOR JUSTICE

An old man walked with a cane, dressed entirely in black. He walked alongside his teenage granddaughter, who sported audio speakers on either side of her head while clutching an electronic device. They strolled through an outdoor market.

"Life in the South is simpler without motherboards and mekanations," he explained, reminiscing on how his people used to spend their time serving their families and communities. People were passionate about their occupations, and relationships were forged exclusively between living beings. Digital parents were unheard of. The young girl continued bobbing her head to the latest tunes while the old man continued his lecture.

"Mekanations would have a hard time recharging themselves in the wooded hills and green valleys," he described. In the markets, fresh fruit and vegetables were available for purchase, and people still shopped in specialized stores for clothing and household items. The All-Mark monopoly that dominated the North was nowhere to be found.

"That's why," he paused, turning to his granddaughter. "Young lady, are you listening?"

The young girl quickly stashed her device back into her pocket.

"Y-yes, Baba," she lied.

The old man sighed. "I see you have one of those… portable video screens. What do you call it? Eye-Mod, was it?"

She hesitated before exclaiming, "No, Baba, it's the latest iGod! It knows everything and can do anything. I use it connect with my friends and stay up with the latest trends!"

The old man said nothing, and they resumed their walk together. He preferred to socialize in the ways he always had.

"You know," he began, "don't they say those things cause mental problems?"

She straightened her back. "Y-yes, Baba, but only if you get hooked on it. Not me!"

The two of them pushed a cart filled with groceries as they continued through the market. To their right, they came across two small children walking with their parents. The youngsters, no older than three or four, scampered around in circles, raising their electronic devices into the air, mimicking the movements of cartoon characters on their screens. The timing was too perfect. Coincidentally, dolls resembling those characters were available for purchase at a nearby toy store, with the screens even indicating the nearest vendor using GPS technology. The parents attempted to negotiate with their kids but failed miserably.

"You see?" The old man shook his head. "Who wouldn't feel depressed dealing with all of this?"

In the northernmost region of the continent, in an upscale apartment, a white-collar worker prepared himself for a meeting. He pressed a button on a mirror, and a suit materialized over his body. He quickly made his way to his office, which conveniently was in the next bedroom.

"I wonder what's on the news," he whispered to his device.

He put on an artificial-reality headset from SurgeLab Electronics. His visual field was instantly flooded with bright lights, large text, and ominous music. Images of people being beaten and killed by law enforcement appeared on his left, while endless news articles on drug use and disparities in crime between the poor and rich scrolled on his right.

"Oh, this is terrible," he muttered, swallowing hard as he stared into the next flashing notification. "But I should learn more about this."

As he nodded his head or blinked his eyes to different areas of his visual field, more articles and videos surfaced. Each article painted the perpetrators of the worst crimes and the victims of the most heinous atrocities as people of darkness. Mugshots of individuals with darker skin were the only ones shown, ranging from murder to shoplifting and speeding. A red blinking notification appeared at the bottom right of the screen, capturing his attention. The screen was then taken over by a video of a GAIA police officer violently handcuffing someone from the South. The video had already reached two million views.

"OK," he said, feeling beads of sweat forming on his forehead, "just one more video before getting to work."

A notification to his left caught his eye. This video had three million views.

"Wow, never seen this one before!" he exclaimed. The video was titled "Patriot Payback" at the top. It showed a crowd of maybe a dozen light-skinned rioters burning and looting the homes of darker-skinned people. They group appeared organized, their actions were brutal, and the view count was skyrocketing. The comment section encouraged wannabe vigilantes to share their thoughts and pass along similar videos to others. The man's foot began to tap against the ground, and his heart raced with a mix of excitement and anxiety. After consuming his daily dose of the news, he was now prepared to work as a GAIA software programmer.

Not too far away, deeper in the metropolitan area, a business executive was on her break. She strolled past levitating vehicles and crowds of pedestrians, casually sipping on a nutritional supplement smoothie. Suddenly, a device caused her entire body to vibrate.

"Oh, I'd better see what's new today," she remarked, her face lacking any noticeable emotion.

Out came her viewscreen from her purse, and almost immediately, an army of ads assaulted her senses. Despite their flashy appeal and urgent notification chimes, she remained numb to their effects. A variety of products promising happiness, beauty, and freedom aggressively vied for attention on the screen.

"Same old, same old," she muttered to her device, continuing to walk. Then, something caught her eye. "Oh, what does this say? Major announcement?"

This product was different. It caught her attention more than the others. She nodded her head toward it, signaling her interest.

Five advertisements filled up the screen, each featuring the same exact product. It was a medication used for bleaching genomes, touted as being based on Markan technology, but customized for at-home use on Ziffea.

"Oh, it's from a different planet? I need to know more," she remarked out loud.

As she spoke, her device listened. Models displaying before-and-after shots paraded across the screen, while scientific-sounding announcers claimed that these products could bleach a person's epidermal properties to a light-blue shade and lighten hair follicles to an even paler color. The product was dubbed BetterThanBrown or BTB, and it was conveniently available at health food stores, pharmacies, beauty stores, and other establishments that catered to individuals concerned about their appearance, thanks to targeted search engine algorithms.

"Oh, that's strange," she muttered, attempting to close the advertisement. Despite her efforts, it stubbornly continued to loop and play. *Must be glitching again*, she thought to herself, slightly annoyed.

On the metanetworks, societal media played an integral role in popularizing BTB chemicals, hair straighteners, biochemical surgeries, and other products meant to change the natural genetic appearance of darker-skinned people. It only took a few days for the algorithms to influence search engine results with associations between words like "beauty" and images of emaciated, light-skinned models. Bleached societal media influencers racked up views like never before. Anyone could be touted as an epitome of beauty so long as they did not spend too much time out in the sun.

Fortunately, none of the members of Black Mountain used societal media. The way it tracked users made it too risky. The same could not be said for the various members of the Community. Even the most ardent supporters of Black Mountain gradually stopped passing by their camp at the beach. Food donations got less frequent. Mechanics and engineers who used to volunteer their tools and skills to Atkon stopped showing up. Supporters told Black Mountain they feared being threatened or extorted every time they left home. It seemed increasingly likely that no successor to the *Raven* would ever fly. The only supporters who were not obstructed were those who used advanced virtual machines and private networks to access the metanetworks.

One day, however, Atkon excitedly called Zoticon over. "Remember that Hydron clone that liquified and seeped through the ship until it made it right up to the bridge?"

"Yes, what about it?"

"Well, each time he regenerated, that gave me an opportunity to remap his aura."

"So what does that do for us?"

"I was running searches relating to what the scanners gave us about the mechanical code in his energy signature. Then I cross-referenced that with information received from our partners in the Community."

"Well?" Zoticon snapped. "What did you find?"

Atkon pouted. "AnansiBlu can explain."

Zoticon sighed. He turned to Anansi, who stood off to one side. "Well?"

She adjusted her glasses. "We found the location of Zi-Tai's headquarters."

Zoticon almost fell to his knees. This was far more than he'd expected to hear. He swallowed hard, struggling for once to compose himself. There were fewer things he was prouder of than his skill at hiding his emotions. He cleared his throat to give an appearance of calm professionalism. "Good."

"Good?" Ann appeared behind him. "This is wonderful! Come on, we have to share this with the team!"

"Show me what you got," Nani said. BlackBlob and FireArm stood beside each other ready to spar.

"Alright," FireArm launched toward her. "Take this—"

BAM.

FireArm was knocked to the ground so hard that he tumbled a few meters. Pushing his gloves into the ground, he jumped right back up to face his sparring partner.

"Wha'appen man? Yuh neva even touch mi." NaniMaroon waved above him with her boxing gloves and whimsically pranced through the air.

"Next!" she announced, grinning. "Ah weh yuh ago, kom back yah, Fiyah! Mi can tek on di two ah unnu rite now!"

BlackBlob charged at her. He threw punches that she easily parried before sending him twirling into the air and then onto the floor with a right hook. He landed with a thud, and FireArm went to his side to help him up.

"I don't get it. How do you hit so hard?"

"I'll tell you my secret, but you gotta fight me for it!"

She leapt into the air, hurdling into his direction. FireArm got to his feet and immediately jumped away. Nani drove her heel right into the spot he had just moved from. Her attack threw a cloud of dirt into the air.

"C'mon man! Ah wha unnu ah gwan wit'?!"

Nani was sparring with both of them at the same time. FireArm launched forward with controlled strikes, but she shifted out of his range. BlackBlob followed up with jabs from the left and fierce straight punches that were blocked and deflected just as quickly.

"Harder!"

Nani sped up, increasing the pressure on both of them. A series of light jabs psyched FireArm out. While he was disoriented, she switched over to take on BlackBlob, punishing his missed punches with a powerful front kick that sent him flying backward. Then, she spun around and went back to work on FireArm again, throwing jabs that forced him into a defensive position. When he covered his upper body, she instead drilled a left into his abdomen.

"Oof!" He stumbled backward.

"Harder! Why are you fighting?"

FireArm stepped closer and attempted to launch an uppercut—but missed. "What do you mean why am I—Oof!" Another body blow caused him to crumple. He took a few steps back and stumbled. Meanwhile, BlackBlob struggled to catch his breath.

"We don't have time to play around!" she yelled. "Think about it. Why are you two here?"

FireArm thought about the question. The words "I trust the universe" came back to his mind—not as an answer to her question but as a feeling in his spirit. He shook his gloves and got back into his fighting stance.

BlackBlob felt his breathing return to a steady rhythm. The words "I am brave" echoed in his mind. A feeling of excitement shot through his limbs. He jumped up, wound up his right arm, and went back into his peekaboo posture.

Both youths thought deeply on their purpose. Their eyes showed determination. Their movements carried a different kind of energy.

Nani advanced on them. They bobbed, weaved, and dodged all of her fists. She fired off attacks at them until the heat of her movements melted her gloves. "Yea man! Ah now unnu ah get it!" She laughed.

Suddenly, Nani could no longer dodge their punches. The image of planet Ziffea appeared in FireArm's eyes. He thought of other children like him, who would be going off to war and never have a chance to experience their childhood. BlackBlob thought of all the people who had been oppressed and held back from realizing their dreams. Both of them thought about the future and whose future it was meant to be. FireArm felt freedom in his heart and launched his right fist. BlackBlob felt a strong sense of belonging and channeled it into his left. Putting the will of the future into their fists made the force of the two punches finally break through her guard.

BANG!

Nani stumbled, and one of her knees hit the ground. She placed one of her hands, the glove on it destroyed, on her knee. "Woiieee," she squealed. "Lawd god, dat a 'ell of a *tump*!"

The two youths looked down at their gloves. The hands they had used to punch Nani were completely exposed, and the areas of impact around their gloves were corroded. FireArm's face was solemn but glowing as he stared at his exposed fist. BlackBlob gave a half smile and fist bumped his friend with the other glove.

Ann watched them from afar. A tear streamed down her face. "The time for justice has come," she said in a loud, clear voice. As if they had expected her, the three younger Fighters turned and looked at their teacher.

"We leave at sundown."

ANANSIBLU

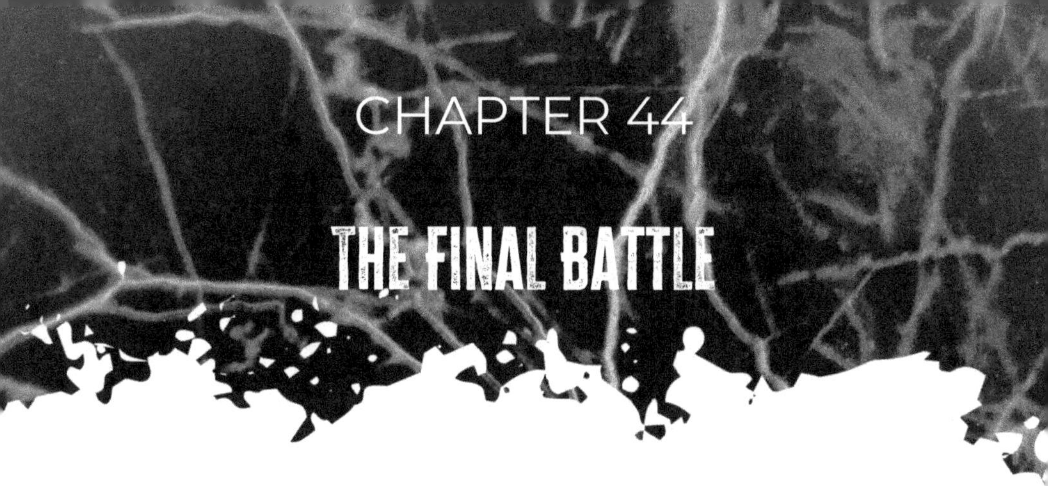

CHAPTER 44

THE FINAL BATTLE

"It's just as we expected," Zoticon whispered. "We have to inform the others."

AnnRoticon nodded. She walked over to the Fighters as they meditated around the fire. When she had told them earlier to get ready to leave at sundown, she had not anticipated the latest development. They would need the strength that meditation gave them even more now.

The meditation circle was nearly finished. Ann waited a moment, until she saw the Fighters' eyelids start to flutter.

"Not to interrupt you all..." she began.

"We've finished," said Anansi, looking up with a smile.

"Fighters. Zi-Tai has begun its full-scale invasion of the South."

FireArm opened his eyes and looked at her with determination. "Because they cannot find us, they are trying to exterminate support for our cause."

BlackBlob opened his eyes and exhaled with focus. "We now have no choice. Our mission moves from sabotage to annihilating the enemy."

Zoticon now came up behind AnnRoticon. He looked over at Atkon, who was still hunched over their portable viewscreen. "Atkon," he called. "Are you ready?"

Atkon, startled, turned toward the group, nodded, and picked up two suitcases lying on the sand beside them. "I tried to make the colors appropriate for the task at hand," they said, handing one suitcase to Zoticon and the other to Ann.

"Zoticon of Black Mountain North, these are the colors of red, black, and green. These outfits will fit the requirements of your squadron. Red is for the blood in our veins, black is for the people, and green is for the future." Zoticon took the suitcase and handed the clothes within to FireArm and BlackBlob.

"AnnRoticon of Black Mountain South, these are the colors of gold, black, and green. These outfits are based on the requirements of your squadron. Gold is for the sun above us, black is for the struggle for our people, and green is for the land that we cherish." Ann opened the suitcase, removed her outfit, and handed the remaining ones to Anansi and Nani.

"I was only able to save a few books from the library," Atkon explained, "but these are colors that held significance for revolutionaries a long time ago. I wove in metal fragments from the *Raven* so that she could guide and protect you on this mission. Please change as soon as you can. I will lead the way once you are ready."

The other members of the team thanked them. Handling the heavy fabric for the first time and hearing about the significance of the colors gave FireArm a strange sense of déjà vu. It was as if he had heard these words before, but in a past life. He changed into the clothes and stood for a moment in front of the mirror. The design perfectly matched his vision from a few days earlier. It was a loose-fitting black jumpsuit with baggy legs and open sleeves. Where the sleeves opened, and where the bottom hem of the pant leg was rolled up, were reddish-orange designs. On both sleeves, two extensions of the material pointed out like four featherless wings. Each of these burning wings was intended to counter the corresponding threat from Zi-Tai. He felt a new sense of elation, one that connected him to generations of his forebears.

FireArm looked at Zoticon. After the elder Fighter put on his red vest, he extinguished the fires, thanked the land for hosting them, and asked Her to forgive the damage that the Zlon had caused to the environment. Were those tears in his eyes? He was search through the broken pieces of the *Raven* that had washed up on the shore. They would not be able to bring these remnants with them. They would have to leave everything behind. FireArm now realized that Zoticon might have always had a sensitive side, but this was the first time he'd shown it so openly. He reflected on what might have caused this change. FireArm thought about the night before.

"Hah!" BlackBlob launched a series of punches.

"C'mon!" FireArm caught each and every one of them.

They took turns practicing combinations on each other. They moved with the fluidity of machines. No, even better than that. Their precision transcended anything a mekanation could ever achieve. Their routine took them to the sky, to the ground, and pushed every cell of their bodies to the limit. FireArm knew they were at their best; they operated as a single unit. Now, without a doubt, he believed they were ready to strike back.

After their sparring match, he and BlackBlob had seen Zoticon pouring a liquid from a bottle onto a piece of scrap metal from the ship. The three moons shone high above the old man, reflecting a silvery light off the parts of the water not covered with pollution and dead plant life.

"Sir?" BlackBlob couldn't help himself.

FireArm looked at his partner in shock. BlackBlob dared to disturb this man? FireArm readied himself for a scolding.

But nothing of that nature came out. Zoticon turned to face them, but there was no upset in his face. It was almost as if he had expected them to be here and to see him doing this. His eyes looked different. He spoke slowly to them as the liquid continued to fall. "This is called *libation*," he said. "Long ago, our ancestors did this to honor those who transitioned to the next realm."

The last drop hit the sand. The two youths walked toward him. They saw now what he had been pouring the liquid onto.

FireArm was startled. "What? This can't be!"

BlackBlob was stunned too. "For real?" he exclaimed.

The liquid had fallen on a physical photo. Somehow, a photo of Willo and Blaze had turned up among the wreckage. They looked the same age as they always had, but their smiles were genuine; they had still been a team when the photo was taken. It must have been years ago, FireArm thought, when they first joined Black Mountain.

Zoticon looked at the picture without picking it up. "They were my students," he said. "May their souls find peace," He looked at FireArm and BlackBlob. "I did not know I would lose them, at least not yet." Suddenly, he stopped in his tracks. Frozen, seemingly in deep thought. And then his eyes opened wide. "Wait. Could it be?" He gazed out over the water for a moment, then turned back to his young students. "The oracle must have known this all along."

"The oracle?" FireArm asked.

"Yes, she was the one who let us know we would find the both of you. You two were selected for this. The oracle knew Willo and Blaze would not make it."

"Whaat?" BlackBlob blurted out. He covered his mouth, not intending to voice his surprise so loudly.

"As Fighters," Zoticon explained, "we have powers of chrono-spatial manipulation, as Anansi must have explained during your orientation. The oracles have an even greater mastery over their six powers. Not only can they use our techniques, they can even see the end before the beginning."

"But why are you only telling us this now?" FireArm asked

Zoticon stared sternly at him. "I'm not like Ann, I don't believe in fate. We only make good decisions or bad ones. I didn't want some prophecy to get to your heads, but now... Well, I figured it's now or never."

BlackBlob and FireArm looked at each other.

"We have been fighting Zi-Tai for some time," Zoticon went on. "We have lost a lot of students. When AnnRoticon communed with the oracle, she was seeking an answer to how we could finish Zi-Tai once and for all." He looked toward the stars. "It was our master teacher who called us Black Mountain. Our purpose is to bring the planet to its highest point, even though we come from its darkest soil. We inherited his dream to rid the world of suffering." He clenched his fist. "I say this now so you understand that there will be a time—in the very near future—where it will be up to you, the both of you, to save this world.

"Don't let your inner doubts get to you," he added, looking straight at FireArm. He stepped forward and put a fist to the young man's heart. "Trust the universe." Then he took a step to the side and pressed a fist to BlackBlob's chest. "Be brave."

He looked at the picture on the ground again. "Honor the sacrifices of those who came before you. Even if you didn't know them like I did, just know we would not be here without them."

Now, watching Zoticon put out the fires and give thanks to the land, FireArm thought back to that moment in the night. He was still thinking about it a little later as he stood in line with the rest of the squad.

Zoticon, AnnRoticon, and Atkon looked at the four soldiers lined up in front of them, proud and powerful in their new uniforms.

Together, three voices yelled, "Affirm!"

Four voices called back. "Defeat the enemy wherever he appears!"

Atkon decisively pressed a key on their handheld device. "The final battle begins. Let's go!"

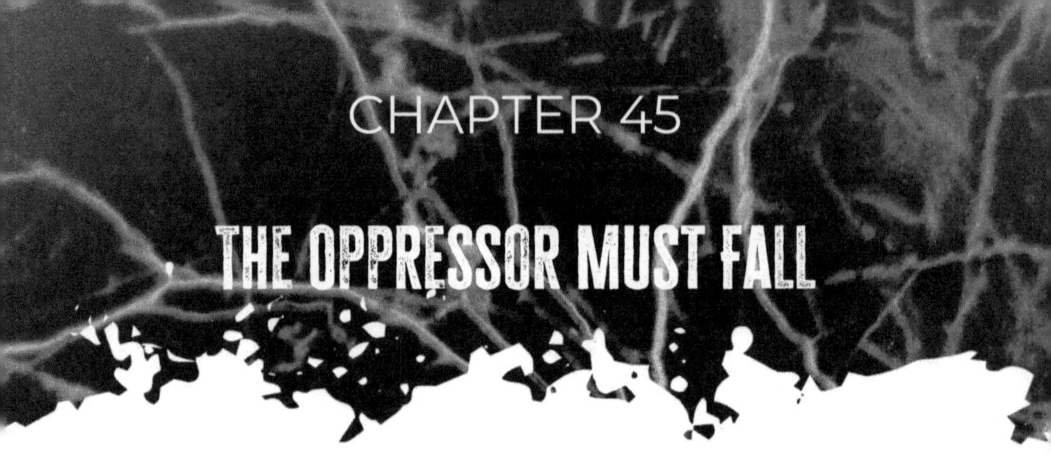

CHAPTER 45

THE OPPRESSOR MUST FALL

Bending their knees, Atkon pushed off the sand and flew straight into the air. The two squadrons followed suit, forming V-shapes on either side of him. They soared full speed ahead into the air, penetrating the clouds, soaring toward the North to confront the enemy of the world.

FireArm's thoughts wandered. Had his training really been enough for the final battle? Had he changed enough? Would his traumatic past rise up again in the heat of battle and cripple him? He could not voice his concerns. The team's speed of travel made the wind too loud. This wasn't the time to play around, anyway. He couldn't let his doubts weigh down the rest of the team. With his worries slightly more under control, his thoughts drifted to their supporters. *What would happen to the Community? Would they survive? Would Black Mountain's efforts really change anything? Would any of them make it out alive?*

He looked below and saw the clouds. He looked above and saw the stars. His eyes went to his left, and he saw BlackBlob. His friend turned his head and gave a nod. That was what he needed. In that moment, FireArm felt that he was no longer alone in his thoughts. He looked ahead and saw Zoticon. He reflected on how many battles the elder Fighter must have survived, how many he must have thought would be his last. He saw Zoticon turn and nod his head as well. Startled, he wondered if his mind was being read. But no, this level of synchronization with the team was what they had all been working toward from the beginning. They were on their way to put an end to the enemy that had taken away Zoticon's home and now threatened this planet. He could feel the power in his fists. He would bring that power to Zi-Tai.

BlackBlob, too, was thinking about the lives that needed to be saved. He thought of all the nameless supporters who had sacrificed resources to help them. Some of them may have been related to his own parents. He thought about how he would make the world a better place for the next generation. *By any means necessary.*

It did not take them long to cover the distance between the two continents. The strong wind behind them seemed like divine providence, but the mission became perilous as they reached the North. The Fighters lit up the sky like comets. Without the *Raven*'s cloaking, they could be sighted and targeted from any direction. This would not be a stealth mission, but an all-out war. The world was watching, and so were their enemies.

Almost as soon as they crossed into the North, anti-aircraft fire lit up the sky like a wall of candles ahead of them. "Shields up!" cried Zoticon.

Atkon flew a little lower and surrounded them with a wide electromagnetic shield to block the projectiles, but they could not protect them completely. There was too much fire from below. Atkon's shield could only reduce the chances of someone on the team being hit by the overwhelming barrage.

Zoticon's squadron broke off to the left and danced through the maze of bullets. AnnRoticon's team banked to the right. Zi-Tai's new anti-matter technology, which had destroyed Willo and Blaze, was on all their minds. Each Fighter knew the risk, knew that the slightest miscalculation could end the mission. Zoticon yelled with all his might, "Return fire!"

Atkon dropped the shield, providing the opportunity for the team to go all-out. While swooping in and out of harm's way, each Fighter focused on as many targets as they could. They created mental pictures of the trajectory, location, and orientation of each cannon. After setting their intention and charging their spiritual energy, a bombardment of rainbow rays of light homed in on their targets. Explosions shattered windows and blew wreckage far up into the air.

Dozens of targets were evaporated in a matter of seconds, silencing the ground artillery and leaving a trail of flames, craters, and indistinguishable metal parts lying in the streets. The only lights visible were the streetlamps and the multitude of fireworks that fell onto the city below, and the only sound to be heard was the seven Fighters cutting through the wind. The results of their training were evident. Not a single civilian was touched, but every hostile mekanation met its fate.

>*The tower is directly ahead!*< Atkon spoke into the fleet's mind as loudly as they could. Even if the Fighters could not see it, they felt the pressure inside them, telling them the target was near.

The oppressor of the planet would fall that night, or all would be lost.

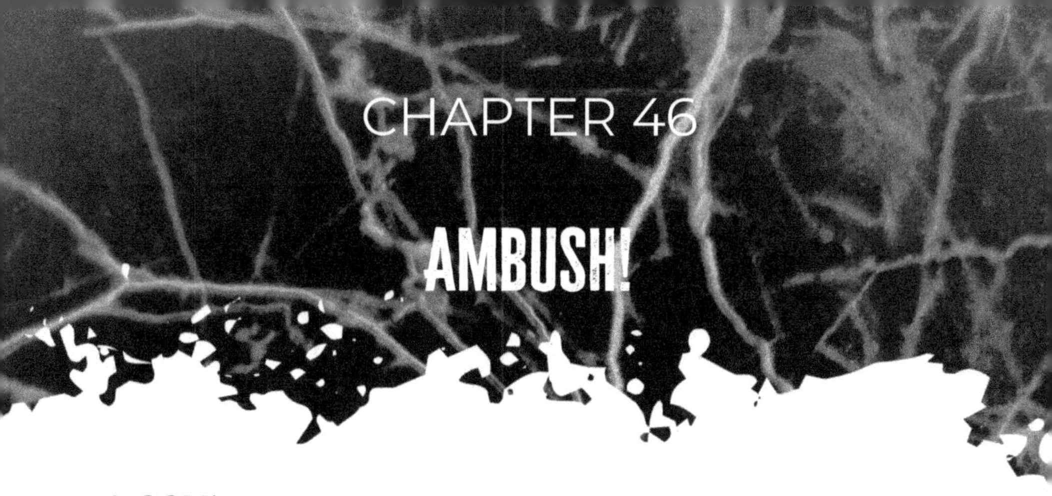

CHAPTER 46

AMBUSH!

FOOM!

As the Fighters descended, the skyline came into view. Steel skyscrapers gleamed in the moonlight and seemed to rise up in defiance, but FireArm and the rest of the team blew past them, shaking the windows, challenging their dominance of the skies and making even the streetlamps wave to and fro. In the lead, Atkon dodged barriers and dead ends, guided by downloaded urban sprawl maps provided by the Community's best hackers. On the inside of their eyes, Atkon saw colored markers and points of guidance indicating the exact location of the enemy's headquarters. As they flew through the night, the trail of their auras glimmered overhead, like lines of neon light stretching into the distance.

Suddenly, they came to a maze of overpasses, roads, and highways. On their right, plasma-thrust assault choppers weaved between the passing buildings, flickering in and out of sight. They flew parallel to the Fighters, avoiding contact for the moment. FireArm watched them with caution. Were they preparing an ambush? Was the team heading exactly where the enemy wanted them to go?

<*I got this!*> Anansi communicated telepathically to the team, soaring high above the formation to gain a bird's eye view of their stalkers. She rose high and looked down at them from the height of the skyscrapers. They were traveling together, perfectly coordinated like a school of fish. She leaned to the right, and from her hands rained down a multitude of tree-trunk sized icicles that impaled cockpits, ruptured engines, and sent rotors spinning through empty roads. In the space of a moment, their pursuers were devastated. Clouds of smoke and fire littered the pavement. Anansi, still flying higher than the rest, spotted a

line of armored vehicles assembling up ahead. Putting her fingers toward her temple, she transmitted a message to Atkon.

<*Graviton battle tanks up ahead! That's what those copters were waiting for!*>

Atkon, in turn, relayed the message to Nani.

<*Mi agu mash dem up!*> she mentally conveyed as she sped ahead, surrounding herself in a red aura. She burst through the air and sent a shockwave through the streets below, racing past rail tracks, fuel depots, and storage facilities, then into an open parking area. As she broke into the launchers' line of sight, their turrets swiveled toward her and fired volley after volley of powerful munitions. They punched holes through the buildings behind her as she weaved and bobbed. She quickly glanced behind herself. The buildings she'd passed looked like steel cheese graters.

FireArm saw the damage too. *They look like apartment buildings,* he thought. They must have been full of civilians at this time of day, but Zi-Tai's forces had never cared about collateral damage to people or to the environment. *They will end up blaming this on us again. We have to stop them!*

Seeing the devastation, Nani turned to face the incoming threat. Toward the wind, she yelled, "Ah wha unnu a gwan wid? Tek dis!"

She descended sharply, slamming the ground and running as fast as she could, keeping as low as she could. She rushed toward the enemy while a barrage of amber bullets tore through the air above her, each barely missing and only making her increase her speed. She kept running. The force of her feet hitting the pavement left craters in the ground. Dirt, debris, and pieces of white motherboard tiles shot into the air behind her until she reached the first graviton battle tank. She forced a fistful of fire clear through it. *BAM.* Then the second. *BAM.* Then the third. *BAM.* Soon, she had melted through all twenty of them. Explosions lined up behind her until she leapt into the air once again to rejoin the formation.

They continued their flight through the enemy lines until they approached a clearing entirely made up of motherboard tiles. Up ahead, a tower loomed on the horizon. There it is, FireArm said to himself, just as Atkon announced, "Dense cluster of enemies detected."

The buildings around them grew smaller, and they flew into one of the dense city's few remaining open spaces, preserved to keep a buffer between the populated districts and the army base they were now approaching. As the fleet pressed on, two giant black spheres appeared in the distance on either side. They floated ominously with deep humming noises and loomed over the white landscape lit up with the lights of thousands of motherboards. Each sphere was the size of a stadium. All around their circumferences were silver hatches. One by one, each hatch opened, and packs of aerial armored drones poured out of them, blotting out the night sky and hiding the three moons.

The top of a third sphere rose before the tower in the distance, but this one did not leave the ground, only rising until its hatches lined up with the terrain. The hatches opened and armies of tanks and mechanized infantry poured out, launching barrages of mortar shells, rockets, and energy weapons in the direction of the fighters.

<*Shields!*>

Atkon generated a large field of energy once again, forming a four-story wall of energy ahead of the Fighters. This shield penetrated the screen of flashing lights and explosive material and plowed through the artillery and ammunition.

Still, the sheer number of them required drastic measures. <*Ann,*> Zoticon communicated to his sister, <*we need your critical strike for this.*>

At once, her body began glowing from her crown to the base of her spine. A glorious light emerged from her hands, rivaling the combined brightness of the moons above. The power of her focus caused ripples to form in the clothing of all of her comrades and wind currents to push waves through own her cape and garment. <*Cover me, Anan, Nani! Take out the one in the front!*>

<*Affirmed!*> Anansi and Nani sped ahead to confront the ground forces. They stayed low, dancing through the air and evading enemy fire while hurling rapid beams of soulforce energy toward the encroaching army. Above them, Atkon led the way, providing cover for FireArm and BlackBlob.

As they sped forward together, AnnRoticon braked in the air. Zoticon pulled up beside her. "Just like old times?"

"Just like old times."

Steeled by the memory of losing the fight against Zi-Tai on their home planet, Marka, determined not to let history repeat itself, intent on righteous revenge, AnnRoticon stretched out both her arms in opposite directions. One hand faced the orb to the west, the other aimed to the east. A bright light emanated from each hand, and boulder-sized swirls of energy coalesced around her palms.

By now, the swarm of drones had grown and were on the verge of closing in. Zoticon placed his open left palm ahead of himself and his right palm out to the side. A dark-purple energy swirled out and formed what looked like blades the length of short swords ahead of his fingertips. His movements defied reality. Even before he moved, dozens of drones had evaporated in explosions. The sheer speed and force with which he swung his forearms created a space that prevented any of the drones from getting within ten meters of AnnRoticon, while at the same time slicing and destroying any mechanized enemy that even approached that range. The blades cut and diced scrap metal, defeating countless enemies and protecting his sister. The empty circle around AnnRoticon gave her plenty of space to charge her attack.

"Ready?" Zoticon asked.

"Ready."

Zoticon jumped as far and as fast away from her as he could. As the drones started to close in on her, AnnRoticon yelled at the top of her lungs. "Critical Strike: The Light of Khonsu!"

The ground trembled and cracked into hundreds of pieces. Even at a distance, FireArm and BlackBlob had to close their eyes to the blinding light that emanated from behind them. When the blaze subsided, FireArm turned around and tried to make out what he could amid the torrent of destruction. The two black spheres were slowly sinking toward the ground. Each had a gigantic rupture in the center. The shredded interiors of the holes left the motherships looking like two gigantic tires in the sky. They crashed to the ground, throwing up huge piles of dirt amid large plumes of smoke and a storm of mechanical debris.

>*Keep your eyes on the road, gentlemen,*< Atkon cautioned. >*The light will blind you.*<

<*Oh, ri-right!*>

FireArm and BlackBlob turned around to face what lay ahead.

Looming in front of them rose the final target.

NANIMAROON

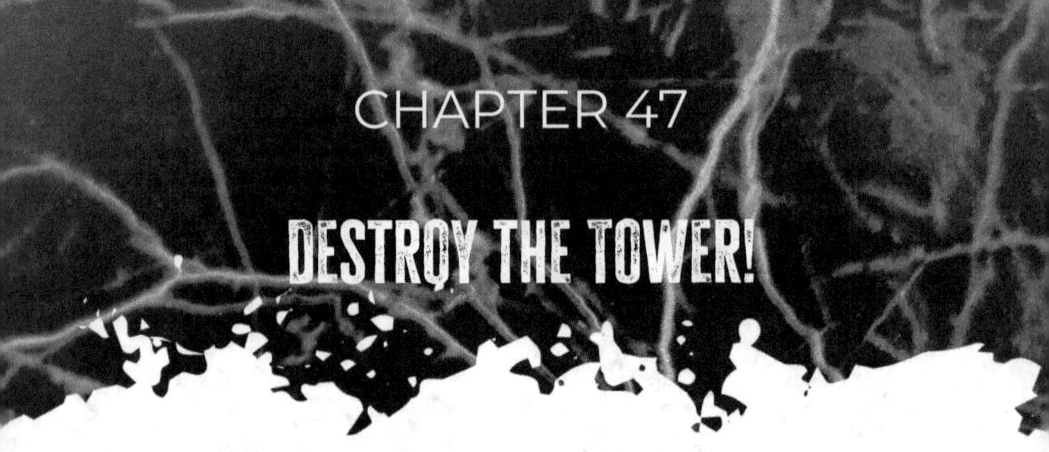

CHAPTER 47

DESTROY THE TOWER!

"Fire, there it is!"

The tower lay directly ahead of them, its thirty stories pointed straight toward the sky. There, the Fighters would find the enemy of the world, the base of operations for the military wing of Zi-Tai. This was the central command for the attack on the South. Somewhere deep in the bowels of the tower was the C.O.R.E., the central generator that controlled Zi-Tai's whole network of motherboards. Destroying it would not only put an end to the invasion of the South but also cripple Zi-Tai's control over the North. If they could find and destroy it, it would mean the beginning of the end of Zi-Tai's whole planetary project.

But it wasn't going to be easy. The tower was the most heavily fortified site in all of Ziffea, but as Zoticon and the team now realized, this was the mission the oracle had picked FireArm and BlackBlob for.

"Daahlin, let's do this!"

Anansi and Nani broke off in opposite directions to encircle the enemy's main line of defense. They maneuvered skillfully and with agility, avoiding enemy fire while protecting themselves with soulforce shields. Anansi launched freezing shockwaves that ripped through the ground and made it impossible for the armored vehicles to aim straight. As the motherboards beneath them ruptured, an intense frost took over, freezing the ground troops in place. On the other side of the tower, Nani surrounded herself with a mass of intense heat that disintegrated the ground beneath her. As she smashed through their defenses, her punches created seismic waves that ruptured the ground and swallowed the mekanations and the smaller vehicles. Then she sped through the larger mechanical foes like lightning striking through the sky. Beneath the remaining Fighters, explosions erupted all over the tower's grounds.

The enemies' defenses were waning and they were no longer the main targets of the anti-air gunfire. Atkon lowered their shield and spoke without telepathy. "From here on, you will be on your own," they warned.

"But what are we supposed to do *on our own*?" FireArm asked.

"See the tower?"

"Yeah."

"Destroy the C.O.R.E.."

"Destroy the C.O.R.E.?"

Before Atkon could explain, a swarm of mekanations that resembled Hydron clones burst out of the tower and rushed toward them. "I'll take them on," Atkon said. "You two must continue the mission!"

Atkon fired into the swarm and peeled away from FireArm and BlackBlob, luring the mekanations away from the two youths as they continued to fly toward the tower. They fired surges of electrical current into several of them at a time. For a moment, they looked badly damaged. Then they rotated their bodies, reconstituted themselves, and resumed their pursuit.

FireArm could hardly believe his eyes. These were the same kinds of clones that had invaded the *Raven* with Willo. How could machines still function after getting hit with 100,000 volts of Atkon's soulforce? *No time to question it,* he thought to himself. *Just defeat the enemy!*

Behind him, he watched Atkon engage at close quarters with dozens of the clones. They fought exactly like Willo. Some fired blasts from their arms. Others got in close enough to throw punches. Atkon kept all of them at bay until the sheer number of attacks overwhelmed them, with punches and swarming attacks that became impossible to block or deflect.

"Atkon!" BlackBlob shouted, looking back at the midair fist fight.

BZZZTT!

From within the swarm came a big blast of blue electrical energy. Atkon's body was surrounded with a sphere of lightning and shockwaves, which vaporized the attackers where they stood. They did not regenerate. Atkon emerged from the sphere of energy unharmed, then spoke into BlackBlob's mind. <*Don't worry about us. Fight for the people! Fight for the planet*!>

"Right!"

"Let's go!"

CHAPTER 47 | DESTROY THE TOWER!

BlackBlob and FireArm pressed on, aiming for the top of the tower. That would be where it was most vulnerable. If they could gain entry from the roof, they could proceed to the core somewhere down below from inside the tower's defenses. As they neared the roof, they saw a large capsule elevator begin to quickly descend into the center of the building from what appeared to be a penthouse.

"Fire," BlackBlob smiled nervously, "this is it."

FireArm looked back at him. "We gotta completely destroy everything!"

"Let's get to work!"

Their bodies became charged with light. Glowing with their auras, they flew to the top of the ivory-colored tower. The penthouse was in complete disarray. Broken computer pieces and other bits of technology littered the floor.

"Shyaah!" FireArm let loose a stream of kicks to one side of the building. Each kick beat out like the flap of a hummingbird. Every time he lifted his leg, flames shot from his feet, melting through reinforced steel and turning the concrete into rubble and dust. His fiery soulforce carried a deep black aura of determination.

"Oraaah!" BlackBlob, meanwhile, flew to the other side of the building and fired a barrage of fists loaded with an equally dark flow of energy. His punches left craters and eroded the walls with a force like the ocean. Each punch shot shockwaves through the structure. Columns collapsed, and large fragments of the building fell to the streets below.

They hit the building with all their might until the whole structure collapsed under the sheer force of their blows. Dust clouds arose from the demolition. As the dust dispersed, it revealed a large, dark sinkhole. The two dove toward it, then froze in midair. At least a kilometer of the tower remained intact below the ground!

"We ain't done yet," FireArm yelled.

"Find the core," replied BlackBlob, "and destroy it!"

They nose-dived into the center of the underground tower. The inside was flowing with luminescence and energy, brightening and dimming at a rhythmic pace. They charged deep into it at full speed. Power cords and cables that had fallen from above lay in disarray everywhere, and live wires waved and whipped around the two young Fighters as they descended.

They surrounded themselves with protective auras and flew parallel to where the elevator shaft had been. It was now empty and inoperable due to the destruction above. They dodged pieces of stray debris while diving down into the bowels of structure. As they plunged deeper into the heart of the tower, deeper into the planet, they broke through to a large, open, cylindrical room. They looked below. They had finally found it. The Central Operating Resource Engine. The C.O.R.E. Protected by a thick layer of tempered glass, a huge orb pulsated with a force that alternately shone blue and white. Large ripples of energy were visible at its center.

"Look!" BlackBlob called to FireArm. "This must be how they steal the energy of the whole planet, it's just like Uncle Zot taught us!"

The orb was about the same size as the black orbs that had housed the enemies above, but this orb was brimming with light and seemed to be planted firmly in the bottom of the room. Debris from the destroyed tower had landed on some of the computer equipment around the base of the orb. The walls and what was left of the ceiling were covered in motherboards that emitted an almost blinding glow.

BlackBlob and FireArm descended cautiously to about halfway to the bottom of the room, then hovered right above the C.O.R.E. They focused their energy on destroying it, but there was no telling how it might react. If they were lucky, it would crumble to nothing, but for all the two Fighters knew, it might explode and take them with it. Given its reputed power, it might take the whole city with it. All they knew was that it had to be destroyed.

Intent on their mission, neither youth heard the huge steel door open below them or saw the flying exosuit of armor that rushed up until the three-story silver threat was almost upon them.

The colossal figure was encased in thick sheets of metal alloy that glimmered in the reflective light of the orb. It carried a long, laser rifle about ten meters long, but instead of attacking them at once, it used booster jets on its feet to rush up past them. Inexplicably, it then stopped and hovered above, as if studying them.

Peering up, the two Fighters saw the dark silhouette of a pilot seated in the middle of the craft, protected by a thick, tinted windshield. The giant suit moved gracefully through the air. As they watched, its right arm lowered the laser rifle away from them while the palm of its left hand stretched toward them as if signaling for them to stop.

FireArm assumed a fighting position. “The hell is this guy?”

BlackBlob went into his. “And why isn’t he attacking us right away?”

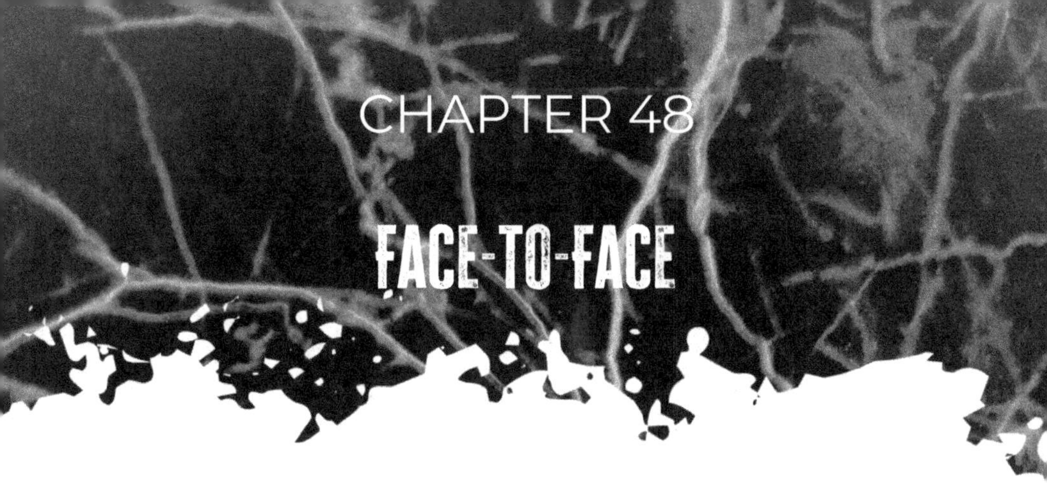

CHAPTER 48

FACE-TO-FACE

For a moment, the two Fighters stared at the armored exosuit. The three floated in the air. Nobody moved. No one said anything, but FireArm had a heavy feeling in his heart. The pilot of that machine was the only thing between them and their goal, and whoever they had not come in peace. But what was the raised hand all about? Was he telling them to stop? Why? Would destroying the orb come with unintended consequences? Were they about to destroy the planet they wanted to save?

Suddenly, the silence was broken by a deep, harsh voice that echoed throughout the underground complex.

"Get out of here immediately. You don't know what you're doing."

"Why should we stop?" BlackBlob yelled back.

"If you destroy the C.O.R.E., you will have made yourselves the enemies of the people."

The enemies of the people. Where had FireArm heard that before? Yes, it was what they called the Fighters back at the orphanage. Memories flooded into his mind—mekkies showing them pictures of "terrorists" destroying infrastructure, supposedly killing people indiscriminately. He thought back to his doubts when he had first been brought aboard the *Raven.* Then he thought about how they had reached this core. *Didn't we nearly destroy a city to get here? Are we really the saviors we've been told we are?*

He is right. Look at the devastation you caused. We are the terrorists, after all.

FireArm placed his hands onto his head. The voices in his mind had returned. They had not finished tormenting him. As if sensing his doubts, BlackBlob looked toward his comrade and yelled, "Fire!"

CHAPTER 48 | FACE-TO-FACE

Phutais had been watching the two young Fighters carefully from the cockpit of the large combat exosuit that encased his body. He had always governed more by shrewdness and cunning than by force. *That one doubts his conscience,* he told himself. *I could put holes through them right now, but they are too close to the C.O.R.E.. If that blows up, it's all over.*

The mechanized suit holds out its left hand and gestures diplomatically. "Why do you want to disturb the peace that we have built here? You are not the saviors of this planet. *We* are. We put an end to war, and now you want to start another?"

BlackBlob sensed his companion weakening. He couldn't let that happen. He stared straight at their enemy. "You're the ones ruining the world," BlackBlob shouted with tears in his eyes. "You poisoned the water, and you're ruining everyone's lives. You're not bringing peace, you're turning the planet into a giant waste dump!"

Blob is wrong. Who will believe that you fought for justice when you destroyed a city? Are you really sure you didn't kill any civilians?

FireArm slammed his hands into his forehead. "Stop it!" he yelled.

Phutais smiled. "*If I defeat him psychologically, he will be no threat physically,*" he said to himself.

BlackBlob looked back at his friend. He couldn't give up. Not now. He had to be brave! He pointed decisively at his adversary. "We are fighting for our future generations," he yelled.

Phutais thought, *You don't deserve to reproduce.* But out loud, he replied, "We are fighting for world peace."

"So why do you got so many drones, tanks, and anti-matter bombs, then?" BlackBlob shot back.

Phutais looked at the dashboard of his craft and glanced to the left of his console. A video screen showed that the number of drones and tanks on the battlefield was steadily decreasing. Red numbers lit up on the console with X marks over the spherical battleships and reinforcements.

BAM.

Phutais slammed his hand into it, and the screen shut down. The force of the blow made his whole metal suit wave and shake in the air. His frustration and rage filtered through to his piloted machine. The armor's hand clenched into a fist that shook with fury.

FireArm saw this external sign of the pilot's anger. Wait, he told himself. Something is not right about this guy. His words don't match his actions.

No. Don't think about that. You're the only crazy one here.

The voice grew louder. FireArm breathed in and exhaled, silencing it. For the moment, at least. He closed his fists and struggled to maintain his composure.

BlackBlob watched. "He's trying to get into our heads!" he shouted at his friend. "Fight it off, bro!"

"Enough!" yelled their enemy. He aimed the laser rifle at them. "If you get in the way of our future, you will join your ancestors!"

BlackBlob's eyes grew wide. His aura increased with the strength of a waterfall. "Oh, you don't want this smoke," he yelled back at the giant machine, then he turned back to his partner. "FireArm, deal with the C.O.R.E., this dude's right about to get folded!"

"Sorry, Blob," FireArm shouted back. Then he burst into tears. "I... I *can't*."

"You can't? What are you—? OOF!"

The enemy's flying suit burst toward them, smashing into BlackBlob and sending him flying toward the wall. He slammed into the white, plated surface but partially broke his impact with his feet. THUNK. Large slabs of metal fell toward the equipment that surrounded the base of the C.O.R.E.

"Ugh, how could a thing that big move that fast?"

Leaving the dazed Fighter alone for a moment, the metal armor turned its attention to FireArm. Seeing this, BlackBlob tried to warn his distracted comrade. "Get out of the way!"

BAM.

Before FireArm could look up, a backhand from the giant machine tossed him spinning through the air. He slammed into the metal slabs and was half-buried in his own imprint on it.

"I will deal with you first," the voice announced from the loudspeakers. "There is no room for the weak in our future." The craft pointed its rifle toward FireArm, still stuck inside the mangled wall.

"Nah, not gonna happen," came BlackBlob's determined voice.

Time stopped. BlackBlob charged toward the machine and hurled a closed left fist at its metal arm. It passed through effortlessly. When time resumed, fragments of metal wire and mechanical components were flying through the air. The severed arm still gripped the rifle as it tumbled down and cracked the protective glass around the C.O.R.E.

Watching this, Phutais felt something. Something he hadn't felt for a very long time. What was this? Fear?

FireArm's jaw fell open and his eyes widened. He could only stare at the damaged machine. "Blob!" he yelled.

"What?"

"You did the invisible magician thing!"

"I did?"

"You fools!" Phutais sneered, recovering his composure. These two children weren't going to stop him. It was unthinkable. He directed the machine's left hand at Blob, sending him flying with an open palm. Swiftly, the machine then retracted its hand to reveal the barrel of a cannon that fired a powerful surge of electricity toward the two Fighters.

"What do you call it? Uh? Protection!" At the last moment, BlackBlob formed a shield of soulforce around himself and his companion. The cannon fired torrents and torrents of energy into the shield, but with each barrage, its barrel peeled and ripped a little more, unable to withstand the sheer force of its own blasts.

"FireArm, don't listen to him, just fight back!"

BlackBlob grabbed FireArm's collar and launched a fierce back kick into the protective shield. It propelled itself straight toward the giant craft, exploding its left arm. As the exosuit recoiled from the impact, screws and bolts from the disintegrating arm flew into the cockpit's windscreen. The reinforced glass could not be shattered, but the result was worse. It was instantly covered with a maze of tiny threads that prevented the stunned pilot from seeing out of it.

"Lemme get you outta there," BlackBlob told FireArm while the mobile armor was momentarily distracted.

THUNK.

Several pieces of the motherboard collided with the floor below. Some of them fell and further cracked the protective glass of the C.O.R.E., but FireArm was dislodged from the wall.

"Bro, we *need* you!"

"I know, man."

"Tell me what's going on!"

Don't say a thing. He will reject you. He will hurt you.

Along with the mocking voice, lashes of past memories invaded FireArm's psyche. A glimpse of a tiny, younger version of himself came into his mind. The child reached a hand out to him, and he reached a hand back—but before they could touch, the image vanished. FireArm focused on his breath again, and his mind grew still. The voice momentarily receded.

"Dude, listen," he said, looking at BlackBlob, "I've got all these voices in my head."

"Bruh," BlackBlob replied, looking earnestly into his friend's eyes, "we *all* got voices in our heads. C'mon, man!"

FireArm looked at him in disbelief. Was this true? Did it mean he wasn't crazy? That his mind was not the problem?

"Your therapy session is over!" The protective windshield of the mobile armor flipped open as its pilot knocked it loose and jumped out. As soon as the man left it, the exosuit flew toward the Fighters at full speed. At the last minute, BlackBlob pulled FireArm out of the way, and it exploded on contact with the wall of motherboards. Loads of metal slabs tumbled to the ground. The two Fighters regained their position in the air and looked back at their enemy. He was floating in midair.

"Wait, what?" BlackBlob exclaimed, his jaw hanging open. *It can't be,* FireArm thought to himself. *He's a Fighter, too?*

Frustration, surprise, and confusion ambushed the minds of the two youths. Had this man once completed an initiation ritual like they had? If so, how could he use these sacred powers to enslave people instead of freeing them? The answer to these questions would need to wait, FireArm told himself. The team was still fighting overhead, and he and BlackBlob had a job to do. He focused on his breath and focused on his target.

The enemy's lanky body was well-toned and covered entirely in metal. He raised his three-fingered fists ahead of himself, his fighting stance exuding the confidence of more than a century of combat training. His white technogarment and mask shone like polished silver. Two rows of small packages formed a red X on his chest. He reached into one of these and extracted a syringe. "It's time to do away with you pests," he yelled as he injected the syringe into his neck.

BOOM.

A surge of soulforce energy flooded the area. A bright gray light emanated from him. His muscles strained against his technogarment and stretched it to its limits. With a grin, he gazed at his opponents, raised his head in the air, and shouted with a voice that echoed throughout the room, "LIGHT POWER!"

CHAPTER 49

DEFEAT THE ENEMY

BlackBlob's eyes grew wide. FireArm closed his fists to stop them from shaking. Their adversary was swirling with white energy, and his aura grew larger with each second, reflecting like a second sun off the shiny white slabs of motherboard that lined the room. The only clearly visible structure in the blinding light was the blue orb that continued to pulse at the bottom of the room.

After a moment, the brightness of the enemy's aura shrank into a more concentrated glow around his solar plexus. BlackBlob was nearly overwhelmed by the force of his enemy's aura. His legs shook. *Snap out of it!* he told himself. He shook his head and remembered his training, then put his arms in an X position across his chest. "I am *brave*!" he yelled as a swirling haze of pulsating black and blue energy enveloped him. A few seconds later, it shot out like a cyclone around him. His fists clenched and, fighting stance intact, he launched himself toward the enemy. He threw a rapid flurry of his best punches at his opponent—who effortlessly blocked them.

"Useless!" he yelled in triumph as he parried BlackBlob's attacks. "Is that your best?"

The masked menace took the offensive with a side thrust kick to the chest that sent BlackBlob flying back into the wall. The young Fighter changed course midair and broke the impact with his feet, smashing through a whole row of motherboards that tumbled toward the C.O.R.E.. Undeterred, he leapt from the wall and charged right back at his adversary.

BlackBlob threw another flurry of punches as he closed in on him, but this time he augmented them with an extra measure of soulforce. Surging masses of energy splashed against his opponent without damaging him. BlackBlob threw more punches, but each one was deflected or blocked with one single open palm. No matter where he punched, his blows were absorbed or deflected.

"None of your attacks can harm me," snarled the enemy Fighter. From his other hand, he produced an explosion of energy that went off like a grenade. BlackBlob dodged it just in time, then retreated some distance and raised his left hand to fire a blast. Just then, another explosion knocked the hand away.

"Ack! What? I can't even aim at him?" he exclaimed.

The authoritarian let out a guffaw. "You fool. Your weak spirit means nothing to my superior technology."

BlackBlob shook off the pain from his bruised hand. His glove had been completely destroyed. "If a fist fight is what you want, that's what you'll get!" he declared fearlessly.

He swooped in close to the towering foe again, but his opponent brushed aside every single attack with minimal movements of his body and only one hand.

FireArm watched the battle from the sidelines. *What if he's right that we all have voices in our heads?* he thought. *What if I've been wasting my time thinking there was something wrong with me when there never was?*

You can't fight him. There is something wrong with you. You'll never fix it!

The sight of his friend's courage destroyed FireArm's doubts. He thought about BlackBlob's determination all through their training and how much they had both grown since they first met.

No. You're going to get hurt!

Don't fight anyone stronger than you!

Are you crazy?

FireArm heard the voices, but this time, he did not oppose them. He welcomed them. He realized they could not hurt him. "*How am I supposed to tell the difference between my trauma and my intuition?*" he asked himself.

With trust, another voice from a higher place declared.

He placed his arms in an X formation. "I can trust the *universe*!" he shouted out loud as a swirl of darkness and fire enveloped him. An eruption of heat surged from him through the room. The enemy turned his head momentarily to witness this. He had been blocking BlackBlob's attacks with ease, but now he pulled back.

"Another sheep for the slaughter?" he declared. Then, he delivered a side kick imbued with a blinding burst of energy. BlackBlob blocked it with both arms, but it sent him flying toward the other end of the room. This time he was heading headfirst into the motherboards. FireArm watched as his friend accelerated toward the opposite wall. As the young Fighter stood distracted, their adversary quickly turned and sped in FireArm's direction.

You're going to die.

"Not yet," FireArm shot back, then he glanced back toward the far side of the room. BlackBlob was moments away from hitting the wall.

Instinctively, FireArm launched himself at his friend. Behind him, the enemy Fighter floated motionless, as if frozen in time. An instant later, FireArm found himself between BlackBlob and the wall, holding his comrade in his arms. Stunned, BlackBlob looked at him. "Bro! You did it, you did the secret technique!"

"I understand it now. This technique is not for fighting, it's for *rescuing*!"

"Rescuing? Who needs rescuing?"

"Protect me!"

FireArm flew to the top of the room and charged up a blast.

"I don't get it—What are you doing?"

FireArm glared at his adversary with newfound energy. "Even with all your military, guns and bombs, you still can't take away our spirit!" he scoffed.

"How *dare* you!" yelled Phutais. His rage amplified his aura. No one had ever spoken to him like this, and survived. "Your head is mine," he screamed, raising his hand.

BlackBlob saw the hand go up and knew it was too late. FireArm was directly in the line of fire and would never be able to react in time. The next blast would be fatal.

"No!" BlackBlob told himself. He wasn't going to let that happen.

Suddenly, everything slowed. As the nearly invisible projectile emerged from the enemy Fighter's palm, it seemed to hang motionless in the air. BlackBlob swooped above, grabbed FireArm, and carried him away as the projectile crawled toward the spot where FireArm had just been. And then, just as suddenly as it had slowed, time was restored. The enemy's projectile slammed into the far wall and exploded safely there. An avalanche of motherboards shattered and fell toward the center of the room. FireArm and BlackBlob dodged them easily, but when the massive pieces of metal tumbled toward the orb's protective glass cover—

CRASH

—it fractured and split open. The naked orb below was completely exposed. The masked man looked down at this, scarcely able to believe his eyes. He cried, "What do you think you're doing?"

Looking up at his opponents, he saw a surge of projectiles heading his way. He dodged them and responded by hurling back a multitude of explosive attacks of his own. FireArm and BlackBlob took turns firing, rescuing each other, and firing once more. Each explosion caused more sheets of metal to fall through the fractured glass cover into the core. As the damage mounted, it began to blink and stutter.

"Keep firing!" BlackBlob yelled.

FireArm launched more blazing beams of energy that descended like shooting stars. The enemy moved quickly enough to avoid them, but he couldn't stop more debris from hitting the C.O.R.E. He shot back rapidly, now with both hands, but the two youths used the chrono-spatial technique again and again to protect one another while more and more chunks of metal fell into the massive energy center. Their adversary blasted all that he could, but there were too many. Suddenly, warning lights began to flash, and a mechanical voice announced, "ATTENTION. CRITICAL DAMAGE SUSTAINED."

The enemy whipped his head toward the C.O.R.E. It was flashing blood-red, indicating irreparable damage.

"No!" he thundered. "This can't be happening!"

In a frenzy, he plunged though the fractured glass around the C.O.R.E. in a desperate attempt to dislodge some larger shards of the motherboards that had mortally wounded the core. He tore them loose and threw them to the side of the room as fast as he could.

BlackBlob yelled, "Now! Let's stomp 'im!"

"Shyaaah!"

The two youths raised one fist each and unleashed their most powerful streams of soulforce upward. Using the momentum of their spirit energy, they executed two devastating dive-kicks from the top of the expansive room toward their adversary's head. Sensing their approach, he attempted to block both their feet with one hand, but he couldn't repel them. The sheer force of their momentum was too overwhelming. They pushed on, driving his feet deeper into the mass of energy. As he sank, his entire metallic body began to shimmer and blink. He was being absorbed into the C.O.R.E.!

FireArm and BlackBlob disengaged and flew upward before they too were swallowed up by it, dodging more of the falling sheets of metal that plunged past them to puncture and tear the C.O.R.E. even more.

"You fools—NOOO!"

As the enemy struggled, sparks of high-current electricity spread throughout the bottom of the room. In a fit of rage, he slammed his fists down into the core, but that only created a chain effect. Huge crackling sounds erupted below him. Pipes filled with wires burst out of the walls as fire and electrical currents consumed the C.O.R.E and everything around it.

An enormous explosion sounded deep below the room. FireArm looked at the motherboards around him. Their white light started to flicker and blink. Many shut off completely. BlackBlob looked above and saw the walls starting to cave in.

"Let's get the hell out of here!"

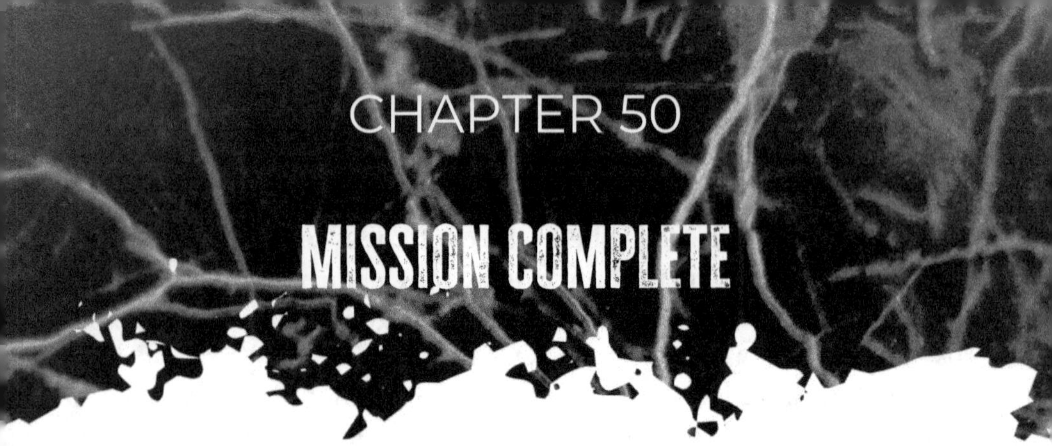

CHAPTER 50

MISSION COMPLETE

FireArm and BlackBlob raced toward the absolute darkness far above them. In the half-light that surrounded them from the rising explosion below, they watched the remaining walls of the tower collapsing. Everywhere they looked, motherboards were crumbling under the energy surge created by the enemy's enraged attempts to extricate himself from the C.O.R.E. But his frantic struggles had only further disrupted it, swallowing him like quicksand into a metallic grave that consumed the space around him until it reached a critical mass.

Using the contrast of the darkness above them and the light from the explosions below, the two youths flew upward. FireArm threw a barrage of spiritual energy to clear the space above them, while BlackBlob created an energy shield to stop the walls from closing in.

They raced upward and upward. Deactivated lights and gun turrets lay on the sides of the walls. The motherboards no longer provided their luminescent white glow. Instead, they were swallowed up in the surge of devastation that was rushing to the surface behind the two heroes.

The roar and heat of the explosion grew closer. FireArm's blasts couldn't keep up with the sheer quantity of falling debris, and BlackBlob's shield weakened under the weight of it.

You're not going to make it!

FireArm yelled back, "I know you're scared, but I love you, little buddy!"

Time slowed to a crawl. FireArm reached over and held BlackBlob, carrying him through stones and metal sheets that seemed suspended in the air. They passed stationary electrical currents, wires, and other fragments of the tower's walls. They maneuvered past slabs of concrete frozen in the air and tons of metal that would have prevented them from escaping, were it not for the chrono-spatial technique. Finally, they entered the final section of the tower. Above, the clouds had parted. The light of the moons shone down on their dark skin.

BOOM!

The instant they emerged from the top of the tower, time resumed. A massive fountain of fire emerged from the crevice they had just escaped. The city was completely dark. They could no longer hear gunfire, explosions, or the sound of warfare. FireArm landed with BlackBlob in his arms, placing him down a safe distance away from the burning tower.

BlackBlob looked at his friend with a raised eyebrow.

"What?" FireArm asked.

"Bro, did you say 'I love you' to me back there?"

"What are you talking about?"

"Down there. Didn't I hear you say you say 'I love you, little buddy'?"

"Hey, that wasn't for *you*, that was for the voice in my head."

"Ohhh. OK. Fine."

There was silence.

"Wow. Really? Are you disappointed?"

Above, they saw Atkon waving to them. They flew up join the rest of the team, who were picking off the last drones and mekanations. Many of these remnants seemed to have gone haywire, performing random functions rather than targeting the Fighters. The light from the motherboards was completely extinguished. What only moments ago was a battlefield now stretched out to the horizon like a giant black checkerboard. In the distance, FireArm and BlackBlob saw the giant black orbs that had housed the drones and autonomous vehicles. They now looked like large sunken planets on the horizon. Smoke and scrap metal littered the land. Thousands upon thousands of metal carcasses lay everywhere.

The Fighters were taking no chances. They followed an alternate route out of enemy territory at a much higher altitude to avoid any reinforcements that might still be active. Their caution turned out to be unnecessary. Atkon, keeping watch through their internal radar system, detected no further enemy signals. As far as they could see, the whole city was as dark as could be.

They were almost surprised to have defeated the enormous power of Zi-Tai in a single epic battle. They'd known that the tower, and the mysterious C.O.R.E. that lay beneath it, were the heart of Zi-Tai's dominance over the planet, but the total reliance of the corporation's massive tentacles on that one machine, and its mastermind's sheer arrogance in arranging things in that manner, was a bonus they had never dreamed of. Through collective effort, the will to challenge reality, and sheer determination, they had done the unthinkable. They had saved their planet from the world's oppressor.

Eager to be home, they flew back to the southern camp as fast as they could. The silence beneath them as they traversed the North was eerie, but after this victory, an invincible confidence had arisen within them. BlackBlob thought about how the safest place in the world was to be flying in this formation. FireArm observed a quietness in his mind that felt unfamiliar but natural. None of the Fighters said a word during the flight back, but not due to any regret. AnnRoticon had ordered their silence, to grant space for meditation and for gratitude for the will of the universe. They were all going to make it back home, safe and sound. For this, there was a deep, shared sense of gratefulness.

Eventually, Atkon's map guided them to their campsite. Before touching down, they saw naval and aerial units of Zi-Tai retreating north. As they fell back, FireArm realized, they were spitefully doing as much damage as they could. He could see craters on the ground that violated the landscape and gave off the smell of combat. Although he could see blood, the vengeful rampage of the retreating forces must at least have ended quickly because of Black Mountain's efforts in Azor City. Their mission of intimidation must have been called off as soon as they realized they no longer had a commander to report their bullying back to, or even a C.O.R.E. to protect them.

The Fighters approached the crescent beach, and one by one they touched the ground. None of them wasted any time changing out of their technogarments and getting some rest. Their bodies were weary. They deserved every bit of peace they could get. FireArm found his bed, and his head found its pillow. He didn't even have time to reflect on the battle before sleep overtook him.

He awoke to crowds of villagers approaching with gifts of food and drink. The sounds of rhythmic music and people singing, dancing, and laughing brought a smile to his sleepy face. Nearby, he saw Ann laughing with Anansi and Nani. The three ladies were gifted a large pot of rice and peas from the local villagers. Pots of steamed cabbage, callaloo, and ackee were lined up on the dinner rack. Ginger beer, mauby, and carrot juice flavored with rum were on the second rack. Nani smiled. "Looks like we'll be having our post-mission meal after all!"

FireArm was thanked by more people than he could remember. Many of them embraced him and kissed him, crying tears of joy with no reason to hide them. He had never experienced this level of gratitude for anything he had ever done. It was so overwhelming that he had to take breaks to compose himself. After some prodding and with support from BlackBlob, he agreed to be hoisted up along with his friend on the shoulders of the stomping, hollering, dancing revelers. BlackBlob yelled over at FireArm, "So much for us being unknown to the public!"

The sun shone above, warming the hearts and minds of all that it reached. Throughout the day, more crowds from the surrounding communities made their way to the beach. Some had dark skin, some light. Some had curly hair, others straight. All of them showed their love in their own unique ways. Some journeyed by foot, bringing other gifts beyond food and drink—artwork, charms, scarves, plant medicines. People brought what they could to show appreciation with more than just world-dollars.

FireArm and BlackBlob stuffed their faces while Anansi and Nani checked out the headwraps, essential oils, and ointments. Ann flew through the air, taking some small children on short trips over the trees while Atkon high-fived those members of the Community who felt more at ease with public spaces. FireArm looked off into the distance. Seeing the sun about to set against the glistening ocean, he reflected on what freedom felt like and what a world without the prison of Zi-Tai would be like.

Then he asked, "Hey, where's Zoticon?"

EPILOGUE

UNDEFEATED

After finishing their meals, they tidied up before formally thanking the remaining Community members for their generosity. As the crowds left, a gentle silence descended. The air felt light and safe. The smell of sage wafted through the camp.

Anansi gently placed the incense holder on a small altar. Nani set down meditative mats and chairs. They took turns speaking about what the victory meant for them and honoring the memory of their fallen comrades and the *Black Raven.* They spoke about the sacrifices and challenges of their journey with Black Mountain, and thanked the ancestors for their power, wisdom, and guidance.

Then they talked and joked about how they would spend time vacationing deeper in the South and working with the Community's AI models to help recreate and expand the *Raven*'s lost library. They imagined a hard-earned vacation where they would learn everything there was to know about the rich cultures and traditions they had helped to safeguard. With a laugh, Nani looked forward to all the new recipes she would discover. Her mouth watered thinking of jalapeños and wasabi. Anansi visualized herself reading books under the cover of palm trees. They would finally be able to see the world they had saved yet still knew little about.

Afterward, BlackBlob and FireArm walked to the site where the ceremony would take place.

"You know..." FireArm said a little hesitantly. "Thanks for helping me out back at that tower."

He looked at his brother-in-arms. His expression grew lighter as he saw the warmth on BlackBlob's face.

"Hmm... Remember when we first met, and you said we weren't friends?" BlackBlob crossed his arms and gave a fake pout. "Well, I think I deserve an apology!"

"Let's be clear," FireArm smiled, "that was kinda funny though."

"Bruh, it took a whole-ass final boss battle for you to get a sense of humor? Wow!"

They laughed. For the first time in his life, FireArm felt truly and fully part of something greater than himself. He had learned to trust others. He had found people worth trusting. Doubts still remained, but rather than suppressing the voices, he had learned to engage with them. To heal with them. After all he had gone through at the orphanage, this proved that the bullies had never taken his spirit from him.

"Not gonna lie"—FireArm glanced at Blob—"you really came out swinging in the end. That battle brought out the best in you."

"Heh." BlackBlob smiled. "I guess so." The thought that they had been able to master their techniques and use them to benefit others brought warmth to his heart. He was a world away from the slap his "mother" had once given him. Rather than being a problem child, he was a protector of the planet. He had helped clip the wings of Zi-Tai. "As the old man would say," Blob added, pumping up his chest, "I guess now we have *found our purpose*."

They were still chuckling when a voice came from behind them.

"That impersonation was somewhat inaccurate." They jumped and turned, shocked, to find Zoticon standing there—and were even more shocked to hear a hint of laughter in his voice. "Come," he said, "there is a mandatory debriefing ceremony, and you must participate."

BlackBlob looked at FireArm. They both raised their shoulders and followed. Led by Zoticon, they walked to the clearing, still thinking about how far they had come. It wasn't much more than a year, but it felt like a lifetime. The tides of time had changed them. They had new responsibilities, new powers, and a new purpose.

The entire team was now in the clearing, each sitting however was comfortable for them.

Uncle Zee sat down behind a large desk, and Auntie Ann walked over to him. "Ahem!" Nudging him with an elbow, she gestured to one of the shelves. "Go on," she said.

Zoticon, sighed. "All right, fine." He reached into a cupboard beside the desk and brought out a black box. He placed it on the desk as the team huddled around. BlackBlob's eyes widened. "Did you get us a gift for all our trouble? I don't believe this!"

"What is it?" FireArm asked.

"Open it," Ann said.

"OK," replied FireArm. He opened the latch and peeled a folded cover from the top. Peering into the box before fully opening it, he noticed the smell. "Umm, something in here smells sweet," he said. "Like sugar?"

"You're lying," BlackBlob exclaimed. "You got us a gift?"

"Just get on with it," Zoticon said.

BlackBlob leapt in between FireArm and opened the lid the rest of the way. Inside was a cake surrounded by candies and other confectionary.

"Wait a minute, don't tell me *you* made this?" BlackBlob kept back a laugh.

"Why wouldn't I have made it?"

"Sir, it's just—it's just, I never saw you as a baker."

"What's the matter with you? I bake all the time. I do it for my self-care."

FireArm pointed at the center of the cake, where the word *CONGRATULATION* in multicolored icing stretched from one side to the other.

"Sir, um, I think you spelled it wrong," FireArm said, his eyes tearing up.

"It looks like he ran out of space and had no room for an S," BlackBlob said.

"Not at all," Zoticon said. "I prefer it this way. This was your first completed mission where everything actually went right, so since you only completed one, you only get one congratulation. Complete more and we'll see about additional congratulations."

The youths looked at each other.

"It's his way of making a joke, guys." Ann giggled.

They all burst out laughing.

"Whooo," BlackBlob wheezed, "is that what we call jokes nowadays?"

Anansi and Nani laughed too, but they were interrupted by the sound of a blade cutting through air. Zoticon's hand was surrounded with a black and purple aura. A pointed tip of spiritual energy emerged. FireArm leapt back quickly and assumed his fighting pose.

"Whoa whoa whoa, it was just a joke!" BlackBlob said, stumbling backward. "Right?"

"What's wrong with you?" Zoticon looked at them with one raised eyebrow. "We don't have any knives. I'm just going to cut the cake."

The youths looked at each other in silence again. "Wow," they said simultaneously, after a moment.

Ann laughed. "C'mon, guys," she said, producing some plates from behind the desk.

"I guess we're going to have to get used to these quote-unquote *jokes* from now on."

Zoticon's eyes smiled at his fighters. "Maybe you just might," he said.

After enjoying slices of cake, the team gathered together and meditated until the last piece of ash dropped from the incense stick. Ziffea's three moons coated the land in a soft, silvery light. Ann stood by a lamp, sipping herbal tea. Sitting in a lounge chair, Zoticon took sips of black coffee while FireArm and Blob playfully fought over the last slice of cake.

"All right, let's debrief," said Zoticon, taking a last sip of his coffee.

The youths were used to debriefings by now, but this one was different. There was a lightness in the air. Not only did they manage to discuss everything without any fear of judgment, but Zoticon provided feedback and suggestions for training. FireArm felt understood and comfortable. BlackBlob spoke confidently about his mistakes. They discussed the possibility of new missions. Ways that they could help rebuild what was lost. To restore and protect the strength of the global South.

"You guys really saved the day in that final fight," Nani told them.

"So did you catch the name of the Fighter at the bottom of the tower?" Anansi asked.

FireArm and BlackBlob looked at each other. "Nope," said FireArm.

"He put up quite a fight, but he didn't introduce himself," BlackBlob added.

"Do you remember what he looked like?"

"I don't know, he was a tall guy in a white suit."

"Oh well, I guess it's not important," Anansi mused.

And with that, the great leader of Zi-Tai, his century-long endeavor, and his quest for absolute victory was over. The High Commander's name was erased from the world with no possibility of ever being known to them.

"I forgot to ask," Zoticon said. "How does it feel to have saved the world?"

"Saved the world?" FireArm asked.

"Whadya mean?" BlackBlob added.

"Exactly that," Zoticon replied. "You are heroes now."

"So we protected billions of people?" FireArm said as he stared out over the ocean.

"Yup, "Ann said. "There is no chance that Zi-Tai will be able to restore the grid, at least for another decade or so. The mekanation project is over for now."

"Really?" BlackBlob asked. "I mean, I'm a bit sad because I was raised up with one of those bots. I called him *Dad*."

Atkon closed an electronic device. "I don't mean to be harsh, but I am 100% certain that he was programmed to call you *son*."

"But will Zi-Tai really be OK with all of this? I'm sure they'll be pissed at us for a long time," BlackBlob said.

"Let them be," Zoticon said and stood up.

FireArm looked at him. "What about those mercenaries? Death-Dweller and Tri-Spectre? Don't you think we'll clash with them again?"

AnnRoticon seethed at the more mention of her nemesis. "Zoticon, listen. They betrayed us in the past. They will betray us again," she said with unaccustomed firmness. "They have left us with no other option than to destroy them."

Zoticon looked down at his empty palm and then clutched it into a fist. "I understand how you feel. So we will crush them when they return. We have no choice but to win every time. What's the motto?"

"Defeat the enemy wherever he appears," they all replied in unison.

"We owe it to our ancestors," Zoticon responded.

"No doubt," FireArm said.

"I feel you," BlackBlob added.

Ann passed out cups and poured a red liquid into each of them.

"What's this?" BlackBlob asked.

"It's Red Drink—Hey! Don't drink it yet!" Anansi said.

"Sorry!"

"Ahh, the sweet smell of sorrel," Nani said, sniffing her cup and smiling.

Zoticon gripped his cup, then raised it up. "We might not be able to change the past, but this revolution will bring a future that our ancestors could be proud of."

"The ancestors are undefeated," AnnRoticon exclaimed.

"Undefeated!" the team repeated.

That night, every one of them slept peacefully. Zi-Tai's planetary power mesh, the network of control nodes ran from the C.O.R.E. that FireArm and BlackBlob had destroyed along with its creator, had been rendered useless. Without it, Zi-Tai only had the remnants of its army of mekanations to rely on. They could perhaps defend some scattered outposts of empire, but they could no longer control the planet. At least not unless another all-powerful visionary leader came along.

The wings of Zi-Tai were clipped, with no leader at the helm and no one to keep them in line. As a result, the four remaining members had no reason to resume their meetings. Telron found this situation preferable, as it allowed him to govern without any scandals that could be linked to him. Harbush also preferred not to take orders so that he could spend more time giving them to his corrupt subordinates. Meanwhile, Meridian dedicated much of her time to the lab, focusing on the development of GAIA units that could one day surpass her master's plans. As for Maiden, she disappeared into the shadows, after withdrawing large sums of world-dollars from Zi-Tai's bank accounts.

There was a power vacuum in the world, and it would take some time to restore a proper balance. But one thing was for sure: The colonizers could no longer hold sway over the planet, at least for the foreseeable future. FireArm felt lighter in his heart, knowing that he had found trust in others. BlackBlob felt a sense of release in his spirit, knowing that he now had a real family around him. Zoticon's faith in the future had been restored. AnnRoticon looked proudly at her brother. There was hope once again that the world could return to its original rhythm. The trauma of suffering had been repelled.

On that fated evening, the sky was clear, the stars were shining, and Black Mountain beamed with pride.

FIREARM AND BLACKBLOB

ABOUT THE AUTHOR

David Archer is a Black Jamaican African Canadian from Montreal Canada. He is an anti-racist psychotherapist who specializes in treating complex PTSD and racial trauma. He seeks to demystify mental health and increase the number of Black and anti-racists of all races to enter the mental health field. He holds a degree in computer science, a bachelor's in Psychology, a master's in social work, and a master's in couple and family therapy.

Certified in EMDR and Brainspotting therapies, he utilizes technologically advanced forms of mental health treatments to help people from diverse backgrounds, races and social identities. His expertise has led him to deliver presentations on an international scale at conferences, facilitate impactful workshops and trainings, and provide clinical guidance for therapists across the profession spectrum—from student-therapists to seasoned experts. Notably, some of his writings have become required readings for therapists seeking trauma-informed and evidence-based practices.

David Archer's highly acclaimed book, "Anti-Racist Psychotherapy: Confronting Systemic Racism and Healing Racial Trauma," delves into the intersection of mental health and systemic racism. It explores revolutionary perspectives on dismantling systemic racism, decolonizing mental health practices, and understanding the neurobiological consequences of anti-Black racism.

In "Black Meditation: Ten Practices for Self-Care, Mindfulness, and Self-Determination," Archer writes about essential skills for cultivating a positive Black racial identity. This collection of practices serves as a resource for those who might not have access to an anti-racist therapist, encouraging them to explore concepts of race, personal growth and cultivating a positive self-concept.

His third book, "Racial Trauma Recovery: Healing Our Past Using Rhythm and Processing," Archer introduces the groundbreaking integrative clinical framework called Rhythm and Processing (RAP) Strategies. This innovative approach goes beyond traditional talk therapy, by incorporating interventions that involve taxing working memory and memory reconsolidation approaches. By using these modern methods hundreds of people have found their way to deep and permanent recovery.

And Black Mountain Fight for the Future is the fourth one. Yup. The one you're reading. Thank you for reading it.

To connect with David Archer, access more content, or inquire about professional consultations or workshop presentations, please visit:

- Website: https://archertherapy.com
- Facebook: https://facebook.com/archertherapy
- Instagram: https://www.instagram.com/archertherapy/
- YouTube: https://www.youtube.com/@archertherapy
- LinkedIn: https://www.linkedin.com/in/archertherapy/

If you like any of his work, please like, subscribe, write reviews and get the word out. Let's make a difference for the next generation of therapists and therapy-seekers. Thank you!

OTHER BOOKS BY THIS AUTHOR

If you liked *Black Mountain*,
you might also like the books that inspired it.

Anti-Racist Psychotherapy: Confronting Systemic Racism and Healing Racial Trauma
Link: **https://amzn.to/3b0iqvT**

Black Meditation: Ten Practices for Self-Care, Mindfulness, and Self-Determination
Link: **https://amzn.to/3JEnhm7**

Racial Trauma Recovery: Healing Our Past Using Rhythm and Processing
Link: **https://amzn.to/3C8HY89**

LET'S WORK TOGETHER

David Archer is available for podcasts, presentations, and trainings.

Let's deliver the message of Anti-Racist Psychotherapy and Racial Trauma Recovery to those who need it.

Email me at david@archertherapy.com for more information. EMDR therapy certification, workshops, and free resources (mailing list, videos, and recorded podcasts) are available at:

https://www.archertherapy.com

You are invited to view and download these resources.
Be well, stay healthy, and take care.

www.ingramcontent.com/pod-product-compliance
Lightning Source LLC
Chambersburg PA
CBHW071416200726
48294CB00002B/411

* 9 7 8 1 9 9 8 8 7 1 0 1 8 *